Dead Reckoning

HISTORICAL FICTION BY C. NORTHCOTE PARKINSON
PUBLISHED BY McBOOKS PRESS

Dead Reckoning

C. Northcote Parkinson

RICHARD DELANCEY NOVELS, NO. 6

McBooks Press, Inc.

Ithaca, New York

Published by McBooks Press 2003
Copyright © 1978 by C. Northcote Parkinson
First published in the United States by Houghton Mifflin Co., 1978
First published in the United Kingdom by John Murray Ltd, 1978

Cover painting: *Naval Ramming 1811, The British Warship "Hermes" Rams the
French Privateer "La Mouch."* Courtesy of Mary Evans Picture Library.

Library of Congress Cataloging-in-Publication Data

Parkinson, C. Northcote (Cyril Northcote), 1909-
  Dead reckoning / by C. Northcote Parkinson.
    p. cm. — (The Richard Delancey novels ; no. 6)
  ISBN 1-59013-038-3 (alk. paper)
  1. Delancey, Richard (Fictitious character)--Fiction. 2. Great
Britain—History, Naval—19th century—Fiction. 3. Napoleonic Wars,
1800-1815—Fiction. 4. Guernsey (Channel Islands)—Fiction. I. Title.
  PR6066.A6955D43 2003
  823'.914—dc21

                                                        2003005458

Visit the McBooks Press website at www.mcbooks.com.

Printed in the United States of America

9 8 7 6 5 4 3 2

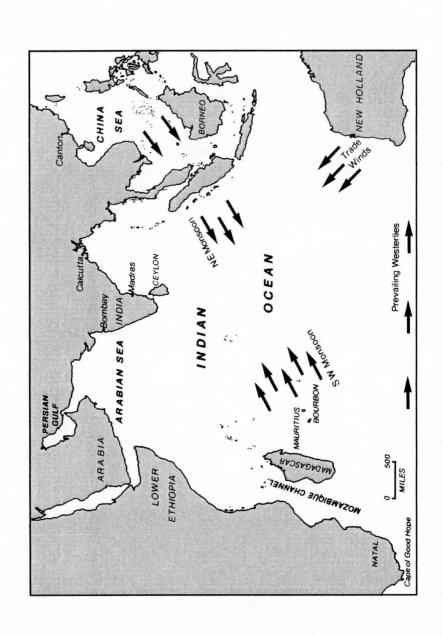

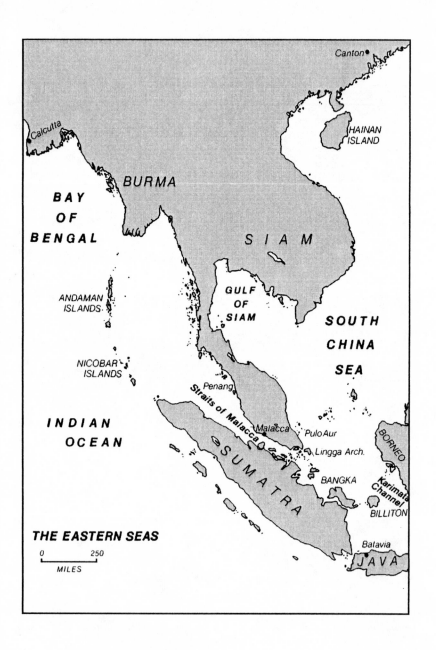

Canton

HAINAN
ISLAND

Calcutta

BURMA

BAY
OF
BENGAL

SIAM

ANDAMAN
ISLANDS

GULF
OF
SIAM

SOUTH

CHINA

SEA

NICOBAR
ISLANDS

Penang

Straits of Malacca

INDIAN
OCEAN

Malacca

Pulo Aur

Lingga Arch.

SUMATRA

BANGKA

BORNEO

Karimata
Channel

BILLITON

THE EASTERN SEAS

0   250

MILES

Batavia

JAVA

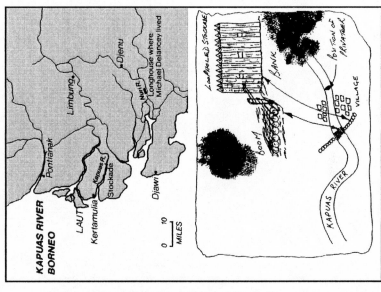

KAPUAS RIVER
BORNEO

Pontianak

Limbung

Djenu

Nuri R.

Longhouse where
Michael Delancey lived

LAUT

Kertamulia

Kapuas R.

Stockade

Djawi

0   10
MILES

WALLED STOCKADE

BANK

POSITION OF
PRIVATEER

VILLAGE

BOOM

KAPUAS RIVER

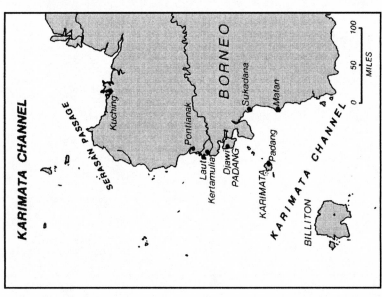

KARIMATA CHANNEL

SERASAN PASSAGE

Kuching

BORNEO

Pontianak

Laut
Kertamulia

Djawi
PADANG

Sukadana

Matan

Padang

KARIMATA

KARIMATA CHANNEL

BILLITON

0   50   100
MILES

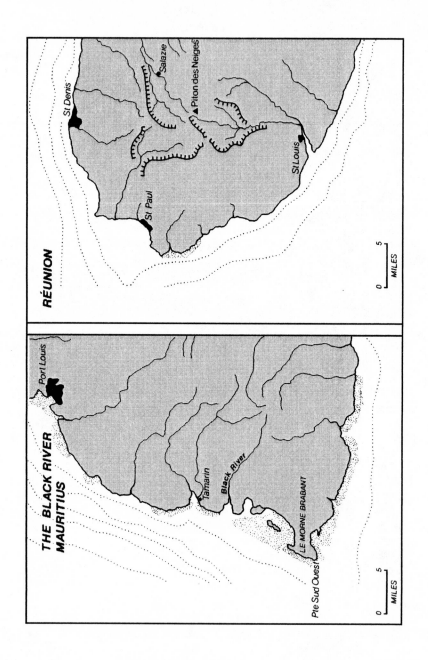

THE BLACK RIVER
MAURITIUS

Port Louis

Tamarin

Black River

LE MORNE BRABANT

Pte Sud Ouest

0   5
MILES

RÉUNION

St Paul

St Denis

Salazie

▲ Piton des Neiges

St Louis

0   5
MILES

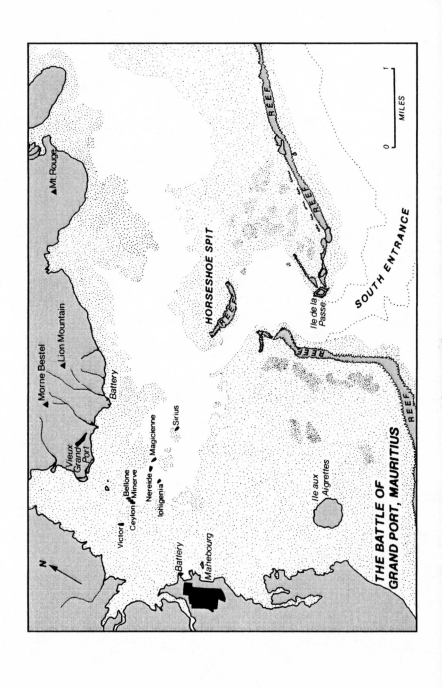

THE BATTLE OF
GRAND PORT, MAURITIUS

HORSESHOE SPIT

SOUTH ENTRANCE

REEF

Mt. Rouge

Lion Mountain

Morne Bestel

Battery

Vieux
Grand
Port

Victor

Bellone
Ceylon
Minerve

Nereide
Iphigenia
Magicienne

Sirius

Ile de la
Passe

Ile aux
Aigrettes

Battery

Mahebourg

N

0   1
MILES

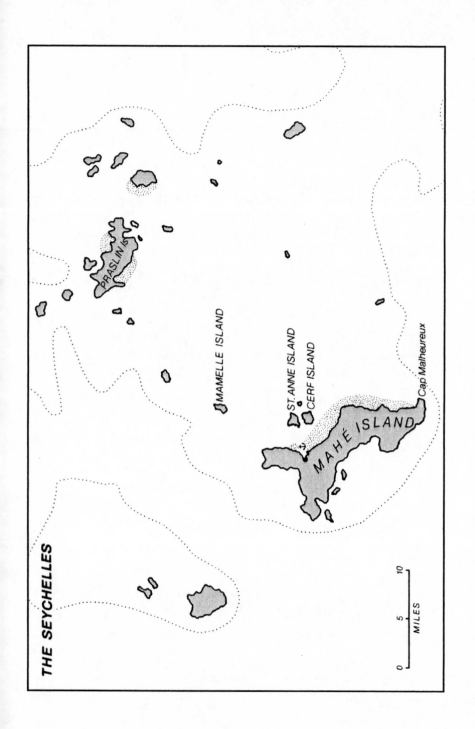

THE SEYCHELLES

PRASLIN IS.

MAMELLE ISLAND

ST. ANNE ISLAND
CERF ISLAND

MAHÉ ISLAND

Cap Malheureux

0   5   10
MILES

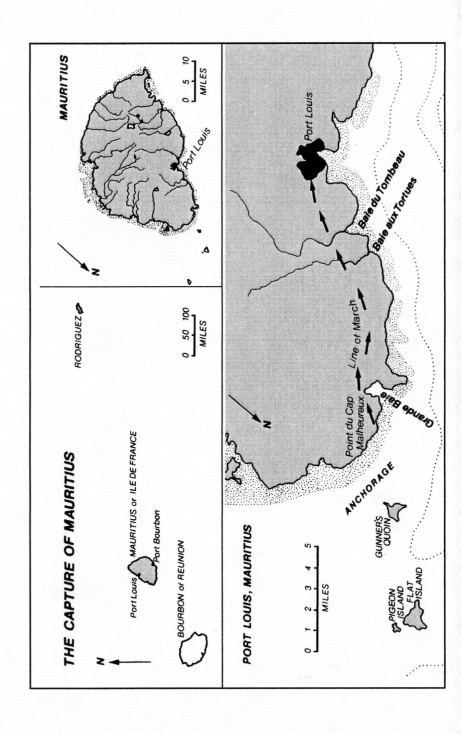

THE CAPTURE OF MAURITIUS

MAURITIUS

RODRIGUEZ

Port Louis   MAURITIUS or ILE DE FRANCE

Port Bourbon

BOURBON or REUNION

N

0   50   100
MILES

Port Louis

N

0   5   10
MILES

PORT LOUIS, MAURITIUS

Port Louis

Baie du Tombeau

Baie aux Tortues

Line of March

Point du Cap
Malheureux

Grande Baie

ANCHORAGE

GUNNER'S
QUOIN

PIGEON
ISLAND

FLAT
ISLAND

N

0   1   2   3   4   5
MILES

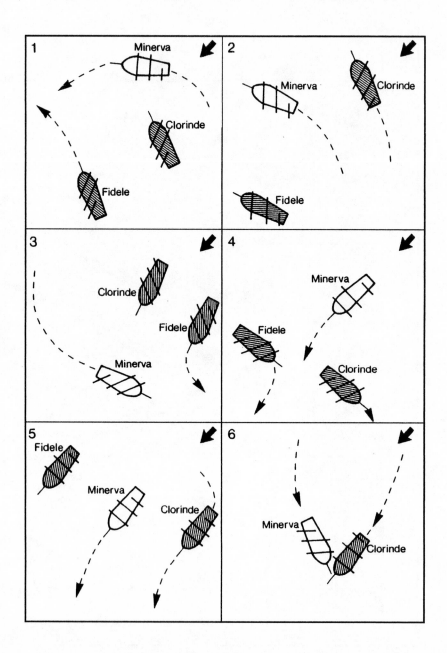

Chapter One

TO THE INDIES

"**I** AM HAPPY to inform you, Captain Delancey, that you have been appointed to command the frigate *Laura* of 32 guns. She is refitting at Portsmouth but should be completed next month. Perhaps you know the ship?"

"No, sir. I am honoured, however, by the Board's confidence in me."

"She is an old ship," the First Sea Lord here referred to a document, "though far from being the oldest. She is one of the *Amazon*-Class ships and was Thames-built in 1773, mounting twenty-six 12-pounders and a dozen 24-pounder carronades. She measures 684 tons, is established for a crew of 215 and is 126 feet 3 inches long on the gun-deck. Her recent service has been in the West Indies, from which station she was brought home for repair. She is a useful ship of her class, handles well and was last commanded by Captain Chastleton, who died last year at Bermuda. The *Laura* is to be stationed in the East Indies but is more immediately to sail on a particular service, forming part of a squadron under the command, as Commodore, of Sir Home Popham. He is presently in town and you will, no doubt, wish to call on him. Good-day, Captain, and I wish you every success."

Delancey made his bow and withdrew, going to collect the essential documents from the outer office. Then he was in White-hall and walking slowly towards Charing Cross. The East Indies!

The idea of it might seem attractive on a cold autumn day but there was much else to think about. It was the most distant station, remote enough to be forgotten, a place where fortunes were made by the fortunate, a place where many died and where others gained promotion. A few years back he would have welcomed the prospect of visiting the mysterious East. As a lieutenant or as a captain not yet posted, he would have seen it as a great opportunity but he felt now that the posting had come too late. He was already on the captain's list, depending only on seniority for his further promotion. He already had a small estate and a modest independence. Above all, he was married. There were officers, he supposed, who would take their wives with them to India but he could never be one of them. To see Fiona losing her beauty, becoming sallow, suffering from dysentery, dying of fever—all this was unthinkable, a risk to which she should never be exposed. But the alternative was a long separation. How could a marriage last with the husband away for years? Marriages did survive that test, as he knew, and the more easily if there were children. But he and Fiona were still childless and he wondered if it was fair to desert her for as long as four or five years. Was it not asking too much of her? It would be long enough, good god, for him! But he had his profession, his frigate, his men to look after, his King's enemies to fight. She would have only a house and garden, her friends to entertain, her dog to exercise, her letters to write. He had been married now for three years and he and Fiona were still deeply in love. He was still apt to wonder what he had done to earn such happiness. He could remember a time when his friends were telling him that his fortune was as good as made; that a match was possible which would bring him lands and wealth and the protection of a great family. He might have dined with admirals, made friends with ministers, picked his own 38-gun frigate and chosen his station. He had perversely rejected that prospect, if it really existed, and had married a young woman without relatives or estate, an actress who was not even legitimate, a girl with nothing to offer but outstanding beauty, strong character, and native intelligence. This, he had been told, was the end of his high prospects in the service. He would be employed, to be sure, while the war lasted but he would have only a mediocre ship (like the *Laura,* and he could picture her) packed off to a distant and fever-ridden station. There would be no knighthood for him, no Order of the Bath, no presentation to the Sovereign. He had no regrets on that score. Fiona meant more to him than any honour the world had to offer. He would make the same choice once more if the clock were to be put back, leading him to make the same decision again. And yet he would have liked, in a way, to have an assured and brilliant future. People might sneer at Fiona's background and he supposed that they did, an actress, at one time, being thought little better than a prostitute, but he would have liked to see her take precedence of them all as Lady Delancey. More than that, she could play the part more gracefully than the majority of those who had been born to it.

Although moving in no glittering circle, Delancey and Fiona were no longer compelled to lodge at his old address in Albemarle Street. They were now the guests of Colonel Barrington, whose town house was on the west side of St James's Square. A widower and now crippled with gout, the Colonel was little seen in society these days. He had, however, a wistful admiration for Fiona and a liking for Richard, they having been originally introduced to him by Delancey's American cousins. The Colonel was always very ready to lend them his carriage, of which he himself made little use, and this allowed the Delanceys to appear with an air of affluence at the few functions to which they were invited. Delancey, as on this occasion, was happy to walk the short distance from the Admiralty to St James's Square and would have thought it no hardship to walk from Westminster to St Paul's. He was coming to realize, however, that no man of fashion would walk so far and that he might have to mend his ways. Or did it matter? Their stay in London must soon end. The result, moreover of his posting to the East Indies would be to confine poor Fiona to their home in Guernsey. She could not well appear in London without him and this would deprive her of much that she valued and not least the theatre. As a former actress she loved going to the play, so she and Delancey had been keen patrons of Covent Garden, Drury Lane, and both of the theatres in the Haymarket. Fiona's idol was Mrs Siddons, whose provincial appearances, extending to Bath, would hardly bring her to St Peter Port in Guernsey. The more he thought about his immediate future, the more depressed did Delancey become. To refuse the command of the *Laura* would ruin his career in the service; to accept it might well ruin his marriage. Such were his gloomy thoughts as he paced along Pall Mall. Fiona would be waiting to hear the result of his visit to the Admiralty. How, for heaven's sake, was he to tell her?

Fiona! The mere name had still, for him, a magical quality. She was very lovely but her beauty mattered less, perhaps, than her vitality. She could not enter a room without everyone turning towards her. She was normally smiling but with a special warmth for her friends and a bright-eyed touch of mischief on occasion and a look, as if sharing a secret, which she kept for children. She was not clever in the more obvious sense but she was always kind, so much so that Delancey had never known her speak ill of anyone. What was it that set her apart? Her way of doing or saying the unexpected? The way she danced where others seemed only to shuffle or plod? There was nobody in the world, he knew, who resembled her at all.

Delancey turned the corner into St James's Square and was admitted by Colonel Barrington's servant, who took care of his hat, cloak and sword. It was a splendidly proportioned hall panelled in white, floored in black-and-white chequered marble and with more than a hint of the East, with elephant tusks, a tiger-skin rug by the fireplace, and a portrait of Warren Hastings (a copy of the Reynolds portrait) at the end of the stairs. Before he could go upstairs to the drawing-room, the old, white-haired, red-faced, and spectacled Colonel hobbled out of the library and asked him how he had fared with their Lordships.

"I am posted, sir, to the *Laura*, of 32 guns, a frigate destined for service in the East Indies."

"Zounds, I hardly know whether to call this good news or ill. The frigate is a bigger ship than your last, to be sure, but—the East Indies! For your good lady this will come as a disaster. Can you not refuse the appointment?"

"No, sir, not if I am to remain active in my profession. The *Laura* is bound, first of all, on a particular service. Were I to refuse this opportunity I should scarcely be offered another. It would be different for a man with independent means or with great parliamentary interest but, lacking either, I must take what I am given and make the best of it."

"I see that and my hope must be that this voyage will make your fortune as many another fortune has been made in the East. We shall see you as a Nabob yet! But for how long will you be overseas?"

"Four years would be the average, sir, I fancy, but five or six years would be nothing out of the way."

"S'death! Don't say that to your good lady in as many words. Tell her, dammit, that the war will end in a year or two—as well it may—and that peace will lead to your recall."

They were standing in the hall and at this moment Fiona appeared from the first-floor drawing-room and stood at the head of the stairs.

"Pray what is this conspiracy, gentlemen? Can I not be a party to it? Quickly—what is the news?"

"I am to command the frigate *Laura* and go on a particular service; afterwards to the East Indies."

There was a moment of silence and then Fiona exclaimed:

"See how well you are thought of! No secret expedition can sail without you! And once the business is concluded you will be chosen to bring home the dispatch. That's how it will be!"

She was so lovely, so eager, so young. Delancey was halfway up the stairs by now and Fiona was halfway down. She was in his arms, laughing and crying at the same time.

"Depend on't, I shan't be away for long."

"Of course not, my love . . . a few months at most!"

"Forgive us, Colonel." said Delancey, "we have urgent matters to discuss."

They went to their room and Delancey did his best to comfort her. They both knew exactly what this posting could mean but neither would admit it. Each was thinking, although neither mentioned the name, of a Captain Jennings, an acquaintance they had made at Lady Hertford's Ball. Jennings had been eight years on the East Indies station and had returned a man of some wealth, successful in prize-money, retiring from the service and becoming Member of Parliament for a pocket borough in Cornwall. But his India Stock and his Hampshire estate had been dearly bought, for he was a mere wreck of a man, sallow-faced, thin and trembling, the victim of hepatitis and malaria. For all practical purposes he was finished save as a silent vote in the government's interest. Was this to be Delancey's fate? He was a fine man, Fiona knew, healthy and vigorous, but the same could once have been said of Jennings.

From thinking of Jennings, Delancey went on to think of his own elder brother Michael, who had gone to the East Indies and had never come back. He was dead, most probably, there having been no news of him for years. How many went to the East and how few of them were seen again! In his arms that night, Fiona cried for a while and then resolved bravely to make the best of it.

"When you have sailed, my love, I shall go back to Anneville. And do you know how I have it in mind to pass the long months until you return? I shall make ours the finest garden in the Channel Islands! Do you remember our reading together how Mr William Shenstone, the poet, laid out his gardens at the Leasowes? He was never a rich man but he so contrived matters that his gardens became famous and were visited by people from far and wide. When you come ashore I shall say 'You are now the owner of a garden which has been painted by the best-known artists and described in verse by the most celebrated poets!'"

"And what shall I do for you in return? I cannot promise to bring you riches. All I can promise is to draw and paint the landscapes of Asia, collect and press the foreign flowers, and try to bring back with me all of the East that was worth going to see."

They were very close to each other during the following weeks, each clinging to a love which was so threatened, each knowing that their time was short, that the refitting of the *Laura* was inexorably nearing completion. They had soon to leave London, saying good-bye to Colonel Barrington and other friends and taking up temporary residence at the George in Portsmouth. Delancey had already secured the appointment of Nicholas Mather as his first lieutenant, with the Hon. Stephen Northmore as master's mate, with Topley and Stock as midshipmen. From his last ship, the *Vengeance* (28), he had managed to bring a few men, including Luke Tanner, his coxswain, and John Teesdale, his steward. His other officers and men were strangers to him and had still to arrive; many on the lower deck had still, indeed, to be recruited. The *Laura* herself was out of dock but still being rigged, fitted, equipped, and stored. There could be no denying the ship's age but Delancey knew that she would look well when painted and varnished. Fiona was insistent that Richard should have good cabin furniture with a carpet and curtains, with new and better cutlery, glass and plate. Under pressure from her, Richard had already acquired a new uniform in London and he was now made to buy a dozen more shirts and stockings and a new cocked hat. With a settee in his day cabin and decanters on his sideboard, he was beginning to look like the senior officer he had now become. As soon as she was in the ship Fiona found that all the men in sight had become her slaves; the carpenter and sailmaker to begin with, followed by Teesdale and his assistant Fuller, the gig's crew and all the boys the ship could muster. Even workmen from the dockyard would make any excuse to be near her. The final result was a set of captain's quarters such as Delancey had seen before but never possessed.

When the *Laura* dropped down to Spithead, Fiona insisted on sleeping aboard so as to discover what it was like. "Look!" she cried in the morning. "When we went to bed the Isle of Wight was here on this side, and now it has moved round over there! I find it all *most* confusing!" Mather, who was staying at the Star and Garter, came to dine with the Delanceys at the

George. Over the port Fiona encouraged him until he was almost witty. Asked how he had managed to remain a bachelor, he explained that for a first lieutenant to marry would be a sort of bigamy, he being already married to his ship. Considering this idea, Fiona had to allow that *Laura* was at least a feminine name. She hated to think that he had once been married to *Vengeance!* Seeing Mather's look of dumb admiration directed towards Fiona, Delancey could hardly picture him as the firm disciplinarian he knew him to be. He thought himself lucky, however, to have one key man on whom he could rely. The purser was at first the only other officer appointed, a colourless man called Arthur Finch but one who evidently knew his trade.

Delancey had met Sir Home Popham in London, calling on him as etiquette required. He was received with a cordiality which was also dismissive and he saw little of the Commodore, therefore, until he arrived at the George. As from that time Delancey began to realize that Sir Home was a most unusual character. He was known chiefly in the service as the inventor of the telegraphic signalling code which had just been adopted. By a little inquiry, however, Delancey established the fact that Popham had commanded an Austrian Indiaman, had served ashore under the Duke of York, and had been knighted by, of all people, the Emperor of Russia. He was active and clever, as most seamen had to admit, but some old and peevish officers questioned whether he was reliable. He impressed Delancey as very much a man of the world, moving easily among the great and regarded among them as an authority on matters scientific.

"Glad to have you in my squadron," said Sir Home to Delancey. "I should like you to meet my other officers: Captain Donovan of the *Diadem,* the ship which wears my pennant, Captain Josias Rowley of the *Raisonable,* Captain Byng of the *Belliqueux* . . ."

They all bowed to each other and the Commodore explained that the squadron would include four sail-of-the-line, a 50-gun ship, three frigates, a sloop, and a gun-brig. These would have to escort a fleet of transports, in which troops would be embarked, and there would also be a large convoy of merchantmen. They were to be joined presently by Major-General Sir David Baird, a fine soldier with long experience in India. Did Delancey know the General? Delancey did not, except of course by reputation. Sir Home went on:

"When his name was mentioned to me by the Prime Minister I ventured to say that he could not have made a better choice. Now, like everyone else, you will be wanting to know the object of our expedition. Well, I must not tell you! No one is to know other than the General and myself. Security is all important and we count upon the effect of surprise. I hope, by the way, that your ship has been issued with signal flags of the latest pattern?"

The supper party which followed was a pleasant occasion and Delancey gained a very solid respect for Josias Rowley, who seemed to be an admirable officer in every way. About Popham he could not quite make up his mind. He found himself guessing at the expedition's object. With a Commodore and some obsolete 64-gun ships there could be no naval battle in prospect. No attempt was to be made, then, on enemy territories in Europe. But why a sepoy General? Then he remembered that Baird had served at the Cape of Good Hope in 1795 when it had been captured during the last war. It had been handed back to the Dutch as a result of the peace treaty and now the time had come to take it again. Baird and Popham knew the Cape already, so did Rowley and Byng. Yes, it would be the Cape, the ships and men being carefully chosen and the *Laura* added to the squadron as an afterthought, being destined for the East Indies after the

Cape was in British hands. He thought it likely that the squadron and convoy would sail in separate divisions and reassemble somewhere on the way to the Cape. Would the Dutch put up much resistance? He hardly thought it possible. Given the choice between French and British control they would probably choose the latter, knowing pretty well what to expect.

When able to rejoin Fiona, Delancey told her that he had been well received by Sir Home Popham.

"He sees himself as a great man, on a level with ministers and general officers. He is certainly clever, diligent, and attentive to the welfare of his own men. He does his best to prevent his seamen using bad language—I wonder with what success? I have been told that he is a Fellow of the Royal Society and I can well believe it. He was very civil to me."

"So he should be, my love! He must have noticed how well you look in your new uniform, made this time by a fashionable London tailor."

"He could look at nothing else, being consumed by jealousy. He would have done better, though, to see you in the gown that you are wearing. What stuff is it?"

"A sprigged muslin, dear—what else?"

"Some people would think it scarcely decent."

"It is meant to be only barely decent."

"On decency I insist. Remove the gown this instant! . . . How does it come off?"

"Very readily, my love. I'll show you . . ."

They were never more in love than at this time, aware as they must be that their time was short and that their separation might be long. There were moments when Delancey would mutter something about quitting the service but Fiona would not hear of it. She was the more cheerful of the two, doing her best to hearten him. He must remain, she insisted, the gallant captain she had fallen in love with—unless, indeed, he could return from the Indies as an Admiral.

"You forget, love, that I not long since became a post-captain! It will be enough for me if I return from the Indies with both arms, both legs, and nothing essential lost."

"It will be enough for me if you return *soon!*"

When the *Laura* was nearly ready for sea, Delancey was given sealed orders. He was to escort a group of West Indiamen down Channel and break the seal on reaching a certain latitude. "To the *West* Indies?" Fiona exclaimed, "But that is surely to go the wrong way? No one has provided their Lordships with an atlas!" Delancey had to explain that nearly all the outward-bound trade must set off in the same direction, separating only when the South Atlantic had been reached. There was little risk of interception because the French fleet which had been lately at sea was now back in Cadiz and blockaded there. "There let it stay!" said Fiona but Delancey doubted whether it could stay there for long. The French ships could not be supplied at Cadiz and so would be forced to sea, where Lord Nelson would be waiting for them. There would be a battle and this should hasten the end of the war. On this note the two lovers parted, Fiona standing at the Sally Port and Delancey saluting her as his gig pulled away from the stair. She was still there, a forlorn figure, still waving, when the gig passed behind some anchored ships and was lost to view.

"It's dreadful, this part of it, ma'am," said a middle-aged woman, addressing Fiona. "My husband is boatswain of the *Hercules* and has been mostly at sea these twenty years. I am used to being without him but I never get used to this moment when the ship sails. I'll feel better in a day or two. It'll be the same with you, ma'am, you'll see." Thus consoled, Fiona presently went on board the Guernsey packet and set off for the island which was now her home. She would not worry, she told herself, she would not grieve nor complain of loneliness. The more she was occupied the more quickly the time would pass. In a year or two—perhaps, for all she could tell, in a matter of months—the *Laura* would be back in Portsmouth. It was her cue—as they used to say on the stage—it was her cue to be very brave indeed. Back in Guernsey she laid ambitious plans before old Carré, her gardener, who advised her to hire some extra staff. So a boy called Pierre was recruited and was the target for much abuse from the cook and the indoor maids. By the time of Richard's return, Fiona told herself, it would be a home and garden to be proud of.

On a cold and foggy day in November Fiona heard the church bells ringing in the distance and supposed that there must be tidings of victory. The servants heard rumours but more reliable news was brought later in the day by old, bronzed and white-haired Captain Savage. As soon as he was shown into the drawing room, he came out with it:

"Good and bad news together, ma'am. The French and Spanish fleets have been all but destroyed in a battle off Cadiz but Lord Nelson was hit, shot by a musket-ball and died soon afterwards. No victory as complete was ever known, ma'am!"

"Thank God that Richard wasn't there!"

"He would rather have been present, depend on't, ma'am. But frigates play little part in a general engagement. He will gain more credit, I dare say, where he is. Have you heard from him yet?"

"No word yet, Captain Savage. He sailed as one of a squadron 'on a particular service,' under the command of Sir Home Popham. He could be at the North Pole and I none the wiser!"

"My guess would be that he is at the Cape of Good Hope. I heard some rumour of it and that would seem to be the most likely place. There were troops, you see, under General Baird, which could only mean that a landing was intended. We took the Cape before and gave it back to the Dutch. I fancy that we'll take it again and decide, this time, to keep it."

"Let's hope that we take it quickly and easily and that the Commodore sends the *Laura* home with his dispatch. But how sad about Lord Nelson! He was well liked and so much the hero! Poor Lady Nelson!"

"Lady Nelson? Ah, yes—Lady Nelson, to be sure. A sad day for her and indeed for all of us."

"But surely this victory should hasten the time when peace is made?"

"I dare say, ma'am. But you must remember that the Emperor Napoleon, as he calls himself these days, has still the upper hand in Europe. We have not defeated him on land."

"Oh, dear, I suppose not. So you think the war will go on for many more years?"

There was no resisting the appeal of the girl's tearful eyes.

"I expect Napoleon will tire of it and decide to live at peace with his neighbours."

"Wouldn't that be good news? He must see in the end that fighting does no good and that it is better to be friends."

"Yes, to be sure. He'll see reason before long, depend on't. Then we'll have Richard home again, he and many others who have been at sea for so many years. It would be good to be at peace again."

Then the newspapers came with Collingwood's dispatch and

all the details of ships taken and men killed or wounded. It was the end of February 1806 before news came of General Sir David Baird's conquest of the Cape of Good Hope and there came soon afterwards two letters from Richard; one written from Madeira, the other written from Table Bay. The first read as follows:

December 14th 1805 *Funchal, Madeira*

My dearest Fiona—We are at this beautiful island and it has been good to go ashore after nearly three weeks under sail. Madeira is mountainous, the ground rising from the coast through vineyards and so through wooded foothills up to the high peaks which are volcanic, I have been told, in origin. With Fitzgerald and Mackenzie, our surgeon, I resolved to reach the summit. We were mounted on small, wiry ponies, each followed by a Portuguese boy with a stick. So steep was the way in places that I feared we should fall over backwards. When we dismounted, however, and paused for breath, I examined the poor beasts' hooves, which are fitted, I saw with iron spikes. Without these the ascent would have been impossible and even with them it was hard enough. The view from the top was sublime but I was nervous, I must confess, when we began our descent. My thoughts were of you, concluding that while it is creditable to have a husband killed in action, it is far less romantic to become a widow as a result of his falling off a pony in Madeira and so rolling down the mountainside. All was well, however, and we are enjoying fresh vegetables and fruit. I have also done the usual thing and shipped some wine for use during our further voyaging. The Indiamen ship wine here to sell, eventually, in England. Madeira that has gone to China and back is said to have matured as if it has been six years in the cask, such being the effect of the ship's motion and the changes of climate. I shall bottle some of it especially for you.

On board the *Laura* we are getting to know each other and the crew is shaping well. Mr Mather is the perfect first lieutenant, Fitzgerald an agreeable messmate, and Greenwell does his best. Fitzgerald, I should explain, is Irish and from Wicklow, attractive in his manners and accent, quite a good officer but rather quarrelsome. Greenwell began on the lower deck and is a good practical seaman but nothing more. Sevendale of the Royal Marines is rather taciturn, but is, I suspect, a very good officer. Mr Ragley, master, is elderly and inactive. Soon after we dropped anchor here Sir Home Popham announced that there would be an examination for those who might aspire to the rank of lieutenant. The *Laura* had three candidates, Northmore having already passed, and there was a frenzy of last-minute poring over Hamilton Moore's classic work. The examining board was formidable but I think perfectly fair, with Byng of the *Belliqueux,* Edwards of the *Diomede,* and Josias Rowley in the chair. The result was very much what I expected. Topley and Stock both passed but the stolid Wayland, senior to both of them, failed in navigation and seamanship. My nightmare is to see all my good officers promoted and find myself left with men I cannot trust to prevent the ship falling overboard. One or two of the other midshipmen are promising but the rest are mere children. Northmore is signals officer and did well on the voyage hither from Portsmouth. Our seven West Indiamen were kept tolerably together and responded (eventually) to our suggestions about making more sail. I have a great deal of sympathy for the masters of merchantmen. We impress all their best hands and then blame them for poor sail drill! I had them to dinner one day when we were becalmed and consoled them with plenty of wine. They voted me a very good fellow after that and I thought more highly of them!

Madeira is a delightful island, perhaps the most beautiful I have seen, but the mischief is that ships call here on the outward and never on the homeward passage. So I cannot entrust this letter to any ship bound for England but must trust to luck and hope to fall in later with some vessel going in the right direction. When it finally reaches you it will bring my kind regards to all our friends in Guensey, to Lady Saumarez, to old Savage, and to Sam Carter too if you should see him. Above all, it brings my love to you. You will probably have heard that men-of-war in Eastern waters have sometimes fallen in with a Spanish register ship bound from Acapulco to Manila, bringing riches to the captain and some useful sum in prize-money for every man on board. People may have pointed out to you that such luck as that may come my way and that we shall end with our town house in St Peter Port. You ask little in that way, I know, but I beg you not to heed those who predict for you so prosperous a future. Why do I say this? Because I am not one of those to whom good fortune comes easily. What comfort you have (all too little for your deserving) we owe mostly to my capture of the *Bonaparte* just before the last war ended. I was lucky then but years may pass before I have such another windfall. As for a treasure ship, we find that such a prize falls, more often than not, to the son or nephew of a Commander-in-Chief, an early-promoted youngster whose ship just happens to be there, by the merest chance, when the Spaniard comes in sight. What little success I have I shall have to earn and perhaps deserve. As Shakespeare makes Henry V say: "We are but warriors for the working day. Our gayness and our gilt are all besmirch'd, With rainy marching in the painful field . . ." He thus paints me to the life! Let no one persuade you, then, that I am like to return as a Nabob from the Indies. It will be enough for me if I can come back unharmed and with credit. One thing you may depend on is that I shall never throw men's lives away to make a name for myself. On this note I shall end but will write again from a different port of call, sending my second letter by the same ship, very likely, as will carry this.

Remember me to all my friends and believe me

Your most affectionate husband,
Richard Delancey

Delancey's second letter to his wife was dated from Table Bay on January 14th 1806, and was entrusted (like the first) to H.M. Ship *Diadem*, which also carried the dispatch in which Sir Home Popham announced his conquest of the Cape:

My dearest Fiona—Now you can be allowed to know on what particular service the *Laura* was sent overseas. I was not myself informed until after we had sailed from Madeira but had made my guess before that. The result was that my seamen were taught their arms drill by our marine sergeant and my officers and midshipmen were instructed by Mr Fenner on how to serve as infantry. There was some grumbling at first, seamen muttering that they had never reckoned on becoming sodgers or lobster-backs, but they learnt their drill in the end and even held their own (or very nearly) in a competition against the marines with the purser holding the stopwatch and the surgeon as judge. It was as well we did this because we had to provide a detachment for service ashore and they did very well under Fitzgerald's command and were 'specially commended by Captain Byng. I myself did not go ashore until the fighting was over. When I did so it was to find the colony in our possession again—and what a lovely place it is! Capetown has a delightful climate and is overlooked by the impressive height of Table Mountain. Inland the farms are built in the Dutch style and are so picturesque that I made sketches of several and lacked only the time to turn them into proper water-colours. Do you remember drinking Constantia at a dinner given by Sir John and Lady Warren? Well, I have now visited Constantia itself, the vineyard from which it comes and where I bought some of the wine which is excellent. So I think well of our conquest and feel that we were foolish to have given it back after its previous capture. Wine of that quality is wasted on the beer-drinking Dutch and we shall do well in future to keep it for ourselves. You will be glad to know that we have lost very few men in killed or wounded, the *Laura* having lost none, and that nearly our whole damage was sustained by the *Leonidas* of 64 guns, which grounded while attempting to cover the landing with her broadside. Unfamiliar with Saldanha Bay, Captain Watson took his ship closer to the shore than was prudent, following the example of the *Encounter* and *Protector*, smaller ship for which there was depth enough. The result is that the *Leonidas*, which was to have escorted the China Fleet back from Canton, is now ordered home for repair. Some other ship will now have to go to China in her place but the rumour is that Sir Home, having some further operation in mind, refuses to detach any ship-of-the-line, nor even the *Diomede* of 50 guns. Should this be the truth, as seems not improbable, I may yet be able to boast that I have been to China. Nothing is decided yet and I would not have dared say so much in a letter were it not for the fact that the mail will go home with Captain Donovan together with the Commodore's dispatch and so will not fall into the enemy's hands. I could only wish that Sir Home would write another dispatch, amplifying the first, and this time make me the bearer of it. This does not seem likely! I comfort myself, however, with the thought that the Cape is now in our hands. For years past the French island of Mauritius or the Ile de France has been the base for cruisers and privateers, some of them having had great success against the country trade in the Bay of Bengal or the Straits of Malacca. Some of these marauders have been taken but the only effectual remedy, as everyone knows, must lie in the capture of Mauritius itself. Now the Cape is ours we are brought within shorter range of the French islands and can blockade them as a first step towards their eventual conquest. When they are taken, fewer men-of-war will be wanted in the Indian Ocean and the *Laura* may well be one that can be spared. That is still my hope and I comfort myself with the thought that we may be together again before the year's end. When I first knew that the *Laura* was to be stationed in the East Indies I had at first the wild idea that you might come out in an East India-man and join me at Madras. But this, I had to tell myself, was an idle dream for, apart from every other objection, we could have no certainty that the *Laura* would ever be sent there. As things are, I have at least the knowledge that you are safe in your home, surrounded by friends and neighbours. That goes some way—but only a little way—to console me for the sad fate that has parted us. A little good luck may come my way but I shall not spend all my energies in seeking it. I have work to do and must end this letter by assuring you once more of my love and asking you to believe that I remain,

> *Your most affectionate husband,*
> Richard Delancey

Fiona was made happy for a while, then months followed without a letter—one had failed to arrive as she afterwards realized—and when the next came it was dated from Canton.

March 11th 1806   *Whampoa*

My dearest Fiona—Each letter of mine comes to you from a greater distance! Short of crossing the Pacific I could not be much further away from my beloved. My consolation is that all further voyaging is likely to bring me nearer to you. I see myself engaged henceforth in services which will bring me home again, first to the Straits of Malacca, then to the Bay of Bengal and so to Mauritius and back to the Cape. Or is that too much to hope? Let me tell you, in the meanwhile, of the events which brought me here. The damage sustained by the *Leonidas* led to the *Laura* being sent to take her place as escort to the China Fleet. I came here by the shortest route through the Straits of Sunda, seeing little or nothing of the Indies. So here I am in China! If I were to write for a week and make drawings for a month

I could do little justice to all here that is strange and fascinating. Let me tell you first, however, about Sir Home Popham. He would seem to have conversed at the Cape with the master of an American ship who assured him that the people of Buenos Aires are ready to rebel against Spain. On this slender evidence Popham came to the surprising conclusion that he must go to their aid, attempting in fact the conquest of South America. All this was rumoured before I left the Cape and I fancy that he put this wild plan into execution soon afterwards. We are left to wonder what their Lordships of the Admiralty will have to say about this romantic scheme! By the time you read this you may well know the whole story, court martial and all. I always felt a little doubtful about Popham but no one can accuse him of lacking enterprise. Were I to follow his example I should set off now to attack Manila or attempt the annexation of Japan, but I am a more humdrum sort of officer and will do no more than I am ordered to do. My task is merely to escort the East Indiamen back from Canton, not in itself a very hazardous adventure. Where I shall risk my life is in eating Chinese dinners and enjoying the hospitality of the East India captains. What I shall never achieve is a knowledge of the Chinese language or any real understanding of Chinese manners and etiquette. So far, you will be glad to learn, my health has not suffered from the climate. More than that, I brought my frigate here with a healthy crew, few of them sick and only one man dying from consumption. This record, I should suppose, is rather too good to last but you may depend upon my being careful about overexposure to the sun.

The Chinese, I am told, are jealous of strangers and

intent on preventing them learning much about their country. No European is now allowed to settle in China, only the Portuguese having their settlement at Macao. The East India Company maintain a group of representatives, the supercargoes, who can live in their factory at Canton during the period of the year when their business is done. The East Indiamen which form the China Fleet are of the 1200-ton class, perhaps the finest merchantmen in the world. They might pass at a distance as smaller ships-of-the-line but they are armed only as frigates, having no lower-deck guns. The captain of an East Indiaman is called the Commander and holds a rank equivalent to Colonel in the Company's service. The senior captain is called the Commodore and has the duties of Admiral for the period of the voyage. None but the Company's ships can round the Cape under the British flag but there are other merchantmen called country ships which are owned by shipowners in India and mostly in Bombay. Some of these are fine ships, built in teak which is in some ways a better timber than oak. There are country ships here as well as Indiamen and it is these which bring opium from India. One cannot approve the traffic in this drug but those engaged in it will point out that the Chinese, if not supplied by them, would obtain their opium from some other source; and this is probably true. In these seas, as in the Indian Ocean, we have the monsoons, south-westerly winds in summer, north-easterly in winter, and one does not try to work against them. So we wait in Canton River until the north-easterly monsoon begins to blow, as from which time all trade goes southwards and westwards from here to India or from here to the Cape. At the moment, with the south-

westerly still blowing, we have ships still entering the river
and bringing us the news from India and Europe. I could
thus have heard from you had you any reason to suppose
that I should be here. But after the north-easterly monsoon
begins to blow all this northward traffic stops, the flow of
trade (and information) goes from here southwards and we
shall go with it; the mischief being that we shall then lack
warning of anything the French may intend while they
know from day to day exactly where we are. Our strength
is known, our approximate date of sailing is known, and
so is the route we are more or less bound to follow. We are
too strong for the French privateers, though, and no frigate
even would dare to intercept us. A ship-of-the-line would
be a very real threat but there is none at Mauritius according to our latest intelligence. The likelihood is, therefore,
that our voyage will be uneventful and that Britain's tea
supply may be assured for another twelvemonth together
with the China-ware out of which to drink it and the bamboo tables on which some people balance their cups and
saucers. The bamboo, I find, comes as what is called dunnage, the packing which fills up odd spaces in a ship's hold
and so prevents the cargo shifting. The dunnage belongs
to the first mate, who sells it to the dunnage merchant
when the cargo is landed. You see, I am learning all the
secrets of the East India trade! I have learnt, for example,
what happens to much of the tin which is mined in the
Malay kingdoms which face on the Straits of Malacca.
Beaten out thin, it is pasted on cardboard joss-sticks which
the Chinese then burn as a religious symbol. I suppose that
this is no more remarkable than the growing of tobacco in

Virginia so that people can burn it in London or else (among gentlemen) use it as snuff.

This letter will go by a country ship which is to sail earlier than the main fleet. It brings with it all my love for you, all my longing that we were together and all my hopes that we may be reunited before long. Take great care of yourself and write to me some day care of the government at Prince of Wales Island (also called Penang). I think it almost certain that I shall be there before long—more probably there than at Madras. I have bought you some gifts but will not attempt to send them, resolving rather to bring them to you in person, trusting you to be patient. While asking you to be patient I may add that I am anything but patient myself. I miss you far more even than I knew I would. It seems an eternity since we parted and it will seem another eternity before we meet. Remember me kindly to my friends and believe me,

Your most affectionate husband,
Richard Delancey

Chapter Two

CHINA FLEET

THE HONOURABLE East India Company's Hong or Factory at Canton faced the river but with a space between in which merchandise was being checked against invoices, weighed, and sorted. A little uncomfortable in full uniform, Delancey left his launch at the quayside with Mr Northmore and threaded his way between the boxes and bales, finally reaching the palatial building which was the headquarters of the China trade. He was shown without delay to the President's office where he found assembled the Select Committee of Supercargoes, four in number, attended on this occasion by Captain Woodfall, Commodore of the season's fleet. The President or Tyepan was Mr Thornton, grey-haired, thin-faced, and elegantly dressed. Next to him, on his right, was Mr Inglis, middle-aged, red-faced, and spectacled. On his left were Mr Grant, sallow and sleepy, and Mr Baring, young and alert. They held the best-paid and most enviable appointments in the Company's service and were all closely related to the more influential directors. Delancey had met them all but had not seen much of them since his arrival. Henry Woodfall, by contrast, he knew quite well, they having dined together on four or five occasions. The Commodore he had found to be a quiet man, reserved and apparently shy but a good seaman and easy to work with. The President's office was in the Chinese-Corinthian style with high windows, expensive candelabra, and a large portrait in oils of Queen Charlotte when young.

It overlooked the river with its turmoil of junks and sampans and was next to the general office in which the clerks had their tall writing desks.

"Good morning, Mr President," said Delancey, "good morning, gentlemen. I come in response to your letter of March 14th, marked 'urgent' and 'secret.' In what way, sir, can I be of service to the Honourable Company?"

"Good morning, Captain Delancey." replied Mr Thornton. "We are most grateful to you for coming here so promptly. You know Captain Woodfall, I think? Good. Well, we are met here in secret session—close the door, please, Mr Baring, and tell Mr Hartley that we are not to be disturbed—we are met to discuss an urgent and most disturbing communication we have just received from the Governor of Prince of Wales Island. It came by the country ship *Sarah,* probably the last vessel of the season. The Governor has good reason to believe that the French at Mauritius or the Isle of France have recently been reinforced by an 80-gun ship, the *Tourville* under Captain Roux, together with a new-built and powerful frigate, the *Romaine* of 44 guns. From the same reliable source he has learnt that the *Tourville* has been sent out with the express purpose of intercepting the China Fleet. This report must be based on rumour but the Governor points out that it would be folly to send an 80-gun ship on any ordinary cruise of commerce destruction. We must, I think, accept the fact that this danger exists. On this assumption we must decide what to do. One suggestion already made is that the China Fleet should avoid the usual trade route, keep clear of the Straits of Malacca or Sunda, and head for one of the other straits: Bali, perhaps, or Lombok. Mr Inglis reminds me, however, that this was suggested the year before last when we were faced with a similar threat, and a majority of the commanders were against it because of the navigational hazards. He suggests that they would be of the same opinion still, and I incline to agree with him. What do you feel about this, Captain Woodfall?"

"I agree, sir, with Mr Inglis. I should be strongly against taking so valuable a fleet into more or less uncharted waters. The other commanders would, I think, support me in preferring to sail, as planned, for the Straits of Malacca."

"Should we adhere to that plan we must assume that we shall have the *Tourville* to reckon with. Had the *Leonidas* been here, as expected, we should have little cause for concern. In place of the *Leonidas,* however, we have only the *Laura*—a fine ship in every way, let me hasten to add, but still only a frigate. Her being here is fortunate, nevertheless, in giving us the advice of Captain Delancey, a very distinguished officer. Pray give us the benefit of your experience, Captain. Are you of the same opinion as Captain Woodfall?"

"Yes, sir. I agree that the fleet should go through the Straits of Malacca and the more so in that a more formidable escort may be provided at Penang. It would be as well, however, if we can suggest to the French that our convoy has a stronger escort than we can actually provide."

"How are we to do that?"

"Well, sir, the French may not know that the *Leonidas* was damaged in Saldhana Bay. For all they can tell, she might be entering the river now."

"Won't they know of her arrival in England?"

"Not of necessity. Nor can they be certain that no other ship-of-the-line has taken her place."

"Forgive me, Captain." said Mr Baring at this point, "but I must ask whether a 64-gun ship, whether real or fictitious, would be thought a match for the *Tourville?*"

"No, sir," replied Delancey, "but an action with a 64-gun ship, whatever the result, would leave the *Tourville* in no state to pursue the convoy."

"But what if the *Tourville* were accompanied by a frigate of the larger class?"

"The Indiamen could, between them, beat off a frigate. In my opinion, sir, the presence of the *Leonidas* would be enough to discourage the French. After the recent battle off Cadiz I should suppose that the French morale is low."

"So you think we should try to suggest that the China Fleet is well escorted?"

"That is what I advise. What do you think, Captain Woodfall?"

"I agree, but I wonder how you propose to set about it?"

"The first step is to start a rumour. The second step is to disguise one of the Indiamen as a 64-gun ship. The third step is to disguise the *Laura* as an Indiaman."

"But surely," protested Mr Thornton, "to disguise the *Laura* is to weaken the convoy's appearance again?"

"True, sir. But the Frenchman who meets with the fire of one Indiaman, the *Laura,* will not be eager to engage the others."

"I see," said Mr Thornton. "If we agree to this plan, Captain Woodfall, which of your ships shall we transform into a man-of-war?"

"I incline to propose the *Upton Castle.* That ship's commander, John Tarleton, was formerly a lieutenant in the Royal Navy."

"Very suitable. Well, gentlemen, we have a plan to consider. Do we accept it? Mr Inglis?"

"I agree to accept Captain Delancey's proposal. I suggest, however, that the *Upton Castle* should borrow some extra men, perhaps from the country ships."

"Mr Grant?"

"Agreed."

"Mr Baring?"

"I concur, but this rumour needs to be precise and we need to agree on our story."

"Very well." replied Delancey. "The *Leonidas* of 64 guns, commanded by Captain Barnett, dropped anchor two days ago at the anchorage off Lintin Island, following a slow passage from the Cape via the Straits of Sunda. She is not coming up the river but will rendezvous with the China Fleet off Macao. If we each of us pass this information to two other persons—in strict confidence, of course—the rumour should reach the French without delay."

"Well, sir," said Mr Thornton, "we are all agreed. I leave you, Captain Woodfall, to make detailed plans with Captain Delancey, keeping me informed about the expense involved. I wish to thank you, Captain Delancey, for your able assistance. The meeting is adjourned."

Woodfall accepted a seat in Delancey's launch and they went down the river together, leaving the *Earl Camden*'s cutter to follow.

"What," asked Woodfall, "is the essential point in disguising the *Upton Castle*?"

"The essence of the disguise is to give her a battery on the lower deck. She has the ports painted in black. We need to add the port-lids in red and the guns to project."

"Very well. We can find planks ashore for the port-lids. I am not quite certain how to make counterfeit guns."

"Saw up some old or broken spars into three-foot lengths, then fit them to the dummy ports and paint them black."

"Yes, that would serve our purpose. If we do that, however,

in the main anchorage at Whampoa, we shall be seen and a second rumour will follow and contradict the first."

"I know, I thought of that. Our best way will be to let the *Upton Castle* sail ahead of the rest, assume her disguise at sea, and come into the Lintin anchorage as the *Leonidas* (64) with her proper ensign flying. I'll lend Tarleton my carpenter's crew."

Somewhere astern there was a volley of Chinese crackers accompanied by wails of grief.

"Is that your boat in trouble?" asked Delancey.

"It is my coxswain up to mischief," replied Woodfall. "Each junk has devils clinging to her stern, and each foreign craft has even more devils. If you cut across someone's bow you add your devils to his. If you pass under her stern his devils are added to yours and you have to frighten them off with fire-crackers."

"So what has your coxswain done?"

"He has collected the devils from a succession of Chinese craft and then transferred the lot to that junk he has just passed. They are furious!"

They passed between flat rice-fields where women were working under wide-brimmed hats. They saw a succession of willow-pattern pagodas and patient fishermen. The oars dipping steadily, they eventually came to the line of moored Indiamen in the Whampoa anchorage. There were fifteen of them and a dozen country ships, regularly spaced and all in very good order. As a possible prey to the French the fleet was plainly worth millions.

The *Upton Castle* sailed three days later with a full cargo, also with the *Laura's* marines, carpenter and sailmaker, with Mr Topley as signals officer, and twenty volunteers from the other ships. These supernumeraries boarded her after dark and her place in the line was taken by one of the larger country ships. On the following day Captain Woodfall, as Commodore, gave a dinner party for the other commanders, with Delancey as guest of honour. After the cloth had been removed and while the decanters were in circulation, Delancey was invited to address the others on the subject of tactics.

"Commodore, gentlemen," he began, "we have been told that a French man-of-war, the *Tourville* of 80 guns, may attempt to intercept the China Fleet with or without the help of a frigate or frigates. As escort we shall have the *Leonidas* of 64 guns, which will join us at Macao. We shall also have the *Laura,* but she will take her place among the Indiamen and will be the rear ship in the line of battle. The *Leonidas* will take up a windward position level with the *Earl Camden,* between her and the enemy—".

"Forgive the interruption," said Captain Miller, "but how do you know where the *Leonidas* will be? Her captain may have other ideas and he—pardon me—may be senior to you."

"No offence taken, my dear Miller. I happen to know that Captain Barnett is junior to me. To proceed, then, the *Tourville* will be confronted by a worthy opponent. She will not, I think, come to very close range."

"Why not?" asked Captain Wardle.

"From fear of being surrounded by Indiamen and so prevented from breaking off the action. Supposing, however, that one Indiaman should fall behind the rest, being plainly mishandled, the captain of the Tourville would be unable to resist the temptation. He would direct a frigate to cut her off."

"What if he had no frigate?" asked Wardle.

"He might then try to cut her off himself."

"With what result?" asked Miller.

"He would have such a reception that he would quit the field of battle. If *that,* he would say to himself, is the weakest of the Indiamen, undermanned, ill-treated, badly commanded, I would rather avoid the rest of them. Make all sail for Mauritius!"

"Are these tactics sure to succeed?" asked the Commodore.

"No tactics are *sure* to succeed," replied Delancey, "we can only do our best."

A long discussion followed, with nuts arranged on the table in order of battle and the French mustard pot representing the enemy. All the probable manoeuvres were described with the appropriate signal for each. When the party finally broke up Captain Miller took Delancey aside and said quietly: "I rather suspect that the *Leonidas* may have some resemblance to the *Upton Castle*."

"Keep that suspicion to yourself then. I want the right rumour to go ahead of us. People expecting to see a 64-gun ship will readily believe that what they see is what they expected to see."

"You can rely on me, sir. I'll not share my doubts with any-one else."

Delancey now decided to take the *Laura* down to Lintin Island and disguise her in private, away from the Whampoa waterfront. Before quitting the anchorage he paid a farewell visit to the President of the Select Committee, reporting on the progress of the work to be done.

"Have you put one of your lieutenants on board the *Upton Castle?*" asked the Tyepan.

"No, sir. I thought of it and then reflected that the chief mate, Mr Elton, might resent it. So I sent them a midshipman as sig-nals officer."

"With your carpenter's crew?"

"Yes, sir. With full instructions about manufacturing dummy cannon."

"What you can't produce is dummy smoke."

"No. But we bought some Chinese fireworks, which produce

a fair imitation of musketry. We think we can show a flash effect at lower-deck level."

"You have a good man in Captain Tarleton."

"Very true. Once a man-of-war's man always a man-of-war's man. He is spoiling for a fight!"

"Not, I hope, to the point of an ill-considered temerity?"

"He may err in that direction, sir, but I rather approve his belligerence. The deception will be complete if the escorting man-of-war is straining, as it were, at the leash."

"I hope you are not underrating your opponent!"

"We shall see. But I shall be very surprised—not to say offended—and possibly killed—if the French really press home their attack. Put yourself in their place, sir. Their last action against us led to the destruction of their fleet and the capture of their Commander-in-Chief. They are not in the mood to hazard all on the throw of the dice!"

"Well, Captain, I wish you a good voyage and the best of luck."

Off Lintin Island the *Laura* was repainted as an Indiaman. Delancey had expected Mather to recoil with horror from the desecration but he suddenly revealed a taste for theatricals. The frigate was to be not merely a merchantman but the least presentable ship in the fleet. Soon after the transformation had taken place the *Upton Castle* appeared in her new paintwork and drew from the *Laura* a round of applause. Tarleton had under his command as formidable a 64-gun ship as could be seen anywhere. Her lower-deck ports were open and fairly bristled with artillery. In earlier life Tarleton must have dreamt of commanding a ship-of-the-line and now he was almost making the dream come true. His commissioning pennant was hoisted, his white ensign flew at the mizen-peak, his marines were drawn up with bayonets fixed, and his recognition number, correctly signalled, was accompanied by the firing of a lower-deck gun (in fact, a Chinese firework). He was plainly ready to fight the world and Delancey made the signal Psalm 35:8: "Let destruction come upon him unawares; and let his net that he hath hid catch himself: into that very destruction let him fall." Five minutes later the *Upton Castle* replied with the signal Jeremiah 20:11, which turned out to read: "But the Lord is with me as a mighty terrible one; therefore my persecutors shall stumble, and they shall not prevail: they shall be greatly ashamed: for they shall not prosper: their everlasting confusion shall never be forgotten."

"Not bad," said Delancey to Northmore, "but I wonder who thought of that one—Captain Tarleton or Mr Topley?"

"I think, sir, it would be Topley. He has listed suitable quotations by chapter and verse and arranged them alphabetically. That one will have come under the heading 'Confusion.'"

"Indeed? Mr Topley is a promising officer and I incline to think that he is right. If all goes well, the confusion of the *Tourville* shall indeed be remembered."

"And where, sir, will the French ambush be laid?"

"Near the entrance to the Straits of Malacca, where an interception is certain."

Was he really as confident as that? Would he sight the French off Pulo Aur? And would they launch a half-hearted attack, remaining at long range so being unable to have a clear view of the *Upton Castle?* Luckily for his peace of mind, he had a great respect for Woodfall and Tarleton. As for the Indiamen, they were in a position to fire a great number of guns. Whether they would hit anything was another matter. They were wretchedly undermanned, as he knew, with crews which included Goanese, Chinese, and Malays; and the *Upton Castle* would not be much better in this respect than the others. Native seamen were well able to do the simpler tasks on deck but they were of little use in battle and few of them had the physical strength needed for working aloft. The East Indiamen could be made to look formidable, above all by assuming and keeping a tight formation, but it would be unwise to expect much else from them. They were the finest and certainly the biggest merchantmen under the British flag. From the point of view of British trade and insurance, from the viewpoint of Leadenhall Street or Lloyd's Coffee House, the successful interception of the Indiamen would be an almost unthinkable disaster. And all that stood between the French and the China Fleet was the frigate *Laura* with Delancey's ingenuity and Woodfall's presence of mind. Pondering the odds as he paced the deck, Delancey reflected that he had been dealt a poor hand of cards—and the stake was tremendous.

The French appeared to windward off Pulo Aur when the convoy was nine days out of Macao. Delancey's heart sank when three sail were reported and sank still more when they were identified later as a ship-of-the-line and two frigates, one of the largest and one of a smaller class. The *Tourville* flew a Commodore's pennant and was commanded (as afterwards known) by Etiènne Garnier. The larger frigate was clearly the *Romaine,* the other was finally identified as the *Charente.* It was the last-named ship which was ordered to reconnoitre the convoy, approaching near enough to be fired upon by the *Upton Castle.* It was evening and Garnier decided to defer his attack until the following day. What he could see was a well-formed line of fifteen Indiamen with an escorting man-of-war and a dozen country ships forming a cluster to leeward. The man-of-war appeared to be a smaller third-rate, no match for the *Tourville.* The numbers were entirely consistent with the reports he had received and he was not surprised to see the man-of-war. One of Popham's ships had been damaged at the Cape—that much was known—but he would almost certainly have sent another and she would have had time to reach Canton before the change of the monsoon. He noticed, finally, that the sternmost Indiaman was half a mile from the next ahead. The convoy was under easy sail, as if ready to give battle, but that last ship was still unable to keep in station, being probably a dull sailer under an inexperienced master. Was that likely, though? Well, it was quite possible. The appointed master might be sick or might have died. The captain of the *Charente*, Jean Delisle, reported that this last Indiaman was poorly handled. His study of her, through the telescope, failed to reveal the fact that she was towing a sail astern. But Garnier, while accepting the laggard at her face value, was not quite certain about his chief opponent. Could she be a disguised Indiaman? Such a trick had been played before. In the final resort her real force could only be tested in action.

At daybreak the situation was almost unchanged, the convoy moving slowly southwards, but the sternmost ship had dropped still farther astern and could be seen attempting to make more sail. A signal was being made from the man-of-war, enforced by the firing of a gun. Garnier decided to grasp his opportunity. Directing Delisle in the *Charente* to cut off the laggard, he himself made sail towards the British man-of-war, keeping the *Romaine* in his wake. Once the man-of-war was under fire, he could then send the *Romaine* to cut off the next two Indiamen. If he took only the three of them it would be a considerable success. Were the British man-of-war crippled, on the other hand, he could pursue the convoy for days, capturing the Indiamen one by one until Penang was reached. After their recent victory the British might well be complacent, not realizing that the

French ships were gaining in efficiency. In the past there had been bad relations between officers of the old regime and men of the revolution. There was growing up, however, a new generation of seamen, men who had never known the old regime and who saw Napoleon as a more or less true successor to Louis XV. The *Tourville* was in very good order and the *Charente* was in some ways better. They were able to give a good account of themselves. The *Romaine* was only mediocre, although a very fine ship. One way and another, Garnier could see himself as a minor hero in the history books, one of the men who restored French morale after the recent setback. He was a small and excitable man, energetic and zealous, with a mop of curly, dark hair. He ordered his men to clear for action and then made a tour of the gun-decks, accompanied by fife and drum. He told the gun-crews that they had a chance now to strike a blow for the honour of France.

Garnier was outwardly eager to report a success but inwardly anxious to avoid defeat. The last thing he wanted was a confused battle in which he would find himself surrounded by Indiamen. They might not individually amount to much but there were fifteen of them. His hope had been that they would scatter during the night but this was not their plan. They were still in line of battle under reduced sail, daring him to do his worst. It was plainly a situation in which fire should be opened at long range, using his heavy guns to best advantage. If the British man-of-war were counterfeit this would be apparent from her reply. Meanwhile, the *Charente* would make short work of the wretched Indianian so far astern of the rest. Garnier had Captain Peynier under him as captain of the *Tourville,* a nervous man who bit his nails and had a bad influence on his superior. The point to establish, he said, was whether their immediate oppo-

nent was firing guns from her lower deck. If she were, the ship
would be what she seemed to be, a third-rate of the smallest
class. If she were not, their opponent could be classed as a merchantman, perhaps with a reinforced crew but no more
formidable than a frigate. He appointed a junior officer to observe
the enemy's fire through a powerful telescope. "Vignot," he said,
"you will report at once when you have evidence either way."
When the *Tourville* opened fire, however, at extreme range, there
was nothing to report because the British guns were still silent.
Another broadside roared out, making the deck shudder beneath
his feet, but Vignot could see nothing but the splashes made by
the French shot, mostly falling short. There was a pause of five
minutes while the two ships converged and the range lessened.
Then Peynier decided to try again, his next broadside doing
some little damage but still without eliciting a reply. Peynier
knew very well what his opponent's plan would be. The first
broadside was always the most carefully aimed and the most
effective and the British were seldom willing to waste it at long
range. But there was surely no merchantman in the world so disciplined as to hold its fire for ten minutes? Their opponent was
not merely a man-of-war but one commanded by a resolute disciplinarian; this was, surely, obvious. There was no response
from the British for another five minutes. At last, watching
intently, Vignot could see the flashes from the British gun-muz-
zles—flashes visible on *both* decks, followed by billowing smoke
and followed again by the thunder of the cannon. He reported
at once to Captain Peynier. "There are flashes visible on the
enemy's lower deck." Peynier repeated this information to the
Commodore. "That settles my first problem," he replied. "I shall
not close the range any further. Continue the action." This order
was obeyed but the nervous Peynier actually kept further away

with the result that his next broadside fell short again. There was no important damage on either side, at least none visible, but the *Tourville* was hit three or four times, two seamen being wounded. No guns were fired from the Indiamen which were still placidly heading southward in close formation.

If the *Tourville* was handled with excessive caution, the *Charente* went into action with every sign of confidence. Captain Audenet half expected the Indiamen to tack in succession or even tack together, coming to the rescue of the lame duck. But she was apparently left to her fate and the French frigate headed so as to cross her bows. It was the classic situation of the snake and the rabbit. It is true that the Indiaman altered course in time to avoid the enfilade but this might well have been inadvertent, the result of mere panic. Coming down on his prey, Audenet was almost shocked to see all the evidence of ill-discipline and ignorance. The Indiaman opened fire at long range but her guns were fired singly and at long intervals. Through his telescope the French captain could see a group of men hurrying from one gun to another. Half the cannon were not even manned and the shots fired all went high and wide. As for the sails and rigging, there was a bird's nest appearance, the foresail partly furled and a staysail apparently collapsed across the after-hatch. Some ladies were seen on the quarter-deck and were, with difficulty, made to go below—one reappearing later in apparent hysterics. Some civilian passengers surrounded the captain, urging him, no doubt, to surrender. A distracted-looking officer was apparently trying to quell a mutiny with drawn sword and one mutineer seemed to be trying to strike the ensign. Other seamen on the forecastle seemed to be drunk. Captain Audenet decided that the prize was already his and that he wanted to have her undamaged. He ceased fire, therefore, and tacked so as to take up a position across his victim's bows. This time he succeeded and was rather amused to see the Indiaman's foresail come partly down with a run and flap uselessly in a tangle with the fore-staysail. He gave orders for lowering the boats and boarding the prize and then, through his speaking-trumpet, called on the Indiaman's crew to surrender. A figure now appeared on the Indiaman's forecastle and shouted back through his own speaking-trumpet: "What do you say?" Audenet repeated his demand, wondering what scene of confusion there must be behind the flapping foresail. His victims did not even know how to surrender! He hailed them once more: "Haul down your colours—or else I'll sink you! Haul down your miserable flag!"

On board the *Laura*, Delancey now gave the order for his men to man the starboard battery. Behind the foresail which momentarily hid the scene from her opponent the frigate sprang to life, every man running to his action station. The tangle aloft began to sort itself out and the ship began a slow swing to port, gradually presenting her broadside to the *Charente*. Too late, the French frigate's first lieutenant saw what was going to happen. "Back to your posts!" he yelled. "Prepare to open fire!" shouted the captain. "Look out!" bawled a dozen other voices but the general reaction was far too slow. Delancey could now be seen on the *Laura*'s quarterdeck and his drawn sword, sweeping round, pointed at a quarter-deck carronade. It fired and then, after a count of five seconds, the entire broadside fired all but simultaneously. There was a crashing of woodwork, a whistle of grapeshot, a screaming of the wounded, and a babble of orders. "Fire!" shouted the first lieutenant. "Make all sail!" bawled the captain. The Frenchmen were still trying to organize themselves when the *Laura*'s second broadside followed the first and with murderous effect. Her decks littered with dead and wounded, the *Charente* managed to break off the duel and pull clear of her antagonist. Audenet then made all sail to rejoin his Commodore, making the signal that he had sustained a loss of thirty-four dead and seventy-one wounded. Seeing this signal, Garnier ordered the *Charente* to resume her station in the line. He had now to decide what to do next. The *Charente* had walked into a trap and it was a mistake he could not afford to repeat. He was puzzled over his own opponent, observing that his own ship had so far sustained relatively little damage. Was she really a man-of-war? But then there was that other ship with a Commodore's pennant. Could she be the real escort? There had been a trap—the mishandled ship lagging astern—but was that the only trap? If the *Tourville* were handled as the *Charente* had been, he would have to end his cruise and return to the Ile de France. He decided to break off the engagement and allow the convoy to go on its way. By nightfall he was out of sight to the southward and the China Fleet was heading for the Straits of Malacca.

On the following day, in calm seas, Woodfall gave a dinner for Delancey and the other commanders. Healths were drunk in an atmosphere of mutual congratulation. John Tarleton was something of a hero and made a suitably modest speech. A ceremony then followed in which Delancey was made an Honorary East India Commander. Longhurst, commanding the *David Scott,* the ship ahead of the *Laura,* who had enjoyed the nearest view of Delancey's skirmish, was lyrical in his description of it.

"At one moment there was chaos with a ship in utter confusion, badly commanded, ill-trained, ill-disciplined, tottering somewhere between a mutiny and surrender. Then came the transformation scene! In a minute there was a frigate in action, every man at his post, every gun manned and armed. Then—crash—came that first broadside! I never saw anything like it!

The French did not know what had happened to them. And before they had recovered their wits the next broadside hit them. That ship was completely silenced and I wonder now that you did not go on and capture her. A success like that, frigate against frigate, would have earned you your knighthood."

"I'll admit I was tempted," replied Delancey, "and I agree that the frigate could have been captured. But remember, please, what I had been told to do. My orders were to escort the China Fleet from Macao to Penang. Had I taken that frigate, the French Commodore would have retaken her and would, in doing so, have attacked the convoy. Look at it from his point of view. In intercepting the China Fleet he loses a frigate, captured by an apparent merchantman! There is no comparable event in history. He is left with two alternatives. Having broken off the engagement, he can shoot himself before the court martial can assemble, or else he must go into battle and recapture that frigate regardless of the cost in lives and damage. How would the battle have ended? With the capture of the *Tourville?* I doubt it. But the result, whatever happened, would not have been consistent with the convoy's safety."

"But what if the *Tourville* had been taken?" asked Tarleton. "We might picture her surrounded by Indiamen, unable to escape and fired on from all directions. What a story that would have made, what an event for the history books!"

"That is all very well," said Delancey, "for a navy captain like you, commanding a ship-of-the-line like the *Leonidas*. A fire-eating man-of-war's captain need not count the cost. We East India Commanders—" (there was a roar of laughter at this point) "we—East India Commanders look at the matter differently. We were not sent out here to fight with the French. Our orders were to fetch tea from Canton and deliver it safely to the East India

Docks in London River. That is what we are doing and any escort provided is to help us achieve our purpose. Captain Longhurst reminded me just now that my capturing a French frigate in a single-ship duel would have earned me the honour of a knighthood. That is probably true but I was not sent to the East in search of honours, nor am I the man who should receive them. The knighthood, if there is one, should go to Captain Woodfall, the Commodore under whose pennant we were all proud to serve. Allow me, sir, to anticipate events and give the toast 'Sir Henry Woodfall!'"

Back on board the *Laura,* Mather reported on the dinner he had given for the officers and midshipmen. "Morale is high, sir," he concluded. "The effect of that pantomime, followed by those broadsides, has been excellent. We all see the *Laura* now as a crack ship. It is only a first-rate crew which can pretend to be hopeless. We had every reason, sir, to be proud of them."

"I *am* proud of them. But remember this, Mr Mather, the crew is now at its peak, fresh from Europe, healthy and up to strength. This is too good to last. We shall presently feel the effects of tropical illness, losses, invaliding, early promotion, recruitment of native seamen, and general lassitude. The real test will come in a year's time and in the year after that. We cannot hope to be as good as we are now. Our hope must be that we shall still be better than the other side."

No longer in line of battle, the China Fleet was sailing up the Straits of Malacca with the *Laura* under easy sail to windward. The distant blue mountains on either side rose above the clouds and the sea was alternately in sunlight and shadow. It was very hot and humid as compared with China, the equator being not far to the south of them. Awnings were rigged and rules relaxed about uniform, even officers wearing only shirt and trousers. Mather had a group of midshipmen taking bearings with the sextant.

Delancey walked aft and left them to it. How was he going to do without Mather? He was fortunate to have kept him for so long; for long enough, indeed, to have trained the midshipmen. He himself could never have done that so well. Fitzgerald, on the one hand, lacked the patience and Greenwell lacked the knowledge. The *Laura* would presently drop anchor at Penang and there, as he guessed, his troubles would begin. There would be malaria, to begin with, desertion quite possibly, and a general wastage of men who could not be replaced. He was lucky to have fought that action when he did, using tactics he would never dare use again while on this station. At Penang he would almost certainly receive fresh orders. He would probably hand over the China Fleet to another and stronger escort. He would have to call on the recently appointed Governor. He would also have the opportunity of writing his next letter home. He would do better, in fact, to write the letter beforehand, knowing that he would be busy from the time of his arrival there. So he went to his day cabin and began:

March 28th 1806 *Straits of Malacca*

My dearest Fiona—I please myself with the thought that I am nearer to you each day, and could only wish that this would, of necessity, hasten the day on which we shall be reunited. I suspect, alas, that their Lordships will have other work for me during the months to come. We have had some success, however, during the last few days, having saved the China Fleet from an attack by three French men-of-war, one of them the *Tourville* of 80 guns. We could not have out fought the French but we achieved a theatrical success and one which would have won your professional approval.

We have in the *Laura*—and I suppose there is in every ship—a fair amount of amateur acting talent. On the way to China, when we were sailing steadily with the south-westerly monsoon behind us, the starboard watch put on a performance of *The Rivals* by Richard Brinsley Sheridan, a play in which I know you have acted (as Julia, I think?). It was really very well done and several of the midshipmen did famously in the women's parts. I became aware, any-way, of the talent we had available.

On the return voyage I decided to transform the *Laura* into an Indiaman and we agreed, further, that she should be the worst ship in the fleet, ill-trained, ill-handled, slow, and useless. When I explained my plan to the officers I read them a part of Shakespeare's play *The Tempest* (Act 1, Scene 1). You know the scene "All lost! to prayers, to prayers! all lost!" Then I assigned them their parts in our own little play.

When faced by the enemy we were to stage a scene of utter confusion, a nightmare of disorder with more than half the crew hidden below decks and the rest behaving like madmen. Cannon would be fired but aimed wide of the target, sails were to fall on the deck, men were to mutiny and fight each other—there was to be a scene wor-thy of Drury Lane. The success of this production was possible only because the crew was highly disciplined and trained by Mr Mather, the ideal first lieutenant. I could never have risked a scene of confusion if there had been any danger of the confusion becoming real.

Calling upon our acting talent, we presented the very picture of chaos, the characters on stage being some of them civilians and some of them ladies (with costumes made for *The Rivals*), some of them in a state of mutiny and some of them drunk. So our opponents, in a French frigate of about the same force, declined to take us seriously. They ceased fire and awaited our surrender. At that moment we suddenly pulled ourselves together and fired two broadsides which nearly sank them. This ended the battle, the French concluding that where the worst ship was so dangerous the best ships must be invincible. Their Commodore took himself off and will discover before long that he is the laughing stock of the Indian Ocean. With our losses confined to two men slightly wounded, I flatter myself that our farce has been a success. Let me add that I have no plans for staging a tragedy.

We are approaching Prince of Wales Island, a settlement which has recently been elevated to the rank of Presidency, complete with Governor, Council, and Garrison. There are further plans for making it a naval base with facilities for building men-of-war. It remains to be seen whether these plans will answer. We spoke with a southward-bound country ship yesterday and I learnt from her that Sir Edward Pellew (the Admiral under whose orders I am placed) is there on a flying visit from Madras. He is one of the best seamen of the day with a great reputation in gunnery and tactics. He may well think up some service for me which I had rather avoid! He will be much concerned over the damage being done by French privateers which operate from Mauritius. The most active of these is a ship called the *Subtile* commanded by the famous Pierre Chatelard, who has so far avoided all efforts to capture him.

We capture other privateers from time to time and our prizes are then sold for the benefit of the captors, much to the profit of people like myself. After changing hands two or three times the privateer vessel, which is usually ill-designed for anything but privateering, is then repurchased by her original French owners and sent forth again to prey on our shipping. It would be in the public interest to destroy them on capture but this we cannot afford to do. I should add that we in the *Laura* have so far made nothing. We might have earned, and we may even receive, the thanks of the East India Company but this will do nothing to pay our mess-bills.

On this subject I should add that we have now recruited a number of Chinese servants. I have one to do my laundry and the wardroom officers have three, one of them a cook. So we have Chinese dishes on occasion, and we add to these a variety of tropical fruit. One of these, the durian, has a pleasant taste but a most offensive smell and has to be eaten while holding one's nose!

We have just sighted Prince of Wales Island and I am wanted on deck. So I will close this letter, meaning to tell you in my next letter how much you mean to me and what misery it is to be so far from you and for so long. Pray remember me to my neighbours round Anneville.

And believe me still,

Your most affectionate husband,
Richard Delancey

Chapter Three

THE TASK

D ELANCEY had been invited to dine at Suffolk House, Prince of Wales Island, and his host, Mr William Phillips, had asked him to bring one of his officers as a fellow guest. Greenwell had been his choice and Delancey, having hired a two-horse palanquin, told this officer what to expect. He had to confess to himself that Greenwell was not the ideal fellow guest, being round-shouldered, haggard in appearance, and tongue-tied in company. Delancey had supposed, however, that the experience would be good for him. Leaving the harbour area they could see, looking back, the *Albion* (74 guns) at anchor, together with the frigates *Duncan* and *Caroline* and the sloop *Seahorse*.

"Mr Phillips," he explained, "is Collector of Customs and Land Revenue. He is not a Member of Council but he affects a superior style of living. He plans, I have been told, to make Suffolk House a smaller copy of the Governor-General's palace at Barrackpore. It already has a park, it seems, and begins to look out of the ordinary. The dinner to which we have been invited will follow a pattern set by the Dutch in Java. You are used to curry, I know, but this will be something more elaborate. It is usual to drink beer with it rather than wine and it is followed by a Malay dish of sago, coconut milk, and gula Malacca."

"What is gula Malacca, sir?"

"A sort of molasses derived from the palm tree. It has a cooling effect after the curry—not that Malay curry is so very hot, compared at least with what they have at Madras."

"Seems to me odd, sir, that people who live in so hot a climate should like curry at all."

"Well, they have the spices and so maybe incline to make use of them. Our fellow guests on this occasion will include Sir Edward Pellew, Captain Macalister, and a number of Mr Phillips's colleagues in government."

"I hear, sir, that the Admiral was a guest last night on board the *Earl Camden*."

"Yes, and Captain Woodfall deserves the compliment. We are fortunate to be serving under Sir Edward's flag. Did you ever see him before?"

"No sir. Like everyone else I've heard tell of him for years past. When he was a captain I have been told that he could race any midshipman to the topmast-head, giving him to the main-top. He is remembered as the man who sank the *Droits de l'Homme* and who rescued the crew of the *Dutton*, East India-man, when she was wrecked at Plymouth."

"Yes, he is an almost legendary character. But he is Commander-in-Chief for the first time and has no easy task. He has about thirty ships in all and has with these to defend all the commerce of India against the French cruisers and privateers."

"Wouldn't he do better to capture their base?"

"This is, no doubt, what he would prefer to do. But for that he needs the co-operation of the Government of India. They have not so far seen fit to provide the troops. If they were to lose a few Indiamen they might think differently."

The two sturdy ponies from Acheen in Sumatra were plodding more slowly as the track grew worse. On one side was a pepper plantation, on the other an area of virgin jungle with immensely tall trees and, beyond them, the distant summit of Penang Hill. Their vehicle stopped for a few minutes while the Malay syce went to inspect the planks of a dubious bridge. It was then that Delancey became aware of the noise, the call of the birds, the continuous sound of the cicadas, the rustle of the treetops. There were also myriad scents, the less acceptable coming from a Chinese hovel by the wayside from which a slant-eyed child gazed at them in solemn wonder. It was hot and humid and the two officers had removed their uniform coats and loosened their cravats. Presently their syce returned and their journey was resumed. Ten minutes later they entered the grounds of Suffolk House, which could be seen on the rise to their left. Delancey and Greenwell now put on their uniforms, adjusted their cravats, and reached for their hats. Curving up the hillside, the drive finally brought them to their destination, a timber-built, palm-thatched, white-painted house in the local style. A veranda surrounded it on the first floor and there was an open-sided room over the carriage port into which their carriage was driven. Indian servants came forward to open the vehicle's door and the visitors were ushered upstairs to find their host awaiting them on the first floor. He was a youngish man with a red face, in shirtsleeves and holding a wine glass.

"Come in, gentlemen, come in! Captain Delancey, your servant. And this officer? Mr Greenwell, I am happy to make your acquaintance. And do please remove your coats and loosen your cravats. It is hot enough in this climate without being overclothed as well!" Delancey and Greenwell discarded the garments they had just put on and bowed to the company at large. "And now you must meet my other guests. I need not introduce you to Admiral Sir Edward Pellew, nor perhaps to

Captain Macalister. Allow me, however, to present Mr Hobson, Mr Robinson, Mr Erskine, and Mr Ibbetson. Captain Laurence of the *Albion* . . . Mr Riley of the Admiral's staff, Mr Barstow of the *Duncan* . . ."

Sitting down, Delancey found himself next to Captain Macalister, a Member of Council and Commander of the Company's troops in the island.

"I am interested to meet someone of your name, Captain Delancey. It is not, I should say, a common name and yet there is—or was—another Delancey in the East Indies. Could it be a relative?"

"I had an elder brother who went to sea and to India but I have heard nothing from him for years and had assumed that he was dead. He was mate at one time of a parsee-owned country ship out of Bombay but that was when I was a midshipman. Is he really still alive?"

"There was a man of that name here in Georgetown and he had certainly been mate in a country ship. He sustained some injury, however, which brought him ashore as a ship's chandler. He was here for some years and I remember him quite well. Then he went to live on the mainland, in Kedah. I last heard of him in Malacca but was told at the same time that he had left there. Your brother—if it is your brother—would seem to be a rolling stone. Does that sound like the character you knew as a boy?"

"Yes, sir, I think it does. He was a good seaman, I fancy, but wild and unruly, seldom out of trouble."

"Well, now you mention it, the Delancey I knew had a rather dubious reputation. I cannot recall now whether anything was proved but his departure was welcome, I think, to the government. He had children by a Malay and finally deserted her and them. He is not a relative who would do you credit and I shall not mention the possible relationship to anyone else."

When dinner was served Delancey found himself on the Admiral's right. Pellew was a vigorous man of middle age, with piercing eyes and hearty manner, somewhat running to fat but looking like the great seaman he was known to be. Their first meeting had been merely formal but the Admiral now studied Delancey with some care.

"I am glad of the chance that has made you my neighbour at dinner," said the great man (but was it mere chance?). "I have heard about you from Woodfall, on whom you have made a great impression. By his account you saved the China Fleet!"

"He is too generous, Sir Edward. Most of the credit should go to the Commodore himself and not a little to the other commanders."

"That is not their opinion, and I have learnt more from them than from your report."

"I excluded from my report all mention of tricks we may wish to repeat."

"We'll never dare repeat that one. I take your point, however, and applaud your brevity. Your immediate reward will be a good dinner. Look at that—our opponents in line ahead!"

The dinner table had been laid in a central room, opening on the veranda at either end and cooled by a through breeze and by the punkah overhead. The Admiral, on their host's right, was being offered rice, to begin with, from a large wooden bowl. The white-uniformed servant who carried it was followed in succession by thirty-one other servants, the leaders bearing dishes of curried meat, chicken, or fish, with the more junior servants bringing up the rear with the sambals (chutney, bananas, prawns, cucumber, and so forth). Mere politeness compelled each guest to take a little from every dish and even the most cautious ended with a small mountain of food on the plate. Those who had begun with too much temerity were puzzled at the end about where to put the last delicacies which were offered. Wine was provided but most people preferred beer. They were soon mopping their foreheads as the curry had its effect and many began to feel unbearably replete.

"Rice fills you up," the Admiral explained, "but the effect wears off, leaving you with some appetite for supper. One feels at this stage that one will never be hungry again!"

Hardly were the first plates empty before the column of servants re-formed for a fresh attack, but few would accept more than a token replacement. Then the toasts were proposed, to the King, to the Royal Navy, to the East India Company, to the prosperity of the island. By then the sweet was being served with a cooling effect and with it the formalities were relaxed.

"For your skirmish with Commodore Garnier you deserved a good dinner," said the Admiral to Delancey, "but you also deserve a relief from convoy duty. Perhaps you will have heard the name mentioned of Pierre Chatelard, commanding the *Subtile?*"

"The French privateer? Yes, sir."

"I want the *Subtile* destroyed."

"She will not be easy to take, sir."

"Nor is it enough to take her. I want her burnt, sunk or completely wrecked."

"And that is to be my task?"

"Yes, I think you are the man to do it. In the ordinary way we treat privateers like mosquitoes. We have some sort of mosquito net to keep them out of particular places like the Bay of Bengal. We slap at them when they bite us. We never plan a systematic hunt for one particular mosquito. But this man Chatelard has gone too far. I mean to detach a frigate with no other duty, her orders to destroy the *Subtile*. I need a captain with brains and I think you should be the man. Have I made a good choice?"

"I may be as good a man as the next. But it is not a task that everyone will want. A privateer is not a Spanish register ship from which to make a fortune. She is not a French frigate from the capture of which a captain might gain credit. Out of a privateer destroyed we cannot even make prize-money. I have given some thought, however, to the problem posed by Pierre Chatelard and have reached one conclusion. It is this, that Chatelard acts upon information received from spies on shore, one of them probably in this settlement."

"Why are you so sure of that?"

"Because he has no failures. If one of our sloops were to turn pirate, the first merchantman her captain saw would have naval escort, the second would be too heavily armed, the third would be too fast, and the fourth would be in ballast. The *Subtile* is never outsailed or outgunned. She appears in the right place at the right moment, clearly as the result of good intelligence."

"One might think that you had commanded a privateer."

"I did command one, years ago."

"That being so, you are the very man I want. I shall give you your orders in writing tomorrow but their substance I give you now—"Find and destroy the *Subtile*." Do you think you can do it?"

"I think it probable, sir. But you must be prepared to accept a heavy loss of life. Cruising among the islands will lead to sickness among my crew, the result of proximity to all these pestilent swamps. Destroying the *Subtile* may mean the destruction of the *Laura* as well."

"A heavy price, I must confess. But I have to confront the government, the merchants, and underwriters and they leave me no alternative."

"Would you think it wrong of me to ask for a reward?"

"What do you ask?"

"For the *Laura* to be sent home."

"I'll do my best. Failing that, I could transfer you to the Cape, as a move at least in the right direction. By next year we may regard the *Laura* as worn out. She would have been built in— let's see—in about 1775? At the beginning of the last war?"

"No, sir—in 1773."

"Thirty-three years . . . yes, she's an old ship. She should be sent home in 1808 at latest and this I shall be prepared to recommend."

"Thank you, sir. My chances of locating the *Subtile* would be greatly improved if your staff could list the prizes she has taken and the location of each capture."

"Tell Riley what you want. I gather, by the way, that Chatelard has been extremely kind to his prisoners; they all live to tell the tale."

"The good privateersman is always humane, sir. He thus encourages merchantmen to surrender without a fight."

"You know the trade too well, Delancey. I wonder you gave it up!"

"To be a successful privateer, sir, one needs to be on the losing side. Our privateer commanders made fortunes during the last war. It is the French who have their opportunity in this."

"And that's a fact and be damned to them!"

It was late afternoon when the dinner ended, everyone more than replete. As if by magic the different carriages began to appear at the door. Waiting their turn to say good-bye, Delancey and Greenwell could look across the straits to the mountains on the mainland culminating in Kedah Peak; the green carpet of jungle trees darkened by a cloud shadow moving slowly towards them. As they watched, the peak was blotted out by greyness. The wind had risen and the air felt cooler as they left. "If you ask me," said Greenwell, "I think it is going to rain." As their carriage drove off the two officers, who had donned their uniform coats before leaving, removed them again, reflecting that these garments existed in the East only for the purpose of a very fleeting ceremony. The sky presently darkened and a few drops of rain fell, at which their syce, smiling broadly, produced two umbrellas made of oiled paper on a bamboo frame.

"A cheap imitation," said Greenwell. "I could wish that I had my boat cloak."

"On the contrary," replied Delancey, "I have been told that the umbrella was invented in these parts and took this form, of which the European version is the copy. As for your boat cloak, you would be as wet with perspiration in it as you are going to be without it."

"I see what you mean, sir."

Abruptly and without further warning the downpour began, such rain as Delancey had never seen before. It fell solidly as if thrown down by invisible buckets. They were wet through in a matter of seconds and no conceivable umbrella or cloak could have made the slightest difference. Rain drummed and bounced on the track, cut through the foliage of trees, and turned each ditch into a miniature river or torrent.

The whole world had turned, seemingly, to water, a fact

which gave amusement to their driver if not to the ponies. The vehicle was finally brought to a halt under a clump of trees which offered a little protection. Ten minutes later the rain stopped and the sun came out again, turning much of the water into vapour. In the atmosphere of a Turkish bath the journey was resumed and the two-horse palanquin brought them back to the water-front near the fort, the point from which their journey had begun. Delancey had been given a great deal to think about.

Calling next day on the Admiral, Delancey was given his written orders and told to victual his frigate for a six-month cruise. The flag lieutenant gave him, in addition, a list of captures made by Pierre Chatelard. To this was added a sealed letter, to be opened after the capture of the *Subtile,* authorizing him (he was told) to proceed to the Cape. A further sealed packet was to be opened after twelve months if the *Subtile* should have eluded him. Armed with these various orders, Delancey said good-bye to the Admiral with a certain finality. "Remember," Sir Edward concluded, "I don't want to have the *Subtile* as a prize. I don't want to have Chatelard as a prisoner. I merely don't want to hear of them again!" Going back to the *Laura,* Delancey placed the list of captures alongside the chart and neatly marked them in with the date of each. He dined alone that day and spoke to nobody, returning continually to the chart and studying what he must try to see as a pattern. The art of the thief-taker, he told himself, is to forecast the future crimes of one whose past crimes reveal a certain habit. If the same man broke into houses A, B, and C, we may know something at least about his preferences and methods. What could he tell, in the same way from a list of prizes taken?

The list read as follows:

Ship	Location	Cargo	Date
Oriente	Bencoolen	Cloth	July 7th 1805
Jehanzier	Tenasserim	Rice	August 1st 1805
Macaulay	Cape Rachado	Cinnamon and Pepper	August 13th 1805
Jambalasse	Pulo Bintan	Nankeen and Tea	September 23rd 1805
Lowjee	Billiton	Pepper	October 4th 1805
Gunjawar	Malacca	Nankeen	October 17th 1805
Jarah	Pangkor	Rice	November 8th 1805
Fortune	Sandheads	Opium, Rice, Wheat, Piece Goods & Specie	January 21st 1806
Ganges	Bassein	Pepper	January 30th 1806
Susannah	Little Andaman	Indigo	February 19th 1806

One thing apparent from the chart was that Pierre Chatelard's most valuable captures had been among the latest; probably the *Susannah* and the *Ganges*. These were the losses which had spurred the Calcutta merchants into activity and protest. The next point of interest was the apparent length of the cruise. No ship could remain so long at sea without returning to base for supplies. A man-of-war could refit at sea with the aid of a supply ship but a privateer could rely on no such system. The *Subtile* had sailed from Mauritius, but could not possibly have refitted there, or anywhere so distant, between October 28th and January 21st. That period represented, nevertheless, a break in her activities. In theory, Chatelard might have been merely unlucky during those weeks. But Delancey thought that unlikely. It was far more probable that he had withdrawn then from the trade routes in order to refit at some chosen port of call. How long would such a refit take? Pierre Chatelard was, he remembered, a man of the old regime who had been at sea before the revolution. He would almost certainly choose to be in port for Christmas with sucking pig as the chief item on the menu. Allowing time for the seasonal festivities he would want a month ashore, roughly the month of December. His chosen port must therefore be within three weeks' sail of the Sandheads and at no greater distance from Pulo, Pangkor. The distance might be something over two thousand miles. It could not be in the Andamans or Nicobars. He doubted whether he could use a harbour in Sumatra without the fact being known in Penang, and the same argument applied almost equally to Java. The *Subtile,* he concluded, must have a secret base in Bali, Lombok, or Timor. But Timor, come to think of it, was too distant . . . His thoughts turned to Borneo, to a thousand miles of unexplored and imperfectly charted coastline. But much of this, he argued, would be too far away. The ideal base would be somewhere, surely, between Cape Datoe and Cape Sambar, somewhere more or less equidistant from the Straits of Malacca and Sunda. To search that area would be to cover six hundred miles of coastline with little or no help from the primitive inhabitants. Before attempting such a search he would need better information than he now possessed.

Delancey thought now, as he paced the deck, of Chatelard's system of intelligence. Suppose he had spies ashore at Bassein, Penang, Malacca, and Palembang, how could they communicate quickly enough with their employer? Take the case of an opium ship, laden with rice, wheat, piece goods, and specie (in addition to the drug). She would sail from Calcutta in January or

thereabouts and call at all the major ports right down to the
Lingga Archipelago, collecting tin, pepper, rattan, wax, and betel-
nut before going on, eventually, to China. If the *Subtile* had a
rendevous near Lingga, how could an agent at Malacca ensure
that his information would arrive in time? In point of fact the
only opium ship taken by the *Subtile* had been intercepted off
the Sandheads, in the approaches to Calcutta, but what about
the *Macaulay*, taken off Cape Rachado? Could news of her coming have been sent from Penang? It was true, of course, that an
opium ship would lose time in discharging and shipping cargo
but the boat which conveyed the message might equally lose
time in finding the privateer. Was there a native boat suitable for
the purpose? He decided at this point to take Mather into his
confidence. After all, if he himself were to go down with fever,
it would be Mather's task to destroy the *Subtile*. So Mather needed
to know all that his captain had been told or had guessed. Nor
was Mather unhelpful when consulted.

"I should not have thought that the ordinary native boats
were built for speed. I suspect that the bamboo slats in the sails
of the Chinese craft give them some capability of working to
windward. Sampans are slow, I should say, and the Malay prahus
no better. But there was something I heard recently which might
have a bearing on this problem. A lieutenant in the *Seahorse* had
been ashore somewhere in the Riau Strait—maybe Pulo Bintan
or thereabouts—and visited a Malay village where the men raced
model boats against each other, betting on the result."

"I never heard of that. But why is this relevant?"

"Well, sir, the boats were perhaps two feet long, each with
an outrigger and a float on the end of it."

"Yes?"

"The outrigger enabled each boat to carry a vast sail area in relation to its size. They could sail at a remarkable speed. The officer who had seen this tried one of these boats against his six-oared cutter. Pulling their utmost, his men were outdistanced each time, and still outdistanced when they hoisted sail. He was surprised at the result of these trials and wondered whether the Malays ever built full-size boats of the same pattern. If they did, he thought, they would be just as fast. But the Malays he questioned could give him no sufficient answer to his queries on this point, probably because they did not understand him."

"Mr Mather, I am obliged to you. I understand that there are boats at Madras with an outrigger, called catamarans and designed so as not to upset in the surf. But success with a model is not quite the same thing as success with an actual boat. For one thing, no one is drowned when a model capsizes!"

"Very true, sir. But if there are small craft with an outrigger and a large sail area, they could be very fast indeed. They might not be suitable for the ocean but could work up a great speed in the Straits of Malacca. Should we see a craft of this kind we shall have the clue, perhaps, to the plan which Chatelard follows."

"I agree. We should learn nothing, however, from intercepting such a vessel. She would carry nothing in writing, of that we may be sure, but her mere presence would show us how the trick is done."

What further information they could obtain about catamarans in Far Eastern waters was contradictory and confused, some people having heard that such craft existed but none claiming to have seen them at sea. By one account they had once been common but had more recently gone out of fashion.

While still refitting and shipping provisions at Penang, Delancey received the following letter from the Admiral:

Sir—Captain Stavely of the *Seahorse* has recently been admitted to hospital with a serious illness, since when a medical board has reported that he must be invalided home. It is now my duty to appoint an acting captain to that ship and I have decided to promote Lieutenant Nicholas Mather into the vacancy in recognition of your success in the recent action against the French ships *Tourville, Charente,* and *Romaine.* You will accordingly direct Lieutenant Mather to assume command of the *Seahorse,* giving him the acting commission enclosed herewith. You will no doubt wish to promote one of your other officers as first lieutenant and one of your young gentlemen to the vacant lieutenancy. If you will submit the names for promotion I shall make out the acting commissions accordingly . . .

With this letter before him, Delancey reflected that this moment had long since been inevitable. He could not have expected to keep Mather any longer and had been lucky indeed to have kept him for so long. Now he would have to make do with Fitzgerald as first lieutenant, a handsome, black-haired, thin-faced man much admired by the ladies, a man with an attractive Irish accent but a poor replacement for Mather, an officer who was good in battle but no pastmaster in day-to-day training and management. At this point the deterioration of his crew would begin. His acting-lieutenant would be the Hon. Stephen Northmore, over the head of Wayland, who had failed the examination, leaving Topley next in line. Northmore would make a good officer, of this there could be no doubt. But what if Fitzgerald were promoted or killed? Greenwell would be hopeless as first lieutenant and Northmore would lack the experience. Losses, moreover, had begun on the lower deck, a petty officer and three seamen invalided out (all members of the one boat's crew), one seaman drowned, and one marine private deserted. So it would go on, with no replacements to be found. In the meanwhile, he must congratulate Mather and wish him joy on promotion. He sent for him at once and came to the point:

"Mr Mather, it is my, pleasure and privilege to hand you your acting commission as Master and Commander of the *Seahorse,* succeeding Captain Stavely, who has been invalided home. I suggest that you call on the Admiral now and go on board the *Seahorse* tomorrow in the forenoon, returning to this ship for a farewell dinner at which your messmates will say good-bye to you. For my part I must thank you now for all your past service under my command. I could not have had a better first lieutenant. I am totally confident of your fitness to command your own ship and I look forward to hearing of your being made post. I shall do all in my power to further your career and have no doubt that it will be not merely successful but distinguished."

More unnerved than Delancey had ever seen him, Mather stammered his thanks and withdrew. Interviews followed with Fitzgerald and Northmore, with Greenwell, Wayland, and Topley. A weakened team had to re-group so as to face the future. If only Greenwell had any personality, if only Wayland had any brain!

The Admiral sailed next day for Madras, taking his squadron with him and leaving the *Laura* to complete her refit and proceed on her mission. The farewell dinner for Mather was followed next day by a farewell dinner on board the flagship. All seemed very quiet after the squadron had gone. Leaving Fitzgerald to find his feet as first lieutenant and leaving Northmore to have his new uniform made by a Sikh tailor in Georgetown, Delancey spent time ashore making discreet inquiries about possible enemy agents. He found that Penang had been visited last year by a slightly suspect European who had described himself as a missionary and who had presently been asked to leave. If his object had been to set up a network of native agents there was little hope of identifying his representatives in Georgetown. There were swarms of tradesmen there, Chinese, Eurasian, and Indian, and almost any one of them might serve his purpose, few of them feeling any particular allegiance towards the East India Company. One government official, the Assistant Secretary, proved particularly helpful—being fluent in Malay—but he offered little hope of finding the needle in this particular haystack. He knew of the Malay type of catamaran but had never actually seen one in Penang harbour. Nor could he see that such a craft could serve any useful purpose, whether for fishing or for trade. That Pierre Chatelard should have a system of intelligence seemed to him very possible and he promised to look out for any sign of espionage. He told Delancey what he knew about Borneo but admitted that he had never been there. He was evidently a keen antiquary and told his guests at dinner one day that the ancient capital of Kedah lay buried somewhere in the jungle, perhaps near the foot of Kedah Peak. He had heard stories about it and had been shown one or two carved stones said to come from there. The conversation centred presently on the future of Prince of Wales Island. Trade was flourishing there but the place, it was now clear, was far from deserving its reputation for health. Many had died recently of malaria and there had been too many deaths from the liver complaint. The one certain fact was that seamen fared better at sea or even in harbour if prevented from going ashore. On land there was nothing as fatal as the pestilent swamps which surrounded many a river mouth. What no one could understand was why Georgetown, surrounded by recently cleared jungle, was as unhealthy as it was proving to be.

As the process of refitting and victualling came to an end Delancey had the opportunity to write home.

April 25th 1806   *Prince of Wales Island*

My dearest Fiona—My last letter, of immense length and full of detailed information, went with a man-of-war to Madras but the opportunity occurs to write again, entrusting the letter to a ship which should reach home even sooner. Our stay here is nearing its end, the chief event being the promotion which has deprived me of my first lieutenant, Mr Nicholas Mather, whom you will remember. The promotion was more than justified but I cannot persuade myself that his replacement will leave me with so little to do! It is all too likely that we shall have other losses and that I shall have to work harder as time goes on. You might suspect that I might as readily fall sick as anyone else but I never think that at all likely. I feel (wrongly, no doubt) that I am indispensable and that, whoever goes sick, it must never be me. I dread the moment, however, when I become, in effect, my own first lieutenant because I was never very good in that role and have been spoilt for years by having, in Mather, the perfect deputy. This is a beautiful country and I have been royally entertained by the folk who are stationed here. I have made a friend of one rather junior official, Thomas Raffles, who is clearly the government's chief source of inspiration and energy. Some more senior men think of themselves as in exile from London or Calcutta but this is his first overseas appointment and he is fascinated by everything. He has a charming wife called

Olivia and a delightful Malay-style house full of native documents, and curios. With his help I have picked up some
slight acquaintance with the Malay language and some
slight knowledge of Malay institutions and folklore. All this
may be useful in the months to come. But you will ask at
this point how many months must pass before I begin the
voyage home. The answer must be that I have no idea. In
more cheerful moods I say '1807.' When sunk in gloom,
which is not very often, I groan '1810.' I am now to be
employed on 'a particular service.' You last heard the phrase
applied to Sir Home Popham's conquest of the Cape. On
this occasion the service is different to this extent that only
my own ship is involved. All else is secret and I must say
no more lest the enemy should see this letter. Do you
remember young Northmore? He now dons his uniform
and wears his sword as acting lieutenant and I expect to
see my other midshipmen similarly transformed, boys made
into men with a stroke of the pen! I wonder how they will
do as officers and then I remind myself that older men long
ago had as many doubts about me, and perhaps with more
reason! Mine was a chequered career, God knows, but I am
now a grave and responsible officer, older than most people on board, and no youngster can imagine that I was once
of his age and thought (at one time) to have no future at
all. I shall reveal no important information if I tell you that
I shall presently visit Malacca, for long the chief city in the
Straits of that name, fortified by the Portuguese but now
dwindled in importance. It is said to be picturesque and I
may be tempted to portray its crumbling glories in water-
colour. I have made several sketches of Penang but will not

attempt to send them home. You shall hear of all these places some day when seated by the fireside at Anneville and our friends will mutter to each other "How tedious the old man is with all his tales of the East!" This thought warns me to curtail my description now and end this letter, asking you to believe me still, and always,

Your most affectionate husband,
Richard Delancey

Chapter Four

BORNEO

THE *LAURA* was at anchor off the town and port of Malacca and Delancey was paying his courtesy call on the Company's Resident, Captain William Farquhar, who had governed the place since its capture from the Dutch in 1796. He was a rather pedantic Scotsman, a little pompous on first acquaintance and seemingly embittered by the slowness of his promotion. His knowledge of the country and of the Malay language was profound and he knew all that was to be known about the local trade and commerce. He knew about Chatelard of the *Subtile* and gave careful thought to the system of intelligence upon which his operations might be based. He acknowledged that Chatelard might have an agent in Malacca, perhaps some Dutch Eurasian with French sympathies, perhaps some Javanese trader working merely for pay. With twenty thousand inhabitants, it would not be easy to find the spy among them. As for a fast outrigger sailing canoe, he had seen nothing of the sort but had to confess that he had made no study of the native small craft. When asked about Delancey's brother, Michael, he was more forthcoming.

"There was a man here of that name when I first arrived. We thought at first that he was French and planned to take him into custody as a possible revolutionary. It appeared, however, that he was a native of Jersey, speaking English with only a trace of a foreign accent. He had been at sea but had sustained some back injury and came ashore, setting up in business as a small tradesman. His shop, I remember, was near the bridge and he lived with a Malay woman who had several children by him. I supposed at first that he was addicted to drink or drugs but was told by the police that he was merely eccentric. He was said to be especially interested in the primitive people of Malaya and was often to be seen practising with a blowpipe."

"A blowpipe?"

"Yes, a weapon used mainly in hunting. I have one here." The Resident took a slender dark-coloured stick from a corner of the room. Delancey saw that it was over five feet long, hollow, and shaped at one end like the mouthpiece of a bugle. His host took a dart made of bamboo, sharp at one end and fitted at the other end with a pith 'cork.' Inserting the dart, which exactly fitted the blowpipe, Farquhar inflated his cheeks and blew with pursed lips into the mouthpiece, like blowing the bugle but with an almost explosive puff. The dart was embedded an inch deep in the woodwork on the far side of the room.

"It is not lethal in itself," Farquhar explained, "but the point is dipped in poison from the Ipoh tree. They use the same sort of blowpipe in Borneo, I am told."

"Do the Malays use it?"

"No, they are more advanced in the ways of civilization. Nor do they live in the jungle. They live along the riverbanks and use firearms. Here, for example, is a small 'lela' or brass swivel gun of the type they mount in their war prahus." He pointed to a rather ornate weapon of almost modern appearance.

"Perhaps they learnt about firearms and cannon from the Por-tuguese?"

"They had no need! The Malays had artillery before the Portuguese reached the Indian Ocean. I have sometimes wondered whether cannon were not actually invented here. This town, I believe, is where spectacles were first manufactured. People ingenious enough for that might have invented cannon as well."

"But why do you think that probable?"

"Well, they had the blowpipe which embodies all the principles of the firearm except for the explosive. Their Chinese friends and neighbours had the gunpowder. It would require no genius to combine the two ideas. In one way, of course, the blowpipe is superior to the firearm for it is silent. The expert will seldom miss at twenty yards but if he does the monkey or parrot—or human, for that matter—is still unaware of the danger and may be the target for another shot. When Malacca was taken by Albuquerque in 1511 the Portuguese suffered more casualties from blowpipe darts than from the defenders' artillery or elephants. They did not die immediately, of course, the poison often taking an hour or two to produce a fatal result."

"How interesting!" said Delancey. "But my brother, from what you say, would seem to be no more eccentric than you or I."

"I am not sure about that. He had gone native, as one might say, and may even have become a Muslim. He went away rather suddenly, no one knew why, but left his Malay woman here. His chandler's shop is kept now by a Tamil but he is still, I suspect, the owner of it."

"I envy you, sir, your knowledge of the country. When at Penang I was similarly envious of Mr Raffles."

"Raffles? Well, he speaks Malay but cannot write it, nor has he been in the country very long. One must give him the credit for being at least interested. Francis Light, the founder of Penang, was the last man who understood the people of the Straits. The present government there is so absurdly overstaffed that the officials only meet each other. They will die before they can tell a Chinese from a Malay."

"Several have died already, sir, the place being far less healthy than was at first supposed."

"Aye, they are discovering what I could have told them, that malaria appears as soon as you fell the jungle. Let it alone and you can avoid the disease—except, of course, in the coastal swamps."

At the end of an interesting conversation Delancey obtained from Farquhar the loan of a Portuguese police sergeant called De Souza who spoke Malay and was indeed a native of Malacca. With De Souza as guide he soon found himself outside the shop where his brother would seem to have lived. There were some noisy children in the street, possibly his own nephews and nieces, and De Souza's inquiries finally led him to the Malay woman with whom Delancey's brother had lived. She was fat and middle-aged but must once have been attractive. She was also suspicious, apprehensive, and shy, resolving to divulge the minimum of information about anything. After many evasions and periods of silence, she finally admitted to having known Tuan Delancey. Where had he gone? She said at first that she did not know. After further questioning she said something about the islands to the south. De Souza suggested Riau, Lingga, Bankka, Billiton, and Celebes but she merely shook her head. Could she mean Borneo? She again shook her head but with less emphasis. Delancey suggested some place-names in Borneo; Sambas, Singkawang, Djawi, Pontianak, Matan . . . Watching her carefully, Delancey thought he detected some slight response to the name Pontianak. At this point De Souza intervened, pointing out that the final "K" in Pontianak should not be pronounced. When he said the word correctly there was a long pause and she finally muttered "perhaps." She was now asked why he had gone there. The conversation which followed was so long and frustrating that Delancey's attention wandered to the shop's stock in trade and finally to the Tamil shopman. "Would *he* know?" he asked finally, and De Souza repeated his question in Malay. Another long conversation followed and De Souza finally offered Delancey what little information he had gleaned from these two sources:

"So far as I can understand, Tuan, and I know no Tamil, this woman's husband knew of some tribe, some people, who needed his help. Or else perhaps they would be led by him. He went to join them, meaning to return some day. I am not at all sure of this but I can get no more out of them. I think, but I'm not certain, that he had been to this place before."

Delancey thanked the woman for her help and gave her some money. She looked more cheerful after that and actually volunteered a further bit of information. Her Tuan had not gone alone but had other men with him in a war prahu. At that point the interview ended and Delancey asked De Souza whether he had ever seen an outrigger boat at Malacca. Here again there were language difficulties and Delancey had finally to make a drawing on his sketching paper. By the time he had finished he was surrounded by an admiring crowd, few of whom identified his boat as such, but one Malay broke into rapid comment which De Souza finally translated. "He says, Tuan, that there is such a boat here now, drawn up on the beach, and that it comes from Bintan." This meant nothing to Delancey but De Souza said that Bintan was in the Straits of Singapore.

Led by their Malay guide, Delancey and De Souza walked southward along the beach and presently found the catamaran

pulled up under some overhanging palm trees. Her crew were
not to be found but everyone agreed that they were not local
men. Was the boat used for fishing? No one tried to answer that
question but all agreed that a boat of this kind must sail very
swiftly. A fisherman suggested that the boat's owner might use
it to visit his relatives. Delancey did not pursue his inquiry any
further but thanked De Souza for his assistance and presently
went back to his ship.

   He felt certain now that his guess had been correct and that
Chatelard's success was due to information received. That it was
delivered by fast-sailing catamaran seemed more than probable,
and Bintan was central to the area in which the *Subtile* was
known to operate. What was strange was that such clues as he
had to Chatelard's base and his own brother's whereabouts
pointed alike to the western shores of Borneo. He wondered
wildly whether his brother might turn out to be a French spy.
Then he rejected the idea as absurd. His brother might be eccentric, romantic, dissolute, or even deranged; he would not believe
that he could be disloyal.

   Before sailing from Malacca, Delancey was introduced by Farquhar to a retired Portuguese priest who had made a study of
the aboriginal folk of the Malay Peninsula and the islands of
south-east Asia. This was Father Miguel Silvestre, small, white-
haired, and diffident, with eyes agleam behind his spectacles, an
Orientalist of some note. In his missionary efforts he had found
that followers of Islam were seldom if ever converted to Chris-
tianity, that Chinese paid little attention to his preaching but that
the primitive tribesmen had only the crudest kind of nature wor-
ship and were therefore, in theory, fair game for missionary
effort. The basic difficulty was to learn enough of their language
to approach them, a difficulty made worse by the fact that each

tribe seemed to have its own dialect. After many years of effort Father Miguel could point to no considerable body of converts. He could, however, claim to have collected a great deal of information.

By means of using an interpreter (for the priest knew no English) Delancey managed to gain some knowledge of the aboriginal and other tribes of Borneo. Along the coast and up the rivers of Borneo there were Malays, Javanese, Bugis, and Chinese, usually living under the rule of a Malay Sultan: such rulers being established at places like Balikpapan, Pontianak, and Sambas. Further inland were the aborigines, the Kayan and Kenyah people of the Batang Kayan River, the Murut and Kelabit tribes, and the Sea Dyaks or Ibans who live on the northern tributaries of the Kapuas River. Certain Malay tribes had taken to piracy, notably the folk on the Kapuas River owing allegiance to the Rajah of Limbung. Their war prahus were based on Kurtanalia, south of Pontianak, a place within easy striking distance of the Karimata Channel, itself the approach to the Straits of Sunda. In all this piratical activity the Sea Dyaks up the River Nuri played no part and their patron, the Rajah of Djawi, was equally innocent. There had been wars in the past between the Kapuas Malays and the Nuri Sea Dyaks but the pirates had won and the men of Djawi had been compelled to make peace and pay tribute. In the light of this information it seemed to Delancey that Chatelard might base his operations on the Kapuas River, having reached with the Rajal of Limbung some agreement which gave the Kapuas Malays a share of the booty taken. If this were the situation, Chatelard was in alliance with pirates of the most cruel character, and this shed a new light on his character and motives. Before their conversation ended, Delancey asked Father Miguel whether he had known that other Delancey who had lived at Malacca. It soon appeared that they had been at least acquainted. Where had he gone? Father Miguel had been told that he was in Borneo, somewhere near Pontianak. Why had he gone there? The reply to this was hesitant but the priest thought that Michael Delancey, of whom he obviously disapproved, had some plan for trading with the Ibans, presumably in damar and rattan. He knew no more than that and of Chatelard he knew nothing at all. At the end of his inquiries Delancey had learnt all too little about Chatelard's plans for commerce destruction. He knew enough, however, to start making a plan of his own.

Quitting the anchorage off Malacca, Delancey took the *Laura* southward down the Straits, calling at every port and questioning each merchantman he met. He could obtain no news of the *Subtile,* last definitely seen off the Little Andaman, and so had no idea whether she was ahead of him or behind him. Off Lingga, however, he saw for the first time a Malay catamaran at sea. Northmore called him on deck and handed him the telescope with the words "something of interest, sir!" For her size the outrigger canoe carried an extraordinary press of sail and was coming up astern of the *Laura* at a remarkable speed. The frigate had been under easy sail but Delancey now decided to make a race of it. "Mr Northmore," he said, "crowd all sail and see if you can keep ahead!" It was a beautiful day with bright sun and high-piled cumulus cloud, a stiffening breeze from the north-east and a glimpse to starboard of Tanjong Djabung. The crew hurled themselves into action as the orders were shouted. "Set the top-gallants! Way aloft! Haul taut and make fast! Set the royals! Set the flying skysails! Set the foretopmast staysail! Set the flying jib! Set the weather stunsails!"

For an hour it looked as if the frigate were holding her own. Then the breeze began to slacken and the outrigger canoe began to creep up, being seen on the *Laura's* windward quarter and then on her windward beam. Despite every effort that could be made the Malay craft began to draw ahead. Studying her through his telescope, Delancey felt pretty confident that she was the boat he had seen on the beach at Malacca. She had a crew of three and was going like the wind. Delancey had an insane impulse to sink her but realized that his whole theory was guess-work and that he had no solid fact to justify a suspicion, let alone a brutal gunfire. The *Laura* was fairly out sailed and the native craft vanished into the distance. Orders were then given to reduce sail and the voyage continued under all plain sail.

Delancey considered that his commissioned officers must now be taken into his confidence. If he were to die it was essential that they should know what his plan had been. He invited them to dinner and talked to them while the decanter circulated, reading first the orders he had received.

"So our task is to find and destroy the *Subtile*. Note, please, that it is our only task. Were we to hear of some other opportunity—a possible prize, a French sloop, say—we should not be entitled to go after her. Nor must we bring the *Subtile* in as a captured enemy privateer. Our orders are to destroy her and this we shall do. We have, however, to find her first. Studying all the facts available to me, I have come to the tentative conclusion that Pierre Chatelard has some sort of base in western Borneo. He has certainly been around the Straits for over a year without returning to the Ile de France. He must have refitted somewhere close to his cruising ground. There is evidence, moreover, that he has good sources of information and that news reaches him quickly about any possible prey. I think you all saw the native craft which overtook us earlier this afternoon. My guess is that Chatelard receives intelligence and warning by just such a fast-sailing craft and probably by that one. Having no such system of communication myself, I am compelled to rely upon mere guess-work. You will realize, gentlemen, that I am very much in the dark and it may well prove that all my guesses have been incorrect."

"Forgive me, sir," said Fitzgerald, "Were you not tempted to intercept that outrigger craft with a well-aimed cannon?"

"I was tempted," said Delancey, "but I resisted the temptation. If that racing canoe is what I think she is, her movements will tell me something of what I need to know. My present conclusion is that the *Subtile* is ahead of me, not astern. That catamaran is sailing towards her employer, not away from him and that, I assume, is why she is in a hurry."

"I could wish, sir," said Fitzgerald, "that we knew what message she is to deliver."

"But is that so difficult?"

"It is difficult, sir, for me."

"Perhaps Mr Greenwell could tell us?"

"Not me, sir," said Greenwell, with eyes downcast.

"Mr Northmore?"

"She might warn Chatelard that the *Laura* is heading southwards."

"That much is clear from today's sighting. But the message almost certainly informs Chatelard that the opium ship *Fort William* has left Malacca and will call at Lingga and Palembang."

"How can the French agent know that?" asked Greenwell, astonished.

"How do I know it?" asked Delancey in turn. "He will surely know what is common knowledge. So that Chatelard will receive at the same time news of a possible prize and warning of a possible danger. Can we guess from that what he is likely to do?"

"Sail for Palembang?" asked Fitzgerald hopefully.

"I doubt it," replied Delancey. "You forget that he will have other sources of intelligence and the news of other possible prey. I should guess, however, that he will keep away from the Straits of Sunda and will try to discover what we mean to do. We must expect to be watched by his native spies, including those we have seen already. But the point will come—and may have come already—when he comes to realize that a frigate has been sent to deal with him. What will he do then?"

There was a silence and then Northmore said: "He might hide at his base."

"He might indeed," replied Delancey, "but that plan fits ill with the character of Pierre Chatelard in so far as it is known to us. I do not see him as a man who would hide himself. He is more likely to do something." There was another silence as Delancey looked from one to another of his officers.

"Well, gentlemen? What should we expect him to do?" Since there was no response, Delancey had to answer his own question. "Did none of you ever play hide-and-seek? If Chatelard guesses that we are going south to look for him he will surely decide to go north. Our heading for the Straits of Sunda will be his cue to make for the Bay of Bengal. He will be off the Sandheads when we are off Bencoolen."

"So your plan, sir, will be to double back and cruise off the Sandheads?" Fitzgerald was evidently relieved to find so simple a solution to the problem.

"Well, that is one possibility," Delancey admitted, "but it is not the alternative I prefer. Chatelard began his present cruise in late December or early January. He may go north again but my guess is that he must return to his base in May or June. If we can locate his home port that is where we shall wait for him."

When the party broke up Delancey realized how much he was missing Mather. Of his present officers only one, Northmore, had any brains and he, of course, lacked experience. What drudgery it was to help them see the obvious! Mather would have known at once what the alternatives were. Was his plan the right one? Who could tell? It was at least based, however, on a process of reasoning. Should he really have turned northward again after being sighted by that damned outrigger craft? The objection to that lay in the choice of passages. No, the better plan was one based on the fixed point, the place (if he could find it) to which Chatelard must return. He had narrowed that down to a definite stretch of coastline. What he lacked, however, was a man who knew the country—someone perhaps like Father Miguel. He would need to ask questions and could hardly do so without an interpreter. He himself had a few words of Malay but he realized that a knowledge of Dutch would have been of more immediate use. He turned to the chart again and put himself in Chatelard's place. "If I still commanded a privateer and wanted a safe harbour on the west coast of Borneo, where should I begin to look for it?" At Sukadana or Padang? Or up north around Mempawak or Singkawang? No, it would be better to find a complex estuary with islands and creeks among which to hide. This thought brought him back to the confused coastline between Pontianak and Djawi, a mere hundred miles of it. That would be the first place to look; and there, incidentally, if anywhere, he might expect to find his missing brother. He wondered whether there was really any point in finding Michael, who probably needed no help and was happy in his own fashion, but he was still fascinated by the way that inclination and duty were leading him in the same direction. If

Chatelard had a base for the *Subtile,* Michael was the very man to know all about it.

A week later the *Laura* sighted Borneo just north of Pontianak and began a cautious approach through poorly charted waters. With the leadsman in the chains and with barely enough canvas to have steerage way, Delancey brought the frigate to what should have been, by all reckoning, the mouth of the Lava River on which Pontianak is placed. He finally dropped anchor opposite a belt of canebrake and mangrove and sent the launch in to investigate. Completely hidden to view from a distance, the rivermouth was finally located by the rush of fresh water and the *Laura* brought to a new anchorage near by. Pontianak was some ten miles inland but Delancey decided against taking his ship up the river. He took the launch instead and was able to sail for most of the way. When the breeze died away his men rowed the last mile or so under a hot sun, Delancey reflecting that Pontianak was almost exactly on the Equator.

When he sighted the place, sited in the angle between two confluent rivers, he was astonished to see that Pontianak was a city as well as a seaport. In the city proper was the Malay settlement centred on the Sultan's palace and this was faced by two Chinese towns, one on either riverbank. Opposite this metropolis were moored a cluster of Chinese junks with two enormous vessels towering over the rest. Guided by a Malay prahu, the launch was brought to a landing-stage opposite the palace, where Delancey, Northmore, and Stock were met by a Malay chief, who presently showed them into the Sultan's presence. The principal reception hall was of great size and centred upon a carpeted dais. On the dais stood a long table at which Delancey was presently seated, being offered tea and sherbet by way of refreshment. His

elderly and richly dressed host, the Sultan, was polite and vol-
uble but Delancey's few words of Malay did not serve the purpose
of a serious discussion. As interpreter the Sultan produced a Chinese youth who spoke Dutch and Delancey came to understand
that Pontianak was under Dutch protection and that the only
men-of-war which called there were under the Dutch flag. All
efforts at interpretation failed at first but there finally appeared
a Malay boy who spoke English and who asked, on the Sultan's
behalf, why his visitors did not speak Dutch. Delancey admitted, in reply, that his ship was not Dutch but claimed that he
was friendly with the Dutch—a people with whom he was actually at war. The interpreter evidently explained to the Sultan that
his visitors were French for the atmosphere improved even if
mutual comprehension did not. The Sultan knew nothing, it
transpired, of any other man-of-war frequenting the coast.

On the subject of another European called Delancey he
was equally ignorant but he called into consultation a Malay
chief who perhaps held some office equivalent to chief of police,
who remembered a trader who might have been the man sought
but who had long since gone elsewhere, perhaps to the village
of Laut. With no other information forthcoming, Delancey was
relieved when supper arrived, making further conversation needless.

The meal comprised chicken and salt fish with a dozen different curries, basins of rice, jars of pickles, and, later, sliced
pineapple and cake, accompanied throughout by cool, sweet
sherbet poured from an enormous jar. The crew of the launch
were simultaneously entertained in an open-sided shed close to
the beach, being given as much curry and rice as they could eat.
All went to sleep soon afterwards but Delancey roused his men
in the small hours, determined to reach the estuary before the

heat of the day. Aided now by the current, they dropped down the river as the sun rose and were back on board the *Laura* for breakfast.

There was little wind that day and the frigate, heading South along the coast, was again overtaken by a native craft. This time it was a fishing canoe with branches of the coconut tree instead of sails. The branches were spread fanwise and held in place by a bamboo rod and the crew consisted of one Malay holding a steering paddle. On the following day what little breeze there had been died away and Delancey dropped anchor opposite a mangrove swamp. He was becalmed again on the following day, progressing southward only by the aid of a short-lived morning and evening breeze. All this coast looked much the same, with level alluvial swamps backed by more distant jungle trees. It was steamingly hot and seamen were distressed even under the awnings, few of them able to sleep much at night. At last, with a few men already sick, the frigate came within sight of the small village of Laut.

Drifting rather than sailing, Delancey brought his ship to within half a mile of the village. It was a calm, hot day, with a mist on the flat, mirror-like surface of the sea, the land revealed only by its jungle trees. Laut, like Pontianak, was under Dutch protection in theory, but passing ships, as he knew, would usually ignore the fact. He decided to send in a boat, bearing a message for Mr Michael Delancey. This mission was entrusted to David Stock, whose cutter was faithfully reflected, each dipping oar blade making a visible disturbance. Over an hour passed before the cutter was seen again and the oarsmen were dripping with sweat when they came aboard.

Reporting on the quarter-deck, young Stock handed the letter back and stated that Mr Delancey had been in Laut and had done business there but had gone. A Chinese merchant who knew some English had told him that Tuan Delancey had gone southwards along the coast to Djawi or Matan. Delancey decided at once to follow but dead calm delayed him for two days more. Then at Djawi, eighty miles further south, he sent in a boat again. This time Stock came back with the news that an Englishman had been there but had gone inland some time ago—perhaps two or three years since—accompanied by several Malays. This time the information came from an Indian tradesman who had once lived in Malacca. Delancey now decided to follow up this clue and bring the frigate in closer to the shore.

The day was windless and the *Laura* was finally towed in by her boats, dropping anchor opposite the village, the inhabitants of which lined the shore to watch. Almost at once a sampan came off from the land and headed for the frigate with several passengers on board. As the distance lessened it became apparent that the visitors included a minor Malay chief, perhaps the village headman, distinguished by headcloth, sarong, and kris, two other armed Malays, a Chinese towkay, and the Indian with whom Stock had already conversed. Delancey ordered a one-gun salute, the parading of a marine guard, and the piping of the side.

Impressed by this reception, the party from the shore were led to the captain's cabin and offered some refreshments, alcoholic and otherwise. All chose to squat on the deck while the preliminary courtesies were exchanged, the Indian acting as interpreter and the Chinese merely bowing and smiling. The Malay chief finally asked why the *Laura* was honouring Djawi with a visit Delancey replied at once that he wanted to buy provisions; pigs, poultry, fruit, and so forth. There would, it appeared, be no difficulty over this, provided that payment was made in dollars. After some further discussion about prices, Delancey made very casual mention of an Englishman who had come to Djawi, he believed, from Pontianak. There followed a muttered conversation between the visitors, the question having evidently upset them. After some minutes the Indian asked "Why you want to know?" To this Delancey replied "He is my brother," a reply which led to another discussion in Malay. There was evidently a family resemblance, to which the Indian drew attention, for the fact of relationship seemed to be accepted. The Indian finally replied "He left here long ago."

No further information could be extracted so Delancey went on to ask about a French ship with many guns called the *Subtile*. Without the need for any discussion all at once shook their heads. The Indian went on to emphasize that no French ship had ever been seen near Djawi. Watching their faces and noting their unanimity, Delancey concluded that they were lying and had agreed beforehand what lie to tell. He expressed his regret, therefore, adding that he had been prepared to pay a thousand dollars for information about the *Subtile*'s usual port of call. What a pity, he said "that no one was ready to help him. He could think of no simpler way of making money. He would have to go on to Matan where he supposed that people might be readier to accept money without having to work for it. Much could be done with a thousand dollars. One could buy a fishing boat with it. One could set up one's son in business. One could provide a dowry for one's daughter. But, there, if no one wanted the money . . . He changed the topic of conversation and asked about the health of the Sultan of Limburg. His guests looked upset again— it was far from obvious why—and went into secret conclave. After a prolonged discussion the Indian was empowered to answer, rather sulkily, "He very well." Delancey talked again about pigs and poultry and so brought the conference to an end on a happier note. The sampan presently returned to the shore, a plan agreed for shipping provisions on the following day.

As the light was failing that evening a sampan appeared along-side and a boatman hailed the ship. There was only one passenger this time, the Chinese who had said nothing on the earlier visit. His English was now fluent and he had clearly understood all that had taken place. He had occasion to spend two thousand dollars, more than he happened to have at the moment and more than he could borrow except at an extortionate rate of interest. He knew something about a French ship, something of which his friends were ignorant. He also knew the whereabouts of the Englishman who had left Djawi . . . Delancey regretted blandly that he had only a thousand dollars to spare, having to spend so much on poultry, eggs, and fruit. At the end of a prolonged discussion the Chinese agreed to accept fifteen hundred dollars, telling Delancey all that he wanted to know. He finally drew a sketch-map of the Kapuas River (north of Djawi) and made a cross on its more northerly channel, a few miles from the estuary. There, he explained, the French ship came to refit with the Sultan's permission. As for the Tuan who was the Captain's brother, he had gone up the Nuri River and was living at a kampong on the way to Djenu. Another sketch-map was drawn to show where the kampong was and a drawing added to indicate that the kampong was really a longhouse; a village, as it were, under a single roof. If this information was correct, Delancey's brother was living with the primitive folk of the interior, which seemed likely enough in view of Michael's reputed interests.

After the Chinese had received his reward and gone, Delancey was pondering the information so far gained when a sharp challenge was heard forward and it became obvious that another boat

was alongside. He walked forward to inquire and saw by moonlight another sampan, again with one passenger, the Indian who
had formed part of the previous deputation. He did not come
aboard but called softly that he now remembered some fact
which the Tuan Captain might like to know. He knew that he
could count on a suitable reward—say, fifteen hundred dollars—
and that the whole transaction could remain a secret. "Too late,
my friend," said Delancey and bade his visitor good-night. An
hour or so later came another challenge and the sound of another
boat alongside. This time it was a Malay prahu, its only passenger the Malay chieftain whom Delancey had already met. He
called to Delancey that he did, after all, have some knowledge
which might be of interest to the Tuan. It had slipped his memory that morning but had come back to him since. Now, about
that thousand dollars . . . "Too late, my friend." said Delancey,
"*selamat jalan.*" He turned in that night with the feeling that he
had made some progress with his mission.

There could be no doubt that the information received about
the Kapuas River was correct. For Delancey's purpose, however,
it was insufficiently precise. Where, exactly, did the *Subtile* refit?
Neither the river nor the coast itself was charted and the diagram he had gave no idea of distance. Dared he send a boat up
the river? Obviously not. Its presence would alarm the Malays,
who would find means to warn Chatelard that his base had been
discovered. His better plan would be to procure a Malay prahu
and send it up the river with a single officer in Malay costume.
Who was he to send? Wayland, perhaps, master's mate? Or Topley? Topley had to some extent proved himself. So maybe
Wayland should be given his chance? Or would he make a mess
of it? He thought that the risk was worth while provided that
Wayland had a good petty officer at his elbow and two armed

seamen to keep the Malay boatmen in their place. As a first step, Delancey sent for his commissioned officers and told them what had to be done.

"I propose to send one small party to reconnoitre the Kapuas River and fix the position of Chatelard's base. I propose to lead another and larger party up the Nuri River, leaving Mr Fitzgerald in command of the ship. If you have questions to ask, now is the time to ask them."

"Might I ask, sir," said Fitzgerald, "whether the boat expedition up the Nuri River is not a suitable task for the first lieutenant?"

"In the ordinary way, it certainly is," replied Delancey, "but the man whose help we need happens to be my brother. I have, I think, the best chance of persuading him to do what I want."

"But isn't the other patrol more proper for a commissioned officer, sir?" asked Northmore.

"It is, but I can't spare a commissioned officer. Mr Wayland is the man I can spare. Should I be lost, it is important that the rest of you know what Wayland has been sent to do. You will be present, therefore, when I give him his orders. Pass the word there for Mr Wayland!" A few minutes later Wayland reported, a burly young man with fairish hair, a red face, and an earnest, well-meaning expression.

"Mr Wayland," said Delancey, "I have been told that the French privateer *Subtile* is based upon a shore establishment set up in the Kapuas River. I propose to destroy her while she is refitting there. Towards doing this the first step is to locate her base, making a rough chart of the river and indicating where the *Subtile* will be. This must be done secretly, without the knowledge of the Malays whose alliance Chatelard has secured. I propose to hire a Malay craft with the necessary four oarsmen and entrust you with the mission, assisted by Coxswain Ellis. With him as petty officer you will have two armed seamen but all, like you, in Malay costume. Having made a chart and placed the *Subtile* in position on it, you will report back to me here at the mouth of the river. What will you need apart from your personal arms and those issued to your crew?"

"Well, sir, I'll need provisions for a week, a tent of some sort, ammunition for all arms carried, cooking utensils, and bedding."

"Is that all?"

"All I can think of, sir."

"You are forgetting your mission. You will also need paper, pencils, pens and ink with a board to use as desk, a sextant, telescope, compass, chart, and a piece of canvas to protect the equipment. Add to that a Malay dictionary and a notebook in which to keep a log."

"Yes, sir. Very good, sir."

"You will leave before daylight tomorrow and should make your preparations now, darkening your skin and purchasing for each man a Malay baju, sarong, and headcloth. What do you know of the language?"

"Very little, sir."

"Then you will have to learn quickly. Off with you."

Wayland withdrew and Delancey turned to face the other officers.

"He must do the best he can. I could not spare anyone else. Now I must detail the crew for the launch, complete with a midshipman. I'll take Burnet, I think. It will be good experience for him. We shall need a gun in the bows, Mr Fitzgerald, and canvas enough to make an awning, with axes, saw, hammer, and nails and plenty of spare rope and twine. See to it, please. Yes, and detail Lakin as coxswain. I'll want two marines with a musket and cutlass for each seaman, and two pistols each for myself, Lakin and Burnet."

There was a great deal of work to be done but both boats, the hired Malay craft and the launch, were away long before daylight, the one with men disguised but the other with every appearance of a man-of-war boat, lacking only the British ensign.

The Nuri River narrowed quickly as the sea was left behind. It was placid, with a slow current, the jungle coming down to the banks on either side, fringed in places by a belt of mangrove swamp. There were blue hills in the distance with, above them, a high-piled bank of cumulus cloud in white and grey. All was very still, the only noise to be heard being the regular splash of the oars and sometimes a few words exchanged among the launch's crew. By Delancey's reckoning the launch would have about sixty miles to go, following a right-hand tributary ten miles below Djenu. The boat's present speed would be four miles an hour so that it would be a two days' pull, allowing for time to rest the oarsmen. There was an hour for dinner spent on a shell beach below a small headland.

At nightfall the party camped on a small sandy island only twenty yards from the swampy shore. They were plagued by mosquitoes, which the smoke from the camp fire did little to disperse, and there were alligators to be seen on the far bank of the river. Delancey had allowed himself one luxury and only one: a piece of mosquito netting with which to cover his head at night. Frustrating the mosquitoes, it added to the heat and left him the more exhausted. He roused his men in the small hours, hoping to make good distance before the heat of the day began. By that evening they had in fact reached the point at which the tributary joined the main river, having seen only the occasional Malay kampong with a few fishing craft glimpsed in the distance. They camped again near the confluence and spent another night fighting the mosquitoes, this time in a clearing which had once been planted with rice. Early next day they passed close to a village built on piles over the water where swarms of naked children played with dugout canoes. An hour later they saw a long roof among the trees, set back from the river, and Delancey concluded that this was his destination.

The longhouse, approached by a path from the riverbank, must have been over two hundred feet long. The living quarters were on a platform some ten or twelve feet above the ground and under a steep attap roof. There were some padifields beyond and some goats and poultry wandering around. The primitive inhabitants, nearly naked, gazed at Delancey and his men with curiosity but without fear. They had plainly seen Europeans before and Delancey guessed that there were Dutch traders to be seen, on occasion, at Djenu. The diminutive men who came to greet the visitors were evidently Ibans or Sea Dyaks and quite ready to offer hospitality. They were short, dark men, strongly built, wearing only a loincloth or sirat but with blue-black tattooing on their bodies. Some of them wore a sheathed parang, rather like the West Indian machete. They led Delancey to the end of the longhouse where there was a shaky bamboo ladder. Leaving his four seamen to squat in the shade, Delancey climbed the ladder and found himself in a wide veranda stretching the whole length of the building. This, he could see, was the village street in which people met, conversed, and worked. Opening on to the veranda, on his left, were a succession of rooms in which the families slept. He realized at once that this was the coolest building he had entered since coming to the East. The air space between ceiling and roof provided insulation while the sketchy nature of side-walls, partitions, and floor allowed air to circulate freely throughout. He looked about him with interest, The inhabitants to be seen were mostly bare-breasted women and naked children, the men having presumably gone out to work, fish, or hunt. They looked up as Delancey passed but were too well mannered to stare or point and some were too shy even to smile. He strolled past successive groups at work, each falling silent as he passed, and looked into successive rooms, most of them unoccupied. An older Iban, self-appointed guide, was trying to explain something to him but in a language of which he knew nothing. He pointed, however, and Delancey, following the indication, went on to the end of the longhouse. There, in the last room of all, clad in tattered shirt and trousers, a bearded and haggard European lay asleep on some rice matting. So wild was his appearance that Delancey could only with difficulty identify his brother Michael. Beside him was an opium pipe and his was evidently the drugged sleep of an addict. Considered as a possible ally, Michael was completely useless—so much seemed obvious. For all practical purposes he might merely be regarded as dead.

Chapter Five

LOCATING THE ENEMY

RICHARD DELANCEY knew all too little about drug addiction but he supposed that Michael must eventually wake up, perhaps later in the day. Would he then take more opium? He thought of removing the temptation but decided to leave a note instead. On a piece of paper he wrote in capital letters: YOUR BROTHER RICHARD IS HERE TO SEE YOU AND WILL CALL AGAIN TOMORROW. Propping this note where Michael must see it, he walked back the way he had come, greeting the folk he saw with a wave and a smile. The Ibans were friendly enough but he had no means of conversing with them, or of gaining their friendship. His main problem was how to keep his men occupied for perhaps two days and this he solved on his way back to the boat.

"After dinner," he announced to his boat-crew, "we shall build a proper landing-stage here, felling the timber as necessary and making it long enough to bring in a prahu alongside. This will be our gift to the people of the longhouse whose guests we are."

The rest of the day was spent in this useful activity, the Ibans watching with amazement as the structure took shape. Before dark they came down in procession and brought with them a supper of chicken and rice with some potent, sickly, and bitter-sweet liquor called tuak served in coconut shells which Delancey made his men treat with extreme caution. They slept ashore that night and work was resumed in the morning, the landing-stage being finished off with a hand-rail and an attap roof to keep the sun off. Whether the lbans thought it an improvement he was never to know but he thought that they were, initially, more surprised than grateful. While the work neared completion Delancey went up to the longhouse again and went once more to the room at the far end. Michael, he found, was awake but in an ugly mood.

"You!" he growled. "You! Why must you come here? Why seek me out? Why couldn't you let me be?" He fell back on the rice matting and mopped his forehead with a trembling hand. "I've had enough of your rotten world with its governors and captains, its cravats and stockings, its customs and laws. I'm through with it, d'ye hear? I'm done with it, and I'll have nothing to do with your rotten war either, nothing at all. There are the French with their revolutionaries and rebels, their renegades and ruffians, and here are the British with their King and their Company, their Articles of War, and their articles for sale. Ah, I was part of the system once, chief mate and in line to become master. I was a gentleman once but could take no more of it and came ashore. I've moved further and further away from the whole stinking system, coming at last to join my friends on this remote river. And who comes to drag me back to the treadmill? My own younger brother! You, Richard, the one of us who obeyed the teacher, kept to the rules, never stepped out of line! But let me tell you that you are wasting your time. I shan't leave with you. I shall stay here where all is quiet. I'll smoke another pipe and presently forget that you exist. You come too late, Richard, you come too late . . ."

"You are quite wrong, Michael, I haven't come to drag you away. I think you are quite right to stay here. I am happy to

think that you have found peace. I like your friends and neighbours and only wish I knew more about them. What is your
position here? Are you the chief of the tribe? What can you do
for these people?" It was some time before Michael took in what
Richard was trying to say. For some minutes he merely repeated
himself, muttering "Why go back to Georgetown or Malacca? I've
had enough of all that. My life is here and I live among friends
. . . What can I do for them, you ask? Is that it?" He had come
to the point but he drifted off it again, vowing once more to stay
among his friends. "Why are they my friends? I'll tell you, I'll
tell you. I'll not hide from you the fact that I can speak their
language. It wasn't easy, so don't think it was. She taught me,
you'll understand, word after blessed word. Now, these people
are head-hunters—bloody savages as some people would say. But
head-hunting is religious, really, it helps the padi to grow. If it
looks like a poor crop you go out at night and return with a
head or two, taken from another tribe. But a Malay head will do
very well and a European head may be better for all I know. You
should see our collection—I did something to improve it. So
now I can tell these people what to do. I see that they are given
a fair price for their rattan. I give them quinine when they need
it. I persuade the Rajah's tax-gatherer to let them alone."

"But haven't your people lost some of their best hunting and
fishing country?"

"So you have heard about that? Yes, they used to have longhouses on the Kapuas River but were driven away by the Malays.
They would have fought but these Malays had been given muskets by the French. So the Dyaks ran away and made their homes
here. Some would fight even now but I tell them not to fight
against men with muskets. Their chance may come, I tell them,
but they must be patient."

"Their chance *has* come, Michael. The Malay pirates are going to be attacked from the sea. That gives your Dyaks a chance to attack them at the same time from the land. In that way they can recover the Kapuas River for themselves."

There followed a long and tedious discussion, greatly prolonged by Michael's inability to concentrate. His attention continually wandered. At one time he spoke of his boyhood in St Peter Port, of old Le Poidevin with whom they had gone fishing, of the crazy and leaking boat which was once their pride, of the time they were nearly caught robbing an orchard. He talked of the Malay woman with whom he had lived at Malacca, of the country ship in which he had been chief mate, of the stupid prejudices observable in the officials of Penang. Humouring him, Richard kept bringing the conversation back to the subject of the Dyaks and their claim to the Kapuas River. He eventually secured Michael's promise to call the elders of the tribe together that evening. He had a proposal to put before them and Michael was his only possible interpreter.

That arrangement made, the two brothers shared a meal, the Dyaks at the same time providing a pig for the boat's crew. Michael ate little and Richard saw that he was a sick man, his health undermined by malaria and opium. To enlist his help seemed an almost hopeless task. They were presently joined, however, by a Dyak called Penghulu Kanyan, evidently the chief man of the tribe, with whom Richard presently established some form of understanding. Kanyan, like Richard, knew a little Malay and Michael acted as a somewhat unreliable interpreter. When told of the attack to be made on his Malay enemies, Kanyan showed keen interest, evidently seeing the possibilities.

Richard showed in pantomime how the Malays would be firing in one direction while the Dyaks would approach them silently from the other. The difficulty was clearly to be one of timing and this again must depend upon the movements of the French privateer. By Delancey's calculation the *Subtile* ought to refit in about June. Supposing she had entered the Kapuas River, how long would the Dyaks take to move overland from the Nuri River? The path through the jungle might be twenty miles, if it followed the most direct route (but would it?), added to which must be the distance up the Nuri and down the Kapuas; possibly fifty miles in all or roughly five days' march. Allowing time for the message to reach the Dyaks, Delancey thought that a combined attack might be launched seven days after the *Subtile* had reached her base. Kanyan seemed to agree that five days would be sufficient for his march but Delancey wondered whether he had really understood the arithmetic. He went over it again, drawing a map in the earth near the longhouse, and persuaded Michael to repeat the whole narrative in the local dialect. It then transpired that Kanyan would have to consult with other chiefs living in other longhouses. He could make no final decision until a general meeting had been held. He could make no promise but he thought it probable that war against the Kapuas Malays would be agreed. They would do nothing, however, until they received the message. Added to the recapture of their territories, the Dyaks would have the plunder of the Malay settlement, a place enriched by the activities of the *Subtile*. Delancey's message might be expected in two or three weeks' time.

Delancey said good-bye to his brother that night, explaining that he would begin his return journey long before first light. Michael was more composed at the moment of parting, showing even some regret, but was evidently ill and unlikely to live for long. Kanyan, on the other hand, was at the new landing-stage when Delancey's men embarked. He was carrying a blowpipe as a sign of his warlike intent and accompanied by other men similarly armed. For a surprise attack falling on the rear of a force already engaged they had, Delancey reflected, the ideal weapon. There was a friendly parting by torchlight and then the boat was pushed off and went downstream. The oars dipped in rhythm but with unequal power and Delancey soon realized that some of his men were unwell. He quickly relieved two of the oarsmen, who were plainly feverish, and replaced them by two marines. By midday one of the marines had the same symptoms and was replaced by the coxswain, the tiller being given to young Burnet. That night they encamped again on a small island, by which time another seaman was sick. They set off next morning with four men ill and ended with five lying in the bottom of the boat, Burnet taking an oar and Delancey now the helmsman. By the evening they had reached the *Laura* and Delancey asked at once whether Mr Wayland had returned. "No, sir."

Fitzgerald reported, "Coxswain Ellis had come aboard but reports that the others were all killed by the Malays."

"Very well, Mr Fitzgerald, I have at least five men sick, probably with malaria. Tell the surgeon to look after them. Send Ellis to my cabin to make his report—and I think you should be present when he makes it."

Five minutes later Ellis reported, clutching a roll of paper, and told a confused story.

"We passed a kampong called Kertamulia, sir, and Mr Wayland said not to stop there 'cos we might be recognized. We hit a sandbank, though, and had some trouble getting the boat off. While we were doing this a Malay boat came near us, so near that the boatmen must have seen that we were not Malays. Our boatmen talked with theirs, too, and must have given us away. But Mr

Wayland said to push on, it couldn't be helped, and we came that evening to the place where they career that French privateer, a shingle beach with a useful fall of the tide and a line of sheds or godowns as they call 'em on the starboard side of the river. Further down the river, two or three cables distant or maybe a half mile, they have a regular stockade with a fence down to the river on either side and some cannon mounted. They have a boom there to draw across the river from one stockade to t'other. There were no Malays around that evening but they appeared next day, a lot of'em armed at that. I was ashore to look more closely at the capstans and suchlike when I heard the first shots fired. There was a lot of shouting after that and I knew that things had gone wrong. Then I saw Mr Wayland running my way and all covered with blood. I fired my musket at the Malays who were after him, and they retreated again. Then there was another shot, rather distant, and Mr Wayland fell dead, dropping this roll of paper, which I picked up. I hid after that in an empty hut, knowing that the others must all have been killed. Later that night I crept out and found a sort of canoe and drifted in it down the river, passed Kertamulia, and so reached the river-mouth. Then I paddled out to the ship and made my report to Mr Fitzgerald, sir, who told me to show this paper to you."

The roll of paper, when flattened out, revealed a quite useful diagram of the Kapuas River, indicating the position of the stockade and dockyard some two miles above Kertamulia and nearer the sea than Delancey had expected it to be. A second drawing showed some detail of the stockade but this was unfinished and stained with blood. Delancey thanked Ellis and dismissed him, turning to Fitzgerald for any further information he could add.

"Well, sir, Ellis forgot to report that a Malay woman helped him paddle that canoe and went off in it after he came aboard."

"Was she pretty?"

"Pretty, sir? Well—yes, I suppose she was, and quite young too."

"I see. And what do you think of Ellis's story?"

"I think he did quite well, considering."

"Do you? For myself, I don't believe a word of it."

"What really happened, then?"

"Ellis deserted the party in order to sleep with this Malay girl. He was with her when the party was attacked and remained in her hut until the fight ended. She then took him in her canoe— he picking up this map on the way to it—and went down river, he in the bottom of the boat and she answering challenges from the stockade or other craft. The man is lying but this map luck-ily tells the truth."

"Shall I put him under arrest, sir?"

"Certainly not. We have no evidence against him. His only certain offence is in being a bad liar, lacking the brain to make up a better story."

"I'm afraid that Wayland's little expedition was something of a disaster."

"Not at all. It was a success, giving me the information I wanted at the cost of three lives. The other information I wanted will probably cost me five lives. In this world, Mr Fitzgerald, there is a price to pay for everything. For the destruction of the *Subtile* the price is going to be heavy."

On May 24th the *Laura* was through the Karimata Channel and cruising on a line between Dending, in Billiton, and the island of Kebatu. If Chatelard wanted to pick up a final prize before returning to the Kapuas River, this might well be the area in which he would operate. On the other hand, it was just as likely that he would make straight for his base, already satisfied with the captures he had made. He could also, far that matter, cruise in the Karimata Channel itself. The argument against this possibility was that the Karimata Channel is a hundred miles wide whereas the *Laura,* placed where she was, had only thirty-five miles to patrol. As Delancey saw the problem, Chatelard would prefer a near certainty to an outside chance. He saw Chatelard as that sort of man. Events, however, were to prove him wrong.

Early in June he intercepted a valueless Dutch merchantman bound for Java. She had on board three Englishmen, the master, first and second mates of a country ship captured by the *Subtile* off Billiton a few days earlier. Chatelard had rid himself of these prisoners by putting them on board the Dutchman, having no wish, obviously, to take them into the Kapuas River. Delancey released the Dutch ship, being unwilling to spare a prize crew, and headed north again for the Karimata Channel. Having put his three Englishmen on board a country ship bound for Calcutta, he at last obtained his first distant glimpse of the *Subtile.* She was to windward of him on a northerly course and Delancey recognized her at once from the descriptions he had heard or read. He went in chase but soon realised that she was a faster ship than the *Laura* and superbly handled. By nightfall she was at once further to windward and further ahead. Dishearteningly, moreover, the privateer had gained this distance without any special effort while the *Laura* had crowded all the sail she had. Annoying as this might be at the time, Delancey had at least the satisfaction of knowing that he had been right not to seek the *Subtile* in the Bay of Bengal. He could never have overtaken her without the aid of another man-of-war. With two ships he might have trapped her against the land but he had not been given the force needed. So he was justified in seeking to pinpoint the privateer's base. He felt certain, moreover, that Chatelard would now be on his way there. Having taken one more prize and having sighted the *Laura,* he would surely conclude that his cruise was over. This would be his cue to vanish, refit, and rest, assuming that the frigate would have gone by the time he emerged.

There was no sign of the *Subtile* by daybreak but Delancey felt justified in making directly for the Kapuas River. Were Chatelard tempted to take another prize it was just possible that the *Laura* might be there before him. Having been mistaken once about Chatelard's possible plans, Delancey was now less confident of his guess-work. It was clear, however, that he must head for the Kapuas River and wait.

But how was he to know if the *Subtile* had already entered the river? His first instinct was to call at Djawi and ask that question of his Chinese informant. But could the news have reached him in time? And might not the *Subtile* enter the river while he was at anchor off Djawi? Given the choice, he wanted to deal with the privateer at sea rather than in the river. She was, in herself, no match for the *Laura* but ashore the odds would be more even, the French being reinforced by their Malay allies. To attack that stockade would be to risk heavy losses from battle and disease. The Dyaks might help but would they appear on the right day and would Michael be fit enough to direct them? The Dyak alliance had seemed real enough when it was discussed with Kanyan but did it really amount to more than a vague possibility? Would the other tribal elders agree to it? Were they able to deliver the attack?

The best plan beyond question was to intercept the *Subtile* at the river-mouth, and Delancey plotted his course accordingly,

sighting the coast just before sunset on June 10th. There was a
faint sea-breeze and the *Laura* came slowly into the anchorage
and finally dropped anchor in eight fathoms. There was a period
of minutes during which the jungle trees were lit for a moment
by the purple sunset, and then, quite suddenly, it was dark.
There was nothing to be seen on that moonless night and nothing to be heard except the murmur of fresh water against the
ship's side. Delancey gave orders to clear for action and beat to
quarters. After going the round of the gun-deck he had a final
word with his lieutenants.

"I have reason to believe, gentlemen, that the French privateer *Subtile* will soon try to enter the Kapuas River. All lights,
including battle lanterns, are to be extinguished. We must maintain complete silence, every man at his post. We shall then be
in position to engage her should she make the attempt."

"But will Chatelard try to enter the river at *night?*" Fitzgerald
clearly thought the idea absurd.

"I don't know, Mr Fitzgerald," but I think it possible. Chatelard knows this river very well. His preference, no doubt, would
be to enter in daylight but what if he knows that the *Laura* is
on his tail? In that event he would want to enter unseen and
therefore after dark."

"But can he be aware, sir, that we know about his base?"

"Yes, Mr Fitzgerald, he can. His Malay friends, who are in
touch with him, may have taken our men prisoners and learnt
something from them."

"But our boat's crew were all killed, sir."

"We have only Ellis's word for that and I don't believe a word
he says."

"So you think, sir, that the *Subtile* may be approaching the
river-mouth now."

"I don't think it probable. But we should look very foolish if Chatelard were to make the attempt and we were all in our hammocks. I have told Mr Stock to have the flares ready to ignite at a moment's notice. Our first broadside should follow five seconds later. Our object must be to cripple the *Subtile* at the outset."

Removing his shoes so as to step silently, Delancey prowled the decks, ready to reprove anyone who coughed or shuffled. The silence, however, was very well observed and he finally returned to the quarter-deck and took post near where young Stock had his well-shrouded lantern. Hours passed and it was nearly four o'clock when Burnet whispered, "Look, sir—there."

The boy pointed but Delancey could see nothing at all. "A sail, sir."

Could the lad be imagining things? "How distant?"

"A half-mile, sir."

If there was anything there, it had to be the *Subtile*. No other ship in the world would attempt the Kapuas River in darkness. Some tense minutes passed, Delancey worried to think that his eyesight was failing, and finally young Stock whispered, "I see her now!" and pointed in a slightly different direction. The bearing had changed with the enemy's approach. Delancey sent Fitzgerald to alert the gun-captains and repeat the order for silence. Then he strained his eyes until, finally, he glimpsed the enemy and heard the leadsman singing out after each cast. He now saw with surprise that there were dimmed lights aboard the privateer. In the still night he could hear men at work or in conversation, having no thought of imminent action. The *Subtile* must now be within four hundred yards, the range diminishing . . . Then there was a shout from the other ship and Delancey knew that the *Laura* had been seen. "Flare—*Now!*" he said to Stock, and the whole scene was suddenly illuminated, showing the *Subtile* on course to pass the *Laura*. In that split second Delancey could see that she was a beautiful ship in immaculate order, commanded by an artist in his profession. "Fire!" said Delancey to the gun-captain of the aftermost quarter-deck carronade, and "Flare!" to David Stock. The whole broadside followed, making the frigate shudder and reel. The effect of surprise could not have been more complete.

Delancey was to say afterwards that the recovery of the *Subtile* did Chatelard infinite credit. He was in battle before he had even cleared for action. Many a commander would have hauled down his colours to avert the impending massacre. Far from surrendering, Chatelard drove his men to their guns and made some sort of reply to the *Laura's* second broadside. The scene on board the privateer must have been one of indescribable confusion and bloodshed. After receiving the third broadside the *Subtile* slid past her stationary opponent and was soon outside the *Laura's* arc of fire. "All hands make sail!" shouted Delancey but the order was obeyed too slowly. Some minutes passed before the pursuit began and the *Subtile* was still the swifter ship of the two.

Three more broadsides were fired at the retreating enemy, whose stern-chasers replied, but the range was lengthening and little damage was done. Ten minutes later the action ended abruptly as the frigate gently ran aground. The depth of water on the bar of the river was sufficient for the privateer but not for her antagonist. By the time the *Laura* had been refloated, not without difficulty, the morning light silhouetted the jungle trees and the *Subtile* had vanished from sight.

Delancey anchored the frigate in deeper water and called for casualty and damage reports. There were seven killed and eighteen wounded, four of them unlikely to recover. There was some damage to the rigging and to the bowsprit and five shot holes

to plug, all above the waterline. The frigate was little the worse
for the encounter but the privateer, it could be assumed, was little better than a wreck.

After making his report, Fitzgerald offered to complete the
Subtile's destruction.

"Let me take the boats in, sir, and finish her off while the
French morale is low."

"Thank you for that offer, Mr Fitzgerald. I shall be glad to
see you perform that service but not immediately. I shall make
the attack in a week's time."

"But the French will have recovered by then. They will have
strengthened their stockade, sir, and mounted their cannon
ashore."

"That is true, Mr Fitzgerald. You are forgetting, however, that
we have the Malays to deal with. Their morale is unaffected
because they have not even been in action. The sound of firing
will have brought them to the scene in force. After a week during which nothing has happened, they will begin to drift away
again. They never have provisions for more than a few days.
Then I shall try again to achieve surprise."

Soon after daybreak the *Laura* was under sail, presently dropping anchor again off Djawi. Once more a sampan came off from
the shore, this time with just the one passenger: the Chinese
from whom Delancey had gained the vital information. Although
Djawi was nearly forty miles from the Kapuas River, the Chinese
already knew about the skirmish at the river-mouth. Wasting no
time, Delancey came straight to the point. Would his Chinese
friend like to earn another five hundred dollars? He would
indeed. Would he then make it widely known that the *Laura*
was now on her way back to Malacca and Penang?

Assuming that the *Subtile* had been put out of action, and

being short of supplies, Delancey had decided to quit the neigh-
bourhood and go north. He had called at Djawi for poultry and
fruit but had to leave again almost immediately. So far as the
Malays were concerned, the coast would be clear from tomorrow. Could the Chinese ensure that this news would reach
Kertamulia? There was no difficulty about that, it seemed, the
Chinese having business contacts all along the coast. He had no
love, Delancey thought, for the Malays of the Kapuas River and
had already guessed what Delancey meant to do. It would be a
pleasure, the Chinese said, to see that Delancey's plans became
generally known. There followed some everyday transactions,
enough to explain the *Laura's* presence at Djawi, and the Chinese went happily ashore.

Sailing before sunset, Delancey dropped anchor next morning at the mouth of the Nuri River. Sending for Topley, he told
him that he was to take a written message to Mr Michael
Delancey. He was to command the cutter but Mr Burnet would
be his pilot, having been up the river before, and his coxswain
would also have had that experience. The object of the expedition was to persuade the Dyaks to attack the Kapuas Malays in
one week from today. Topley was to be back at a rendezvous in
four days and should be able to report that the Dyaks were on
their way.

As soon as the cutter had been lowered and had rowed off,
Delancey plotted a course for the island of Pedjantan. He had
watered there before and thought the place suitable for a landing exercise and for rehearsing the attack on a stockade.
Fitzgerald was brave enough but did he know how to deal with
a boom so placed as to block a river? He might not have known
the secret before the exercises began. He certainly knew all about
it before they came to an end.

The *Laura* was back on the Borneo coast in time to rendezvous at nightfall with Topley's cutter at an unfrequented bay
on the north side of the Nuri estuary. Three of the cutter's crew
were sick but Topley was able to report on a successful mission.
He also brought with him two Dyaks, one of them a minor chief
and the other a young man who was to act as the chief's run-
ner. He had seen the Dyaks begin their overland march and
reported that Michael Delancey had gone with them and knew
the exact day on which their attack was to be staged.

"But why did you bring these Dyaks with you?"

"I thought that they might serve a useful purpose and Mr
Delancey agreed with me. The elder Dyak is called Tedong and
he knows the Kapuas River, having formerly lived on its banks.
The younger man, Sochon, is a good hunter and able to travel
quickly through the jungle. You will notice, sir, that he wears
the head-hunter's sword with a staghorn hilt. When the attack
is launched Tedong may act as guide and Sochon might try to
make contact with the Dyak force under Kanyan."

"A very good idea, Mr Topley. And you think that Kanyan
will be with us when the day comes?"

"Yes, sir. He and others seem to be bitter against the Malay
pirates."

"And is my brother in good health?"

Topley hesitated over his choice of words, anxious to tell the
truth without giving offence.

"He is not very strong, sir, but he wants his Dyaks to regain
their territory. I think he will keep going until the campaign is
over. He might fall sick again afterwards."

"Thank you, Mr Topley. You have done very well, using your
brains and showing a readiness to take responsibility."

Two more days were spent in training and in drawing up a

detailed plan. The central problem was the removal of the boom, without which the boats could not attack the *Subtile*. Delancey decided to storm the stockade in three stages. There would be, to begin with, a feint on the left. Then the real attack, on the right, would be directed against the end of the boom on that side and would culminate in the ropes being cut and the timber parts set adrift. In the final stages the boats would pass through and form line abreast for the assault on the privateer.

For the main attack Delancey detailed four groups, all under the direction of Mr Fitzgerald. One group would give covering fire with musketry. Two groups, left and right, would place scaling ladders against the stockade, climb them, and deal with the defenders by means of hand grenades. The last group would also have scaling ladders, would pass between the other groups and, crossing the stockade, would cut the boom adrift with their axes. This last group must be led by an officer, inevitably Mr Greenwell, and the two grenade parties would be led, respectively, by Topley and Stock. The gunner, Mr Woodley, would lead the feint attack, assisted by Midshipman Burnet. The boats, each commanded by a midshipman, would finally go though—led by whom? There must be one officer left in command of the ship and this would normally be the captain, but Delancey decided to direct the whole operation and lead the boats himself, ordering Northmore to stay on board the frigate. This was a difficult decision to make but he realized that the assault on the privateer would have to be planned on the spot. He could not know, to begin with, whether the French would be on the stockade or on board their ship. He supposed that Chatelard would have to divide them, but in what proportion? The Malays again were an unknown quantity. As pirates they would know little about fighting but they might be numerous. Of their strength he could make no estimate at all. Nor could he assume that the Dyaks would intervene effectively. They might, but his plan could not be based upon them. Supposing they did not appear and supposing that half his men were lost in storming the barricade, which was then found to be manned only by Malays, all further operations would have to be cancelled, at least for the time being. Who but he could take that responsibility? No, he must direct the operation as a whole and lead the final advance in person.

Delancey explained his plan of attack at a final conference attended by all officers down to the rank of midshipman. He had a large diagram pinned to the cabin bulkhead and drew arrows to show what had to be done by whom. When all questions had been resolved the officers withdrew but Fitzgerald returned at once to say that Mr Northmore wished for an interview with the captain. Delancey agreed to see him, knowing perfectly well what the young man was going to say. Some protest was inevitable and Northmore, white-faced and trembling, made a passionate plea to be allowed to take part in the operation. He felt disgraced, he said, to be left out of it.

"Mr Northmore," Delancey replied, "I should have been disappointed in you had you failed to protest at this moment. We are on the eve of an enterprise which should reflect credit on all who take part in it. In all I said just now, with the others present, I assumed that our efforts would succeed. But now, with none present except Mr Fitzgerald and yourself, I want you to consider the possibility of failure. I should not ordinarily talk about that but I am paid to think about it and about every other possibility. Assume now that we attacked at daybreak and found that stockade impregnable, defended by numerous cannon and by a thousand resolute opponents. By midday our losses include all officers and over a hundred men. The survivors make their way back to the frigate, many of them wounded and all exhausted. It then becomes the duty of the officer who was left on board to sail the ship back to Prince of Wales Island with only half a crew. Nor should you forget that the *Laura* may be attacked by the pirates while most of the crew are out of the ship. After the boats have gone up the river you will have more to do than bite your nails and wait for them to return. You have made your protest and I have rejected it. You need now to work and plan, listing the men you have and assigning them to the work they will have to do."

"Thank you, sir. I do understand that you have to leave a commissioned officer on board the ship. I exchanged a word just now, however, with Mr Greenwell. I think he would be willing, sir, to take my place."

"Indeed. I wonder why?"

"He thought, sir, that my prospects in the service are better than his. It may be, also, that he is not feeling well."

"If sick he would do better to tell me about it. As for you taking his place, I will not agree to it. I have good reason to allocate the duties as I think best. I have to make decisions. I do not have to defend them in argument. Your request, Mr Northmore, is refused."

Delancey turned to Fitzgerald after Northmore had gone, saying:

"I don't much like the sound of this."

"Nor do I, sir."

"I am not changing my plans, however, nor shall I allow my officers to exchange their duties. We shall attack the stockade at daybreak tomorrow."

Chapter Six

THE STOCKADE

T HE COLUMN of boats was ascending the Kapuas River under cover of darkness. Ahead of the rest went a native canoe with Tedong as guide, bearing a white flag just visible to the next boat, in which Delancey had embarked together with Lieutenant Sevendale of the Royal Marines, Midshipmen Forrest and Ledingham (the former as A.D.C.), the master-at-arms, the boat's crew, the sergeant, and twenty marines. Behind this boat was towed another native canoe with the other Dyak, Sochon, on board. Next came the cutter, with Mr Woodley, Mr Burnet, and twenty-four seamen—the party detailed to make the feint attack on the left. Then came the launch, commanded by Mr Fitzgerald with Mr Topley and Mr Stock and manned by thirty-eight men in all. Last of all came the other cutter with twenty-six seamen led by Mr Greenwell. Mr Northmore had been left with over seventy men in the *Laura* but of that total twenty or more were sick. Complete silence had been ordered and all that could be heard was the dipping of the oars.

Lower down the river the jungle had hedged the river on either side but this gave place presently to signs of cultivation. A small village was dimly seen, its houses built over the water, and then some huts built on a headland. At last, with the first hint of daybreak, Tedong let his canoe drift back and, coming alongside Delancey's boat, indicated to a point ahead where the river seemed to narrow. There were several lights shown there on either side and others, further back, hinted at the presence of a kampong. This was evidently the site of the stockade and Delancey passed the word back for Mr Woodley. As soon as the cutter was alongside, Delancey pointed left and gave the order to advance. Guided by Tedong, the boat went into the bank and disappeared from sight.

After a few minutes Delancey went forward again but more slowly, keeping to midstream and with stringent orders about avoiding noise. The sky ahead was now appreciably lighter with silver now tinged with pink. After what seemed an age there was a single musket shot on the left, followed later by the lighting of a flare. This was the signal for Fitzgerald's boat to draw level with Delancey who pointed right and whispered "Good luck!" Five minutes after the launch had gone in, Delancey told the last boat to follow. Then he told his oarsmen to resume rowing and his coxswain to hold course down the centre of the river, at the same time detaching Sochon, whose canoe headed into the shore on the right. So far all had gone according to plan with a growing sound of cannon and musketry on either bank, later punctuated by the harsher bang of the bursting grenades. Delancey thought to himself that he had gained at least a measure of surprise.

It was growing lighter every minute and the stockades were clearly visible on either side with the boom still in position across the river. The rattle of musketry continued but he could see no activity at the right-hand end of the boom. Adjusting his telescope, he could see the windlass to which the main cable was led but no attempt had been made to cut it. When Tedong returned from his mission on the left, Delancey turned to Midshipman Ledingham, and told him that the main attack was seemingly at a standstill. "I don't know what has happened," he went on calmly, "but I think it possible that Mr Greenwell has been wounded and that his party is hanging back, leaderless. I want you to go ashore in Tedong's canoe, take command of that group, move up to the stockade—which Mr Fitzgerald's men should have cleared—and cut the boom at that end. Off you go and—good luck!"

Good luck was what the boy would need and Delancey knew all too little about his capabilities. He could spare nobody else, however, and played almost the only card he had. He had thought wildly for a moment of leading Greenwell's party himself but he remembered in time that his target was not the stockade but the privateer. He must be ready to lead through in person when the boom had gone. Meanwhile, however, the sound of musketry had begun to slacken and he had the dismal impression that the momentum of the attack had been lost. Outwardly impassive, he thought unhappily of all the things which might have gone wrong. Had there been a second stockade behind the first or had the first one been guarded by a ditch lined with sharp bamboo points? Had Fitzgerald been killed or had his men lost their sense of direction? What could be happening and why did nobody think to tell him what the position was?

He would have liked to recall Mr Woodley from his feint attack on the left but he doubted whether this were possible. But then he had another idea. Could the feint attack become a real one? He wished now that he had another twenty men in hand. He could then have reinforced Woodley and so regained the initiative. All he could do now was to provide Woodley with new orders, which became possible now with the return of Tedong in his canoe.

"Mr Forrest," he said, "I want you to go ashore with Tedong

here and find Mr Woodley. The attack on the right has not so far succeeded. The boom is still in position. So I want Mr Woodley to attack the boom at his end, on the left. He is not equipped for cutting the cable so you will take an axe with you—here it is—and give Mr Woodley what help you can. Off with you!"

After Forrest had gone, Delancey could only wait and curse himself for keeping so small a reserve. Firing had largely died away, with silence on the left and only a few scattered shots on the right. Delancey began to suspect that the whole operation had failed, his men having been launched against a stronger force in a well-fortified position which he had failed properly to reconnoitre. His temptation was to lead his marines against the boom but he resisted it. With the boom still there his boat would be brought to a standstill and would come under fire from either bank. That way lay certain defeat. Or was he defeated already? To the strain of worry was added the further strain of appearing confident and unconcerned.

The day was growing hotter as the sun rose above the tree-tops. He turned to make conversation with his dour marine officer, Mr Sevendale:

"The cool of the day is over."

"Aye, sir, and the heat of the battle is still to come."

"Very true. We have so far been fighting the Malays. I have left the French to you."

"I doubt if they will stand up to us. Privateersmen fight for money if they fight at all. There is no future for these men and they must know it."

"I hope we can soon come to grips with them."

"We have to be patient, sir. In a land campaign half our time is spent in doing nothing. One has to grow used to it."

"I suspect, however, that the French have been active. They will by now have warped the *Subtile* athwart the river and mounted half her guns ashore."

"No doubt of it, sir. Might I be allowed to make a suggestion? If her broadside covers the river I think we should land at a point which is almost out of range, attack on the left and capture the guns that are mounted there. She will then be under an enfilade fire and will have to strike her colours."

"Why attack on the left?"

"You told us, sir, that the buildings and kampong are on the right."

"Yes, that was what Ellis said. I think your suggestion is a good one and I like your idea of turning their own plan against them. We shall follow your advice. What shall we do, however, if the *Subtile* is seen to starboard, bows-on, with her broadside brought to bear on the opposite bank of the river?"

"Our plan in that event should be to land well below her on the right and capture the guns placed on that side. She will then be under an enfilade fire but at even closer range."

"Agreed. Where should we be without the Royal Marines?"

They discussed the alternative plan in greater detail, allocating specific tasks to individual men. By the time each man knew what he had to do some ten minutes had passed. Then the battle quite suddenly revived on the right with heavy fire and the sound of cheering. Watching through his telescope, Delancey saw, at last, a hand-to-hand conflict at the end of the boom. Cutlasses flashed, pistols were fired, and bodies fell into the water. A minute later he could see the rise and fall of an axe. Men cheered again as the last strands parted and the boom swung down-stream, hinged on the other bank. On Delancey's order the oarsmen began to row and the coxswain steered a course midstream, passing just clear of the boom as it drifted past.

The last phase of the action had begun and all depended now on the good direction and sustained momentum of Delancey's attack. From the right flank came the sound of desultory firing, as if Fitzgerald were exploiting his success. From the left flank by contrast there came no sound at all. Ahead, the shining river was empty, curving, gradually to the left. As the oars plunged in rhythm Sevendale ordered his marines to fix bayonets. Five minutes later the river curved to the right and there, ahead of them, was the *Subtile,* unrigged and moored across the river. The privateersmen sighted the boat at the same time and opened fire at long range. Delancey told the coxswain to steer into the shore on their left. Within a matter of minutes he drew his sword and led his party ashore. There was no jungle at this point, nearly opposite the village, but a succession of small fields, some planted with padi and others grazed by goats.

Leaving two older seamen with the boat, Delancey ordered six others to act as scouts, he following them at the head of the marines. He came across startled Malays who scuttled away in panic but there was no sort of resistance to his march. After ten minutes, however, he was surprised to hear the French cannon open fire again and wondered what their target could be. Cannon boomed repeatedly and he could smell the powder as the advance continued. At one moment he was blundering through a hen-run, at another he was all but falling over a solitary pig. In such close country it was impossible to see more than a few yards ahead but it was easy to keep parallel with the river and as easy to guess from the gunfire how far they had still to go.

When the sound was deafeningly close the seamen ahead of him fell back a little and Delancey halted the marines. "Rest for three minutes," he said and the men sat down, checked their priming, and regained their breath. Going forward cautiously, Delancey peered round a tree and saw the enemy's position. There was the *Subtile* with her broadside wreathed in smoke, firing down the river (but at what, for heaven's sake?).

Nearer at hand were three cannon in position on a low headland, so placed as to cross the fire of four more cannon on the opposite side of the river. These were not in action but all were manned by Frenchmen and a young officer was busy with a telescope. Delancey went back to the marines, deployed now at regular intervals. "Fifty yards to your front," he said to Sevendale. "When you are ready—attack!"

"Advance!" said the marine officer and led his men forward at a steady pace. Delancey followed with his armed seamen three on either side of him. Two minutes later Sevendale shouted "Charge!" At that instant Delancey burst through some bushes and saw the marines already among the French seamen, who had been taken by surprise, few of them even armed.

While the French were killed or captured, Delancey's men manned the nearest cannon and aimed it at the privateer's stern, some twenty yards distant. To miss at that range was impossible and the first shot went through the *Subtile* from stern to forecastle. By then the marines had the other two guns swung round in turn, one aimed at the *Subtile* and the other at the guns on the far bank of the river. The remaining marines engaged the privateer with their muskets and stopped the French rallying to her defence. It was at this moment that Delancey had his first glimpse of Chatelard, a small dark man who seemed to be everywhere at once. Of his energy and courage there could be no doubt at all but his men were plainly dispirited. Rallying men from the main deck, he attempted to mount a couple of sternchasers but nothing came of it. He tried to bring small-arms men to the stern of the ship but they mostly ran forward or below. Sword in hand he drove a few of them aft but Delancey turned to Sevendale and pointing, said, "Shoot him!" Grabbing a musket from a wounded man, Sevendale loaded the weapon, aimed it carefully, and fired. Seeing that Chatelard had been hit, Delancey called on his men to make a final effort. In another few minutes the privateer's colours were hauled down and her guns fell silent. Her own boats were used to take possession of her.

With the *Subtile* taken, Delancey prepared to launch a new attack on the village and shore installations but this proved needless. Fitzgerald appeared on the beach and his men could be seen clearing the storage sheds and magazines. Malay resistance had evidently crumbled after the breaking of the boom. Spared the necessity for further battle, Delancey looked for Chatelard and found him at the break of the quarter-deck, lying dead in a pool of blood. Some twenty-three other dead bodies were visible with fourteen wounded and seventeen prisoners. One of the prisoners, a petty officer, said that there had been sixty-three privateersmen (after many lost by sickness), which would leave eight missing. Having made this calculation and seen what damage the privateer had sustained, Delancey heard a bump alongside and found that the two seamen he had left with the boat had impressed some Chinese as oarsmen and so brought the boat up the river.

"Well done," said Delancey. "But tell me what the French cannon were firing at?"

"At us, sir," explained the elder seaman. "We made the boat look fully manned and rowed out into the river, dodging back when their shot came too close. We thought it would give them something to think about."

"It certainly did that. But how did you man the boat?"

"We persuaded these Chinese to row and we added some clothes and hats hoisted on bits of bamboo."

"There will be extra grog for both of you when we reach the *Laura,* and thank you for your good service this day."

Manning the boat in more regular fashion, Delancey put the Chinese ashore and then landed on the other side of the river, where Fitzgerald greeted him.

"Well done, first lieutenant. Tell me what happened."

"Well, sir, the Malays were on that stockade in force, armed with muskets and a lot of brass swivel guns, the sort you see in their war prahus. The stockade itself was higher than we expected and loopholed for musketry. We suffered heavily before we had our scaling ladders in position. The grenades, however, drove the Malays back and we looked back expecting to see Mr Greenwell's party but there was no sign of it. We were not really equipped for cutting the boom so I sent a petty officer back to serve as guide or, failing that, to bring us a couple of axes. He did not return and has since told me that he lost his way. For the time being I held the line of the stockade and was planning how to reach the boom but then we were attacked by the Malays in force. We beat them off with great difficulty. When they fell back again, Midshipman Ledingham appeared from nowhere at the head of Mr Greenwell's party, sealed the stockade, and made straight for the boom. We kept up a rapid fire while he cut the cable. After that the Malays rather collapsed, withdrawing in disorder and leaving their dead behind. We pushed on against dwindling resistance and reached this village without further loss. We have lost twenty-nine men in all, many of them killed."

"And Mr Greenwell?"

"I have been told that he was wounded but have not seen him since."

There was something constrained about this last statement. Fitzgerald was not telling all he knew. Delancey let it go at that, however, deciding that the time had come to rest.

"With the exception of four sentinels, all seamen and marines have half an hour in which to rest and have a meal from the provisions they carry. After that, we all have work to do."

Delancey sat down in the shade and Teesdale brought him something to eat. He was not hungry, however, nor very talkative, having a great deal to think about. When half an hour had passed he issued his further orders to Mr Fitzgerald: "You will hold this village and the prisoners with twenty men, assisted by Mr Sevendale and twenty marines. You will send Mr Topley back with the launch and ten men to collect the wounded on this side of the river and take them on board the *Laura*, returning with the launch tomorrow after this has been done. Mr Stock, with eight men, will bury the dead, listing them and collecting their weapons and packs, reporting back to you here when this task has been completed. Tell Mr Ledingham to report to me here with two seamen. Now, Master-at-Arms, you will take six men in the cutter, go back along the far side of the river, and find Mr Woodley and his party. I cannot tell you where they are but their orders were to make a feint attack on the stockade. I suspect that they may be in that area still. They must join me here as soon as possible."

Had he remembered everything? Almost certainly not. Nor could he be certain that Fitzgerald would think of what he had forgotten. There were, however, some questions he had to ask, with Ledingham as his first witness. When the youngster reported to him, with two armed seamen at heel, he congratulated him at once on the part he had played. But for his efforts the boom might still be in position.

"Thank you, sir. I think we were lucky, though. Earlier in the action the Malays were fighting like tigers. They even counter-attacked the stockade after it had fallen. Then they collapsed and I had my chance to reach the boom. I can't think why they should have lost heart when they did but it was fortunate for us. Two of my men were slightly wounded in that skirmish by the boom and those were our only casualties."

"You did very well for all that. I am now going to walk back over the battlefield and I want you to tell me what happened. There are one or two things I should like to know."

Leading the way, the midshipman walked through an area of cultivated land broken up by ditches. Crossing the last of these, they came across their first dead Malay, lying face upwards and deprived of his knees (taken no doubt as a souvenir). There was no sign of a wound but his face was that of a man in extreme pain. On an impulse, Delancey turned the body over and saw, between the shoulder blades, the protruding end of a Dyak dart.

"Poisoned . . ." he muttered. "It must take some time to take effect."

"Was he shot, sir, with a blowpipe?"

"He and, I suspect, many others. That is why they suddenly lost heart."

Bodies became more numerous as they came nearer to the stockade, some of them clearly killed by musket shot but others by the blowpipe, all these from behind. Ledingham then showed Delancey where the boom had been cut, where three bodies still lay, all slashed or stabbed with the cutlass but one, face downwards, with a dart in his neck. Going round the end of the stockade, they inspected it from the attacker's point of view. It was still formidable and the scaling ladders were not really long enough. In the middle where Ledingham had gone through, two ladders had been lashed together with spunyarn. The others had shown less initiative and had probably spent their efforts in firing through the loopholes. The Malays would have been fifty yards further back, shooting from behind trees; and that, he thought, was where the Dyaks found them. The British casualties had nearly all occurred in the approach to the stockade, where five bodies still lay and two wounded men unlikely to live. He had hardly examined these before young Stock came to remove them.

"Now, Mr Ledingham, I want to see the position from which Mr Fitzgerald's musket men brought covering fire."

"It must have been somewhere to the right, sir. I never saw it myself."

They walked over in that direction and found the place without difficulty, a dead Malay lying just beyond. He differed from the others, however, in that his head had gone, neatly sliced off. The actual cause of death was a bullet hole through his chest but the Dyaks had been there since.

"Good god, sir!"

"The Dyaks are head-hunters, Mr Ledingham. Now show me the line of your advance."

The midshipman led Delancey back to a hollow opposite the centre of the stockade, screened by bushes and marked by one or two items of equipment.

"This is where I found Mr Greenwell, sir. He lay over there and told me that he was wounded and that Mr Hubbard had been killed."

"Were his men in action?"

"Two of them had been sent forward a few paces. They were about here, sir, behind trees, and just able to see the stockade."

"Were they firing?"

"I rather doubt it, sir. Their fire would have been masked by our own men."

"I see. And what was the nature of Mr Greenwell's wound?"

"I don't know, sir."

Retracing Ledingham's route back to the river bank, they came across the body of Midshipman Hubbard. He had been killed by a long-distance shot fired at some other target and had died clutching his dirk. Telling his two seamen to bring the body, he walked slowly back to the stockade. Ledingham now asked him the obvious question:

"If the Dyaks were so active on our side, sir, why don't we see them?"

"They have gone in pursuit of the Malays. They are head-hunters, remember." The midshipman was sick at this point. Delancey laid a hand on the boy's shoulder.

"It happens later. I mean, they have been killed first."

"Yes, sir. Sorry about that."

"It's partly the smell. We'll go back to the village now."

Adding his two seamen to Topley's party, Delancey began to inspect what had been the *Subtile*'s base. There were still some naval stores in the riverside godowns and these were, very properly, guarded by a sentry. Four other marines were posted outside the hut in which the French prisoners were confined. In the most substantial hut Fitzgerald was making a list of the booty taken, which included the specie out of which the privateersmen were paid.

Walking past all these riverside buildings, with Ledingham still at heel, Delancey came across a smaller hut which would seem to have been used as a prison, being strongly made with barred windows. Here and there some prisoner had scratched his name on the timber uprights.

Looking idly at these marks, Delancey came across the name JO WAYLAND and knew what he had suspected, that his master's mate had not been killed in the skirmish but had been taken prisoner. What had happened to him after that? Where was he now? To this question he resolved to find the answer but he went on to visit some adjacent buildings. These had been designed and furnished for comfort and with ample servants' quarters behind them. One of them had clearly belonged to Chatelard, who would have slept ashore while the *Subtile* was in port. Many of his personal possessions were there and it could be assumed that he had been there the previous night. Another house could have been shared by his officers, who would probably have taken it in turns to sleep on board the privateer. The third and last house presented more of a problem. Its biggest room was furnished like an office with a long table, a desk, and a number of cupboards, all securely locked. On the walls were charts of the Indian Ocean and of the Straits of Malacca, with maps of India, Arabia, and Persia. There was a bedroom but no sign of recent use. When the cupboards were broken open they were found to contain the logs of captured merchantmen, piles of newspapers published in Bombay, Madras, and Calcutta, and sheafs of correspondence found in various prizes. It had been somebody's task to collect intelligence and plan the *Subtile's* campaigns. This was where he had lived and worked but the contents of the drawers of the desk gave no clue to his identity. It was clear that he meant to return or had handed over his duties to someone else. It remained to see what the prisoners would reveal when interrogated.

When back in the village Delancey found that Bartlett, the master-at-arms, had returned.

"I'm sorry to have to report, sir, that Mr Woodley and his party were all killed but two and they badly wounded. I turned those two seamen over to Mr Topley and I have told Mr Stock about the others. It looked to me, sir, as if Mr Woodley attacked the stockade but was himself attacked by Malays who worked round his flank and surrounded him. Mr Burnet and Mr Forrest were also killed, sir. They must have been greatly outnumbered."

"But there are no Malays there now?"

"Dead ones, sir, about a dozen. The rest must have run away after the boom was cut. I followed back the way they must have come but could find no trace of them."

So, much, Delancey thought, for my feint attack, led by a warrant-officer for lack of anyone better. It had served its purpose at a cost of nineteen men killed, including a midshipman, and two men badly wounded. It was clear now that the Dyaks had all kept to the one side of the river. That was why Woodley's party had fared so ill. Without having totalled the losses, he knew now that they were appalling. Nor was the list complete for his men were still ashore, many of them, and might fall sick before they could embark again. Turning from this disheartening thought, Delancey asked Fitzgerald whether he had extracted any useful information from the prisoners.

"Not much, sir. There are seventeen apart from the wounded but three of them are Portuguese from Goa who have answered questions put to them through one of our Goanese who also knows English."

"Good. Now question those three on two points. John Wayland was taken prisoner. What happened to him? There was a man in charge here when Chatelard was at sea. Who was he and where did he go?"

"Aye, aye, sir. What about the *Subtile?*"

"I want you to remove from her everything that would be of use to us—canvas, cordage, powder, stores of every kind. What is not removed will be burnt with the ship tomorrow."

"Couldn't we bring her away, sir?"

"We could but we shan't and that for two reasons. First, my orders were to destroy her. Second, we shall lose more men from sickness every day we remain here. No, she will burn tomorrow and then we quit this place for good."

That evening Fitzgerald reported some further success in his interrogation of the Portuguese. "They say that an English seaman—almost certainly Wayland, from their description—was questioned for days in the prison hut but evidently without much success. Chatelard was very angry and handed him over to the Malays for execution."

"To the Malays?"

"Yes, sir. That seems to have been a regular practice. Before Chatelard came poor Wayland must have been held prisoner by this other man you were asking about. These Portuguese never knew his real name but heard him called Fabius and they agree that he sailed in a ship for the Ile de France."

"So he did, did he? I should like some day to meet him."

"What are we to do with the French prisoners, sir?"

"We shall leave them here, whether wounded or not."

"For the Dyaks to finish off?"

"Or for the Malays to take care of. They will have an easier death than they planned for Wayland."

Next morning the *Subtile* was set on fire and so were all the buildings except one isolated storehouse in which Delancey had told his men to collect everything which might be of use to the Dyaks. Naval stores, by contrast, were sent down to the river in the privateer's launch, Delancey now having boats to spare. While directing this operation, he was approached by a petty officer who said that a European wished to see him. It could only be Michael, who looked completely exhausted and carried a French-pattern musket. With him were Kanyan and Tedong, each with a blowpipe. Delancey hastened to thank them for their support but Michael interrupted him at once:

"You've had help from them. Now they want help from you!"

"In what way, Michael?"

"We have pursued the Malays to a place about eight miles up the river. They have taken refuge in a small island which they have done something to fortify. They still have muskets and ammunition and the Dyaks can do nothing against them."

"I see. My best plan will be to supply the Dyaks with small-arms."

"They won't use them, Richard. They are frightened of the recoil."

"Then we had best give them cutlasses, enough for the purposes of a night attack."

"They need your help, Richard. They need you to give them confidence. They will have no security here while those pirates are alive."

"Look, Michael, my orders were to destroy the *Subtile,* which I have now done. I was never ordered to interfere in a war between Dyaks and Malays. My task here is finished and we shall be at sea again tonight."

"But you owe your success to the Dyaks—you must know that."

"I do know it. But they also owe their success to me. They have what they wanted—heads!"

"What they really want is the Kapuas River."

"They will never keep it unless they are prepared to fight for it. I can provide them with the weapons. You must provide them with the leadership."

"I hate the whole system, Richard, of which you have become a part. I came here to escape from it. Then I thought for a moment that you would be a friend to the Dyaks and help them to regain their lost country. But I was wrong. You are no friend to them or to anyone. You are merely part of the system."

"Have I denied it? But tell Kanyan and Tedon that they'll have their share of all that was taken from the pirates and from the French. Tell them to come and see what they have fairly earned."

Faced with the storehouse, Kanyan and Tedong were more grateful than Michael wanted them to be. They could certainly find a use for all that they had been given. Nor did it appear that they had relied upon further help against the Malays. Given a cutlass apiece, they seemed confident enough in their ability to finish the campaign.

"I'll help them and advise them," said Michael, "but I'll die very soon. And as for you, Richard, I hope that you rot in hell!"

Delancey's final glimpse of Michael was that of a scarecrow figure outside the storehouse from which a procession of laden Dyaks headed back into the jungle. He never saw Michael again and hardly supposed that he could live for long or that he even wished to survive. From their first meeting in the longhouse it was apparent that Michael had reached the end of the road.

In the last boat to leave the scene of destruction, Delancey knew that a final and unpleasant task awaited him. Greenwell's conduct had presented him with a problem to which there was only one solution. He had known instances in which certain incidents had been overlooked but what was the use? The officer concerned had no authority left. No, he had to act at once. He no sooner reached the *Laura* than he sent for the surgeon. "How many men have you under your care, Mr Mackenzie and how many more shall we lose?"

The surgeon presented a list, making a detailed report on those who were still in danger. Having made a rough total, Delancey laid down his pen.

"And how is Mr Greenwell?"

"He has a wound on his right leg, a little below the knee. No major artery was severed but he may have lost some blood before he was bandaged. He is in no danger and is able to walk."

"Was the wound caused by a bullet?"

"No, sir. It is a clean cut, caused by a blade."

"On the inside or outside of the leg?"

"On the outside."

"It was not inflicted, however, during a hand-to-hand conflict."

"No, sir? Then it could have been due to an accident—a seaman tripping over some obstacle while carrying a drawn cutlass. It could, in the same way, have been the result of Mr Greenwell tripping over his own sword." Mackenzie's face was expressionless and his words carefully chosen.

"You did not ask him what happened?"

"No, sir. I did not."

When alone again, Delancey stared for a minute or two at the inkstand. Then he deliberately took a pistol from where it hung on the bulkhead, saw that it was loaded, checked the priming, cocked it, and placed the weapon on his desk. Then he called out "Pass the word for Mr Greenwell," and waited thoughtfully until there was a knock on the door. Invited to come in, Greenwell limped forward, white-faced and trembling, and stood at attention.

"Sit down, Mr Greenwell," said Delancey. "You know why I have sent for you." It was a statement, not a question. Greenwell was staring at the pistol, his forehead shining with sweat, his hands fiddling with a handkerchief.

"Yes, sir."

"There are questions I could ask but what is the point? I should not believe your answer."

"No, sir."

"So it only remains for me to do what I must, Mr Greenwell. I am placing you under close arrest. When a court martial can assemble you will be charged with cowardice."

"I suppose so." The words were whispered.

"I need hardly add that I deeply regret having to take this action. Had the circumstances been different, had a pistol gone off while you were cleaning it—" he glanced at the pistol on the desk—"I should have reported you killed in battle. But I have no alternative. You can see that."

"Yes, sir. I tried, I did my utmost. I couldn't describe the sleepless nights . . ."

"I know. I have always known. But what could I do? You must presently go to your cabin but you had best wait here a little and recover. I need to see Mr Fitzgerald about appointing Mr Northmore as your escort and Mr Topley as acting lieutenant. We sail tonight for Prince of Wales Island. Were we there and were you going ashore, I should have to say—good-bye." Delancey went on deck and gave out his preparatory orders. There was much to do, his crew requiring a great deal of reorganization. While in conclave with Fitzgerald he half expected to hear the sound of a pistol shot. Or did he? Thinking more carefully he realized that no shot would be fired. Greenwell was not that sort of man. He should never, in fact, have been promoted.

"Ready to sail, sir," Fitzgerald reported.

"Very good. Man the capstan. And leave Mr Topley in charge of the deck."

As he went to his cabin Delancey could hear Topley's young voice calling "Heave taut!" The pistol, now uncocked, lay on his desk and he put it back on its hook. Then he sat down to study and absorb the full extent of his losses.

The wounded fell into three categories: those likely to recover, twenty-one; those likely to be invalided, eight; and those likely to die, twelve. He might soon have a crew of about 110 men, a little over half his establishment. And what proportion of these would fall sick as a result of being ashore among the mangrove swamps? Twenty, thirty, or more? His frigate was no longer fit to do battle. In destroying the *Subtile* he had all but lost the *Laura*.

The arithmetic done, Delancey took a sealed letter from a drawer, marked "To be opened after the destruction of the *Subtile*." Slitting it open he read:

H.M. Ship *Albion*
April 19th 1806   *Prince of Wales Island*

Sir—Having accomplished your mission you are hereby required and directed to proceed to Prince of Wales Island where you are to carry out necessary repairs and ship provisions for six months. When ready for sea you will proceed to the Cape of Good Hope and place yourself under the command of the flag-officer commanding there.

I have the honour to remain . . . etc.

Enclosed with this official order was a private note:

April 19th 1806

Dear Delancey—I congratulate you on having destroyed the *Subtile*. I knew that you would do it and I knew that the cost would be heavy. All this I sincerely regret. I should have liked to send you home but I have at least sent you in the right direction. When the admiral at the Cape (whoever he may be) realizes that the *Laura* is worn out, I have no doubt that he will decide to spare you. I thank you in advance for your good services. You will have heard that I am quitting this station and will probably not be in India when you receive this. Should you ever serve again under my flag you will find that I shall always have a high opinion of the man who finally rid me of the *Subtile*. I thank you for all you have done, bless you.

> *With every good wish . . . etc.*
> Ed. Pellew

The *Laura* was back at Prince of Wales Island in October 1806 but required docking, part of her stern-post having decayed. She was docked at Bombay, coming back to Prince of Wales Island in May 1807. The following letter from there was the last which Delancey wrote before he sailed for the Cape:

June 11th 1807

My dearest Fiona—My letters from Bombay will have told you about the *Laura's* time in dock. She now has a teak stern-post and many new knee-timbers and is in very much better state. It is not so easy to make good the losses in men. We had heavy casualties last year and my only recruits

have been Goanese, Lascars, Sepoys, and Chinese. As for
officers, I told you that poor Greenwell was tried here by
court martial and dismissed the service. He is a tradesman
now in Georgetown and I met him ashore two days ago.
Apart from Fitzgerald, my lieutenants are promoted midshipmen, Northmore and Topley. With those two
commissioned and three others killed in Borneo, I have
only two left, Stock (now master's mate) and Ledingham,
and have no idea where I can find any more. I have men
enough to work the ship but would rather not meet with
the enemy. I dare say, however, that they are as ill-manned
as we are, or anyway I must devoutly hope so. If I gained
the good opinion of Admiral Pellew that does me no good
because he is going home and has not offered to take me
with him! I am now ordered to the Cape from which station my letters will reach you the sooner. From what I hear
the ships on that station spend their time blockading Mauritius (or the Ile de France), an occupation which may not
end until we capture the island. Our failure to do so is
mainly the result, I suppose, of the place being so con-
foundedly remote. This letter must be brief, going as it does
by a ship that is to sail in the morning. My next may well
be dated from Capetown. In the meanwhile I mean to climb
the Hill here tomorrow and attempt to make a sketch from
the top. Before ending this letter I must ask you to take
great care of yourself and believe me still

Your most affectionate husband,
Richard Delancey

Postscript. Since writing the above we have suffered disaster. Fitzgerald, my first lieutenant, seems to have had a

quarrel with the surgeon of the regiment in garrison here. They met at daybreak and Fitzgerald was fatally wounded, dying before the ball could be extracted. He was quick-tempered, I know, and may well have been at fault, his opponent, I am told, being slow to take offence but a dead shot with a pistol. Fitzgerald was unmarried but had devoted parents in Wicklow who will be heartbroken over this tragic event. I must feel for their loss but cannot refrain from lamenting my own. Northmore, who must be my first lieutenant, is far too young, and Stock, now to be acting lieutenant, is a mere boy. Or do they all seem children to me because I am becoming middle-aged and cantankerous? They are lucky in their promotion. Had there been a flag-officer here my lieutenant's vacancy would have been filled by a midshipman from the flagship, someone on the Admiralty list, or else a relative of the Admiral himself. I am far from being the senior naval officer here but the other men-of-war are as shorthanded as I am and anxious to retain the men they have. Northmore will have to grow up quickly and I think very well of young Ledingham who behaved gallantly in Borneo.

Surrounded by much younger men I have the feeling that I am needed, that things could go very wrong if I were ill. Having no time to be sick, I remain well! I must admit, however, that I took full advantage of our stay at Bombay, having nearly eight luxurious weeks in harbour and being free to sleep all night. Blockading Mauritius will be more arduous but I tell myself, hopefully, that I should be home in 1808 or at latest in 1809. When I reach home, moreover, I may well decide to stay there!

Chapter Seven

MAURITIUS

IT WAS July 5th 1809 and Delancey was dining with his officers in the wardroom, following the usual Saturday routine. In the chair was the first lieutenant, the Hon. Stephen Northmore, and Delancey, remembering him as a bright fifteen-year-old midshipman, thought him absurdly young to hold so responsible a position. Then he did some mental arithmetic and realized, with a shock, that Northmore must be twenty-four—no, dammit, twenty-five. He was a handsome young man with fair hair, dark eyes, and bronzed complexion. Rather lazy in his younger days, he was becoming an admirable officer, there could be no doubt of that.

Edward Topley, second lieutenant, short, sturdy, and dark, perhaps two years younger than Northmore, would never be quite as good but had become very reliable; far better in that way than Fitzgerald had ever been. David Stock, third lieutenant, a son of the Bishop of Killala, was a born seaman, popular with the crew and endowed with good powers of leadership but with only moderate intelligence. Sevendale of the Royal Marines had proved himself an excellent soldier in Borneo and revealed, from time to time, a quiet sense of humour. Mackenzie, the surgeon, was a competent Scotsman, sometimes teased for his economical habits, and Finch, the purser, was as colourless and efficient as he had been from the first. Present

as guests were young Ledingham and another midshipman
called Lewis, transferred from the flagship as a result of a
quarrel.

The sea officers were all rather young as compared with their
captain, who was forty-eight, but Delancey had trained them all
himself. Or was that true? No, he reflected, they had really been
trained by Mather. It was now for Northmore to train Ledingham and Lewis. He was no such teacher as Mather had been
but he was a good man to copy and Ledingham had already
picked up some of his mannerisms. Lewis had also been heard
to say "Do it right," an expression derived from Stock who had
learnt it from Mather, a man Lewis had never known.

On the whole, Delancey had reason to be satisfied with his
officers. He could only wish that his lower deck had been half
as good. The frigate was very undermanned and the real seamen left were only a handful. His only consolation lay in the
skill of the Chinese servants who did the laundry and who had
provided, as usual, an excellent dinner. Ten days after leaving
the Cape, they had not quite exhausted their fresh provisions.
There were still, for example, some oranges left. As for the
frigate herself, she was all but worn out. Rear-Admiral Stirling
had seen that and had ruled out any idea of sending her to sea
before the end of the hurricane season in March. There is a
point beyond which repair of a ship becomes impossible and
that point, for the *Laura,* would be reached in 1809; at the latest, in 1810. The work carried out at Bombay had merely
postponed the inevitable. Looking around him, Delancey
thought that the ship and her captain were almost equally worn
out. Faced by a new French frigate out from France he would
be lucky to avoid having to strike his colours. If he fought it

would not be to gain glory but merely to survive, he and the *Laura* having grown old together. If he went home in 1810 he would have been five years on a foreign station. It was enough and more than enough.

"Were you ever in Mauritius, sir?" It was Topley asking the question and Delancey had to bring his thoughts back to the present.

"No, my knowledge of the place is merely from hearsay. It is not an easy place to blockade."

"Because of the reefs which surround it?"

"No, because there are three places to watch. The main French naval base is at Port Louis, there is another harbour at Grand Port a dozen miles away, and then a third is St Paul's in the other island of Bourbon; all three places defended by shore batteries. We can't be in strength at all three points and the returning French frigate will head for the one which is open at the time."

"What I can't understand, sir," said Northmore, "is why we haven't captured the islands and ended the nuisance."

"Why, indeed?" replied Delancey. "One possible reason is that the French frigates have had only moderate success. They have captured country ships but have seldom intercepted an East Indiaman. Should the Company lose two or three of its own ships, the Indian governments would begin to take notice."

"Can't the Navy take action by itself?" asked Stock.

"Not if we're to land troops. Those can only come from India."

"But remember, sir," said Sevendale, "that I could land twenty-one marines, or even twenty-two if you count the drummer boy."

"Oh, yes, I should include the drummer boy," replied Delancey, "He could terrify the French militia into surrender. They are said to number three thousand."

"And amount, probably, to nothing." Topley spoke with conviction but Delancey would not agree.

"We cannot be certain of that. Militia regiments in Britain are often little inferior to regular troops. But the same word is often applied to a rustic rabble without discipline or training."

"And some rustics, sir," said Sevendale, "are difficult to train. They often don't know right from left—"

"Let alone right from wrong," added Mackenzie.

"So we shall have to land and inspect them," Delancey concluded, "before we dare pronounce on their quality."

"All the American States have a militia," said Northmore. "A free Negro volunteered to join in New Jersey and was asked whether he would prefer the cavalry. "No, sir," he replied, "When that thar trumpet sounds the retreat, I don't want to be hindered by no horse!"

The conversation became general but Delancey was still wondering about the armed forces of Mauritius. Could they really have transferred their loyalty from Louis XVI to the Republic and from the Republic to the Empire? Could they, at that distance, have absorbed any ideas about liberty, equality, or fraternity? Or did they merely want to live in peace? It was one thing to have names on a list and muskets in an armoury, quite another to have men actually on parade when the alarm was sounded. The one certainty in Delancey's mind was that Josias Rowley, to whom the Admiral had entrusted the blockade of the islands, would never confine himself to sailing back and forth. Captain Rowley, as he remembered him, was one of the ablest men in the service and would certainly pursue a more active course. He would push his patrols up to the high-tide mark and beyond.

"It is all very well to believe in discipline," said David Stock,

"but some officers go a great deal too far. Did you hear of what
happened when Captain Railton joined the *Falcon?*"

"I heard something about it," said Northmore. "Wasn't there
some sort of mutiny?"

"There was the beginning of one. Captain Railton had previously commanded the *Scorpion* and made for himself the
reputation of a taut hand. He was transferred to the *Falcon* when
the *Scorpion* was ordered home. When he read his commission,
the men all refused to serve under him."

"Allow me to interrupt," said Delancey with a touch of asperity, "I'm not sure that I like this sort of gossip. But, having heard
so much you had best hear the end of it. Admiral Stirling went
on board the *Falcon* and asked the men whether any one of them
had served under Captain Railton before. No one came forward.
So they knew nothing about Railton, he asked, except from idle
rumour? This was the fact and they had to admit it. So the men
returned to duty and the *Falcon* sailed with convoy to India."

"But isn't it true, sir, that Railton will flog the last man down
from the yard-arm?" Stock evidently knew more than he had said.

"I have no idea. But I shouldn't condemn Railton on the basis
of lower-deck gossip. I met him only briefly but I am told that
he has a good record. Shall we leave it at that?"

Delancey could not allow talk against a senior officer and
young Stock looked properly ashamed of himself. He and the
others probably thought that the old man was becoming
pompous. The fact remained, however, that Delancey had heard
the same rumours himself. There had been something like
mutiny on board the *Scorpion* and before that in the frigate of
which Railton had been first lieutenant. He wondered for a
moment whether Stirling had acted with sufficient care.

Three days later (July 8th) Delancey wrote to Fiona at some length:

My dearest Fiona—To understand this letter you will need an atlas open at the map of Africa. Alongside Africa, on the right, you will find the big island of Madagascar. Beyond it again you will find the small islands of the Ile de France (also called Mauritius) and the Ile Bourbon (also called Réunion). The Seychelles comprise a group of islands which also, in theory, belong to France. The white inhabitants there number about two hundred, mostly deported convicts, and about twice as many slaves. These islands change each time a man-of-war calls there, but this is merely a matter of hoisting different flags. Failing to capture the French islands, we have had to blockade them, which is tedious work. We are the cats and the mice, at present, are reduced to two, the *Semillante* (32) and the *Canonniére* (48).

The bigger French island is Bourbon or Réunion but it is the other island, the Ile de France or Mauritius, which is the more important. It centres on Port Louis, which is deemed to be impregnable, but there is another harbour, less strongly defended, on the other side of the island. This is called Grand Port and there is a town there called Mahebourg. The interior of the island is mountainous and the coastline is rocky, fringed with reefs which are said to make a landing difficult or impossible. The population is very mixed and includes a high proportion of Negro slaves, used in the cultivation of sugar and coffee. The work of maintaining some sort of blockade is likely to be tedious and quite ineffective in curtailing the depredations of their men-of-war. On returning from a cruise, a French frigate will be warned by signal as to the whereabouts of our blockading squadron and will make accordingly for one of the three harbours available. My plan would be to conquer both islands and so have the chance to go home! I must first, however, secure for myself the appointment of Governor-General—an office which is not even vacant!

Remember me to my neighbours in Guernsey and believe me

Your most affectionate husband,
Richard Delancey

At the end of August 1809 Delancey reported on board the *Raisonable* (64) off Port Louis and was once more in the presence of Josias Rowley. Aged forty-three, Rowley had been in the navy all his life and was the grandson of Admiral Sir William Rowley who went to sea in 1704. His uncle had been Admiral Sir Joshua Rowley, his cousin was a captain now serving in the Mediterranean. Fortunate in his service connections, he had not been quite as lucky in his career. The only battle in which he had taken part was Sir Robert Calder's action off Finisterre, an affair which ended Calder's career and did little for the reputation of anyone else. But Rowley's ability was known and he made an instant impression on everyone who met him. He was a fine-looking vigorous Irishman, with a ready smile but penetrating glance. His ship was in impeccable order, his own appearance to match. He radiated confidence and vitality and was never at a loss. Greeting Delancey as an old friend, he told him at once what the *Laura's* function would be:

"My squadron comprises the *Raisonable*, *Leopard* (50), *Laurel* (22), and *Otter* (16). At Port Louis the French have a powerful frigate, the *Canonnière* but little else. Their other frigate, the *Semillante* had an action with the *Terpsichore* in February—you will have heard about it—and has since been disarmed and dismantled. We hear that she is to go back to France as a merchantman. Plans for the capture of the French islands have been discussed and I have been ordered to collect information about them and more particularly about their state of defence. Were there an effective French squadron at Port Louis, I should find it difficult to reconnoitre the landing places, but we now have our chance. I think it probable that the French will be reinforced and so we must do what we can in the meanwhile. For the task of reconnaissance I need a good seaman with brains and a knowledge of French."

"And one perhaps whose frigate is old and expendable?"

"That, too. Can you do it?"

"Tell me first, sir, what questions I am to answer?"

"There are two questions. First, I want to know where we could land an army. Second, I want to know what resistance we can expect after the army has been landed. Given information on those two points, the staff in India can draw up a detailed plan. We have little idea at present as to what force we need or where we are to put it ashore."

"I understand, sir. And I must assume that we shall need to have contact with people ashore?"

"We have none as yet. We have brought from the Seychelles, however, a man called Henri Lestrange who knows the Ile de France and who claims to have royalist sympathies."

"He is, I suppose, a convict?"

"Oh, yes. His offence could, of course, have been political."

"No doubt, sir."

"He is at present on board the *Otter* but I'll send him to you."

"Thank you, sir. He may well be useful, especially if he is a pilot for the French islands."

"He is not, but he has friends ashore, or so he says."

"I'll do my best, sir."

"Dine with me and meet my officers. The master, Mr Gavin, has made an improved chart of the coast around Port Louis. Learn what you can from us before you work on the problem."

It did not appear, however, that much had so far been discovered about the Ile de France. Its most interesting feature, to the blockading ships, was the signal station on a hilltop behind Port Louis. Apart from that the approach to that chief harbour was defended by an almost invariably adverse wind and a serried row of cannon facing the sea. Wherever a landing was to be planned it would never be there. Lestrange, when he arrived, turned out to be a small, white-faced, and untidy man aged about sixty. He was, he explained, a royalist, opposed to the republicans and even more opposed to the Corsican usurper. He had previously been associated with Oliver de Grandpré of St Malo but had parted company with him when Grandpré made his peace with Napolean. In considering plans for capturing Mauritius, Grandpré had rejected Baie du Tombeau, Pointe aux Canonniers, Grande Rivière, and La Rivière Noire. His advice had been to land at Baie aux Tortues. To do that now was out of the question.

"Why?" asked Delancey.

"Because his recommendation is too widely known. General Decaen will have provided against any landing there."

"What place do you advise?"

"At Grand Port."

"And what sort of resistance might we expect from the garrison and the National Guard?"

"Well, I should judge the garrison to be very weak. I have been assured that only four hundred and ninety men paraded for the funeral of Governor Malartic, every man present who was not actually on the sick-list. The National Guard is supposed to number about eleven hundred but there would never be more than eight hundred actually present, and those ill-trained and poorly disciplined."

Lestrange went back to the *Otter* and Delancey sent for Sevendale telling him what Lestrange's advice had been. They discussed it as they paced the sunlit quarter-deck.

"In my opinion," said Sevendale, "Lestrange is right about Baie aux Tortues. It has been too much talked about. His idea about Grand Port is, to my mind, nonsense."

"Why do you say that?"

"Well, sir, look at the island." Sevendale pointed towards Port Louis, recently renamed Port Napoléon, with wooded hills rising to jagged peaks in the background. "The centre of the island is occupied by mountains rising to over 2,500 feet with a sort of plateau between them. Port Louis is the capital, the place we must occupy. Grand Port is on the opposite side of the mountains with no good roads in between."

"And what about Lestrange's estimate of the garrison and National Guard?"

"It is out of date, sir. General Decaen brought with him well over a thousand more men. As for the National Guard, I should suppose that the paper strength is greater than he supposes but that the numbers do not signify."

"And what landing place would you advise?"

"Well, sir, we must capture Port Louis and we can assume that most of the garrison is there. So we do not want to be too distant, as we should be at Grand Port. Neither, however, do we

want to be too close as at Baie du Tombeau. I should assume
that we shall meet with some resistance wherever we land, that
a message will then go to Decaen, and that he will send troops
to meet us, taking two hours, say, to collect them and have them
ready to march. I think that we want five hours ashore before
those troops arrive. If we allow another hour to deal with the
local opposition, let us call it six hours after landing before our
troops are ready for battle. I consider therefore that the landing
place should be fifteen to twenty miles from Port Louis. The
exact place is a question of seamanship."

"Thank you, Mr Sevendale. I accept your calculations as to
time and distance."

"They are very approximate, sir. I have taken no account of
the state of the roads."

"About that we know too little. Given the right distance, however, we should be in Port Louis on the day after we have landed."

"We should leave it no later, sir, or Decaen will otherwise
have time to withdraw his garrisons from the far side and the
other end of the island."

"And what is the size of force we should land?"

"Two thousand infantry, with artillery and engineers, bringing the total to two thousand five hundred."

"I am most grateful to you. You have evidently given the matter most careful thought."

Delancey knew that he would have to do the rest of the planning himself. Going to his cabin he placed the chart on the table
and studied it afresh. The required distance northwards would
bring him to Cap Malheureux, opposite the island known as the
Gunner's Quoin (Coin de Mire on the chart). The same distance
southwards would bring him to the mouth of La Rivière Noire
or else to La Rivière Tamarin. Neither area offered any sort of

harbour for a ship but both of them seemed to be easily accessible by boat. Which was preferable? The northern coast seemed to offer the better anchorage outside the reef, in ten to twenty fathoms. If that were so, he would have to explore the north coast without showing too much obvious interest in it and then stage a raid on some point to the southward, preferably at about the same distance from Port Louis. Having made these decisions, he issued his orders and sailed on his mission. There followed a week of intensive exploration, with casual cruising each day and boat expeditions each night. Every gap in the reef was tested and measured, with soundings entered on a master chart. It became clear in the end that Mapou Bay was the place for the landing and La Rivière Noire for the testing raid. When the *Laura* finally rejoined the blockading squadron, Delancey was able to make a firm and detailed report. It was accepted at once and he presently took on board a detachment of a hundred specially chosen soldiers under Captain Stenning, Lieutenant Pinsent, and Ensign Hodges. They comprised volunteers from different regiments, all of them now armed with rifles (rather than with the ordinary musket) and they wore a colonial uniform in dark green. They were marksmen whose training had begun at Shorncliffe and ended with boat-pulling and elementary seamanship at Dover. Off duty they affected laxness of discipline and minor eccentricities in accoutrements. Unimpressive as they were in appearance, Delancey was assured that they were demons in battle.

The landing was to take place at daybreak on September 24th. The *Laura* made her approach well after midnight, towing the three large boats which had been supplied for the occasion. There was little moonlight but there was no missing the landing place, which was close to a mountain called La Morne de la

Rivière Noire, clearly silhouetted against the sky. The wind was faint and the frigate went silently through the water, which shoaled rapidly after the river-mouth had been reached. When in ten fathoms Delancey hove to but did not anchor for fear of making too much noise. Somewhere to starboard the French had a battery with barrack buildings some distance in rear, the cannon actually bearing on the place where the boats were to beach. A silent signal brought the landing craft alongside and the infantry scrambled aboard two of them, leaving the third to Sevendale and his men. Ledingham and Lewis went with the troops, Stock with the marines. The frigate's own launch was manned only by seamen, led by Topley, and Northmore, in command of the whole operation, went in a cutter which brought the number of boats to five. Northmore and Stenning were given a quiet word of warning at the last moment:

"Remember, gentlemen," said Delancey, "what we have been told to do. We are not trying to conquer the island. We are not even trying to take prisoners, although two or three would be welcome for questioning. We merely want information on two points. First, we want to know how long it will be before troops arrive from Port Louis. Second, we want to discover whether the National Guard need be taken seriously. My guess is that the artillerymen on the spot will be regular gunners, the infantry supporting them will be National Guard, the troops coming to the rescue will be regular infantry. By tomorrow we shall know whether I am right."

The boats pushed off and vanished into the darkness while the frigate made sail and presently dropped anchor to the southward, outside what he guessed to be the battery's arc of fire. All was silent again save for the noise of the breakers along the shore. As Delancey paced the deck the sky turned pale behind the mountain, which loomed black and menacing. All was silent and Delancey wondered whether his landing party could have lost direction. He reflected, however, that this was impossible. From where they were to land they had only to follow the shore to their right.

He thought again about the men who were leading the attack. Stenning was a gentleman, young and adventurous, who had been in battle before. Pinsent was a promoted sergeant with still more experience. Hodges was a mere boy, under fire for the first time. They were to attack the barracks, leaving the battery to the seamen and marines, whose task it would be to put the guns finally out of action. Spiking the guns was not enough, he had emphasized, and Topley knew exactly what to do.

He peered again into the darkness, seeing nothing but made aware of the scent from the land. What was it? Wild acacia? Trochetia? An hour passed as he paced the deck, the eastern sky turning from pale silver to pale gold. What could have gone wrong? There came at last the sound of a distant musket shot, followed a few minutes later by a volley. After that the firing was continuous. Then there followed the boom of cannon and a splash where the shot had fallen both short and wide. So poor was the French aim that Delancey decided to stay where he was, theoretically a sitting target. The ineffective cannonade went on for twenty minutes and then abruptly ceased.

"Man the capstan!" Delancey ordered and the frigate sailed again towards the river-mouth, dropping anchor again in eight fathoms. Daylight now revealed the union flag hoisted over the battery. From further inland came the sound of musketry becoming more distant, less frequent, and finally dying away. Delancey's gig was in the water and he chose this moment to go ashore.

The distance was about a mile but the tide was making and

the river-mouth soon narrowed to the point where the landing craft were beached and guarded by sentries. Landing there, Delancey followed a path to the right, accompanied by his coxswain and two armed seamen. On his right were the rocks which bordered the river-mouth, beyond them the dramatic profile of La Morne de la Rivière Noire and the *Laura* at anchor. On his left there was thick undergrowth, heavy with scent and loud with the noise of birds and insects. "A beautiful island," he thought, "too good for the French!" It was very hot, however, and he was perspiring freely. After perhaps half a mile he emerged from the shade of trees and was promptly challenged, "Halt! Who goes there?" Remembering the password he answered "Black River," and was allowed to go on, saluted by the boatswain's mate.

As he approached the battery position he heard the sort of noise which he associated with a blacksmith's shop, the clink of hammer on anvil. When he reached the battery, Northmore reported to him. "All well, sir. No casualties, three prisoners. We are knocking the trunnions off and rolling the gun barrels into the sea. All the powder is now wet and we shall roll the shot after the guns. The prisoners are locked in the magazine." He pointed to a stone-built hut in rear of the gun platform.

"Well done!" said Delancey. "Now show me the barracks." They walked back the way they had come but followed a path which branched to the right. This brought them to another sentry post and so to a group of white-painted wooden huts with a stockade on the side which faced the sea. Here Stenning reported to him. "All well, sir. Two men wounded and one wounded prisoner. The enemy fled inland, leaving five men killed, and we have seen nothing of them since."

"That is, since five o'clock?"

"Yes, sir."

"Are there any stables here?"

"Stables, sir? Yes, I think there are."

Stenning led the way to a hut detached from the rest with a half-door and a characteristic smell. There was hay in a manger and some water left in a bucket, with stalls for two horses and every sign of their having been occupied.

"Your wounded prisoner is of the National Guard?"

"Yes, sir. So were the men whose bodies we found."

"So the two horses would be for the commander of the post and his orderly."

"No doubt, sir."

"The orderly will be riding to Port Louis with a message. The commander will have gone with his troops in the same direction but will halt after crossing the Tamarin River."

"Yes, I suppose so."

"How many men will he have?"

"Over a hundred, I should guess, thirty of them gunners."

"So he won't come back until he is reinforced. The orderly must ride, say, twenty miles. Troops must assemble and move in this direction. Cavalry could be here by about two in the afternoon, infantry by about four or five."

"Do they have any cavalry, sir?"

"I don't know. This is our chance to find out. Now I'll have a word with your wounded prisoner."

This sole living and present representative of the National Guard was an insignificant Creole in a rather smart uniform, crippled for life by a bullet through the ankle. Captain Stenning nodded his satisfaction. "I always tell my men to fire low," he muttered. The prisoner explained meanwhile that he was a barber by trade but had been called up some months since, much to his annoyance. He had no love for Napoleon and cared nothing for the glory of France. He could boast now that he was a soldier who had been in battle, but what good would that do him? He would rather have a sound ankle. He was a married man with two children and all he had wanted was to live in peace . . .

As they walked away, Stenning asked Delancey whether it was significant that the prisoner showed so little loyalty towards Napoleon.

"Of no significance at all," replied Delancey. "He was telling us what he thinks we want to hear. But we have fairly measured the heroism of the National Guard. How long did they stand their ground?"

"For about five minutes, sir."

"That is what they are worth, then. The French gunners are better but I doubt whether they have had the ammunition to spare for practice. Their shot came nowhere near the *Laura* despite the fact that they were not themselves under fire."

Delancey joined Northmore at the battery position and shared a meal with the seamen and marines, Then he gave orders for evacuating the post:

"Mr Northmore," he said, "Captain Stenning will remain with his men to meet the French assault when it comes. He has orders to withdraw, however, when attacked. Mr Topley will place his seamen in position to guard the boats. Mr Sevendale will place his men between the boats and the barracks so that the soldiers can pass through the marines' position as they go to embark. The marines will then withdraw in turn, covered by the seamen who are ashore. Is that clear? I shall now return to the ship and leave you in command."

At about three that afternoon there came the renewed sound

of musketry which died away in half an hour. There were single shots after that at long intervals but the firing had died away by nightfall. Delancey saw nothing of the skirmish but had a full report from Northmore when the boats returned.

"The French attacked soon after three and we glimpsed some men on horseback—probably dragoons, armed with muskets. They failed, however, to press home their attack. After a further skirmish, in which two of our men were slightly wounded, the French withdrew again. Captain Stenning then sent out patrols. They reported, on their return, that they had seen camp-fires in the distance, indicating the arrival of troops in force. We embarked after that but without any further contact with the enemy."

"Thank you, Mr Northmore. What is your interpretation, Captain Stenning, of the French tactics on this occasion?"

"Well, sir, General Decaen would seem to have some cavalry, perhaps no more than a troop. When he heard of our landing he sent some senior officer, with a few cavalrymen, to take command of the National Guard and gunners that were already on the spot. This officer, probably a Colonel, spurred them into action, his dragoons setting the example, but little came of his efforts. He was followed by a column of infantry but that failed to arrive before nightfall. The camp-fires our patrols sighted were lit by their troops forming the vanguard, their main body being far to the rear."

"Thank you for a skilful operation in which we have discovered all that we wanted to know at a cost of four men wounded, all likely to recover. Well done!"

When the *Laura* rejoined the squadron off Port Louis, Delancey was able to report the success of his mission.

"The best place for our troops to land would be Mapou Bay,

in my opinion, immediately opposite the Gunner's Quoin, where there would be room for two battalions to land at the same time. The total force needed should not exceed two thousand five hundred men. The initial resistance would be small but French cavalry patrols might be expected to appear in about eight hours. French infantry would not be present in any strength until daybreak of the second day. We need not concern ourselves with the French National Guard, the military qualities of which are negligible."

"Thank you, Captain Delancey, for an admirable report, concise and to the point. Have you anything further to add?"

"I shall report in writing, sir, on our landing at La Rivière Noire, commending the behaviour of all concerned. May I add my private opinion that General Decaen will capitulate as soon as we give him a reasonable pretext?"

"Why are you so sure?"

"Because he has been in exile here. All his contemporaries have been winning glory in Europe, becoming Barons or Dukes of the Empire. He will want his share, only to be gained after a creditable capitulation to superior forces."

"From what I hear, the army he will have to face will be superior enough. Other estimates of the force needed are widely different from yours! That, however, need not concern us. Our task, is merely to put them on shore."

It was not a task to be undertaken in 1809. Lord Minto's approach to the conquest of Mauritius was nothing if not cautious. The plan initially agreed was for the conquest of Bourbon, and the orders for that were not issued until March 1810. The blockade of the French islands continued in the meanwhile, the monotony relieved only by a raid on Bourbon in September; a raid in which the *Laura* played no part, having been left to cruise off Port Louis. When the hurricane season approached Commodore Rowley withdrew to the Cape with his whole squadron. He knew by then that the invasion of the French islands was to take place in 1810. Amidst all the other preparations he ordered a survey on the *Laura,* supposing that she might have to be sent home. It was decided, however, that she was good for another season of blockade duty but would probably have to be broken up at the end of the year. That would not mean the end of Delancey's service in the Indian Ocean, he was assured; he and his crew would be transferred, no doubt, to another frigate. His services had been extremely valuable, he was told, and he was much too good a man to lose.

Chapter Eight

BOURBON

JANUARY 7th 1810   *Simm's Bay*

My dearest Fiona—We have had Christmas at the Cape and I think myself that we had earned it. First, we have occupied the little island of Rodriguez, which offers little but water and is occupied by two French families which are not on speaking terms with each other or with us. It is at Rodriguez that we mean to assemble our armada for the conquest of the French islands. A large army is to be embarked in India but even this impressive force is ordered to move cautiously, conquering Bourbon first, which is very poorly defended, and then going on to invade Mauritius itself.

You will rightly guess that I am to play the central role in the coming drama. In point of fact, my vital contribution is already made. I told the Commodore where to land, at the right distance from Port Louis, the island's capital. I then made a little raid—but I described it, I think, in a previous letter—at a place about the same distance from Port Louis but in the *opposite direction* (so as to avoid drawing attention to the actual landing place—what think you of that for cunning?). I was thus able to give the Commodore a good idea of the time it would take the French to arrive on the scene. I also told him that we need not worry about the French National Guard (or Militia), the members of which, as we had found, would run away if we said, "Boo!" to them. I told him, finally, that the force required is about a quarter of what is now assigned to the task.

Having done all this, I expected to be sent home and given a peerage. At the least, I supposed that I should lead the invasion fleet to the chosen beach. But there is no such gratitude in the world. I was told, kindly but firmly, that the beach must be surveyed by experts in cartography and that the actual landing will be planned by specialists in conjunct warfare, the key men to be sent from England. In actual fact, the Commodore thanked me very nicely and seems to think well of me. You must remember meeting him at Portsmouth—Josias Rowley of the *Raisonable*.

In reading my last letter you may have wondered what the French men-of-war were doing while I was ashore on their territory, chasing off their militiamen and admiring the wild flowers. Well, they had dwindled at that time to nearly nothing. Recently, however, the Emperor (or Boney) has reinforced his squadron at Mauritius with four frigates of the largest class. These form the Division Hamelin, the *Venus* (44), the *Manche,* the *Bellone,* and *Caroline* (all of 40 guns). The arrival of Commodore Hamelin has changed the situation overnight, his frigates being more than a match for most of ours. Our 38-gun frigates are outgunned by the *Venus,* if not by the others, and as for the poor old *Laura,* any one of these French monsters could have her for breakfast.

In times past the directors of the East India Company

have assumed, happily, that an East Indiaman—or anyway a group of them—could stand up to a frigate. In point of fact, moreover, few regular Indiamen have been taken in previous years. In 1809, by contrast, no fewer than four have been captured. This gives the French something to celebrate but it might have paid them better to restrain their ardour, for these losses have changed the whole atmosphere at Calcutta. Hearing of mere country ships lost—vessels belonging to shipowners in India—the Governor-General merely said "Dear me! How tiresome!" But the loss of actual East Indiamen is something entirely different. Bugles have sounded, drums have rolled, and swords have been drawn. Cannon are being dragged to the quayside and horses are being embarked. This time the French at Mauritius have gone too far! Such is the wrath of Lord Minto that thousands are being sent to do what hundreds could do as well!

With all this military activity I could wish that we were comparably strong at sea. The *Raisonable,* needing refit, is to follow the *Leopard* home and I cannot see that we have the superiority we ought to have in the waters round Mauritius.

The end, however, for the French is near, and I shall be unlucky indeed if I am not with you before the end of the year. You must expect to see me older, more weatherbeaten, more easily tired, less easily pleased. Am I wiser, too? As a youngster, I believed that a senior captain must possess all the wisdom of the ages. Being now senior myself I know that this is false. I have learnt caution, perhaps, and I know what to do in a whole range of everyday situations, but wisdom—no, that I dare not claim. I am wise only in having found the perfect wife and in wanting no other lover

while life lasts. So do please believe that I still remain, as
ever,

> *Your most affectionate husband,*
> Richard Delancey

Delancey had hardly finished this letter before he was summoned on board the frigate *Boadicea* (38) and told what part he
was to play in the forthcoming invasion.

"You are to understand, Delancey," said the Commodore,
"that the plan is to invade Bourbon first and use that as base for
the attack on Mauritius. After Bourbon has fallen it is my present intention to leave you there for a time; depriving you, I fear,
of the distinction you might gain in our further operations. I
shall do this for three reasons. First, the *Laura* is no match for
any of the French ships. Second, whoever acts as governor of
Bourbon will need a man-of-war to deal with any French merchantman bound for the island and unaware of its capture. Third,
your knowledge of French will enable you to gain information
in Bourbon which will be of service to us in the invasion of Mauritius. I am sorry to give you what may seem an unheroic task,
but I do not regard your role as unimportant."

"Very good, sir. I assume that the resistance to be expected
at Bourbon will be rather slight?"

"Well, the population amounts to fifty-six thousand but only
eight thousand of these are white or of mixed descent. Slaves
number forty-eight thousand but the French would never dare
arm more than a handful of them. So last year's raid met with
little opposition and I expect the garrison to capitulate soon after
we land. I don't foresee having to storm St Denis with bombardment and bloodshed."

"May I ask, sir, where we are to land?"

"We shall land at two places, one at Grande Chaloupe near St Paul, six miles from St Denis, the other at La Rivière des Pluies, a few miles in the other direction. Bourbon has no harbour, unfortunately, and one has to anchor in the roadstead and land over the open beach."

After some further discussion, Delancey went back to his own ship and began to study the chart. Bourbon, he knew, is about eighty miles from Mauritius, being visible on a clear day. Were the two islands, he wondered, within signalling distance? Bourbon is oval-shaped with St Denis at the north. There is a coastal strip of flat ground and then, inland, the hills rise sharply, the centre of the island being mountainous, culminating in Le Piton des Neiges, over ten thousand feet high and usually covered with snow. He had seen the place from a distance only, thinking it picturesque but of little value without a harbour. It had been formed by volcanoes, he knew, and one of them, towards the east coast, was said to be still active. Sugar was grown there but the place depended on Madagascar for some of its food supply.

He thought of the novel *Paul et Virginie,* describing a sort of earthly paradise or garden of Eden, but then remembered that the setting for this was Mauritius, not Bourbon. He hoped, however, to explore both islands after they had been conquered. That done, he hoped for orders that would send him home. He had served foreign for what seemed like a lifetime.

The conquest of Bourbon was actually a rather tame affair. Rowley's squadron, the *Laura* included, was joined by the troop-ships at a rendezvous fifty miles to windward of Bourbon.

The landings took place as planned, with few casualties, on July 7th and the French capitulated on the 9th. Delancey helped to cover the landing at Grande Chaloupe and then sailed with other ships to take possession of the French merchantmen at anchor in La Baie de St Paul. The prizes were all secured by the evening of the 9th and dropped anchor near the *Sirius* and *Laura*. The prize-money would have to be shared with the squadron as a whole but two of the captured vessels were valuable and Delancey, by way of celebration, asked his officers to join him for supper. They had hardly filled their glasses before they heard some confused shouting on deck, followed at once by a grinding crash and shock. On deck in a matter of seconds, Delancey found that a three-masted schooner, one of the prizes, had collided with the *Laura,* carrying away her bowsprit and foretopmast. After an hour of frantic work in the dark the officers reassembled at their interrupted meal.

"What I can't understand," said Topley, "is how that confounded schooner came adrift."

"She didn't," replied Northmore. "Her prize-master, a midshipman called Millington, was trying to shift her berth."

"What, in the dark? In a crowded anchorage? He must be out of his mind!"

"He is not as popular as he was," Northmore agreed. "He has been sent back to the *Sirius,* where his first lieutenant wants a word with him. But what's the use? His stupid blundering has left us crippled."

"I'm afraid, sir," said Stock to Delancey, "that we have lost our chance of taking part in the capture of Mauritius."

"We had no chance, anyway, Mr Stock," answered Delancey. "We were to remain here, in any case, after the squadron has sailed. But this mishap clinches the matter. It will take us weeks to repair the damage, some of it below the waterline. It is not as if this damned island had a dockyard."

"Was the prize much damaged, sir?" asked Topley.

"Her foremast was over the side."

"I wonder," said Northmore, "whether we could make a new bowsprit out of her foremast?"

"I dare say we can but it will still take weeks. The task, Mr Northmore, will fall on you. I shall have work to do ashore."

After a further conference with the Commodore, Delancey landed at Port Denis with Mr Sevendale, a sergeant, bugler, and twelve marines, armed and supplied for a week. With them came Delancey's coxswain and steward, both armed. Delancey and Sevendale found accommodation at the Hotel Joinville, on the Place du Gouvernement, and the marines, with their sergeant and bugler, were given beds in the infantry barracks.

Delancey then reported to Mr Farquhar, the governor, and to Lt. Colonel Keating, the commandant. His mission, he explained, was to gain intelligence about Mauritius from local inhabitants who might be familiar with that island. Farquhar was only mildly encouraging, Keating rather hostile, but they allowed him to go on his way and promised him two packhorses (if he needed them) from among those found at the French barracks.

His inquiries began in St Denis, however, and were directed, in the first place, towards discovering what had happened to the British prisoners-of-war. There must had been numbers of these captured in various ships and there had been several men missing after the raid on Bourbon in 1809. It finially transpired that these prisoners had been committed to the care of Captain St Michel, who had been commandant of the town of St Denis. When questioned, St Michel admitted that he had been in charge of prisoners. They had been kept, he explained, in a disused chapel at the end of the Rue de L'Eglise. Delancey asked to be shown the place, which turned out to be little more than a barn with some adjacent buildings used as kitchen and guardroom. "Not very luxurious," St Michel admitted with some embarrassment, "but prisoners were seldom here for long. Officers were usually released on parole and the others were exchanged after a month or two."

"Just so," said Delancey, "and was it your role to interrogate the prisoners?"

"Never, sir."

"But they were interrogated, I suppose?"

"No doubt."

"By whom, then?"

"Well, sir—" St Michel seemed to hesitate. "There was an intelligence branch here, headed by a civilian agent."

"And what was his name?"

"I cannot recall."

"You could verify his name from documents in your possession."

"All those papers have been taken from me."

"This agent had served previously in the East Indies, I think. He was once in Borneo, was he not?"

"He might have been. I don't know."

"Is he still on the island?"

"He is not in St Denis."

"But he is still at large. Tell me, did any of your prisoners misbehave, riot, fight, or try to escape?"

"Well, sir, you know what sailors are."

"So you had punishment cells?"

"Yes, sir."

"Show me."

Captain St Michel was middle-aged, running to fat, and constantly mopped his forehead in the heat. With evident reluctance, he showed Delancey some cells opening on a back yard, roughly built and plastered, with small barred windows and strongly made doors. In tropical heat any prisoner shut in such a cell would almost stifle.

"Seldom in use, sir," the Frenchman babbled with evident confusion, "hardly ever occupied. These cells were of value as a threat, you will understand. It was enough, you see, for prisoners to know that these cells existed."

Looking around him, Delancey noticed a black-painted door in the yard wall, leading to a detached cottage. Trying the handle, he found the door locked.

"What lies beyond this door?" he asked.

"A private house, no part of the prison."

"Used for interrogation perhaps?"

"Oh, no, certainly not."

"Where, then, were prisoners interrogated?"

"At the headquarters, I suppose, of the intelligence branch."

"And where was that?"

"I can't remember."

"But you must have sent prisoners there."

"No. They sent for them."

"And brought them back, no doubt?"

"Yes, of course."

"Yes . . . of course. Well, Captain St Michel, I have to thank you for being so frank with me. You will want to return to your office and I, too, have other work to do. Good-bye for the present. I think and hope that we shall meet again."

Early next day, Delancey and Sevendale came back to the prisoner-of-war barracks, this time in civilian clothes and accompanied by Tanner, Teesdale, and a Negro servant from the infantry barracks. There was nobody around at that hour and Delancey now made a more careful study of the place. The cells, he could see, had been recently given a hurried and thin coat of whitewash. The Negro, called André, who had come provided with bucket and scrubber, was told to wash it off carefully. He had also brought an axe and crowbar, with which Tanner broke open the black door. It led, as Delancey guessed, into what had certainly been the headquarters of the intelligence branch. It was almost a replica of that other building he had seen in Borneo. There were cupboards, shelves, and a big table. Papers had been burnt in a bonfire which had been lit in the yard, only a few scraps remaining. A central post in an inner room still had chains attached, with an iron brazier near by and some dull red stains on the floor. After noting these sickening hints of what was meant by interrogation, Delancey went back to the cells to see what marks the whitewash had been meant to hide. Pencil inscriptions were already coming to light. One of them read as follows:

Timothy Wood of ship Coromandel prisoner here 1807, starving, sufcated and some mates nere to daeth God help us†.

Another, lower down and scratched with a nail on the plaster:

Thomas Pendle, Q'master, Prisr 1806 have hurd cries of fellow cuntrymn under torchure to tel all but refused and now silence. It is FABIUS asks the questions.

A third, further to the right and in pencil read:

To hell with Bonypart
BRITONS STRIKE HOME

Leaving André to his work, and telling the others to search again, Delancey next visited the other houses in the street. There was, however, a conspiracy of silence. No one had seen or heard anything to suggest that prisoners had been ill treated. Only one neighbour, a hairdresser, had so much as heard of the intelligence branch and he hotly denied that its members had anything to do with interrogation. There had been such a branch of the government, he admitted, but it was solely concerned with signals. What signals, Delancey asked, from where and to whom and about what? The hairdresser could not answer these questions and was pressed to explain why he thought that intelligence meant signals. He finally produced a sheet of paper which he had found, he said, after the secret agents had left; something which had accidentally escaped the bonfire. On this paper were shown arrangements of flag signals with, opposite each, a special meaning. One signal shown meant "The enemy are off Coin de Mire," another that "The enemy are off Grand Port," a third that "There is no enemy ship in sight." It was instantly obvious that the signals related to Mauritius (not to Bourbon) and that they were to be used from shore to ship. French vessels sighting Port Louis were to be informed about the state of the blockade. Once Mauritius had fallen, these signals might be very useful indeed.

The paper after being copied was sent, therefore, to Commodore Rowley. But how did they concern these intelligence men at St Denis? They might, of course, have devised them. Apart from that, however, they might have been more generally concerned with signals. Brought back to the scene—this time under arrest—Captain St Michel finally agreed that the intelligence branch had been concerned (and might still be concerned) with a signal system which connected Bourbon with Mauritius. They had been busy, he had been told, at Salazie. More than that he firmly refused to divulge.

Delancey went to see Lt.-Colonel Keating, who was frankly incredulous about the possibility of signals between Bourbon and

Mauritius. Red-faced, short, and perspiring, he took Delancey to
the window of his office and pointed inland:

"Look, Captain, the high peaks are almost perpetually hidden by cloud. Mauritius is theoretically visible from these
mountains but is not, in fact, seen on more than one day in
twenty. What is the use of that to someone with an urgent message? And, anyway, how could flags be seen at a distance of
eighty miles?" Delancey could see that the high mountains were
hidden by a trailing canopy of cloud and could not remember
having seen them any more clearly. He turned away from the
window with a puzzled frown.

"Impossible, Colonel, I must confess. Any signal system
would have to depend upon light; indeed, upon a good-sized
bonfire."

"But what does it matter, anyway? We shall have both islands
in a matter of weeks."

"The signals don't matter but there is reason to believe that
the island contains a dangerous French agent. He and his men
were concerned in the interrogation and torture of British prisoners-of-war. I am convinced that he is here."

"Ah, yes. I heard something about that. Where is he lurking,
do you think?"

"At or near Salazie."

"Somewhere near the foot of Le Piton des Neiges . . . You
think he should be tracked down?"

"I don't like to think he is still at large."

"But he may have gone to Mauritius?"

"He might at that."

"So what do you want me to do?"

"Add to your kindness over the two packhorses by lending

me a third horse laden with a mortar, a fourth with mortar bombs, two artillerymen, and two grooms."

"Why?"

"Because the men I am hunting may be in one of the caves above Salazie. I may have to flush them out."

"I see. But you had best take four artillerymen, one of them a bombardier. They will know as much about horses as any groom and are more generally useful. Provisioned for how long?"

"For a week."

"And you have a dozen men of your own?"

"Yes."

"Very well, then, I agree to your plan and will add two chargers, one for you and one for your marine officer." Keating stood to the door and called "Mr Redding!" His adjutant appeared at once and was given the necessary orders. "And now, sir, I'll wish you good fortune. When do you march?"

"At daybreak, sir. And many thanks for your help."

As the little column left the town of St Denis in the cool of the morning, Delancey had the odd feeling of being on holiday. His horse had a comfortable pace and gave him no trouble and he had been at sea for so long that there was acute pleasure in merely smelling the scent of the wild flowers. On the left could be heard at first the roar of the breakers on the coral reef, from the right came the rustling of the sugar-cane. They crossed dry ravines by wooden bridges, passed the village of St Marie, and paused to eat by the roadside.

Delancey had obtained a guide for the mountains, a silent man called Jean, recommended by the proprietor of his hotel, who looked gloomy but certainly appeared to know the way. Going through St Suzanne, they took the turning to the right at St André and pushed on through the fields, the road rising at

first and then descending into a broad valley beyond which lay
the mouth of the ravine for which they were heading. This was
L'Escalier, as Delancey knew, and the valley grew narrower as the
mountains on either side rose higher. Rounding a corner, they
suddenly came in sight of the wooden bridge which crosses the
foaming torrent of La Rivière du Mat. There was a thatched hut
near the bridge and here they camped for the night, lulled to
sleep by the sound of a cascade which fell from a height of fifteen hundred feet and dissolved into vapour before it reached
the ground.

From L'Escalier next day a march of fourteen miles brought
them along the river-gorge to the plateau of Salazie, their destination. The road had long since dwindled to a mere track and,
beyond Salazie, disappeared altogether. It was the wildest place
Delancey had ever seen, desolate and silent, without birdsong or
any other sign of life. There was no village at Salazie but only a
couple of empty thatched huts, offering shelter and nothing else,
surrounded by huge boulders which had evidently been washed
down the mountainside. High mountains surrounded this place,
which centred upon a mineral spring of which he had heard.
Somewhere beyond, he knew, was the Caverne Mussard, the
resort during the last century of a band of runaway slaves who
were all killed or captured by a French officer called Mussard.

It was evening by the time they came to this place, very
exhausted, and Delancey told his men to make a fire in the hut,
which had a fireplace, and show no light outside it. After a meal,
he and Sevendale strolled outside and gazed at the mountains
in the moonlight. It was bitterly cold and they wore their cloaks,
moving briskly to keep warm.

"If they are up there somewhere," asked Delancey, "will they
have seen us coming?"

"I don't see how they could have done. We were not visible between L'Escalier and the point where we emerged from the gorge. We could not be spotted after that because the light was failing. We may be seen at daybreak, however, if we are still here."

"I think you are right. Did you taste the water from the mineral spring?"

"Yes, sir. It tasted filthy. I should suppose that this place will become a health resort some day!"

"Unless the spring is buried in some landslide. I feel myself there is something unstable about all these volcanic mountainsides. All yesterday I thought we might be buried any moment under an avalanche. And all these great boulders must have crashed down at some time or other. We shall have to watch our step when we go up Le Piton des Neiges."

"Very true, sir. It doesn't look too difficult, though."

"No, a climb of some two thousand feet. It will be steep, though, and we shall have a lot to carry."

A few minutes later Delancey suddenly stopped in his tracks and pointed upward. There was a tiny pinpoint of light on the mountainside.

"Quick," he said, "fix the position." Borrowing four bayonets from the marines, they lined up two of them from near the hut and two more at some distance. The light soon vanished but they would be able to see in daylight where it had been.

"It will be in the mouth of a cave." said Delancey. "No one could camp up there in the open but a cave could be habitable if the entrance were mostly walled up by rocks. What we saw might have been a lantern."

"Or a glimpse of the camp-fire when a blanket was drawn aside. The cave will be well below the summit, sir."

"Five hundred feet below, I should guess. If we start at first light we shall be there before eight."

"Have you any idea, sir, how many men we must expect to find?"

"No idea at all. Their leader is the man I want, a character called Fabius. It would be useful to take him alive. We must approach the cave as if attacking a not inferior force and I suppose that we must give them the chance to surrender. I brought a speaking-trumpet for the purpose."

"My fear is, sir, that mortar bombs might start a landslide. So I hope they surrender."

"I've thought about the landslide danger and my plan is to approach the cave from two directions. I shall take the mortar and my two seamen round to the right. You will lead your marines round the left. We must try to keep a ninety-degree angle between the directions of our approach. Should you have to go in with the bayonet, the French will have the rising sun in their eyes. If a landslide should start from the vicinity of the cave-mouth we shall not be in the way of it."

"Very good, sir. Will you give the signal to assault?"

"Yes, I shall tell the bugler—whom you will leave with me—to sound the advance."

"And what about the horses?"

"We shall leave them here together with our provisions, packs, and other gear. Our guide, Jean, will look after them and we shall rally back here after our return from the summit."

"Do we need to go up there, sir?"

"Yes, we do. I think they have had some system of signals between here and Mauritius. I want to know about it."

"Very good, sir."

"One other thing. We must try to approach the cave unseen and unheard. If any one of us trips over a stone and starts it rolling, the French will hear it and escape."

"*Can* they escape, sir?"

"Yes, they could go down the Bras Rouge and we should never have sight of them."

"I'll impress that on my men, sir."

Delancey was woken early by the sentry on duty. It was still dark but the stars shone brightly, unobscured by cloud. There was complete silence in that hour before the dawn, broken presently by the sounds of the camp, horses neighing, and muskets being cleaned. Breathing the pure cold mountain air, Delancey and Sevendale took bearings on their objective with a boat compass and marked the position on the map, returning each bayonet to its proper owner. There was a slight paleness in the eastern sky, a faint breeze, the promise of dawn, and Delancey gave orders for the march. Two reliable marines went first as scouts, followed by Sevendale and, the other marines, the sergeant in rear. Leaving a gap of a hundred yards, Delancey followed with his two seamen, properly armed and, behind them, the gunners with their mortar and its bombs.

Progress was slow, the ground being rough and the mortar, heavy, but Sevendale checked his advance so as to keep touch with the rear party. There was a rest each hour but no slackening of pace as the ascent continued. Presently the stars disappeared and a red glow eastwards turned to gold. So far the little column had been following a track and one probably invisible from the French position. The time had now come to deploy and Delancey, pressing on, joined Sevendale and called a halt. After studying the ground through his telescope, he indicated the two lines of advance and the probable mortar position, within easy range of the cave-mouth.

"I wish to God I wasn't so tired!" said Sevendale quietly.

"You are not the only one," replied Delancey. "We are beginning to suffer from the rarefied air; a sensation to be expected as we approach the height of ten thousand feet."

"So the French will suffer too?"

"No, they will be used to it by now. Are you sure now what you have to do?"

"Aye, aye, sir!"

"Advance, then, and good luck to you!"

Sevendale moved off to the left, he and his men gasping for breath but pressing on. After a short rest, Delancey led his own party to the right. They were showing dreadful signs of fatigue but their situation, as Delancey knew, would be worse when they felt the heat of the sun. There could be no respite, therefore, for anyone. He now led the way, stepping from one rock to the next, doing his best to remain hidden from the enemy. There came a moment when he dislodged a small stone but its fall was promptly stopped by Tanner's boot. After what seemed like a week but was really half an hour, he looked cautiously round a huge boulder and glimpsed the cave-mouth at a distance of about three hundred yards. A little to his right was a hollow which seemed suitable for the mortar and he made a gesture towards it which the sweating gunners were glad to obey. He showed them the target and they aligned their weapon towards it. With Tanner, Teesdale, and the marine bugler he worked a little further forward and studied the cave through his telescope. There was no movement but a thin column of smoke ascended against the cliff-face above. The cave-entrance was screened by a wall of piled stones, lit from the left by the rays of the rising sun. He waited for ten minutes, giving time for Sevendale to cover the distance he would have to go. Then he gave the order to Tanner: "Fire one round at the cave."

The musket fired, the shot whined in ricochet off the piled stones, and the sound echoed off the mountainside. All was silent for a minute or two and then a scrap of white material waved over the wall. With a feeling of disappointment, Delancey realized that the French were surrendering.

He stood up with his speaking-trumpet and shouted to them to come out and lay their arms on the ground. It was doubtful whether they heard him but one dark figure emerged under the white flag and stood there in the sunlight. Nothing further happened and Delancey felt that he must advance to within earshot. Leaving his bugler behind but calling on his two seamen to accompany him, but well spaced out on either side, he walked forward over open ground, well to the right of the cave, coming to a halt again at a distance from it of perhaps a hundred and fifty yards.

Using his speaking-trumpet again, he shouted "Come out and surrender, all of you—lay down your arms and we'll give you quarter. Come out and I'll spare your lives!" He was giving them a very fair chance but they had seen only three of his party, he reflected, and had no certain knowledge that they themselves were outnumbered. As sole response to his summons, the one visible figure disappeared again behind the rocks, the white flag being still shown above them.

Warned by instinct, Delancey shouted "Down!" to his two seamen while he himself dropped on one knee. There came a scattered volley from the cave, the bullets flying uncomfortably close, and Delancey led his men back on hands and knees, pursued by further shots of lessening accuracy at longer range. Back at the mortar position he gave the order to open fire.

Moving up to his old position behind the large boulder, and guarded by his two seamen, Delancey studied the cave through his telescope. Then, looking over his shoulder, he watched a gunner light the fuse and drop the bomb down the steeply elevated barrel of the mortar. Another man checked the lock's priming and a third, after making certain of the aim, called out "Ready." On this report the bombardier said "Fire!" There was a muffled explosion and the bomb rose into the sky. Its slow trajectory was marked by a thin trail of white smoke and Delancey could follow each projectile's rise and fall. The first bomb exploded beyond the target, the next was fairly accurate for distance but went too far to the right. The third was accurate for direction but fell short and failed to explode.

Calling back the corrections, Delancey saw that the French were firing vaguely in his direction but with too small a target at too great a range. Not under fire at all, the gunners were working methodically and their next bomb was fairly on target, hitting the cliff and falling behind the stone wall. Exploding, it blew up a shower of stone fragments. It was tempting to assume that the enemy had suffered casualties but the cave, for all Delancey knew, could have a sideways twist which could have made it sufficiently bomb-proof. There was no further sign of the white flag but a solitary figure bolted from the cave and went to ground, seemingly, among the jumbled stones below it. The next bomb fell short of the cave but the one after that was a direct hit. Delancey was inclined for a moment to be critical of the gunners' performance but he remembered then that there were variations in the quality of the powder used. He also knew that the bombs were subject to changes of wind velocity or direction at the top of their trajectory. There must be misses as well as hits. On the other hand, the enemy's position was becoming untenable. Sensing that the moment had come, he ordered the gunners to cease fire and made the bugler sound the advance. The shrill call came clear in the mountain air and echoed from the cliffs above. He then told his two seamen to open fire on the cave-mouth.

Over to the left, Delancey saw Sevendale appear from among the rocks with drawn sword. A minute later the marines appeared in open formation, marching as steadily as the broken ground would permit. He felt a moment of pride in their appearance and discipline, their scarlet tunics and white cross-belts, their glittering bayonets and their measured tread. He could not doubt for a moment that they were the finest troops in the world. Some musket shots were fired from the cave but still in his direction, suggesting that the assault group had not even been seen. When within fifty yards of the cave the marines, obeying an order, levelled their bayonets and slightly increased their pace.

"Cease fire!" called Delancey to his two seamen. "Sound the charge!" he said to the bugler, and then "Follow me!"

The effect of the bugle call was to attract more firing, one musket ball passing through Delancey's hat and another through the bugler's left forearm. The marines, meanwhile, had gone in with the bayonet. Firing died away and Delancey, rallying his mortar crew and applying a bandage to his whimpering bugler, marched his own group up to the cave. The more heavily laden men had to pause every few yards, gasping for breath, but they eventually reached the mouth of the cave. Sevendale came out of the cave with a trace of blood on his sword-point.

"There were eight of them," he reported briefly.

"All dead?"

"Two are wounded, probably dying."

Delancey followed Sevendale into the cave-mouth and saw the effect of his mortar bombs. It was not a pretty sight. The sergeant was searching the bodies for documents and making a pile of weapons and equipment. Delancey glanced at each of the bodies and knew that the enemy spy, the man he had known as Fabius, was not among them. Sevendale indicated the two men still living. One of them was badly shattered by fragments of rock and lay unconscious in a pool of blood. Without hesitation, Delancey drew his pistol, put it to the man's temple and pressed the trigger. In the high-vaulted cave the shot sounded like the crack of doom. From the back of the cave came an ominous crash of falling rock.

"Wouldn't he have recovered, sir?" asked Sevendale, white-faced, while Delancey reloaded.

"We should have hanged him if he had," replied Delancey. "Let's look at the other one." As badly mangled as the first, this man was conscious and moaning in acute pain. Delancey reached for his water bottle, poured water into the man's mouth, threw some into his face and said:

"Where is your chief? *Where is he!*" The man's eyes were open and he struggled for breath, gasping painfully until he finally whispered:

"He got away—damn him to hell!"

There was no point in prolonging the man's agony. Delancey cocked his pistol, placed the muzzle against the Frenchman's head, and pressed the trigger. The shock loosened another fall of rock. With a voice now painfully cracked and harsh, Delancey suddenly turned on Sevendale:

"Don't just stand there, gaping. The most dangerous of our enemies has escaped. Now clear up this mess and prepare to withdraw, taking all captured weapons and documents. Make a thorough search and see that we leave nothing of value."

"Shall we pursue the man who got away, sir?"

"No."

"And what about burying the dead?"

"Leave them in the cave. Bombardier!"

"Sir!"

"How many bombs have you left?"

"Seven, sir, and one out there what didn't go off, like."

"Pile all eight in the back of the cave. Have a meal after that and wait here for my return. Captain Sevendale, when you have finished with the cave, let your men rest and have a meal. I shall make for the summit now, taking my two seamen with me and leaving you in command. I expect to be back here in about an hour."

These were brave words but Delancey was still cursedly short of breath. Slowly, still gasping, he and his two men made their way up the reddish crumbling lava slope. In another half-hour they stood on the summit, over ten thousand feet above sea-level. They were in warm sunlight on a clear day, standing on a peak which fell away steeply on three sides. All around, the valleys were filled with cloud, from which the other mountaintops rose magnificently. There were patches of snow in the hollows which Tanner and Teesdale gratefully put to their mouths. Beyond the clouds the ocean stretched to a distant horizon, broken at one point by the shadowy outline of Mauritius.

On that side of the peak and facing in that direction was the thing which Delancey had come to see. First, there was a large iron basket, suspended from an iron framework, near which was a pile of firewood covered with tarpaulin and a half-dozen barrels of oil. To the eastward—no, maybe east-north-east—there was a large empty frame, attached to strong uprights and hinged at the bottom. Were the frame covered with canvas it would hide the bonfire from the direction of the other island. Lowering the frame would reveal it, making it possible to signal with long or short exposures, no doubt at a routine hour of the night. Had the system been a success? Delancey thought not, supposing that there would usually be too much cloud. But there was an additional installation, a ten-foot rail, about five feet from the ground, which related perhaps to a different system. It was only when he found the remains of a rocket stick that Delancey could see the point of it.

He understood then that the mountain was often hidden by a relatively shallow canopy of vapour. Fired from the summit at a given hour, a pattern or a series of rockets would burst above cloud-level and might be seen from Mauritius. As seen from Bourbon, if they were seen at all, they would appear as lightning. Of the two methods this seemed the better but the French had evidently used both. Having explained the purpose of this equipment to Tanner and Teesdale, Delancey led the way back to the cave.

"We are ready to move off, sir," Sevendale reported. "In my final search of the cave, however, I found a quantity of live rockets; about thirty of them."

"That's just what there would be," said Delancey. "Have them piled near the mortar bombs." When this had been done he told Sevendale to march his men back to Salazie but keep well to the left. As soon as they had gone, he turned to the bombardier and asked him what was his greatest length of fuse.

"Seven minutes, sir. I've three of them."

"Good. I shall now take the rest of the party to a position over there, nearly level with the cave and behind that red rock.

When you see that we are in position there, I want you to put those fuses into three of the mortar bombs, light them, and then *run!* You should be able to join us before the volcano explodes. Understood? You'll have to *run* as never before but seven minutes should give you time enough."

Under cover at the chosen place, Delancey found himself watching the cave for the last time. He saw the bombardier enter the cave. Some minutes passed. At last the young man came out at the double and began his run for safety. It was no altitude for running, however, and he could be seen to be in trouble, gasping for breath. He was going too slowly, that was obvious, and several minutes had passed. Would it serve any purpose to go to his help? Clearly, none. But why couldn't the man *hurry?* Hours seemed to pass while the bombardier ran as if through a lake of glue. Then, the worst happened. The man stumbled and fell, having probably sprained his ankle. He struggled somehow to his feet, fell again, crawled for a few yards and then tried once more to run. He was still in the open when the cave exploded with a sound of thunder. The re-echoing detonation was then drowned in the roar of an avalanche. Peering from behind cover, Delancey saw the cave disappear as its roof fell in, while the more rounded boulders were vanishing down the mountainside in a cloud of dust. There were fragments of rock coming down from above and the bombardier was hit by one of them, Delancey just managing to dodge another. Gradually the noise subsided and the others went to the bombardier's rescue. His left ankle was sprained and his right leg was broken.

"It was my fault, sir. One of those must have been a four-minute fuse."

"No, bombardier, it was not your fault. Never mind, we'll get you back to camp as well as we can."

With an improvised stretcher made of two muskets, the painful return journey began. It was evening before it finished.

After the evening meal, Sevendale diffidently asked Delancey why he had blown up the cave. His captain looked at him with surprise.

"Didn't you look at that rocky mountainside? To have dug eight graves in that would have taken a week! Nor did I want to carry those blasted mortar bombs back to St Denis. It was far better to use them up. I am sorry, though, about the bombardier and a pity about that damned fuse."

"I suppose it was his own fault?"

"No, it was my fault. I told him to run. I should have told him to *walk!*"

Chapter Nine

DEFEAT INTO VICTORY

WHEN Delancey returned to St Denis, the squadron had gone, leaving only the *Boadicea* and the *Laura*, still under repair. Northmore had done very well, plundering the prizes of cordage and pitch, but his skilled seamen were few and the work was slow. Reporting to the Commodore at his shore headquarters, Delancey was invited to dinner that afternoon. He next reported to the Governor, in whose office he found Lt.-Colonel Keating.

"So the leader of the gang escaped?" said Farquhar with a touch of asperity.

"Yes, sir."

"And is up to mischief, I suppose, in some other part of the island."

"I think it more probable that he will make for Mauritius."

"But how?" asked Keating.

"In an open boat—at night."

"Yes, I suppose that could be done in this weather." Farquhar admitted. "He would, of course, know where to find one. He would be lucky, however, to avoid an encounter with one of our men-of-war."

Delancey shook his head.

"That would not tax his ingenuity, sir. Our frigates blockade Port Louis and Grand Port. He could come ashore at Port de la

Savane or La Baie du Cap. Nor is it open boats our men are looking for."

"Very true," said Farquhar, "and by your account this fugitive is a dangerous man. He will be our prisoner when Mauritius is conquered and our Governor of that island will know how to deal with him."

Delancey kept his opinion to himself but he was not as optimistic about this wondering whether Fabius could be identified or whether a court martial could find any evidence against him. His own suspicions were not based on any real information. It was just possible that the man had been killed in the avalanche but that seemed unlikely. Fabius would have known about the Bras Rouge and his path in that direction would have been clear of the flying boulders. It was typical of the man that he should have escaped after telling his men to fight it out: men he must have known were better as torturers than as marksmen. He decided, silently, to avoid bringing Fabius to trial. He would be killed, he decided, while resisting arrest.

The Commodore had no other guests at dinner and he listened attentively to Delancey's account of his visit to Le Piton des Neiges. He had other things on his mind, however, and was soon talking about his own worries. There were senior officers who would never discuss their own problems, preferring to build up a reputation for taciturn omniscience. Josias Rowley was not one of them. He was Irish and quite prepared to discuss anything. Intelligent, quick-witted, and nervous, he evidently had to confide in somebody and Delancey was apparently the only man available.

"I am not to be the conqueror of Mauritius," he explained. "Vice-Admiral Bertie is coming from the Cape and will supersede me before the landings take place. I am to do the work and he will take the credit. Well, it comes fair in the end, I suppose. I may some day be an admiral myself! But I am responsible in the meanwhile and must hand over to him in a situation which is completely under control. But the fact is that I lack the superiority I ought to have over the enemy. You know that as well as I do. Captain Pym is off Mauritius with the frigates *Sirius, Iphigenia, Néréide, Magicienne,* and the gun-brig *Staunch.* He is barely equal to the French and I must keep the *Boadicea* here so that I can meet the Vice-Admiral as arranged."

"I am doing my utmost, sir, to have the *Laura* ready for sea. She will be hove down tomorrow."

"I know you are. But the *Laura* is no match for any of the French frigates."

"What about the *Falcon,* sir?"

"Another sloop would make no difference. In any case, I begin to fear that she is lost. She had been sent to India with convoy and was ordered to report back to me. She is long overdue and we have had no news of her. In strict confidence, it would not surprise me to hear that her crew had mutinied. You know Railton's reputation."

The meal was finished and they were sitting over their wine but Rowley was on his feet and began pacing up and down the cabin.

"We used to count on a superiority, ship to ship, based on a higher rapidity of fire. But I wouldn't count on that today, not in battle against Hamelin's ships, not in a duel with the *Venus!* And our ships have been out here too long, with depleted crews and too much sickness. The *Laura* is wretchedly manned and you know it."

"The French have their troubles, too, sir."

"To be sure they do but Hamelin has not been overseas for so long as you or I. You might think that I would wish to retain my present command but the fact is that I shall be glad to be relieved. We have in our present situation all the makings of a real setback and I don't want to be the scapegoat should disaster take place."

"I quite understand that, sir. May I ask what orders you have given to Captain Pym for the closer blockade of Mauritius?"

"He is under orders, first of all, to raid the coast and distribute copies ashore of the proclamation drawn up by Mr Farquhar. The object of this is to show the inhabitants that they will be more prosperous under British rule and so weaken the effectiveness of the French militia."

"We have, in my opinion, sir, little to fear from the militia in any case."

"Well, we are doing what we have been asked to do. As for British rule being so advantageous, I don't think that the folk here will enjoy it for long. Lacking any real seaport, this colony is governed at a loss and we are almost certain to give it back when the war ends. Mauritius we shall certainly keep, not because we want the place but so as to deny France the use of it. I discussed with Pym a plan to begin the conquest by capturing the Ile de la Passe."

"The island in the approach to Grand Harbour?"

"Yes, our occupation of the batteries there would make Grand Harbour useless, impossible to enter or leave."

"Is Pym to lead the attack, sir?"

"No, he will direct it, or cancel it, indeed, if the situation should be unfavourable, but the actual capture will be a task for Captain Willoughby. He will succeed if any man can."

"An exceptionally gallant officer, sir."

"Yes, but he is also a specialist in conjunct operations. He is always on shore and drilling his men as infantry. I think, myself—and strictly between you and me—that he plays the soldier too much. It is a good fault, however, from the point of view of capturing the Ile de la Passe. This is a task after his own heart."

"And Duperré's squadron is out of the way?"

"Doing mischief, I hear, in the Mozambique Channel."

"But might return when least expected?"

"Exactly! I'll be glad, Delancey, when the invasion of Mauritius begins. At the moment we have troopships and transports on their way from India and the Cape, and their position could be extremely hazardous. I lie awake at night, thinking of the dangers, and there is nothing I can do to remove them."

Delancey said what he could about Pym being a sensible man and Willoughby never at a loss but he thought, privately, that Rowley's squadron was over-extended, and that the Ile de la Passe was better let alone. As things were, the loss of a single frigate would be extremely serious. All he could do, personally, was to hasten the refitting of the *Laura*.

For the next week or so he drove his men to frantic exertion and told his officers that much might be at stake. When the recaptured East Indiaman *Windham* came into the anchorage at St Paul, the captain brought the news that the Ile de la Passe had been captured but that Duperré's squadron had entered Grand Port and was about to be attacked there by Captain Pym. Commodore Rowley sailed at once in the *Boadicea* on August 22nd but returned to St Paul on the 30th. Delancey reported to him at once, meaning to assure him that the *Laura* would be able to sail on the following day. He found the Commodore in his cabin on board the *Boadicea* white-faced and haggard, with his head in his hands and the chart spread before him.

"The worst has happened, Delancey. We have been defeated in battle."

"I heard something of this in the town, sir. All sorts of rumours are current."

"I am sure there are. But the situation is worse than even the French here can suppose. Four of my frigates have been lost or taken—*four* of them!"

"What happened, sir?"

"The Ile de la Passe was captured and Pym went back to his position off Port Louis, leaving Willoughby off Grand Port with *Néréide* and *Staunch*. He was ashore on a raid when Duperré appeared with the *Bellone, Minerve, Victor,* and two prizes. Willoughby managed to regain his ship and made signals which lured the French into Grand Port—he fired on them as they came in and hoped to keep them there. Then he sent the *Windham*, a retaken prize, to warn me of what he planned—an attack on the French ships in Grand Port before the rest of their ships could arrive. There was a battle in the harbour itself, three of our frigates being forced to haul down their colours. The *Iphigenia* remained but then Commodore Hamelin appeared with the *Venus, Astrée, Entreprenant,* and *Manche*. So our last frigate surrendered, together with the Ile de la Passe, and the French can claim a real victory. When I arrived the whole affair was over. I was chased off again and came back here."

"So your squadron now comprises the *Boadicea, Laura,* and *Staunch?*"

"My total strength! And Hamelin will have added the *Iphigenia* to his squadron."

"But Pym and Willoughby will have crippled their opponents, surely, before they surrendered?"

"They had damaged the *Bellone* and *Minerve,* to be sure. But

I still have to face appalling odds. And what is my task? To restore the situation before the troopships arrive in an area we no longer control!"

"What went wrong, sir?"

Rowley was now pacing up and down the cabin, pausing occasionally to glance again at the notes he had been making. His nerves were on edge and his hands were trembling.

"The first mistake was mine. I remained here and ordered Pym to maintain the blockade. I had good reason to make that arrangement but I was wrong. I should have been in immediate command. The next mistakes were made by Willoughby, the hot-headed fool. Instead of holding the Ile de la Passe with all his forces, he had to go raiding ashore—Pointe du Diable, this place and that, taking his best men with him—even his artillerymen."

"But surely, sir, he had been ordered to distribute the proclamation ashore?"

"Yes, but he'd not been told to do it in person. His first responsibility was for his ship and he should have left the raiding operations to a lieutenant. His trouble is that he can never resist playing soldiers on the nursery floor. Well, he is badly wounded now and taken prisoner, with time to reflect on his folly."

"What about Pym's decision to attack the French ships in Grand Port, sir? Was that a mistake?"

"No, Delancey. What else could he have done? But he need not have gone like a bull at a gate. He could have taken his time and felt his way."

"He supposed, I fancy, sir, that the other French squadron would arrive at any moment."

"Of course—I know that. But he need not have been so headlong. He could have taken time to discuss the situation with Willoughby and study the navigational hazards. The attack was made too late in the day. He could have waited until morning."

"Pym and Willoughby are not, I think, the best of friends."

"I know that. It would not have mattered so much had I been there. Instead of allowing Willoughby to act as pilot, Pym had to take a line of his own. He ran his ship aground, the *Magicienne* also grounded and the *Iphigenia* never closed with the enemy. Willoughby was left unsupported and his ship reduced to a mere wreck, with most of his men killed or wounded. The state of the *Nèrèide* must have been unthinkable—Willoughby is not the man to strike his flag while he has a cartridge left. She must have been a shambles! And the disaster was due, above all, to my absence. I could have prevented it. No, more than that, I could have won a victory . . . It is a sad note on which to end my career."

Rowley was slumped in his chair again, staring once more at the chart.

"I hope you will forgive me, sir," said Delancey, "if I beg to differ from you. It seems to me that you now have the chance to make your name a legend. You believe, sir, that you made a crucial mistake. But don't we all make mistakes? Nelson is thought to have been among our greatest men, but he did not make his reputation by avoiding mistakes. He was in error on a dozen occasions, and it was a tactical mistake that led to his death. I have not your wide experience, sir, but it seems to me that a great leader is not one who is always right, nor one who is undefeated but one, above all, who somehow turns defeat into victory. We judge him, finally, by his reaction to disaster, by his speed of recovery, by his resolve to conquer, and by the way an opponent's smile of self-congratulation turns suddenly into alarm and dismay. I would urge, sir, that your great moment is still to come."

"I wish I could think that possible, Delancey. I may have the will but I lack the means. By the time we can regain the initiative I shall be superseded. In the meanwhile, I must decide what to do. The *Windham* I shall send to Rodriguez, to warn other shipping about the present situation. As for you and me we shall have to stay here and help defend this island. The French have strength enough to retake it and may well make the attempt. We may have another ship before long, I have been told; a fine new frigate called the *Africaine,* her only previous service having been to take our Ambassador to the United States. If she were to join me, we might be able to make a fight of it. The *Africaine* is a fast ship, I have been told, and Corbett is a sail-drill maniac who prides himself on his seamanship. But you are right, Delancey. I should like nothing better than a chance to turn the tables on the French, especially at a moment when they think they have won the game!"

As if to illustrate the French mood of confidence, two of the French frigates (one of them, *Iphigenie,* recently British) appeared off St Denis a few days later. Rowley prepared to give battle, sailing from St Paul with the *Boadicea, Laura,* and *Staunch.* He no sooner sighted the French, however, than he also sighted another frigate which turned out to be the *Africaine,* having arrived most opportunely on the station. The French frigates made all sail for Mauritius, the *Africaine* in hot pursuit and the *Boadicea* following as best she might. By nightfall the *Boadicea* was out of sight from the *Laura* and Delancey could do nothing more to regain his position. As he and Northmore paced the quarter-deck, they could just see the glimmer of distant flares.

"We have set all the canvas we have, sir," said Northmore, "but this is an old ship, too long on the station. The French will never escape, however, from the *Africaine.*"

"True enough, Mr Northmore, but will Captain Corbett wait

for the *Boadicea* to join him? Let's hope to God that he doesn't try to fight the battle by himself."

"He should be able, sir, to cripple the Frenchman and so give the Commodore his opportunity."

"I wonder? Corbett must fight under two serious disadvantages. From what I hear, his gunnery will be poor, with little time or ammunition having been allowed for practice. It is also rumoured that he is extremely unpopular. But note the danger of sail-drill fanaticism at the expense of gunnery. His speed will tempt him to outsail his consort and come up with a superior opponent and then his inaccurate fire will lead to his defeat."

Delancey was to claim afterwards that he had foreseen exactly what would happen to the *Africaine*. Of this action itself he saw nothing at all. When the *Laura* rejoined the Commodore next day it was to find that the *Africaine* had been taken by the French after a tremendous action (in which Corbett was mortally wounded) and then retaken by the *Boadicea*. The *Laura* was present during the campaign which followed but was too slow to play an effective role. First of the forces from India was the frigate *Ceylon*, promptly captured by the French *Venus*. From the Commodore's point of view, this represented the worst moment of all but he reacted with vigour, retaking the *Ceylon* and then capturing the *Venus* herself. There followed what was probably Rowley's greatest achievement, the refitting of his squadron in a matter of days. In the midst of all this activity he found time to invite his captains to dinner and thank Delancey among the rest for his support. Delancey, although equally busy, found time to write home:

September 24th 1810   *Bourbon*

My dearest Fiona—I told you in a previous letter that we

lacked the strength to equal the French squadron we were supposed to hold in check. This proved to be all too true and Captain Pym, with four frigates, was defeated at Grand Port, losing all four ships and leaving the Commodore with only two frigates and two smaller ships. To make matters worse he knew that transports carrying troops intended for the conquest of Mauritius were on their way into an area which his squadron was supposed to control. I have said that he had two frigates but one of them was the poor old *Laura,* of which Captain Willoughby once said rather unkindly, "she is too small to fight, too slow to run away." He was right, however, and my only consolation is that he (not I) is a wounded prisoner of war.

The Commodore should have another sloop, the *Falcon,* but we have no news of her and fear that she may have been lost, perhaps as the result of mutiny. I refused at first to believe the stories about Captain Railton, rejecting them as lower-deck gossip, but I have since met an officer who served with him and have had to confess that his reputation must have been well earned.

Anyway, Commodore Rowley was outnumbered by his opponents and could foresee the arrival of other ships, one by one, each being taken in turn by the enemy. This happened to the *Africaine* and the *Ceylon,* leaving the Commodore in a position which might have seemed hopeless. There followed the astonishing feat by which he recaptured these two frigates and went on to capture the *Venus*—the best frigate on the French side—in an action which lasted only ten minutes. All this he achieved with just the one frigate, the *Boadicea.* If ever man deserved immortal fame it is he. But, surely, you will exclaim, he had the *Laura* to assist him? In point of fact we could not have helped him less had we been stationed in the West Indies or the Baltic. We came within extreme range of the *Venus* a few minutes before she struck her colours, firing one useless broadside so as to claim a share in the victory. The one result of that broadside has been to start a leak in our own ship and one which we have so far failed to trace. We have the pumps going now for an hour or more in either watch.

Now the time approaches for the capture of Mauritius. Vice-Admiral Bertie is known to be on his way with a powerful squadron and a whole army embarked in transports. I think myself that the French resistance will be trifling. So Mauritius must fall and I look forward to visiting that island at leisure. I also have my own motive for going ashore there. There is an elusive character, known sometimes by the name of Fabius, whose career as a secret agent I have traced from Ireland to Borneo, from there to Bourbon. He is now in Mauritius—of this I am convinced—and there is nowhere else to which he can readily escape. The moment is coming, I think, when his story will come to an end, probably before a firing squad.

The landing in Mauritius is to be directed by Captain Beaver, coming out from England with the sole purpose of planning and executing this one operation. He has not arrived yet but his reputation goes ahead of him and I see weeks of activity during which we shall all be speaking a new language. From a drawing up of landing tables we shall go on to talk of sepoy units, cross-covering fire, flank battalions, lascar gunners, the Reserve Brigade, and the picket line. In much the same way there will be soldiers with some grasp of the language (although not the realities) of seamanship. There is no real harm in all this "dreadful note of preparation" but I cannot help suspecting that the mere organization has become an end in itself.

I have written confidently about the coming invasion of Mauritius but it might occur to you to ask why the French have done so little to save it. I have myself wondered about that. What would be the outcome if they sent a squadron out, timed to arrive in November? What if it appeared, offering battle, at the very moment when we shall all be busy with landing tables and landing craft? On the whole, however, I think this a remote possibility. That Napoleon should order some eleventh-hour reinforcement is quite probable but I doubt whether French seamanship is equal to bringing a squadron here together and in readiness for battle. Since we captured the Cape they have lacked any intermediate port at which to rendezvous. Some effort on their part is to be expected but I incline to believe that they have left it too late.

Expect to see me within a few months and expect to find me older and more nearly worn out. To be home again is the main thing and I am not much inclined to seek further service, certainly not on so distant a station. The time is near, I think, when I shall have had enough. With the French nearly driven from the Indian Ocean, prize-money is not to be looked for save in respect of captured frigates. We shall intercept no Spanish galleon between here and the Cape. So you must expect only a moderate fortune in the years to come, enough I hope for your needs but far less than you deserve. Within the confines of my modest means I shall do my best to make you happy and compensate you in some measure for these long years of

separation. Remember me to my friends in the Vale and
believe me still

Your most affectionate husband,
Richard Delancey

Ten days later Delancey was summoned on board the *Boadicea*
and found Commodore Rowley in an expansive mood.

"Well, Delancey," he said, "my period as Commodore is coming to an end. Vice-Admiral Bertie will be here in a matter of
weeks and I shall then be no more than captain of the *Boadicea.*"

"A famous captain, sir, of a famous ship."

"It is good of you to say so. In the meanwhile I have my last
chance to bestow a little patronage. Considering the *Laura* worn
out, I should like you to have the French frigate *Minerve* of forty
guns, assuming that she is taken when the island is ours, and I
should like you to take your crew with you. She will be ordered
to England, undoubtedly. I cannot assure you, in advance, that
the Admiral will confirm this arrangement but I shall recommend it and tell him that you have been offered this new
command and that the offer was made in recognition of your
good service."

"Thank you, sir. I am happy to accept."

"It is just possible that the French will destroy their ships
before they capitulate but that is not what I should expect. The
Minerve is a fine frigate and little damaged. As a ship, she will
do you credit."

"I shall do my best to justify your choice."

"I am very sure of that. It has also been my duty to find a
commander for the sloop—I should have said the corvette—
Trompeuse, recently taken by us and renamed *Nautilus.* She is to
remain as guardship at the island of Bourbon and offers a vacancy

for a master and commander. I hope you will regard it as a compliment to you if I make out an acting appointment for Mr Northmore, of whom I know you think very highly."

"I appreciate the compliment, sir, but wonder whether you have not overlooked the claims of your own officers?"

"No, I have other appointments to make and they have not been forgotten. I think Northmore deserves promotion, young as he may be, and you can tell him that the command is his. I do not think that the Admiral will cancel any acting appointments made before his arrival on the station."

Delancey returned to his ship with conflicting emotions. To command a frigate of the largest class must be every captain's ambition. It was something he had never felt sure of achieving. He would be proud indeed to be captain of the *Minerve.* But what about losing Northmore? What about Topley as first lieutenant? There could of course be worse first lieutenants than Topley, a solid reliable man, but he lacked Northmore's vitality. He could do the work but he could not inspire others. The ordinary course of promotion would also make Ledingham an acting lieutenant, deservedly but a little too soon. Altogether, the ship he had been promised deserved better officers than she was likely to have. Cursing inwardly, he sent for Northmore and congratulated him on his promotion.

"I am glad to tell you that the Commodore wishes to offer you the command of the sloop *Nautilus,* a very good ship of her class, not more than three years old and said to be in very good state. I shall be sorry to lose you, Mr Northmore, but I would never stand in the way of a young officer's promotion provided that he is fit for it. I think myself that you will make an excellent captain and have a distinguished career ahead of you."

"Thank you, sir, for your good opinion and for the recommendation to which I owe this prospect of promotion. I am deeply indebted to you for bringing me forward in the service. Yours has been the example I have followed and from you I have learnt what little I know. I shall never forget your kindness and encouragement."

"And I shall follow your career with continued interest."

"There is, however, sir, a question I have to ask."

"Well?"

"Where is the *Nautilus* to be stationed?"

"She is initially to serve as guardship at the island of Bourbon. I understand that the Governor there objects to the island being left without naval protection. So the Commodore has decided to detach the *Nautilus* for that purpose."

There was a moment of silence and it was evident that Northmore was trying to make a difficult decision. He finally made it and said:

"That being the case, sir, I beg to decline the appointment."

Delancey looked at Northmore as if the young man had suddenly gone out of his mind.

"But you do realize what you are doing? The *Laura* will be broken up and I shall take her officers and crew to the *Minerve*—that is, after she has been taken. She will be paid off in England and you will have to seek another berth. There is no likelihood of your being offered promotion in the Channel Fleet or in the Mediterranean. You can have no certainty that you will even be first lieutenant—you may well find yourself third or fourth. There are many drawbacks about service in the East Indies, as you have discovered by now, but the advantage, if you survive, lies in the prospect of early promotion. All the smaller vessels here, and indeed several of the frigates, are commanded by officers holding acting rank. There is no such promotion at

Portsmouth except for officers with great interest. If you refuse this appointment you may wreck your entire career. Don't make a final decision now. Sleep on it and decide tomorrow."

"You are very good to me, sir, but the truth is that I have decided already."

"I have no words in which to express my astonishment. It seems to me that you are making a possibly fatal mistake."

"You have good reason to think that. Please do not think me ungrateful."

"No, I don't think that—not for a moment. But I should like to know why you are refusing so good an opportunity."

"Well, sir, there is one thing more important to me than promotion—and that is survival."

"I see what you mean . . ."

"I have watched, sir, while the original crew of this ship has dwindled to a handful, the gaps filled somehow by lascars, Chinese, Portuguese, and Malays. You point out, sir, that many of our ships on this station are commanded by officers who hold acting rank. What has happened to the captains originally appointed? A few are invalided but the rest are dead. If I remain on this station for another year or two I shall merely add my name to the list and make room for another acting commander. I want promotion, sir, as much as the next man but I want still more to stay alive. I'll accept the risk of being killed in action or even drowned but I would rather avoid death from hepatitis. In a word, sir, I want to go home."

Delancey ended this interview with a great weight off his mind. He had done his duty in urging Northmore to accept promotion but his efforts, thank God, had failed. And who was to blame Northmore for wanting, first and foremost, a passage to England? It was above all things what he wanted himself.

Chapter Ten

COMBINED OPERATION

THE INVASION fleet had assembled at Rodriguez, sailed from there on November 22nd, and was now on its way to Mauritius. Progress was slow, in light and often contrary winds, but, the sunlit scene was impressive. The sea was covered with ships as far as the eye could see. The men-of-war were in strict formation to windward, the *Illustrious* (74) in the centre, astern of the *Africaine* in which Vice-Admiral Bertie had hoisted his flag. There were eleven frigates in all, the *Laura* among them. To leeward a whole fleet of transports carried the army and had eight sloops as escort. Even the transports kept some semblance of formation and were held to it by a constant fluttering of signal flags and the occasional boom of cannon.

It was the day fixed for a conference of senior officers and boats were already lowered in anticipation of the next order. In, obedience to the first signal from the flagship, the *Illustrious* backed her topsails and dropped to the rear of the line. The second signal was for commanding officers, at which the calm sea was suddenly covered with boats, all heading for the *Illustrious*.

On board that ship there was a tremendous twittering of pipes and manning the side as successive captains came on board. Captain Broughton received them in turn and his first lieutenant ushered them into the great cabin, furnished for the occasion with long tables covered in green baize. Pinned to the bulkheads were charts of Mauritius, plans of Port Louis, and an enlarged sketch-map of Coin de Mire. Central to this array of expertise was a large blank sheet of cartridge paper. Near to this was Captain Philip Beaver of the *Nisus,* who had evidently been there before the signal was made. Resplendent in blue and gold, each with a glittering sword hilt, the captains greeted each other casually, each form of address reflecting the order of seniority. The flag lieutenant supervised the seating, ensuring that Caulfield should be on Beaver's right, and Broughton (as host) on his left.

Seated separately at a table facing the chair were seven army officers, adding a splash of colour in scarlet, black, and gold. They were led by Lt.-Colonels Fraser and Drummond, the others holding staff appointments as Brigade-Major or Adjutant. It was Broughton who called the meeting to order, assuming the chair but giving the place immediately to Captain Beaver, a hatchet-faced, parchment-coloured man with a pedantic manner, heavy eyebrows, and bitten fingernails. He plainly suffered from sleeplessness, overwork, and a recent touch of fever.

"You will be aware, gentlemen," he began, "that there was a conference yesterday called by Vice-Admiral Bertie and Major-General Abercromby. It was attended by staff officers of either service and by civilian advisers with local knowledge. Unfortunately but unavoidably absent was Commodore Rowley, who is still on blockade duty off Port Louis with the *Andromeda, Nèrèide* and *Ceylon.* At that conference the Admiral and General, as joint commanders of the expedition, decided upon a plan for the conquest of Mauritius; a plan of which you will all receive copies at the close of this meeting. I was entrusted with the detailed execution of that plan and I am speaking now on behalf of the joint commanders—with all apologies to those who may be senior to me."

Beaver paused at this moment, looking round the cabin from one face to another. Then he went on:

"I need hardly tell you that the plan is secret, to be revealed only to commissioned officers, and these to know only what they need to know. Now, first and foremost, the fleet is to rendezvous in the area marked with a red circle on Chart A" (he pointed to a chart) "between the Gunner's Quoin and Cape Malheureux. There is holding ground there in from twelve to twenty-seven fathoms. The beach on which the troops are to land is at Mapou Bay, between Cape Malheureux and Fort Malartic, the latter post being about four miles distant. One great merit of this landing-place is that it is well sheltered by adjacent reefs. Its main drawback is that our men-of-war—because of those sea reefs—cannot approach nearer than two miles. Assuming an opposed landing, our covering fire must be provided by guns and howitzers mounted in ships' launches. The landing will take place in daylight and I plan to have nearly all troops ashore by nightfall."

"As from this point I propose to deal with the First Division, going on to deal with the rest. The First Division will comprise five frigates and will land 1,555 infantry, half of them of the 84th Regiment. The landing craft, flats and barges, will be organized in two wings, the right under Captain Briggs, the left under Captain Lye. These boats will be serially numbered from one to forty-seven in arabic numerals. The gunboats will be distributed so as to cover the landing, two in advance, three on each flank and two in reserve; these being numbered from one to ten in Roman numerals. Look now at Diagram I . . ."

At this point a junior lieutenant removed the blank paper, revealing the organization of the First Division.

"This diagram shows the order in which the boats are to

approach the beach. Now, I must insist, from the outset, that this order must be correctly formed and rigorously maintained. Should any of the boats be out of position, the units landed will be disorganized and unable to advance as planned. I can assure you—and I speak from experience—that discipline is essential to success in an opposed landing . . ."

Beaver continued his relentless monologue for two hours. He then invited questions, all those from officers junior to him being answered rather sharply. When various other problems had been solved, Delancey brought forward a suggestion of his own:

"You told us, Captain Beaver, that the disadvantage of landing in Mapou Bay lies in the lack of deep water near the beach. Covering fire will have to come, therefore, from gunboats. In rough weather such fire is likely to be inaccurate and even dangerous to our own side."

"That is correct, Captain Delancey. Certain risks we have to accept."

"We should minimize them, however, if we deliberately grounded a frigate opposite the chosen beach and used her as a solidly based battery from which the beach could be swept by close-range fire with grapeshot."

"An attractive idea but I hardly think that the Admiral would be willing to sacrifice a frigate for such a purpose." He spoke sarcastically, looking round at the other captains for agreement. A number of them smiled and two of them laughed. But Delancey was not to be discouraged.

"It so happens, sir, that the frigate I have the honour to command is worn out and will be broken up as soon as the island has been conquered. I think I may say that she is expendable."

"Indeed! That certainly alters the case. But how near to the beach could you go? Your fire would be ineffective beyond half a mile."

"Agreed, sir. But remember that I can empty the frigate first and bring her in fight. She will be wrecked, moreover, and I need not consider the problem of refloating her. In these circumstances I can probably bring her to within five hundred yards of the shoreline."

"Well, Captain Delancey, I thank you for this offer and am myself prepared to accept it, provided that the Admiral agrees. Any other questions?"

After some brief discussion of minor problems, the conference broke up and its members adjourned for dinner as guests of Captain Broughton.

Delancey found himself sitting between Captains Parker and Henderson, the former a high-spirited young man of good family, the latter a middle-aged officer whose acting appointment was due to Captain Rennie's death from malaria. Beaver sat with Broughton, Fraser, Gordon, and Drummond at the other and more senior end of the table.

"Thank God that's over!" said Parker as his glass was filled, "I thought that Beaver was going to talk until sunset, each hour of it more tedious than the last. I nearly fell asleep and wish to God that I had."

"Captain Beaver," said Delancey, "is a very conscientious officer."

"Conscientious! I would call him a bore. As for that confounded conference, every minute of every hour was ten thousand years of living death! All these details of organization are all very well but you know as well as I do that it doesn't happen like that. All is chaos and then the enemy hauls down the tricolour. Your health, sir!"

Delancey replied to the toast and then turned to Captain Henderson.

"Are you impressed with the staffwork?"

"As much as I ever am. To men like Beaver the plan is more important than beating the enemy. What struck me, however, was that he forgot to ask you the obvious question."

"And what is that?"

"He never asked what you are to do with your men after the troops are ashore."

"True enough, he didn't. My answer would have been that my crew will follow the army into Port Louis and occupy all naval installations before the enemy can destroy them."

"And a good answer at that, saying nothing about your real motive."

"What is my real motive?"

"Isn't it obvious? You want to destroy the *Laura* before the experts can say that she is capable of repair. Oh, I know about her leaking and all that. But you want to make sure of it!"

"And I thought I was being so subtle!"

"With the *Laura* written off, you can shift with your crew to the *Bellone* or *Diomede*."

"But the Admiral, surely, might give either frigate to some follower of his own?"

"He can't give both because he has no means of manning them. You have a crew which will be spare."

"He could distribute my crew and send me home as a supernumerary."

"What, after your noble self-sacrifice at Mapou Bay? He wouldn't dare think of it. No, you will have made yourself the hero of the hour, leading the First Division in under enemy fire."

"But there won't be any enemy opposition. You know that as well as I do."

"You and I know it, so does Rowley and so does Tomkinson, not to mention Willoughby and Pym. We all know it, we who have been blockading the damned island for so long. But the newcomers—the Admiral and Beaver included—know something different. They see us storming the beach under shot and shell, earning knighthoods for the directing staff. You will gain the credit for all the risks they think you are to run. Good luck to you! I shan't be as fortunate this time but I shall have learnt something useful for another occasion."

"You have convinced me that I am an intriguer and a cowardly scoundrel."

"No, sir. You are a brave man and a good officer. I would not have dared to speak so freely if I had not known that. But ours is a service in which we have to watch our own interests. We should fare ill if we relied only on our merits."

"Very true. My motives are a little more complex than you seem to think."

"Of course they are, sir. There will always be several reasons for anything you do. I was a lieutenant until quite recently, as you know, and have gossiped with other lieutenants, yours included. I should never make the mistake of underestimating Captain Delancey."

"Perhaps you overestimate him instead. A health to the heroes who are first ashore at Mapou Bay!"

"I drink to that, sir!"

Captain Parker now claimed Delancey's attention.

"Come, sir, we want your opinion. I have been having an argument with Major Dwyer about the resistance to be expected from the Creole militia." Delancey looked across at the red-faced soldier opposite and bowed slightly. "We have each given our opinion," said Parker, "may we now have yours? How long, will they remain steady under fire?"

"Five minutes."

"Ha! I gave them ten minutes, the Major allowed them half an hour. Your guess is nearer mine!"

"But I am not guessing. I have been ashore here and engaged them."

"You have been *ashore* here, sir?" asked the astonished soldier.

"We of the blockading squadron have all been ashore from time to time. We have been around here for years. But I was particularly ordered to test the prowess of the militia. I engageed them, watch in hand, and reported afterwards that they would stand their ground for exactly five minutes."

"Then they, won't give us much trouble on the beach?"

"They won't be on the beach Major. We know that we mean to land at Mapou Bay but the French have not been told about that. We decided not to warn them. There are, as they know and as we all know, a dozen places where we could come ashore. How can they defend them all? The opposition we may encounter must come from Fort Malartic and it has four miles to come— not too far, if they see our fleet in time. As for the militia, you must remember that these warriors are all sugar-planters, tradesmen, shopkeepers, and clerks. They can't be kept from their ordinary work for months at a time. They won't be assembled, in fact, until our fleet is seen. But how long will it take to collect them, check their names, issue them with ammunition, fall them in by companies, and give them the order to march? What would you say, Major? Four hours?"

"It might be done in four hours if they all lived in a town. But many of these, I should assume, live half-way up some mountainside. I think I should allow ten hours to collect half of them."

"Exactly. So we shall find them in a defensive position somewhere between Grande Baie and Port Louis, and most probably at the Tombeau River."

Later that day Delancey received a message, accepting his plan for beaching the *Laura*. The Admiral was deeply appreciative of his offer and considered it a material contribution to the planned operation. He confirmed the arrangement by which Delancey should transfer with his crew to the *Minerve*, the name of which ship would become *Minerva*. In his reply, sent by the flagship's boat, Delancey proposed that his crew should land and take part in further operations ashore, ending in a position to guard the naval installations at Port Louis. This further proposal was accepted by signal and Delancey began to draw up his own plans accordingly. On this occasion Fabius might find it more difficult to escape.

The landing itself took place on November 29th, the fleet dropping anchor at about midday. After the signal had been made "Prepare For Battle" the ships moved into position and the boats began to assemble as directed.

Delancey had emptied the *Laura* previously, sending all her stores to other ships and she now carried little more than her guns, ammunition, and crew. Looking over the side, Topley remarked that they could at least see what they were doing. This was true enough for the water was crystal-clear and the coral on the sea bottom was perfectly visible in ten fathoms. In perfect weather, with bright sunlight and a good breeze, the *Laura* went ahead of the landing craft, Delancey taking charge of the deck as she passed the gap in the reef and holding a steady course for the chosen beach. The water shoaled as the leadsman gave warning from the chains and it looked at one stage as if Delancey meant to run his frigate ashore. So he did in the long run but his immediate tactics were more cautious. He watched the shore through his telescope for signs of the enemy and then edged further in under easy sail.

The *Laura* was now in six fathoms, soon afterwards in five, the coral sea bottom having given place to shingle, each stone visible from the surface. Beyond four fathoms the ship would have run aground but this must not happen except with her broadside bearing on the land. Foreseeing this moment, Delancey had his boats already lowered and manned and he now used them to tow the frigate sideways, having taken in all sail apart from the mizen staysail and jib. Northmore now went ahead in the gig, sounding continually and signalling the results back to Delancey. Backing and filling, the old *Laura* did well on her last voyage, responsive as ever to the helm, the routine silence broken only by the creaking of the pumps. The frigate was now in four fathoms and Delancey could see, glancing over the side, that her keel was only just clear of the bottom. How far was she now from the beach? Six hundred yards? He must close the range if he possibly could. A signal from Northmore told of deeper water ahead and the ship was made to sidle in that direction. Four fathoms and a half! What should he do?

At this time Northmore's boat was seen rowing back towards the frigate, presumably with something to report. Delancey realized, at the same time, that the First Division must be subject to some delay. Had everything gone according to plan, the leading gunboats should be abreast of him by now. They were still, in fact, near the supporting ship, having had no signal to advance.

Given so much delay, Delancey could beach the *Laura* at his leisure. Through his telescope he could see a lot of movement among the boats; the result, no doubt, of some being in the wrong position. Beaver, he thought, would never allow the assault landing to take place until the organization was perfect. Staff officers, he reflected, are often too much like maiden aunts. The result, anyway, was that he had time to hear what Northmore had to say. Not content with the speaking-trumpet, that officer was coming about to report.

"Sir, I have made what could be a useful discovery. Over there on our larboard bow, at five hundred yards distance, there is an underwater ridge at right angles to the shore."

"There is nothing like that shown on the chart."

"There wouldn't be, sir. We are studying the differences between three and four fathoms."

"That is true. And what is the depth of water on your ridge?"

"Three fathoms, shingle, with a gradual slope on this side, rising from six fathoms and a half."

"And what happens beyond?"

"Another dip and another ridge."

"Thank you, Mr Northmore. A useful discovery. Tell your boat's crew to come aboard. I shall need all hands."

Sweeping the shore with his telescope, Delancey could see no sign of the enemy. Looking seawards, he could see a great deal of activity but no signal for the assault. He knew now that he had time enough.

"All hands make sail!" Delancey's sudden shout took his men by surprise—they had rather expected him to anchor. After a moment of hesitation, the men ran to their stations.

"Away aloft!" There was a rush of topmen to the weather shrouds, followed at once by the afterguard.

"Lay out!" The seamen scrambled along the yards and took position along them.

"Man the topsail sheets! Let fall! Sheet home!" The sails dropped and filled.

"Down from aloft!" The men threw themselves down the shrouds and dashed for the halyards.

"Man topsail halyards!—Haul taut!—Hoist topsails!—Man topgallant sheets and halyards!—Sheet home!—Hoist away!"

As order followed order the sails thundered and flapped and the frigate should, by rights, have been under way. But Delancey had turned the ship into the wind, checking her way until all sails were set. There was a good off-shore breeze with occasional gusts of wind, and Delancey, choosing his moment, put the ship on course for the underwater ridge which Northmore had described. The sails filled, the frigate heeled slightly and gathered way. The bow-wave formed, the water foamed past to become a frothing wake. On her last voyage the old *Laura* looked the part.

She was doing perhaps six knots when she took the ground. There was a grinding and shuddering, followed by a crash as the foretopmast went over the side. It seemed for a minute as if the end of the road had been reached but the sails were still pulling, the shingle underfoot gave way and the ship lurched forward for a further fifty yards before coming to a halt, deliberately and finally wrecked.

Looking about him, Delancey was satisfied with his work. The *Laura* was hard aground on an almost even keel, perhaps four hundred yards from the beach. She had sprung a dozen leaks and her almost empty hold was filling with water as she settled in her grave. The pumps were silent at last. Delancey now gave orders to man the larboard battery and prepare to open fire with grapeshot. He was perfectly placed to blast the enemy off the beach but he knew that there would be no enemy there. He ordered the rest of the crew to unbend the sails, unrig each mast, and send down the yards and topmasts. Naval stores should never be wasted, said Delancey, and hours of work followed for the men not actually manning the useless guns.

Meanwhile the signal had been given and the First Division was at last heading for the shore. It was a splendid spectacle, with all the boats in good order and strict formation. The soldiers were ready to dash through the shallows and cross the beach to where, lining the woods beyond, the enemy might be waiting the order to fire. Delancey admired the scene and inwardly admitted that the staffwork, if fussy, had been excellent. But his telescope vainly traversed the beach for evidence of opposition. Of the enemy there was no sign at all. The troops from Fort Malartic could have been there in position—heaven knew there had been time enough—but that was not, probably, what they had been told to do. As Delancey watched, the first wave of troops landed through the surf, their bayonets glittering as they went forward. The gunboats hovered, looking vainly for targets, and the second wave of infantry followed the first. After the whole First Division had landed there came the dull boom of a distant explosion, away to the right.

"What will that mean, sir?" asked Topley.

"The French," Delancey replied patiently, "have blown up their ammunition at Fort Malartic. It means that the garrison there will fall back on Port Louis."

As a fixed battery, the *Laura's* brief career was now at an end and with it her career in the service. The men on the larboard battery were stood down from their guns, and sent to help dismantle the ship. As this work progressed a gig came alongside, half-full of water, and a young midshipman from the *Nisus* came aboard in some distress.

"I have a message, sir, for the headquarter ship of the Second Division but my gig was in collision with a launch and is sinking."

"I see," replied Delancey. "You shall have the loan of our cutter. Can you tell me why the landing was so delayed?" The boy brightened up at once.

"Some of the troops who were to have been on the right flank were put by mistake on board the *Néréide*, which anchored furthest to the left."

"So Captain Beaver had them changed about.?"

"He would have done, sir, but his gig was swamped while towing behind the *Nisus* and he lost his copy of the signals."

Delancey turned abruptly aside, hiding his expression and clearing his throat. In a rather shaky voice he gave orders to man the cutter. Come what may, he must not be seen laughing at a brother captain. Choking a little, he told the midshipman to complete his errand, leaving his gig to be collected later. Then he hurried to his cabin where he could have the joke to himself.

During the late afternoon, after the last troops had landed, he sent for his officers and gave his last instructions on board the *Laura:*

"The time has come, gentlemen, for us to say good-bye to the old *Laura.* She has done good service and we have been, I think, a happy ship. But the hurricane season is upon us and I shouldn't like to face a hurricane in this old frigate. At this point, therefore, her career ends. Our service together will continue, however, for we are to transfer the whole crew, officers and men, to the captured French frigate *Minerve,* a fine 40-gun ship of their largest class. I suspect that General Decaen will capitulate during the next few days and that the *Minerve* and other ships in Port Louis will be handed over to us undamaged.

"We have three tasks to perform before we can begin to prepare the *Minerve* for sea. We have, first of all, to save all that can be saved of the *Laura*. This will be your task, Mr Topley. I do not think it safe for your detachment to remain on board this ship. She is slowly sinking into the sea-bed and is already three inches lower than when she grounded. So you will form a camp ashore, using sails as tents, landing all necessary stores and using the ship's boats to patrol the ship and prevent looting.

"Mr Northmore, you will command a larger detachment and march your men, fully armed, to Fort Malartic, where I hope you will find shelter, despite the damage done by the exploding magazine. Any carts you find there can be used to bring up hammocks and personal kit. As soon as the French surrender or are defeated, you will march into Port Louis and mount guard over the *Minerve*, posting additional sentries over other men-of-war and naval shore installations. I shall lead the third detachment comprising the marines under Captain Sevendale, with two midshipmen, my coxswain and steward. My object will be to occupy the French signal station on the hill overlooking Port Louis and secure their signal code. You will be responsible, Mr Northmore, for detailing men to the two main detachments and for making all necessary arrangements. Any questions? Very well, then, we shall all meet again when we rehoist our ensign on board His Majesty's ship *Minerva*. Until then—good luck to you all!"

As on a similar occasion in the other island of Bourbon, Delancey had a schoolboy sensation of being on holiday. The *Laura* had latterly been a worrying responsibility and he now had the sensation of shedding a burden. Strictly speaking, he should have led the main detachment himself but he could not resist the temptation to hunt Fabius down. He had, he decided, a score to settle. Fabius would not, of course, be an easy prey. His concern, however, had been with signals and interrogation and these provided the point at which the pursuit could begin. It should end somewhere in Mauritius for there was nowhere else for the man to go. In the meanwhile, the battle for Mauritius was soon over. A skirmish on the day after the landing led to a minor engagement on December 1st and 2nd, which was followed by Decaen's capitulation on the 3rd. By the evening of that day Northmore and his men were in the harbour area and Delancey's party had climbed to the signal station above Port Louis. They found it deserted, with flags removed and all papers burnt. All it afforded was a fine view of the town and harbour.

"Disappointing, sir," said Sevendade, "but does the signal station matter now?"

"Yes, it does. My guess is that Napoleon may have sent more ships to the rescue. They may sail after the island has fallen but before news of its fall has reached France. When they sight the island, supposing it to be in French hands, they will identify themselves and expect to be warned about the whereabouts of the blockading squadron. If they see an appropriate signal, they will sail into Port Louis, not realizing their mistake until they are covered by the batteries and compelled to haul down their colours. If there is no proper response, they will go about and make all sail."

"Where will they go, sir, in that event? They would be short of provisions and water."

"They would make for Madagascar and could not well do anything else. But a clean ship straight from France should easily escape from any pursuit. So it is important for us to make the right signal."

"Can we do that, sir?"

"Yes, we can. We have part of their code, remember, picked up in Bourbon. My fear is that someone here—Fabius for example—will contrive to make another signal from some other point."

"Won't he have fled, sir, to the other side of the island?"

"Not if he means to make that signal. My own belief is that those ships are on their way and that Fabius is somewhere in this town."

They were looking down across the town during this conversation. It was evening and lights were beginning to appear, one of them perhaps in the place where Fabius lay hidden. For the time being Delancey could do no more and he led his party down to the harbour where their new ship lay alongside the wharf in Trou Fanfaron. There he was met by Northmore, who reported that the frigate was excellently maintained and had been almost ready for sea. The commissioning pennant was hoisted the following day.

If Delancey expected a leisurely stay in port during which he could make inquiries into the former treatment of British prisoners-of-war he was quickly undeceived. While work on the *Minerva* was still proceeding he was summoned to Vice-Bertie's headquarters—a building near the small boat harbour—and given an unexpected and urgent task. Behind closed doors and after warnings about secrecy, he was told that the sloop *Falcon* had mutinied and was thought to be in the Seychelles. She was known to have sailed from Bombay under orders to join Bertie's flag. Long overdue, she had been regarded as lost but there had been some sinister rumours, followed at last by some definite information.

"A country ship has reached Bourbon from Madras. Her master, a Malacca Portuguese called Da Silva, reports that his ship was intercepted by a British sloop of war which proceeded to rob him of a number of barrels of provisions. From his description I am led to conclude that the sloop he encountered was the *Falcon*. From the conduct of her crew I am inclined to assume that Captain Railton and his officers are no longer in command. I fear this is a case of mutiny. Have I made myself clear?"

"Yes, sir. But where was the merchantman when this encounter took place?"

"I was coming to that. She was north of the Seychelles and the *Falcon* was apparently heading for those islands."

"Thank you, sir. That would be the sensible thing to do. Their need will be for water. If they sail from the Seychelles it will be to head, no doubt, for Madagascar; a base from which pirates have operated before."

"I wonder, Captain Delancey, whether we should use the word 'Piracy.' Pirates are surely a thing of the past, almost unknown in modern times. Tom Collins had his day but is remembered only in the name of a drink."

"But surely, sir, the robbing of that country ship was an act of piracy?"

"Legally, it was. But it was not the act of people who have chosen piracy as a career. They did not capture the ship or kill the crew. They took—admittedly by force—the stores they needed, and that was all. These men are guilty of mutiny. We do not know as yet that they are guilty of murder."

"You mean, sir, that Captain Railton and his officers may still be alive?"

"Indeed they may. They could have been put on board some craft bound for the Straits of Lombok or Bali."

"So our problem is how to bring these mutineers to justice?"

"We must certainly do that. But we want no gossip in the meanwhile. Mutiny spreads, as you know, by example. When our seamen hear of mutiny they should be told, in the same breath, that the mutineers have been hanged. They should never be allowed to picture mutineers living in luxury on a tropic island with plenty of rum and plenty of girls. There must be no word of this to anyone."

"Very good, sir."

"The next question is—how soon can you sail?"

"As soon as we have completed our provisions and water, that is, by the day after tomorrow."

"Good. I thought you were more nearly ready than anyone else. You took over the *Minerva* rather smartly, didn't you?"

"Minerva was the goddess of wisdom, sir."

"Was she, though? Well, you have a fine frigate, the envy of other commanders. Let us see what you can do with her. Your orders are to sail for the Seychelles, find the *Falcon,* and bring her back, with the mutineers under guard as prisoners awaiting court martial."

"Aye, aye, sir. You will be aware, sir, no doubt, that I have only a minimal crew for the *Minerva.* The *Laura* was herself undermanned and she was a much smaller ship."

"I am aware of it, but what can I do? I have somehow to find a crew for the *Bellone* as well—and God knows how I am going to do that. You must do the best with what you have. Your crew is sufficient, I take it, to work the ship?"

"Yes, sir, but not to man more than the one battery."

"What does that matter? There is no French frigate left in the Indian Ocean. Any other difficulties?"

"No, sir."

"Very well, then. Your reward for this service will be your orders to take the *Minerva* back to England. It would seem from your record that you have been on this station long enough. Half the ships will be going home as no longer needed and yours will be one of them. But deal with the *Falcon* first."

"Aye, aye, sir."

The interview was over but Delancey did not leave the building until he had talked with the flag lieutenant.

"You know, Mr West, what my orders are?"

"Yes, sir."

"And I shall have them in writing?"

"Yes, sir."

"Have we an officer here who has served with Captain Railton?"

"That's a little difficult. There was Hussey, but he has gone. Hollis? No, he was never in the *Falcon*. The one man I can think of is Lord Neville, who now commands the sloop *Actaeon*. He was once with Railton but only for a few months."

"Thank you. I'll have a word with him. One other thing—you know what has been said about Railton—I mean, about his brutality to his crew—would you suppose it is true?"

"That's not an easy question to answer, sir. I never served with him myself. I talked with him on perhaps two or three occasions and he was uncommonly civil. But he has a certain reputation and I have probably heard the rumours that you will have heard. I don't exactly know why I say this—a matter of instinct, perhaps—but I incline to believe these stories. I felt no surprise when I heard this recent report. I have felt for some time that he is—or was—a man whose crew might mutiny. I hesitate to voice this opinion because I could produce no sort of evidence to support it. But Neville should be more definite.

He has the reputation of being unapproachable, a man rather difficult to converse with. You will already, perhaps, have made his acquaintance?"

"We have met but only for a few minutes and on a formal occasion. We talked, I recall, about food."

"He is something of a gourmet, I believe."

"Tell me then—and this is my last question—is there in Port Louis a place where a gourmet would care to dine?"

"There is one, Le Morne Brabant, which serves native dishes. The other places imitate France but with indifferent success."

"Thank you again for your information and advice."

The Viscount Neville did not respond too readily to Delancey's invitation, refusing for that day and finally accepting with some reluctance for the following day, the last on which Delancey would be there. Neville was too often a target for toadying brother officers, and preferred no doubt to choose his own company. He softened a little when told about the curried lobster and the Camaron River prawn but raised his eyebrows when he found that there were no other guests.

He was a tall handsome man with a thin nose, prominent blue eyes and an aristocratic manner. For a gourmet he was surprisingly slim. The room where they were to dine was clean but unpretentious and he looked about him with some distaste.

"I sail tomorrow," Delancey explained, "and this is my last chance of a meal ashore. But I should greatly value your lordship's opinion on the bill of fare. I have made inquiries and have satisfied myself that the meat here is more or less uneatable, except for the venison, which is unfortunately out of season. So we must make the most of what they have, which is fish and fruit. I have ventured to order oysters sprinkled with lime and small clams as an alternative, a crab soup, curried lobster, which is really crayfish, I think, with pomme d'amour palmiste salad and a sauce rouge made of river prawns and onion. There are no mangoes, papaws, or lychees just now but I am told that we can have Chinese guavas, custard apples, and bananas. The wine is imported, my lord, from France and they have a Chablis here which is said to be quite drinkable. I hope we shall not fare too badly. We shall be having the best, at least, of what the island has to offer."

The dinner was not what Neville expected but he was willing to give it the benefit of the doubt. He was dubious about the clams but gave a qualified approval to the crab soup. It was the crayfish which converted him and he became quite human, talking easily about a visit he had paid to Paris during the short period of peace which followed the Treaty of Amiens.

"Before the Revolution," he explained, "the best cooks were all employed by the more prosperous nobles. As a result of the Revolution these same cooks were compelled, in effect, to set up in business for themselves. Their establishments provide the best cookery in the world."

Delancey learnt a great deal about gastronomy before he could lead Neville into talking about Captain Railton. Once he began however, he was eloquent.

"Railton?" he said slowly. "I was his second lieutenant for ninety-eight days. I counted them, you know, and each day seemed to last a year—no, a decade. Then I had interest enough to ensure that I was posted to another ship. Poor Dyer then became second and a midshipman called Pringle was given an acting commission as third. Even now I sometimes have a nightmare, thinking that I am back in the *Falcon*. I wake in a cold sweat, fairly trembling, until I realize where I am. No, I have not forgotten Captain Railton . . ."

"Was he mad, do you think?"

"No; and that is the most extraordinary thing about him. He has his own queer sort of sanity. He is or was the most evil man I ever met."

"Evil in the sense of being cruel?"

"Cruel he certainly is but evil in him goes beyond cruelty. He is hated by his crew but not merely for using the cat. In that respect his log might well prove him little worse than some captains who are relatively popular." Neville looked at his wine glass for a minute, trying to crystallize his thoughts.

"Tell me, Delancey, what quality do seamen most appreciate in their captain?"

"Consistency."

"Just so. They like to know where they are. If it is two dozen for being found drunk, they accept that. What they hate is uncertainty. They could be reconciled to a captain who is always in a bad temper on Monday morning or who hates men with red hair. What they cannot stand is someone who is kindness itself in the morning and a raging tyrant in the afternoon. Railton is a man whose moods are utterly unpredictable. I have heard other officers threaten to flog every man in the larboard watch. Railton is the only captain I have known who could have done it."

"What was the final straw, the incident which induced you to arrange a transfer?"

"It concerned a midshipman—no, he was not even that, a young gentleman volunteer—called John Vesey. He was aged about fourteen but looked younger, a mere child, son of some provincial attorney. He was not particularly bright but Railton made him something of a favourite. We all rather liked the boy and Dyer helped him with his navigation. Railton used to ask his officers to dine with him occasionally—he was not consistent even in that—and I was present one day when young Vesey was another guest. There was no other youngster present and Vesey, I could see, was pitifully nervous. The purser did his best to encourage the boy but he was fairly trembling. When it fell to him to pass the decanter, he spilt some of the wine on the table-cloth and more of it on his trousers. He did not drop the decanter, mind you. There was nothing broken, not even a glass. Railton, however, glared at the child as if he had committed treason. "Mr Vesey," he thundered, "you shall be flogged for that tomorrow!" Under any other captain this would have passed as an idle threat or a rather unpleasant joke. But Railton meant it—as we all knew—and meant it all the more because the boy was generally liked and had been treated kindly even by him. There was silence for a minute or two and then Railton asked me what I thought of the local sea fish—did I like the silver bream better than the "sacre chien," did I believe that eating the cordonnier could give one a nightmare? I knew all about nightmares and hoped then that I was in the midst of one. After all, Vesey was the captain's guest. However, I replied somehow and conversation was resumed. When Dyer was speaking I stole a glance at the white-faced child at the foot of the table. He looked as if he were about to faint."

"And was the boy flogged?"

"No, he went over the side during the morning watch. His death was logged as an accident."

"You have painted for me a lifelike portrait of Captain Railton and I am most grateful."

"I could tell you a great deal more about him, but you have probably heard enough. Why are you specially interested?"

"I am wondering whether the crew of the *Falcon* have

mutinied. One of her officers, the surgeon, is an old shipmate of mine."

"Robertson? He is a good man. But as for mutiny, I have myself no doubt at all. The *Falcon's* crew were bound to mutiny and I could not myself understand why they had not mutinied already. I should incline to assume that Railton is dead. If he is not in hell I refuse to believe that such a place exists."

Chapter Eleven

THE SEYCHELLES

THE *MINERVA* was three days out from Port Louis and Delancey had every reason to feel satisfied with his new command. He had tested her in all normal situations and knew now that she was the finest ship in which he had ever served. In the Royal Navy the 38-gun class of frigates enjoyed a special prestige. They were too big for convoy work, too valuable to be sent on casual errands, too powerful to waste on routine patrols. They might, on the other hand, serve with the fleet or take part in a raid, assist in a bombardment or even fly an Admiral's flag. Bertie, for example, used the *Africaine* as flagship even after the *Illustrious* had joined his squadron.

Delancey had never expected to command a frigate of this class, thinking that they were the preserve of the well-born and well-connected, of men with an "Hon." before their name. But the *Minerva* was an exceptional frigate in her class, mounting 44 guns all told, twenty-eight 18-pounders, fourteen 32-pounder carronades on the quarter-deck, and two 9-pounders on the forecastle. Under the French flag she had been manned by a crew of 360, but she had now no more than 263, barely half of them British. She was much larger than other ships in her class, having more generous space for every purpose. The captain's quarters were spacious, the wardroom impressive, and there was more room for each mess-table and hammock. She was both well designed and well built, dry as a bone and extremely easy to handle. Delancey had come to realize just how fortunate he was.

Delancey had his lieutenants to dine with him and made this the occasion to explain his mission. Over their wine he began by commenting upon the *Minerva:*

"I think you will agree, gentlemen, that we have an exceptional frigate in perfect order."

"Yes, sir," said Northmore, "but what I can't understand is why the French ships are so much better than ours. And whenever we do build a good ship it is copied from one of theirs."

"They owe a great deal, I fancy, to their Academie de Marine and to Duhamel du Monceau who founded their school of ship design. While they applied scientific theory, we left the work to builders who do what was done last time. The French are more intellectual then we are and their dockyards—unlike their fleet— were not wrecked by the Revolution. They are better at thinking, we are merely better at fighting."

"So the ideal ship is what we have, sir," said Northmore, "a French frigate with a British crew."

"Half a crew," replied Delancey, "and only half of it British."

"And no more men to be had this side of the Cape." added Topley.

"So we should be at a disadvantage, gentlemen, if we were to encounter a French frigate of the same class and recently out of her home port. We should do well if we fought her to a standstill. To take her would be virtually impossible."

"But is such an engagement likely, sir?" asked Stock. "The French squadron in the Indian Ocean has ceased to exist."

"Exactly, Mr Stock. So that any opponent we meet must have come directly from France, clean, well supplied, and fully manned."

"But how can such a ship be maintained without a base?" asked Topley.

"She can't," said Delancey. "But Napoleon could send her out before he realizes that his base has been lost. I mention this, gentlemen, as a possible situation. Our gun-drill needs to be more than good. It must be rapid and accurate beyond example . . . It is now my duty to acquaint you with our mission. The *Falcon* is overdue and possibly lost. She was last seen in the vicinity of the Seychelles. My orders are to locate her, if possible, and bring her back to Port Louis."

There was a short silence, broken at length by Sevendale:

"I hope, sir, that I am not speaking out of turn. Do we not have reason to suspect that her crew may have mutinied?"

"There may well have been a mutiny. We must, however, say nothing of this to anyone."

"But the men all know about it!" Stock protested. "It was quayside gossip at Port Louis."

"The men do *not* know about it, Mr Stock, because there is little as yet to know. They may share our suspicions but we should not encourage their gossip."

"Two of them served once under Captain Railton," said Topley.

"I know that," replied Delancey sharply, "Davies and Hewitt . . . but our concern is not with rumours but with facts. Of the facts we must grasp the first is that the Seychelle Islands number between eighty and ninety, spread over an area about sixty miles square. There is only one charted anchorage and that lies between St Anne and Mahé. There is only the one settlement and it is on Mahé, with a white population of about two hundred, mostly deported convicts, and twice as many slaves. Some local trader is resident or magistrate and the place now flies the British flag. The Europeans are French though, and have no special loyalty to King George III. A ship in distress, putting into the Seychelles, would normally drop anchor off Mahé. If her crew preferred, for any reason, to avoid notice, they might take their vessel to one of the other islands and we should be left to ask which."

"And what about supplies, sir?" asked Sevendale.

"The islands provide little beside coconuts, I believe, and sea fish."

"So that a ship which resorted to one of the smaller islands like Praslin or Silhoutte might be driven to visit Mahé in the end?"

"Possibly, but we might by then have gone."

"So we may have to search the whole group?" asked Topley.

"We may indeed. I suspect, however, that wherever the sloop may be, there will be people in Mahé who know where she is. Our orders are to find the *Falcon* and bring her to Port Louis. If there has been a mutiny, it is also our task to bring the mutineers to justice."

"I confess, sir, that I have some sympathy with a crew which mutinied against Captain Railton. He could have driven them to it," said Northmore. "From all I hear of him, he could make a ship a hell on earth."

"If there was a mutiny caused by ill treatment," replied Delancey, "the court martial will make every allowance for provocation and will reduce the men's sentences accordingly. We cannot try and acquit the men over the dinner table. Whatever the fate of the *Falcon* has been, my hope is that we can execute our orders quickly and sail at an early date for Europe. We have all been on this station quite long enough."

Delancey had said what it was his duty to say but he thought afterwards that he had been talking nonsense. Nothing could

justify mutiny, he knew that, but how would he himself have
fared under Railton's command? He hated to see men flogged
and hated still more to be responsible for it, but what was it like
to be the victim? And what would it be like to serve under a
captain who might order anyone to be flogged at any time, perhaps for the smallest mistake, perhaps for nothing at all? He
knew how that midshipman had felt and guessed that his own
remedy would have been the same. He had also talked glibly
about the justice to be expected from a court martial. But were
courts martial as just as all that? And were they really merciful?
The very word "mutiny" aroused a number of emotions including resentment and including fear.

In the last resort a court martial is not concerned with justice but with discipline. Confronted with members of a mutinous
crew, the court assembled at Port Louis would wish, above all,
to prevent their example having a bad effect on the squadron as
a whole. Seamen must not be allowed to think that mutiny
offered a neat solution to their present discontents. They must
rather be shown that mutiny must always end with a noose at
the yard-arm. There would be room for mercy, to be sure. Some
men might be thought relatively innocent, having been misled
by the ringleaders. For them there would be no death sentence
but merely an award of five dozen lashes; an act of leniency for
which they should be grateful. From Lord Neville's description
he knew exactly what these men must have had to endure. Was
he now to be the hangman at the end of the story?

Delancey might not enjoy the role of hangman but what was
the alternative? If he failed to locate the *Falcon*, her crew would
either turn to piracy or would starve to death. There was no
future for them in the Seychelles. Nor would they survive long
as pirates for the British squadron, however diminished, would

now have leisure to deal with them. Was there any way in which he could spare these men? And how, anyway, could that be done without the knowledge of his crew? If they were to know the true story (whatever it was) how could they be prevented from talking about it? And if it were known he would be lucky, he knew, to escape with a mere dismissal from the service. Nor, incidentally, did he like the idea of combing the islands for the missing sloop. These waters had never been charted and his frigate might easily end as a total loss, wrecked on some reef of which nobody had ever heard. He could, in theory, take a local pilot but was there one he could trust? The one known fact about the white population of Mahé was that they had mostly been convicts. He had learnt, however, not to worry too much about any problem which had not actually arisen. He might after all, find no trace of the *Falcon*, which could by now have sunk with all hands. He would deal with the situation when he knew what it was.

The only immediate decision he took was to enter the road-stead at Mahé under French colours. The *Minerve* was recognizably French, after all, even to the spelling of her name, which Delancey had not allowed Northmore to change. He could himself pass as a Frenchman and could hope, in that guise, to gain information which would be denied to a British officer. There should be no reason why French criminals should partic-ularly want to conceal the whereabouts of a British sloop.

On a sultry morning, ten days later, the *Minerva* drifted rather than sailed into the anchorage off Mahé. There was scarcely a breath of wind and the frigate dropped anchor in water as still as a pond. Looking back from the boat in which he was being rowed ashore, Delancey could see his ship completely mirrored, even to the tricolour hanging limply at the mizen-peak. The frigate lay at anchor in a roadstead protected by islands.

Mahé was nearly everywhere covered by coconut trees and tamarisks down to the water's edge. Inland there were forest-covered mountains rising to a peak of some considerable height. It was very hot and humid and quite silent except for the rhythmic splash of the dipping oar blades. A few bystanders stood listlessly near the landing place but more had preferred to lounge in the shade of the casuarina trees behind where the tricolour was hoisted over a hut rather larger than the others in sight. On the far side of the hut stood a saluting cannon, freshly painted black with the tompion fitted and a lead apron covering the touch-hole. There was a rudimentary boat pier made from lumps of coral and the cutter was brought alongside it. Followed by his only French-speaking seaman, a man called Jean-Pierre Cunat, Delancey stepped ashore and was greeted by a bearded islander called Hudelet who introduced himself as the resident magistrate and then presented his clerk, a half-caste called Larue. Delancey had not been able to improvise a French uniform but the heat of the day sufficiently accounted for him coming ashore in white shirt and trousers. His boat's crew, as informally clad, did not come ashore, the boat pulling out for some distance and dropping a grapnel. The seamen were seen to be fishing, which seemed to explain this manoeuvre. Further out a school of dolphins could be seen and flying fish, pursued by seabirds. Delancey was led to the palm-thatched hut under the flag, where he was politely offered bananas, jack fruit, and a glass of palm brandy. He and Hudelet talked at first about the weather which was, as they agreed, excessively fatiguing. Both were fluent in French but neither could be said to have a Parisian accent.

"It would not surprise me, Captain, if there were to be a hurricane. This is the time of year for it and there is often, as they say, a calm before the storm."

"Are hurricanes frequent, then?"

"No, they happen very rarely. Nor are we ever in the actual track of the hurricane. It is the fringe which we experience but that, believe me, is enough. You are fortunate to be in an anchorage that is fairly safe."

"Now tell me the local news."

"Nothing ever happens here, Captain. We have more geography than history. We hear news, however, of the Ile de France, news of the British being defeated in a naval battle. The Emperor will be very pleased!"

"Yes. I have just come from there. The British will talk less now about their plans to conquer the island. They have had a setback, there can be no doubt about that. We may even recover Bourbon from them. Tell me, however, you are often visited here by British ships; have you seen any lately?"

"No, Captain, not for many months."

"To be quite frank, Monsieur Hudelet, we have heard of a British sloop being sighted near here and have been sent to look for her. Has she not been seen?"

"No, monsieur."

"A pity. It may be, however, that you can help us in another way. I wonder whether you have here a trader of some enterprise, one who has been to sea, a man whose business extends to the other islands in the group, a man who makes money and might aspire perhaps to have a ship of his own?"

"I know the man you mean! Henri Flacourt! I am not surprised that you have heard of him. He is an active trader, known even in Port Louis. He has had his losses, you know, but so do we all. Yes, he is ready to take risks, is Henri. He is here now but on the other side of the island at L'Esperance. He could be here tomorrow if you particularly wish to see him."

"Well, yes, I could put some business in his way. I could do with fresh vegetables, chickens, eggs, and fruit."

"All those I can supply myself, Captain."

"Of course. But I should also like to meet Henri Flacourt. I should be most grateful if you would send for him."

"Certainly, Captain, and with pleasure. Heaven knows, I do not seek to preserve a monopoly. Ask anyone and you will find that I am strictly fair and never use my official position to gain any mean advantage."

"Your reputation is well known, monsieur," replied Delancey with a slight bow, knowing that what he said was strictly true. "I look forward to seeing Monsieur Flacourt tomorrow."

Taking his leave, Delancey did not suppose for a moment that any message would go to Flacourt. So he told his attendant seaman, Cunat, to send the same message by another route, giving the bearer a quite generous reward.

On the following day, which was equally hot and windless, Delancey had another interview with Hudelet, who was profuse in his apologies. His messenger had failed to find Monsieur Flacourt, who must be on one of the other islands—as indeed he often was. Flacourt, a short and stout man from St Malo with a Breton accent, appeared before Hudelet's explanation was even complete, and Delancey soon took him aside for a private conversation.

"I have been told, monsieur, that you know the Seychelles very well and are fully aware of all that happens anywhere in the group. Will you have patience if I put to you a purely imaginary case? Supposing—I say, supposing—that a British corvette had put in, not at this island but at another island, her crew might well be short of food and as short again of money. Having spent what money they had, they would offer what else they have of value; a few muskets perhaps, a barrel of powder, even a six-pounder gun with the cipher on it of King George III. They might in the end have to sell the ship herself. All this would depend, however, on the British remaining ignorant of the ship's whereabouts. If her presence became known to the French, on the other hand, such a sloop would be compelled to surrender and her crew would all become prisoners-of-war. The profitable trade in cordage and cannon balls would be brought to an end. Do you follow me, Monsieur Flacourt?"

"Perfectly, Captain. If there were such a ship, her crew might well do as you say, and the arrival of a French frigate would be as inconvenient as you suggest."

"Just so. Now it so happens that a French frigate *has* arrived, altering the whole situation. Now let us suppose that you monsieur, were a merchant who had done business with these poor seamen—we are still discussing a purely imaginary situation, remember, a mere fable from a storybook—you would be able to visit that sloop again and tell these men that they will have to surrender."

"Were I such a merchant who had traded in that way I should indeed know where the sloop is and could deliver a message of that kind."

"In that unlikely event, you would also know what end to the story would be happiest from your point of view. The last act of the drama should see the crew removed and the ship left where she is or at least wrecked in a position where she would not sink. All that might remain would belong, in effect, to you. You could become a rich man, Monsieur Flacourt."

"You make me begin to wish that your fairy story were true. But it seems to me that a corvette such as you describe would already be damaged, unfit for sea and incapable of repair outside a dockyard."

They had been pacing slowly in the shade of the tamarisk trees but Delancey paused at this moment and looked directly at Flacourt:

"I think we should begin to speak plainly, monsieur."

"And why not? When Hudelet insisted on placing that gun near the flagstaff, all secrecy was at an end."

"Do the British seamen realize that."

"They are simple men and believe what I tell them. They imagine that they are outnumbered. Nor do they grasp that their presence here is known not merely to me but to every one on the island."

"Will you take me to this corvette and allow me to speak with them?"

"Only after we have reached agreement about the corvette and her contents."

There followed a long period of negotiation, interrupted only for dinner and ended only when the light began to fail. There were consultations among the islanders after that and they agreed, as Delancey afterwards learnt, that they would rather be rid of the *Falcon*'s crew. Their presence was a danger in itself and a strain on the island's food supply. When Delancey came ashore next day Flacourt offered at once to take him to the *Falcon,* which was, he learnt, at Mamelle Island, a mere ten miles away.

"I see, Captain," said Hudelet, "that you have sent down topmasts and have dropped a second anchor."

"Yes, I feel, as you do, that this may be the calm before the storm. I don't like the feel of the atmosphere. But this anchorage will be a good place in which to ride it out."

"Yes, we have shelter here. Mamelle Island is a great deal more exposed. Flacourt tells me that he is going to take you there. I think we should be able to come to some arrangement."

"A pity that there is no wind to take us there."

"Flacourt's slaves will row you there in two hours."

They took a little longer than that, the Negroes keeping time with a dismal African song and the beating of a small drum. It was a flat calm and the forested shores of Mahé slid by to port. Then Mamelle was sighted and near by a single lower mast showed where the *Falcon* had ended her last voyage. She was not beached on the island but aground on a reef some three hundred yards from the shore. It seemed that the ship was on an almost even keel and that the crew were still aboard. There was no sign of any camp on the island and a wisp of smoke suggested that the ship's galley fire was alight. Clothes lines strung across the waist and fishing lines festooned the forecastle. Little notice was taken of Flacourt's boat, which must have become a familiar sight. Delancey studied the ship's position and told Flacourt that it looked precarious.

"She will shift in the first gale and go down in deeper water."

"I agree," said Flacourt, "and I have told the men to land everything of value. They are unwilling to do that and some of them think that the ship can be saved."

"Rubbish," replied Delancey, "she is a total loss. May I ask, monsieur, whether you speak or understand English?"

"No, Captain, I do not."

"Well, then, I propose to address the corvette's crew in English, a language I speak fairly well. How many of them are there?"

"Eighty-nine, I believe."

"Any officers?"

"Only the surgeon. The boatswain has taken command."

"I see."

They were met at the entry port by the carpenter, Mr Calvert, who sent to inform the boatswain when told that a French officer had come aboard. The boatswain turned out to be an old grey-haired seaman called Hodges with a worried expression, possibly the worse for drink. At Flacourt's suggestion, translated by Delancey, he ordered the crew on deck. From the quarter-deck Delancey made his speech:

"Mr Hodges has given me permission to tell you what your position is. Your captain and officers are presumably dead and all you who are left are likely to face a charge of mutiny; a charge for which the penalty is death. Your ship is badly damaged and will sink during the next gale; which is to be expected during the next few days. Once ashore on the Seychelles, having escaped drowning, you must not expect to be welcomed by the inhabitants, who do not have enough food for you. They may leave you to starve or they may hand you over to the next visiting British man-of-war. As I see your present situation, those who do not drown will starve and those who do not starve will hang. Any questions?"

"Who are you, sir?" asked the carpenter.

"I command the frigate *Minerve,* flying the French tricolour and now at anchor off Mahé."

"You speak English, sir, like a native."

"Thank you, Mr Calvert. I have been in England as a prisoner-of-war on parole."

"Cannot you remove us, sir, as prisoners-of-war?"

"Where could you go? The British have captured Bourbon and Mauritius. They will be here, no doubt, in a matter of weeks. I cannot supply my frigate for a voyage to France with nearly a hundred extra hands. What you ask is impossible."

"What then, sir, are we to do?" It was the old boatswain who asked the question, looking the picture of misery.

"What are you to do, you ask? How are you to save your lives? There is a way. There is only one way. You can put yourselves under my command and do exactly what I tell you. You must obey me, you understand, without question. But please realize, at the outset, that your lives mean nothing to me. I don't care whether you die or how. I leave the choice to you. You can either accept my orders or stay here and rot. Please yourselves! Mr Hodges, I give the men ten minutes in which to decide. Mr Calvert, I want you to show me where the ship is holed."

Ten minutes later Mr Hodges, speaking for the remainder, put himself and them under Delancey's orders.

"Very well, then," said Delancey, "I want the surgeon to report to me." A middle-aged man with a squint came forward and introduced himself.

"I am David Robertson, surgeon of this ship."

"Good. Now, I must know exactly when and how the mutiny took place. Can you tell me the whole story? Or do I need another witness?"

"I think, sir, you should hear what Ned Potter has to say. He was Captain Railton's steward."

"Right. Will you take Potter to the captain's cabin? Now, Mr Hodges, I want all hands employed on emptying the ship. The sailmaker is to take all sails ashore and rig tents for the crew and for storage. The armourer is to take all weapons ashore and

store them under cover with a sentry to guard them. Move everything ashore, Mr Hodges! Make the men work as they have never
worked before!"

In the captain's cabin Delancey found Robertson and Potter
waiting for him. He sat at the table and told them both to sit
down facing him.

"Now, Mr Robertson, I want to know what happened. You
needn't tell me why—I know something about Captain Railton.
You were on passage from Bombay to Mauritius. Where were
you when the mutiny took place?"

"Opposite the Maldives, sir, and about to pass through the
One-and-a-half-degree Channel."

"What was the immediate cause of the mutiny?"

"Railton had sworn to flog the last man down from aloft. In
his hurry to get down, a topman missed his footing, fell to the
deck, and was killed. The captain ordered the men to throw the
body overboard."

"Without proper burial?"

"Yes, sir. The men mutinied that night."

"And Railton was killed? Who else?"

"No one else but the officers were placed under arrest in their
cabins. I was the exception, having to look after the sick. Hodges
took command, with Calvert as first lieutenant."

"And then?"

"Two days later the officers tried to recapture the ship. In the
attempt both lieutenants were killed and both midshipmen.
Three seamen were wounded."

"So Hodges decided to make for the Seychelles?"

"Yes, sir—on my advice."

"But his navigation was not quite equal to it. Now, tell me

this: are any of the men here guilty, in your opinion, of delib-
erate murder?"

"No, sir. Railton had driven them to a point of desperation
but the men who killed him were no worse than the others. It
was his life or theirs and what else could they have done? They
had no grudge against the officers but they had to defend themselves. The officers were all given proper burial, by the way. The
seamen lay great stress on it."

"Yes, I know. Now, Potter, you have heard what Mr Robertson has told me. What can you add?"

"Well, sir, I was close to Captain Railton, being his steward;
his valet as you might say. I watched him go mad, sir, and could
tell that he was getting worse. He was quite a pleasant gentleman, I've been told, sir, when he was a lieutenant. Being a captain
was too much for him, sir. When young Binney was killed I
heard him say "Throw that lubber overboard," and his messmates had to do it. He was raving mad, was the captain, and
didn't rightly know what he was doing or saying."

"Thank you, Potter. Now, Mr Robertson, I want to ask you
this: Would you join me in a plan which will save the lives of
your shipmates? It means running a serious risk and making
some statements which will not be entirely true, but it is the
only way to save lives. What about you, Potter? As steward you
are used to holding your tongue. Will you join me in this plan?"

"Yes, sir," said Potter, and Robertson expressed more decided
agreement.

"If we can avert further tragedy, we must do it, sir. I'm with
you, come what may. What have we to do?"

"Listen. It is my guess that we are in for a gale of wind within
the next few days. During that storm I think that this ship will

lift from where she is and sink in deeper water. I propose to convince myself that she was at sea until then and was wrecked on that day. There will be only two survivors: you, Mr Robertson and you, Potter. You will report to me that the ship has sunk and I shall believe you. During the same gale but on Mahé Island itself an American ship will be wrecked at Beau Vallon and will become a total loss. In that instance the whole crew will come safely ashore and will come to me for help. I shall enter them on board my frigate."

"What, in a French man-of-war?"

"No, I should have explained before that I am a Captain in the Royal Navy. My frigate flies the French flag but is actually British."

"But won't the islanders spoil your plan by telling the true story?"

"Not if they want to keep all the contents of the *Falcon*. If all those naval stores, guns and sails and spars, were salvaged from an American ship in the China trade, everything can be kept by Monsieur Flacourt and his friends. If everything came from a British sloop, the Royal Navy will want to claim it. My guess is that they will support our story."

"God, sir, we shall be grateful to you!" said Robertson.

"Keep your gratitude until later. You'll find that I shall demand a great deal in return. More immediately, explain to the men what I intend. Tell them what their story is to be. Rehearse it with them in the greatest detail. What was that American ship's name, from what port, of what tonnage? What was her captain's name? What was she doing here? They will have to tell me their story and I shall believe it. But it needs to be credible and they must all tell the same story, even to the crew of the *Minerva*."

"But, surely, sir," objected Robertson, "they will be recognized by your men, having met them while in harbour?"

"A few will be recognized. Their story must be that they deserted the *Falcon* and were in the American ship when she was wrecked."

"You will run a dreadful risk, sir, if the truth should ever become known."

"I am all too aware of that. My defence must be that I was credulous, too easily deceived. That I made up the story myself will be known only to you and Potter. I have to trust you. My career depends upon your being completely reliable. Listen now, I am going back to my ship. I shall not see you again until after the shipwreck. In the meanwhile you have two urgent tasks. First, strip this ship of everything which is of any value and put all the stuff on shore, as safe as you can make it from the effects of a possible gale. Then use the ship's boats to take the entire crew to some point on the west side of Mahé—Flacourt will show you where—and fix on the exact spot for your shipwreck. Alter the ship's name on each boat and then send one of them to me with news of the disaster. Afterwards and quite separately, you and Potter report to me that the *Falcon* went down with all other hands. Is that clear? Flacourt will know the whole truth, by the way, and the *Falcon's* boats are finally to be given to him."

Back on board the *Minerva*, Delancey wondered whether he had made the mistake that would wreck his career. Almost foolproof in theory, his plan depended too much on seamen being able to hold their tongues. From a humanitarian point of view, he was doing his best for the *Falcon's* crew but were his motives humane? He knew that they were not. What he wanted was a fully manned frigate which might gain him an eleventh-hour victory over some frigate which might yet arrive from France. He now had the chance to recruit eighty-nine men. Adding these to the men he had would give him three hundred and fifty-two, almost a full complement by French standards and something in excess of a 38-gun frigate's establishment. He would have the best-manned frigate on the station, fit to blow any opponent out of the water. Nor were these men from the *Falcon* such bad material. He had looked them over and could see that they were potentially good men and grateful at the moment for their reprieve. Given a few weeks of intensive gun-drill he would have exceptionally strong crew in an exceptionally fine ship. The temptation was too much for him. Accepting the risk, his career would be at stake for weeks and indeed months to come. After that the risk would diminish. There would be gossip along many a waterfront but who took any notice of what poor seamen may say? Once his crew was paid off it would be difficult to substantiate even the most persistent rumour. His decision had been made long since, really before he left Mauritius. Having found the *Falcon*'s men he meant to keep them.

The gale, when it came to the Seychelles, was the outer fringe of a hurricane which passed far to the south, missing Mauritius as well. The wind was fitful at first, with occasional gusts which died away to nothing. Seabirds made a plaintive cry, big waves crashed on to the shoreline, and there was a general sense of impending drama. When the wind rose to gale-force it blew at first from the south, veered slowly to the west, and finally to the north-east before dying away. The *Minerva* was never in real danger, being sheltered by the islands and snugged down in advance, but the wind rose to a high scream of violence, drowning the distant noise of thunder. The storm reached its peak at night and Delancey, on the forecastle, watched by the illumination of the lightning flashes to see how the cables were taking the strain. There was no sign of chafing and he turned away, wondering about the fate of the *Falcon,* the position of which was far more exposed. If the *Minerva* pitched and rolled, her cordage groaning, the *Falcon* could not last for long. He hoped that all the men had gone ashore before the wind began to rise. His guess was that she would lift over the reef and capsize nearer the shore. If the wind blew from another quarter she might drift further out before she sank. In either event there would be nothing left for anyone to see, which was just as well.

By next morning there was no more than a northerly stiff breeze, which died away towards evening. In this more favourable weather Flacourt's boat, rowed by his black slaves, put off from the shore with two passengers. One was Mr Robertson, the other was Ned Potter. Flacourt solemnly presented them as strangers and Delancey had clearly never seen them before. He met them officially, and very publicly, on the frigate's quarter-deck and listened to Mr Robertson's report.

"So the *Falcon* is a total loss and you are the only two survivors. Are you sure of that, Mr Robertson?"

"Yes, sir. She was wrecked in the gale and went down in deep water. I was fortunate in clinging to a cask and Potter here clutched at a hen-coop. We reached Mamelle Island in the dark, searched the shore this morning, and can assure you that there was nobody there. I am sorry to say that all the others must have perished, Captain Railton among them."

After making a more detailed report, Robertson was signed on as supernumerary assistant surgeon, Potter as assistant captain's steward. On the following day there came news of another disaster resulting from the same gale. Hudelet sent word that an American merchantman called the *Active,* out of Salem, had been wrecked on the west coast of Mahé, all the crew being saved. He asked whether Delancey could offer the men a passage to

Mauritius, for there was no way of maintaining so many men in as poor a colony as the Seychelles. Delancey made no rash promises but he suggested that the castaways should be brought to the landing place the next day. He would talk to them and see what could be done. At the appointed hour Delancey went on shore, this time in uniform and attended by Topley, Sevendale, Ledingham, and Lewis. As he left the ship the French ensign was hauled down and replaced by the British. At much the same time the British replaced the French flag on land. When he stepped ashore he was greeted by Messieurs Hudelet and Flacourt, the former a little reproachful about the original deception. "You need not have distrusted us, Captain. As soon as we heard of the capture of Mauritius we decided to become a British colony. We are on your side and look to you for protection." Delancey accepted this addition to the Empire, perhaps a little absentmindedly, and went towards the flagstaff at which the castaway mariners were assembled; all, as it happened, in their best clothes. He had obviously seen none of them before.

"Fellow seamen," he said, "I am very sorry to hear of the shipwreck which has brought you here. I understand that your ship, the *Active* of Salem, went ashore here during the recent gale. I am glad, on the other hand, that no lives were lost and that you were all able, as I should guess, to save your personal gear. I have been told that ship and cargo were a total loss. Who is the ship's master?"

Hodges stepped forward.

"And the first mate?"

Calvert raised his hand.

"Good. Now, I realize that most of you will be American citizens, neutral in the present war. It often happens, these days, that the crew of an American ship will include some British seamen, men we describe as deserters from the Royal Navy. Attempts are sometimes made to identify these men. Let me assure you at once that I shall make no such attempt. So far as I am concerned, you are all American, with papers to prove it. This being so, you might expect that I would offer you all a passage to Mauritius as distressed seamen, and bring your plight to the notice of the American Consul at that port. Unfortunately, I cannot do that. My frigate is not designed to carry passengers in any number. In the ordinary way, I could report your presence here and hope, for your sake, that some arrangement could be made for your rescue. I learn, however, from the resident magistrate that the food supplies here are very limited. Hospitable as our local friends are, they cannot be your hosts for very much longer. At first I could think of no solution to the problem. It now occurs to me that our difficulties would be at an end if you were all to enter on board my frigate, the *Minerva,* perhaps the finest ship of her class in the world. You would be assured of fair rations, good treatment, and the pay suitable to your rank. If you were all to suppose that joining the *Minerva* meant serving in the Royal Navy until the end of the war, you might well hesitate. I can assure you, however, that the *Minerva* is bound for Mauritius and then for England. She will then be paid off. The Americans here, the majority of you, will then use their papers to prove their nationality and will be exempt from any further service.

"Now, I have made you all an offer. But I want, above everything, to treat you fairly. While I can offer you good berths in a happy ship, I must not pretend that life will be easy. The French have been swept from the Indian Ocean but our passage home must take us near the French coast. I must be ready at all times to meet the enemy. The *Minerva* could always outsail a bigger ship and can as certainly overwhelm any ship in her own class. But an action is not improbable and we must be ready for it. So the choice lies with you, to go or stay. Be clear, however, about this; I take all or none. Now I shall leave you to think it over or take a vote. In ten minutes from now I shall ask Mr Hodges what you have decided to do."

Delancey walked away and conferred in the hut with Hudelet and Flacourt.

"What will they decide to do?" asked Hudelet when the offer had been explained to him.

"They will enter on board the *Minerva*." replied Delancey at once. "What else can they do? Now, about the details. I propose that all the boats saved from the wreck go to you, Monsieur Flacourt, as a farewell gift. I also propose, however, that most of the gunpowder shall be delivered to my ship before nightfall."

"But, surely, sir," protested Flacourt, "you have all the gunpowder you need."

"Not for the amount of target practice this crew is going to have," said Delancey grimly. "Do you agree or shall we take the boats?" The argument ended, leaving only the details to discuss. Then Delancey returned to the meeting and asked Hodges what the men had decided.

"We'll all enter, sir," said Hodges. Turning to the men he then called "Three cheers for Captain Delancey!" The cheers were given and seemed even to have been expected, for all boats instantly pushed off from the frigate and made for the shore. Delancey did not wait for them but said good-bye to Hudelet and Flacourt and took Hodges and Calvert with him to the boat in which he had come.

"I find all this quite astonishing, sir," said Topley. "We are going to have a full crew—something unknown in these waters since the war began!"

"We have certainly been fortunate," Delancey agreed. "We have completed our task, establishing the fate of the *Falcon*, and can presently sail for home."

"What I can't understand, sir, is how an experienced officer like Captain Railton could have wrecked his ship on Mamelle Island—or how indeed he came anywhere near the place."

"Oh, I know the answer to that. We are lucky again in that the only two men to survive are the surgeon and the captain's steward. Mr Robertson assures me, and Ned Potter agrees, that Captain Railton was insane."

"That explains a lot, sir. The best of our good fortune is that these Americans have agreed so readily to enter!"

"I think that Hodges must have persuaded them—isn't that right, Mr Hodges? I regret to say that I can't offer you a master's vacancy on board the *Minerva*. Would you agree to act, for the time being, as second boatswain? As for you, Mr Calvert, I learn from Mr Hodges that you were once a carpenter before you became a deck officer. Would you agree to act, for this one voyage, as assistant carpenter?" Neither of them made any difficulty and it was clear that the petty officer appointments would be simpler still.

A fortnight later the *Minerva* dropped anchor in Port Louis but very near the harbour entrance and well away from the other men-of-war. She flew a yellow flag and Delancey reported to Commodore Beaver (the Admiral having gone) that he had some cases of fever among some men recently entered. He proposed to allow no shore leave for fear of spreading the infection. The Commodore then readily agreed that the *Minerva* should sail for home as soon as possible. She would need some supplies, however, which would be sent to her, and there must be a court of inquiry into the loss of the sloop *Falcon.* In the circumstances, this was very much of a formality because the evidence of the two survivors was quite sufficient to establish the truth. That Railton had been insane was readily accepted but no senior officer wished to lay stress on it. It was enough to take Robertson's word for it that the man had been seriously ill and was unfit for duty. Delancey's evidence fixed the date and place of the disaster. These were the essential facts, they were duly recorded, and the case was closed.

The *Minerva,* meanwhile, was completing her stores and water for the homeward voyage, but still kept in a state of isolation. Among the few officers allowed ashore, Delancey was just leaving naval headquarters one day when he was breathlessly hailed by a young officer on the senior naval officer's staff, "Captain Delancey, sir, the Commodore requests you to have your ship ready for sea as soon as possible. Enemy ships have just been sighted from the signal station."

Chapter Twelve

THE SIGNAL STATION

THE SIGHTING of the enemy came as a surprise to many, but not to the Commodore nor to Delancey. When news reached France of the Battle of Grand Port Napoleon's instinct would be to follow up the victory. It would be obvious to him that Hamelin should be reinforced. He would issue orders to that effect and the Minister of Marine would realize their urgency. The likelihood was that the frigates would sail almost at once and that they would be the fastest and best ships available. Later would come the news that Mauritius itself had fallen. It would then be too late to recall the frigates which would be half-way to the Cape and crowding all the canvas they had. Once in the Indian Ocean, they would approach Mauritius with caution, alert for a possible blockading squadron.

They would look to the signal station and there, sure enough they would see the signal in their own secret code which meant "There is no enemy ship in sight." The British signalmen did not possess the whole code, as Delancey knew, but that was a signal they could make and certainly would; and he could himself claim some credit for the signal. All being well, the French frigates would identify themselves and enter harbour. At some point (but at what point?) they would realize that they had been trapped but it would then be too late. They would be under the guns of the batteries on the Ile aux Tonneliers and Fort Blanc. For the leading frigate escape would be impossible but what if they were far apart? In that event the first ship might find means to warn the others. They would go about and vanish in a cloud of spray.

To provide against this eventuality, Commodore Beaver had stationed two frigates, the *Phoebe* and *Galatea,* to windward, so that they could cut off the French retreat. If the French ships came anywhere near the harbour mouth they would not easily escape.

Having issued his orders to prepare the *Minerva* for sea, Delancey went ashore again to report progress. He was shown at once into the inner office where he found the Commodore in an irritable mood. Beaver looked haggard, grey-faced and thin, a sick man who would never give up. His office was in a turmoil, with orders being scribbled and with messengers coming and going.

"Well, Delancey—did you receive my message?"

"Yes, sir. We could sail this evening but we should not be provisioned for more than a month. The lighters are alongside but we shall not be properly supplied until the end of the week, not even if we work round the clock."

"Well, it can't be helped. If a French frigate enters harbour you must be ready to take possession of her. Now, as you are here, I had best tell you what the position is. We had guessed that Napoleon would try to reinforce his squadron here and we now know, from intelligence sources, that three of his frigates are on the way, the *Renommée, Clorinde,* and *Néréide,* all of their largest 40-gun class. There is supposed to be a corvette with them called the *Fidèle* but I am puzzled about her—the only *Fidèle* we know about is a small frigate. Three sail have now been sighted but we think one of them is a much smaller vessel, a storeship or a prize. If they are engaged by the *Phoebe* and

Galatea, you should sail and join in the action. Our signal station above the town will do everything possible, however, to lure the Frenchmen into the harbour."

"Aye, aye, sir."

"We should know the result of our deception plan in about an hour."

The climax came sooner than that. The Commodore had placed look-out men on the roof and one of them came in now to report:

"Beg pardon, sir. The Frenchmen have gone about and are steering eastwards."

"Damnation! What made them take fright? Could we have been using an out-of-date code?"

"There is another possibility, sir," said Delancey. "They could have received another signal from the shore, a signal of warning to contradict ours."

"Another signal? Made by whom?"

"Made by an agent of theirs still on the island."

"Have they such an agent?"

"Yes, sir, I believe they have."

"I give you then the task of finding him, and I hope you succeed before that third frigate appears. If they lost touch with each other, the third one might be no better informed and possibly less suspicious than the other two. In the meanwhile, these first two will be pursued by *Phoebe* and *Galatea* and we shall hope to have you provisioned before anything else happens."

Back on board the *Minerva,* Delancey took a telescope up to the maintop and began a careful study of the landscape behind Port Louis. There were two mountain peaks, La Pouce and Pieter Both, which he ruled out as likely to be veiled by cloud. At a lower level there were numerous hill features to be seen from out at sea. The trouble was that they were too numerous. He took bearings on several of the more promising and then plotted them on the map, comparing that again with the town plan. It would clearly take days to explore all the possible locations and he presently called Sevendale into consultation. Should he send out several parties? He decided, in the end, to keep the marines together.

"But what about our cases of fever, sir? Aren't we still in quarantine?"

"Our fever patients are recovering," Delancey assured him solemnly. "I think the danger is less. And the need to find this signal station is urgent, with that third frigate on her way. We shall land at daybreak tomorrow and set to work, moving from left to right, covering each possible hill feature. The party will be armed and rations for the day will be issued before we go ashore. I shall be accompanied by Midshipman Ledingham, as A.D.C., and by my coxswain. The military commandant has been told of our mission and has given his approval. We should be on board again by nightfall."

Orders are often easy to issue, sometimes arduous to execute. In this instance the day was hot, the hills were steep, the going was rough, and the result, by evening, was exactly nothing. The same party went ashore on the next day, continuing to search and with as little success. Features which seemed promising from a distance turned out to be covered by jungle. Others were accessible but had no view of the sea. Some, viewed from below, looked hopeful but had somehow vanished by the time they were reached. Remembering how Fabius had treated prisoners in Borneo and Bourbon, remembering the murder he had committed in Ireland, Delancey would not easily abandon the search. He became increasingly anxious, however, as it went on, for the likelihood was that the third frigate would appear before he had located the signal station.

On the fourth day Delancey had the consolation of knowing that the *Minerva* was now provisioned for six months and in all respects ready for sea. On the fifth day he found what he was looking for. He and his party had climbed a minor hill feature, pushing breast-high through oleanders, shaded occasionally by jacarandas, battling through undergrowth and coming out finally on a flat and empty summit, lacking any sign of having ever been used for anything. Men threw themselves, panting, on the stony ground under the hot sun. Sevendale had a word with one of his men who said he was footsore.

Delancey focused his telescope on the distant *Minerva*, looking like a child's toy in a seaside pool. A lighter was just pulling away from her side and he reckoned that it would be the last one. Of the others, the first to recover was Ledingham who went to look at some wild flowers. A few minutes later he came running back to the party, calling out "I think I've seen it, sir!" Delancey followed where the boy led, expecting to have his attention drawn to something higher up the mountainside. But Ledingham ran to the edge of the plateau and pointed downwards.

There, perhaps three hundred feet below, stood a hut alongside a signal mast. They must have passed quite near it as they made their ascent. Its position had been chosen with great care, as was obvious. It was screened by trees on either side, making it visible from the sea on a given bearing but not from any other direction. It could not be seen from below, he guessed, and the mast was painted a dark colour to merge with a background of conifers. He had seen nothing of it from the harbour, nor would anyone see it from the town. It had been set up, he supposed, while the French still had the island and set up, moreover, with a view to its use after the island had fallen. There must have been another place from which signals were sent to Bourbon, a station high up in the mountains. All these signal arrangements were masterly, he concluded, as he focused his telescope on the hut.

Even as he did so, a man emerged from the hut, also with a telescope, and placed the instrument on a tripod. He beckoned to the hut and was joined by another man, who presently hurried to fetch a third. Following the directions in which that telescope was pointed, he could see the glimmer of distant sails. Making the same discovery at the same instant, young Ledingham reported: "Two ships heading for Port Louis, sir." Delancey cursed inwardly, realizing that from almost any other point, the ships would have been visible half an hour ago. They had been screened from him by another hill. He would now have to act at top speed and would probably be too late at that.

"Follow me!" he shouted to the others and led them in a breakneck descent of the hill. The scramble which followed was a nightmare. Choosing what seemed the easiest line, he was foiled by a patch of bog and had to turn in the other direction. This brought him into a farmyard where a small mongrel went into hysterics and pigsties seemed to block every exit. Climbing over a dry-stone wall, which largely fell down, brought them into a lane which led in the wrong direction.

To escape from this, Delancey broke through a bamboo hedge and ran through an orchard beyond which was an impenetrable clump of saplings. He followed these to the right and came to a path which at least led downhill. Here he paused so that his sweating followers might catch up with him. They did so, volleying blasphemy, and he set off again down the hillside. When he paused again, on the banks of a dried-up stream, he realized that he had probably descended to the level of the signal hut and had no idea whether it lay to the left or right. He had to admit to himself that he was lost.

Sevendale, when he came up, was inclined to think that they should go to the left, Ledingham favoured the right, and the marine sergeant had no opinion on the subject. With time so pressing, Delancey divided his forces, sending Sevendale to the left with half the marines, he and Ledingham, with the sergeant and his coxswain, going to the right. Whichever party sighted the signal mast would fire three shots in the air.

Skirting a patch of cultivated ground, he came on a cottage from which an old woman rushed out indignantly, waving her stick at them. When she saw the redcoats she ceased cursing and tried to explain something as she pointed down the hillside. Her French patois was difficult to follow and Delancey could not at first make out what she was trying to say. He eventually understood that she thought they must be hunting a runaway slave—such hunts being a familiar sight—and that she had seen a stray Negro earlier in the day. Delancey explained, while his panting men caught up, that he was looking for a small hut with a flagpole. She was too obsessed with her story to take much notice of his. In his exasperation he lost what was normally a fair French accent and lapsed into the Guernsey patois he had known as a child. In some odd way this actually conveyed something to her. She nodded vigorously and pointed up the hillside, adding some confused advice as to the best route to follow. She had confirmed his worst fear, that he had descended too far, but on the whole confirmed Ledingham's sense of direction.

Thanking her, he turned right beyond her cottage and began to climb the hill again, being grateful for the shade of some trees,

as also for the wind which was now against him. Breasting a
steeper slope, he presently heard, ahead of him and to his left,
a sound which he could always recognize; the sound of signal
flags snapping in the breeze. He paused then, gesturing to his
men to keep silence and deploy. They had best advance in good
order for the need for immediate haste had gone. Whatever they
did, they had arrived too late.

The signal had been made but it was still desirable to catch
the enemy agents. He therefore detached Ledingham with four
marines to make a circling movement to the right, the sergeant
with four more to circle left, while he himself with his coxswain
and three marines gave the others a few minutes start and then
went straight ahead. Drawing his own pistol, he told the marines
to fix bayonets and advance. Moving up a final and steeper slope,
he came out on a small level space with the mast in the centre
and the hut just beyond. Three men were grouped round the
telescope and were looking seawards. To the right of the hut
Ledingham appeared, pistol in hand, two marines on either side
of him. To the left the marine sergeant appeared behind the hut,
which was then surrounded. The manoeuvre completed,
Delancey moved quietly forward, with pistol levelled, and could
now recognize Fabius as the centre man in the group. When
within easy range, he halted and called out:

"Surrender! Lay down your arms. You are surrounded."

Fabius whipped round in a second, reaching for his coat
pocket, but paused again when he saw that Delancey's pistol was
aimed at him. Looking round, he could see that his situation
was hopeless, with fixed bayonets glittering on every side. He
dropped his pistol on the ground and his two assistants did the
same. Delancey's coxswain stepped forward, picked up the
weapons, and searched the prisoners to ensure that they had no

others concealed. He relieved Fabius of a dagger and one of his henchmen gave up a pocket bludgeon. A fourth man had been disarmed in the hut and was brought out by the sergeant under guard. Ledingham went to the mast and hauled down the signal flags. After looking through the telescope on its tripod, he reported to Delancey that the ships had gone about and were crowding canvas. One was a frigate of the largest class and the other a small frigate or corvette.

Fabius looked exactly as he had done on the occasion of their previous meeting in Ireland, a fattish smooth-faced man with the air of an unfrocked priest. His voice was under perfect control and his tone was sarcastic.

"Ah, the good Captain Delancey, as zealous as ever in serving King George the Third—who has gone mad, by the way, or so I have been told. Well, we meet again and I am this time at more of a disadvantage. I must accept my fate as a prisoner-of-war."

"You are not a prisoner-of-war, Mr Fabius, if that is indeed your name. You are a civilian facing charges of treason, spying, torture, and murder."

"And what evidence have you? Gossip in Ireland but not a single witness? Suspicious circumstances in Borneo or Bourbon? The making of a signal in Mauritius? Come, sir, you can't be serious. Your case against me amounts to nothing and you know it. As for treason, how can you show that I am or have ever been a British subject? Bring me to trial and your case will be laughed out of court."

"You forget, perhaps, that these underlings of yours may break under interrogation and betray you."

"How can they betray me? They know nothing about me and three of them can prove that they have never been outside the

Ile de France. No, my friend, your case against me rests upon nothing."

"So you think you will be acquitted and can return to France as an exchanged prisoner-of-war?"

"I am willing to make a bet on it."

"But I am not, Mr Fabius. I now incline to think, however, that you are right. You will never stand trial. There is, as you say, a lack of evidence. Quite apart from that, I shall sail today and could not be present at your trial. Without my evidence, you might well avoid conviction on any serious charge. Nor can I spend any longer time on your case. So your argument leaves me with no alternative. You have reached the end of the road, Fabius, and it only remains to say good-bye."

Contemptuous at first, Fabius had come to realize at last what Delancey intended. Desperate, he shouted, "And you call me a murderer!" before attempting to dash at his opponent. A shot rang out and the man collapsed in a bloodstained heap on the grass, shot through the heart. Delancey's pistol was smoking in his hand but he now returned it to his pocket. "Shot while attempting to escape," he remarked briefly.

"And now we must return to our ship as quickly as possible. Sergeant, fire three shots in the air as a signal to Mr Sevendale. Remain here for half an hour, if need be, and tell him what has happened. Then make for the frigate at the double. We shall be sailing within the hour. Mr Ledingham, search the hut and collect any papers you may find there. Take them back to the ship—and quickly. Tanner, take charge of the three prisoners, tie their wrists behind their backs, and take two marines to escort them on board the *Minerva*. And hurry! Remainder, follow me!"

Picking up the dead man's pistol and searching him in vain

for documents, Delancey set off again down the hillside and now with even more haste. He and his companions had the slope in their favour and the wilder country gradually gave place to farmland and that to the outskirts of Port Louis.

Gasping and sweating, they hurried through the streets, stared at by the French inhabitants and jeered at by the children. When they came within sight of the harbour Delancey was still meaning to report to the Commodore's office but he saw now that there was no time for that. Against a contrary wind, Northmore had already warped the *Minerva* out of harbour, leaving only the launch behind at what had been the frigate's berth. With a final effort Delancey brought his party to the boat and scrambled aboard.

"Push off!" he ordered at once. "And row for dear life!" His marines looked at him with wonder, knowing that he had left so many on shore, but he had already thought how to rescue them. As they passed a storeship near the harbour mouth, he hailed the captain and asked him to send his boat for the remainder of his men. Ten minutes later Delancey was on his own quarter-deck, being greeted by a worried first lieutenant.

"Thank God you're here, sir!" said Northmore. "The signal was made for us to sail as soon as those French ships went about. It was repeated half an hour ago. So I began to warp out of harbour, wondering what to do if—anyway, I can't tell you what a relief it is to see you!"

"You did very well. Mr Northmore. Keep the launch in the water—we may need to send ashore—and let me know when the rest of the shore party comes aboard. I must write a letter to the Commodore. I'll be in my cabin for the next quarter of an hour. Tanner will bring three prisoners on board. You can enter them as landsmen volunteers."

A minute later the captain's clerk was taking down a letter which was dictated at top speed.

Sir—I have the honour to report that the *Minerva* is about to make sail after the French ships which are still in sight from our foretopmast-head. Some members of the crew have still to join but should be on board very soon. I had Vice-Admiral Bertie's orders to sail for England as soon as my mission to the Seychelles had been accomplished and I venture to presume that these orders still hold good. It is my intention to overtake and engage these French men-of-war. Having done so I shall proceed to England as ordered. If I am not authorized to do this you might be good enough to signify your disapproval by hoisting the negative and firing a gun. With the wind in this quarter I should still be in sight after you receive this.

I have the honour to be, sir,

Your obedient servant,
Richard Delancey

Without pausing for a second he went on to add a personal letter which read:

Dear Commodore—When last we met you instructed me to find the enemy agent who signalled a warning to the previous group of French men-of-war. I am now able to report that I found him but not in time to prevent him repeating the trick. I arrived about twenty minutes after the signal had been made. The agent who once used the code-name of Fabius was killed in attempting to escape. Three men with him be entered on board this ship. You will realize that time for me was short. Your signal for the *Minerva* to sail was made before I had found the men I had been looking for and it was all I could do to return on board before Northmore sailed without me! With such need for haste I could never have brought these men to trial or even left them under arrest. There was no time even to explain what their crime had been. Fabius solved a problem for me by his attempt to escape. Of the other three one may be an agent of some slight importance, perhaps from Bourbon. The other two are mere underlings, I think, recruited locally. Without any pretence of justice I have condemned them to serve as landsmen on board this frigate. There is no reason why you should have official knowledge of their fate. As regards Fabius however, someone must collect his body from the stricken field. Here again you need know nothing about it and I suggest that you use some local messenger to deliver the enclosed note to the military commandant. Allow me to thank you for your kindness and assure you that I shall overtake these French ships if it is humanly possible. I write myself

> Your obliged servant,
> Richard Delancey

The enclosed note was written by the captain's clerk in his own (as opposed to his copperplate) handwriting.

This comes to inform you, sir, that French agents have set up a signalling post from which they warn French ships away from the island. Their signal mast is on the hills behind Port Louis and this map will show you where it is.

> *Wellwisher*

Delancey made a hurried sketch to indicate roughly where

the place was. He left it to the commandant to decide for himself why there should be a corpse on the site. No harm would
be done if these soldiers were given something to think about.

He had hardly finished this task before young Lewis reported
the arrival of the storeship's boat. Delancey went on deck to meet
the gaze of a reproachful Sevendale.

"Are all your men on board? Good. Well done! Tanner, give
this letter to the boat's coxswain and tell him to deliver it to
naval headquarters, with a guinea for his trouble. Mr Topley, we
shan't need the launch, after all. Hoist it inboard. Mr Ledingham, take your telescope to the foretop and tell us what you can
see of the French. Give the order, Mr Topley, for all hands to
make sail. Mr Lewis, make this signal and fire a gun: "Enemy in
sight, am going in chase." Where are your prisoners, Tanner?
Untie them but put them in irons. Mr Sevendale, the marine
shore party is to splice the mainbrace and is excused any further duty until tomorrow."

Close-hauled, the frigate was soon under way, with the enemy
just in sight and Mauritius already more distant. Delancey
watched the shore through his telescope and was rewarded eventually by the Commodore's signal of acknowledgement and
"Good luck" spelt out. He knew now, with tremendous relief,
that he was at last on his way home. More fortunate still, he had
a superb frigate, fully manned, with the enemy ahead of him
and a chance to come into Portsmouth in a blaze of glory. There
could be no certainty about it but the frigate he was pursuing
must have been slower, for some reason, than the other two, and
it should therefore be possible to overtake her. It only remained
to train his crew to such a standard in gunnery that they would
be more than a match for any French frigate—and indeed in this
case a match for two of them.

Next day Delancey called a conference of his officers and told them first, the story of Fabius, so far as it was known to him.

"In the ordinary way it would have been difficult to deal with him, if only for lack of time. Luckily he solved the problem for me by trying to escape. So I shot him dead and may hope that any further French ships which approach Mauritius, not knowing that it has capitulated, will fall into our hands. On the day we sailed some seamen were inclined to blame the marines for delaying us. I tell you this story so that all on board will know that the marines did very well and are not to be blamed for any delay. We are now in chase of a French frigate which I suspect is the *Clorinde* of 40 guns. The ship with her is probably the *Fidèle* which is either a small frigate or large corvette. I shall be disappointed if we fail to take them both."

"But—forgive me, sir—the Frenchmen are no longer in sight!" Contact with the enemy had been lost during the night and Northmore evidently assumed that the situation would have been different had his captain not wasted time ashore.

"They are no longer in sight," Delancey admitted, "but that is of no consequence. The point is that we know where they are going. They have made a passage from France to Mauritius without calling anywhere. They have found Mauritius closed to them. So they must be short of water and must find some in a matter of weeks. So they are heading for Tamatave in Madagascar. What else could they do? We have about eight hundred miles to sail and perhaps ten days in which to perfect our gunnery. After that, we may expect to engage the *Clorinde* and the *Fidèle* and compel them both to haul down their colours. So we all know what we have to do."

"Aye, aye, sir," said Northmore, "might we know, sir, what tactics you intend to pursue?"

"Well, I shall assume, first of all, that two frigates will hardly refuse battle against one. I must also suppose that we shall be on the same tack and that the *Fidèle* will be ahead of the *Clorinde*. In this way the French might try to prevent me from cutting off their weaker ship. If I then accept the challenge and close with the *Clorinde*, the *Fidèle* may escape, which is the very thing I must prevent. My aim must be to deal with the *Fidèle* first, crippling her before the real action begins. I shall fail in this, however, if my intention is too soon apparent. Nor should I succeed without men enough to man both batteries, which fortunately I have. It is possible, though not certain, that these French ships may be carrying troops to reinforce the garrison of Mauritius, which will make them more formidable at close quarters. I need hardly tell you that the action I expect may involve us in heavy but unavoidable loss. Apart from any tactical advantage we may secure, all will depend upon accurate and rapid gunnery. Between here and Madagascar we shall practise each day, being fortunately able to spare the powder."

"Sir," said Topley anxiously, "if our first object is to cripple the *Fidèle*, we shall, I suppose, load at first with canister and chain or bar shot. Does this mean that we shall pass the *Clorinde* without returning her fire?"

"I hope that we shall not have to do that but the men should be warned that such a necessity may arise."

"Would it be possible, sir," asked Northmore, "to steer between them?"

"It would indeed, and we should end with one of them on either beam—not a promising situation to be in."

"Should we assume, sir," asked Sevendale, "that the captain of the *Clorinde* is aware of our pursuit?"

"Undoubtedly. He saw us as we came out of Port Louis and

he could see that we were alone. I doubt whether he could have identified us beyond knowing our class."

"I am wondering, sir, what you would have done had you been in his place?"

"Well, I should in any case have made for Tamatave. The alternative would be the Seychelles but he would rightly assume that these will now be in our hands. He must have water before he does anything else. If he has troops on board, as I think very probable, his water shortage will be desperate. He can never risk being crippled in action while his water supplies are all but exhausted. As for his tactical alternatives, I should in his place be planning an attack; but I doubt very much whether he thinks as I do. He will defend himself, I believe, and with the *Fidèle* ahead of the *Clorinde*. If I engage the *Clorinde* the *Fidèle* will try to take up a raking position across our bows."

"And good luck to her!" exclaimed Northmore. "We should teach them not to try that!"

"I think we might, Mr Northmore," Delancey admitted, "but let us not underrate our opponents. That was Captain Pym's mistake—or, anyway, his chief mistake—at Grand Port. We have been defeated once and we must not be defeated again. To ensure victory we need, above all, to improve our gunnery. We can do that in two ways. First, we shall have target practice for all first and second gun-captains, teaching them the need to aim and elevate correctly. Rapidity of fire is nothing if the shots all miss the target. Second, we shall mark out a half-circle round each gun and paint in the degrees. Gun-captains will then be trained to aim on a given bearing."

"What purpose will that serve?" asked Topley.

"To help us fire when blind. If there is a dead calm or very light wind the space between two opponents must tend to fill with smoke. The point is reached—and I have known this—more especially at night—when everyone is firing into the void. But an officer in, say, the maintop, using a fixed compass dial, can take a bearing on the enemy's main topmast, rising above the smoke, judge the distance, and send these figures down to the officer commanding the main battery. He will then order his gun-captains to aim on that bearing at a given elevation. I do not promise a perfect result from that method but we should do better than the other side."

As from this day the gun-drill was relentless. A wooden target was suspended from a fore yard-arm stunsail boom and a cannon mounted on the quarter-deck. Practice continued until every first and second gun-captain could hit the target with two shots out of three. Later, an old cask with a small tricolour on a broomstick was hove overboard and the ship manoeuvred so as to put the target on the beam at musket-shot distance. Time was taken to see how long it took to hit the cask, the guns firing in succession. Once that time for this was reduced to something within a minute, practice was resumed against a cask at half-cannon-shot and finally at extreme range. No fewer than five gun-captains had by then been replaced, others being promoted and others again rewarded.

Some days later two casks were heaved overboard at four hundred yards interval. The frigate then bore up, sailed in a circle, and steered between the two casks with both batteries manned and in action. This was a tricky operation at best and had to be repeated six times before a good standard of accuracy could be achieved. Guns had so far been firing in succession but now the exercises involved the firing of broadsides, guns fired theoretically together. They were never in fact simultaneous and some officers considered that such a practice, if possible, would put too much strain on the ship's timbers. So the volley was usually scattered, with a few seconds between the shots, which were sufficiently together even so to make the ship heel over. Accuracy might be reduced but the moral effect was, of course, the greater.

In the ordinary way Delancey was thought a humane captain, reluctant to punish, interested in his men's welfare, but he seemed at this stage to have changed in character. He had become a martinet from whom it was almost impossible to gain a word of praise. He seemed to rage round the gun-deck, finding fault with everything and making it clear that no one's best was good enough. "The old man was never like this before," said Topley to Northmore in a confidential tone of voice. "We can none of us do anything right."

"Can't you understand?" snapped Northmore. "We are soon to be in action with the odds against us. It is not enough to be good—we have to be exceptional. The captain hates losing men in action and blames himself afterwards for the few he has lost. So he gives us all hell now in the hope of saving bloodshed later on. The best way to save your own men's lives is to blow your opponent out of the water, and that, by God, is what he means to do."

This explanation of Delancey's conduct was soon shown to be correct. Two days before the frigate would sight Madagascar, provided the wind held, Delancey ceased to rage and began to praise. "Well done!" he said to the gun-crews. "This is the best frigate in her class and we have the best crew this side of the Cape!" All was now sweetness and light—provided that there were no mistakes—and men basked in a new atmosphere of encouragement. For the French they now felt a measure of pity, as for men who would never know what had hit them. Delancey's aim was now to give them encouragement, show them that they were bound to win. Sailors' memories are short and they soon forgot all they had been through, taking a new pride in being the invincible crew of a crack frigate, the best of her class. What chance had the enemy, even with two frigates? The *Minerva* was a ship that could beat the world. So satisfied was the captain that he cancelled all further drills and gave the men what amounted to a day's rest, no more being done than the essential working of the ship. There was time for skylarking and a little ceremony when a prize was given to the best gun's crew of all.

Delancey had his officers to dinner and told them that the worst was over and that the training was always more arduous than the battle. Towards sunset the officer of the watch was hailed from the masthead, "Sail on the larboard bow!" Telescopes were levelled and a tiny patch of white was glimpsed for a moment in the light of the setting sun. It was gone again as the sun neared the horizon but Ledingham, as acting lieutenant, reported to Delancey that the enemy should be in sight at day-break. He found the captain writing at his desk and somewhat preoccupied. He merely nodded when given the news, going on to sign what he had written and sprinkle it with sand. Looking up with a smile, he said:

"Thank you, Mr Ledingham. You did well to tell me and you have come at exactly the right moment. I shall want you and another officer to witness my Will . . ."

Chapter Thirteen

ACTION OFF MADAGASCAR

THE ENEMY ships were duly sighted at daybreak, almost a day's run from the coast of Madagascar.

"Will they have seen us, sir?" asked Lewis.

"They should have seen us first," replied Topley, "silhouetted against the sunrise. They will not have seen us last night and we had only a glimpse of them."

"When shall we catch up with them?"

"By this evening at this rate but I fancy they will back their topsails and give battle. They have no hope now of watering before the action and they would most likely prefer to fight in daylight."

"Why, sir?"

"A night action favours the better-disciplined crew."

"And that, sir, we certainly are! We have been taught to do it right! But how do we know that they have not been as well trained?"

"The *Clorinde* is a fairly new frigate, straight from her home port, and has never been in battle. She was sent out to reinforce the French squadron at Mauritius. She finds Port Louis in our hands, her campaign over before it has begun. Morale will be low from a sense of wasted effort. As against that, they have two fully manned frigates to our one. They will also suppose that we are depleted and worn out after years in the Indies. And that is where they will be wrong. Through having a clever captain we are very well manned indeed—with three more men at the last moment! I doubted at first whether those men embarked at Mauritius would be any good. They were sulky when first allowed on deck but changed their attitude after the sulkiest of them had received a dozen lashes. They have worked well since then."

The French were soon seen to have backed their topsails but the wind was light and it took the whole morning to come up with them. Delancey sent his crew to dinner rather ahead of time and did not clear for action until after they had finished their grog. The wind was north-easterly as was to be expected at the time of year, the day was fine, and the sun was hot. The French frigates seemed to be in very good order, the *Fidèle* in the lead as Delancey had expected. The *Minerva* was on a course which would overtake them to windward. Delancey sent for his officers and told them what he planned to do:

"I shall attack their leading ship at an oblique angle without replying to the *Clorinde's* first broadside. At about a cable's distance we shall fire our larboard guns into the *Fidèle's* rigging with bar-shot, chain-shot, and langridge. My hope is that we can then pass ahead of the *Fidèle* and manoeuvre so as to fire our starboard battery into her from a position athwart her hawse, using ordinary shot and firing low. With the *Fidèle* crippled, we can then deal with the *Clorinde*. To your stations, gentlemen—and good luck! Mr Northmore, beat to quarters!"

With the drum beating to the rhythm of "Hearts of Oak" the seamen ran to their guns, the marines fell in on the quarter-deck, the powder-monkeys hurried to the magazine, and the marksmen climbed to the fighting tops. When the drum stopped beating there was complete silence save for the creaking of ropes and the occasional flap of the sails. From the French ships came the distant sound of a band playing "La Marseillaise" followed by the noise of cheering. Delancey made his round of the gundeck, having a word with each gun-captain and saying something to encourage those of the youngsters who looked most scared. "Speed is no good," he repeated, "without accurate aim."—"Every shot must find its mark. Don't shoot for the sake of making a noise."—"Wait for the order to fire."—"Remember the drill—if you make a mistake you can burst the gun, killing yourself and your mates."—"Do it fast but do it right!"—"You can't hide from the enemy's fire, so kill them and their fire will cease!" He was glad to see that the men were cheerful and confident, more certain of victory than he was. Now he was back on the quarter-deck, attended by the master and young Lewis as A.D.C. There was perhaps a quarter of an hour to go before the action would be joined. Watching the French, Delancey told himself that the probable climax of his career had been reached. Over the next few hours his reputation would be made or ruined. About him were the officers and men who might pay with their lives for any mistake he might make; and mistakes, God knew, were possible enough. How long had it been, however, since he went to sea! A lifetime ago he had been a captain's clerk, then a midshipman, and gained his commission at the Siege of Gibraltar. He had at one time commanded a revenue cutter, later a privateer, then a sloop. For years he had been learning his trade and now he was going to be put to the test. Good luck—and a little cunning—had placed him in command of a fast and powerful frigate. More luck and cunning had given him a sufficient crew and gunpowder to spare for practice. And now the moment was coming, had nearly come, when he and his men would be put to the proof.

The *Minerva* was on course for a point just ahead of the

Fidèle. As she closed the distance the *Clorinde* fired a first shot so as to try the range. It fell short, as Delancey knew it would, and there was silence for another few minutes. Then, as he watched tensely, Delancey saw the whole position alter. Following some previously concerted plan, the *Fidèle* changed course slightly and backed her topsails. The effect was to place her to leeward of the *Clorinde,* practically on her larboard beam, and she made sail again as soon as the manoeuvre was complete. The *Clorinde* was thus between the *Minerva* and the *Fidèle* and Delancey's opening move had been thwarted. Or had it? On second thoughts, Delancey considered that the French move had been a mistake. The line abreast was a bad formation, as they would soon realize.

"We'll hold our present course, Mr Ragley, and attempt to cross the *Clorinde*'s hawse at about a cable's distance."

"We could go closer than that, sir."

"I know, but I need a longer range to allow the canister to spread. Hold it as she goes. Mr Lewis, my compliments to Mr Topley and ask him to reload after discharge with the same type of ammunition. After firing at the *Clorinde*'s rigging I mean to give the *Fidèle* the same treatment."

As Lewis ran off the *Clorinde* fired her broadside and it was at once obvious that her gunnery was quite creditable. The *Minerva* reeled slightly under the impact of a dozen hits, a boat being smashed amidships and several men wounded at one of the forward guns. Having done the drill a score of times the gun's crew renumbered and the second gun-captain took the place of the first, who had been wounded.

Delancey ignored the *Clorinde* and held his course, with the range shortening and the French guns firing with greater effect. A second broadside did far more damage, dismounting Number

Seven Gun and wounding the foremast, causing five more casualties and tearing holes in the foretopsail. Delancey had decided upon this plan of holding his fire but he wondered now whether he was right to ask it of his men. Not being under fire, the French were aiming as at target practice . . . He could not change his mind now but he would be in trouble if a mast went. The chances were against it and the risk was one he could accept . . . but disaster might strike at any minute. He might himself be killed, if it came to that.

The French fired their third broadside, the *Clorinde* momentarily enveloped in smoke and the *Minerva* was now hit repeatedly, with another gun dismounted and a fire started—but quickly extinguished—at the break of the forecastle. Sails were hanging in tatters, several marines had been wounded, and a quartermaster killed at the helm. It was at this moment that the captain of the *Clorinde* perceived his mistake. With the *Minerva* heading to cross his bows, he would ordinarily have given the order to wear ship so as to confront the *Minerva* with his broadside, but to wear, in the present situation, would bring the *Clorinde* into collision with the *Fidèle*. If he tried to tack, on the other hand, he would be raked by the *Minerva* and separated from his consort. After one more broadside, the most damaging of any yet, the *Minerva* was clear of the enemy's arc of fire.

From the quarter-deck Delancey could see the Frenchmen clearly and wondered what their senior captain meant to do. And now the *Minerva* was crossing the *Clorinde's* bows. Each gun fired in turn with high elevation, sending a storm of iron through the *Clorinde's* rigging. Canister ripped through her sails, whirling chain-shot cut through ropes, and bar-shot chipped her spars and boom. Hardly any reply was possible and the British gunners did not waste a shot. In that raking position each projectile

had a triple chance of doing damage, the shot which missed the
foremast could still hit the main or the mizen. Unlike the *Clorinde*
the *Fidèle* had space to wear and was now attempting to do so
but the *Minerva* was crossing her bows before she could alter
course. A storm of iron ripped through her sails and rigging and
a further broadside followed before she was able to reply. Almost
at the same instant the *Clorinde,* from a rather greater distance,
poured her broadside into the *Minerva's* stern. There was serious damage between decks, with a number of men killed and
wounded. Mr Ragley fell at Delancey's side and was taken below,
his place being taken by the boatswain. The marine sergeant was
killed and a gun put out of action in the starboard battery.

The *Minerva* and *Fidèle* were now sailing away from the
Clorinde, which ceased fire in order to wear ship, but the *Minerva* soon drew ahead of her opponent, allowing Delancey to
cross the *Fidèle's* bows again and fire once more into her rigging.
Persistence now achieved the desired result, the *Fidèle* losing her
foretopmast. As the *Fidèle* turned away the *Minerva* engaged her,
broadside to broadside, and Delancey had, for the time being,
placed the *Fidèle* between the *Minerva* and the *Clorinde*. His gunners now fired round shot and fired low. Results were immediate
and the *Fidèle's* mizenmast went over the side. As the *Clorinde*
approached, Delancey broke off the engagement and drew away,
hoping that the *Clorinde* would follow. But the captain of the
Clorinde was no fool. He hove-to on the windward side of the
crippled *Fidèle,* evidently resolved that his two ships must stay
together.

Delancey now made a quick round of the ship, making much
the same speech to different groups of sailors and marines:

"Listen, men. There are two enemy ships and we have crippled the smaller of them. It cost us lives and men wounded but

it couldn't be helped. The damage we have done to the smaller frigate should prevent her escaping while we deal with the other one. It also makes it difficult for her to go to the other's help. So we shall attack again now before they have time to finish their knots and splices. Fire quickly but make every shot go home!"

Renewing the engagement, Delancey placed the *Minerva* against the *Clorinde,* broadside to broadside at a cable's distance, thus ensuring that the one frigate would mask the fire of the other. All hell broke loose in an instant as the two batteries thundered. The two ships were sufficiently near to each other for Delancey to distinguish the captain of the *Clorinde,* who seemed to be an active officer, hurrying round to encourage his gunners and making warlike gestures with a drawn sword. Delancey's own sword remained in its sheath and he wondered for a moment why portraits of admirals so often showed them posed, sword in hand, against a background of furious carronade. Why draw sword against opponents seen to be a quarter of a mile distant? Putting the thought from him, he turned to watch what damage his guns were doing. They were firing steadily into the *Clorinde* and seldom going wide or over. He could see the splinters fly from a gun-port, a quarter-gallery smashed in, an empty port where a gun had been, a trail of smoke from some part of the forecastle. The *Minerva,* however, was taking punishment too and the *Clorinde* was adding musketry to the volume of her fire, although at too great a distance to be effective. It certainly looked, though, as if some infantry were added to her normal complement. Some of her cannon were firing wild and high and it might be guessed that her gun crews were forgetting the drill. Other guns were firing well, for all that, and the damage was mounting. One shot smashed the cabin skylight, sending a splinter into the boatswain's thigh. The boatswain was sent below, his place being taken by John Cumner, boatswain's mate, and Delancey wondered how many men had already been lost. More to the point, what sign was there of the *Fidèle?*

"Mr Lewis—take a telescope to the mizen-top and tell me where that other frigate is—you should be able to see her topmast above the smoke." The midshipman was back in a flash, with a report that she was moving slowly and was now on the *Clorinde*'s larboard bow.

"Well done, Mr Lewis. She means to take up a raking position—but I have a mind to give her an unpleasant surprise! Mr Cumner, make more sail! Set the topgallants and forecourse!"

The opponents had so far been in the normal order of fighting under topsails, mizen, and jib, and the effect of the additional canvas was to make the *Minerva* draw ahead of the *Clorinde*. There was wild cheering from the French side and the sound of cannon fire gradually died away. As the smoke slowly blew aside, the *Minerva* was seen to be heading for a position across the *Fidèle*'s bows. The breeze was becoming fitful, the movement on either side was slow, and the *Fidèle* could in the ordinary way have changed course so as to present her broadside to the *Minerva*. But her seamen were hampered by the damage to her rigging. They had cut away the tangled mizen but she was still difficult to handle and her head had only been pulled round by the efforts of her launch. The same boat, joined now by another, was now trying to undo the work it had done but there was no time for this effort to succeed. Worse, the two boats were both sunk by the *Minerva*'s bow-chasers, presenting the *Fidèle* with an impossible situation, her rescue attempts complicating her now feeble effort to avoid the coming enfilade.

There was a relative silence lasting two or three minutes and then the *Minerva* had gained her position and, on Delancey's

orders, backed her topsails and fired her broadside. There was
no further aiming at the French ship's rigging. The round shot
swept along her decks from bow to stem and with terrible effect.
For the second broadside all the guns were loaded with
grapeshot. This was the more to be dreaded in that the French
were desperately trying to bring their ship round, for which purpose her sail-trimmers were on deck. For the third broadside the
guns were loaded again with round shot and the havoc wrought
was beyond description. The *Fidèle* was a wreck but her colours
were still flying and her efforts to come round were beginning
to succeed. Very slowly and under a devastating fire, she was
finally able to discharge her first broadside. It was a gallant effort,
although the effect was ragged, and Delancey at once made sail
again, quickly passing beyond her arc of fire. The rumble of
artillery died away and the second phase of the battle was over.

Delancey now summoned his officers to the quarter-deck and
asked for an approximate return of losses and damage. He had
apparently lost thirty-seven men, killed and wounded, with five
guns put out of action, and a wounded foremast which would
hardly survive a stiff breeze. He could tell himself that his tactics had so far succeeded but the wind was dying away, giving
little scope for further manoeuvre. After studying his opponents
through the telescope, Delancey turned back to his officers.

"Well done, gentlemen. We have crippled both enemy frigates
and neither can escape. We have now to finish them off. The
smaller ship, the *Fidèle,* is pretty well shot to pieces. The *Clorinde,*
however, is still formidable, and especially so at close quarters.
With so little wind we have little freedom of movement. Our
tactics won us the first and second phases of the action but we
shall have to win the third and last round by fighting. We must
be prepared, moreover, to fight both broadsides. I shall try to

sail between the enemy ships, breaking their line, but I shall
probably end with one on either beam. Lack of wind may also
allow the smoke to accumulate and leave us firing blind. We
shall then adopt the practice we have rehearsed, firing on a bearing and at an elevation as directed from the maintop. One thing
I want you to understand is this: it is my intention to bring both
prizes into Portsmouth and nothing the French can do is going
to stop me."

There was a cheer from the men who had overheard this and
the officers dispersed again to their quarters.

"Tack, Mr Cumner," said Delancey, "and steer to engage the
enemy from a cable's length to windward." Delancey could see
that the French ships were again in line ahead but now on the
opposite tack with the *Clorinde* leading so as to protect the *Fidèle*.
The antagonists' approach to each other was very slow and the
course of the action was easy to foresee. As soon as the *Minerva*
was fairly engaged with the *Clorinde,* the *Fidèle* would attempt
to try to take up a raking position across the *Minerva's* bows. To
counter that, Delancey would try to sail between them. Their
reply would be to bear up and he would then have one of them
on either beam. To fight them both at once was something which
Delancey had so far been careful to avoid but it could not be
avoided for ever. He considered fighting the *Fidèle* first but concluded that he had to fight it out with the *Clorinde* sooner or
later and might just as well choose the present moment. Morale
would suffer if his men suspected him of being "shy." He would
fight both batteries and still had the men to do it. He made a
round of the gun-deck, however, and told his men what they
might have to do.

"It is not enough to be good," he reminded them, "your gunnery has to be SUPERB!" "Don't become excited and don't throw

your shot away!" "Let's show these frogs how a battle should be fought!" "Do your duty, men, and we'll have these damned Frenchmen for breakfast!" He felt that he was overacting the part of an operatic hero but the men seemed to respond, cheering him as he passed along the line of the guns. "We'll most likely have the frogs on either beam. It'll be hot work but the hotter the battle the sooner the finish. And then we are bound for home! For home, my lads, and to see all our girls again! For home in triumph, as a ship equal to any two ships on the other side! Make these Frenchmen wish they had stayed in port! See to it that they recognize our ensign when they see it again! Down with the Emperor and long live King George! Down with the tricolour and to hell with the French!"

Back near the wheel, Delancey explained to Cumner the opening move he had decided upon.

"We'll try to sail between them and rake them both. We may not succeed but that will at least prevent the *Fidèle* from raking us. The wind is dying away to nothing. Suppose there is a dead calm and we are fighting with both batteries, could we find men enough to man the launch and tow the ship?"

"I think maybe we could, sir, if we let the lobster-backs replace the seamen on three of the guns. But then we should have no reply to the enemy's musketry. Nor don't I know whether the launch is undamaged—maybe it's holed."

"Mr Lewis," said Delancey, "be so good as to ask the carpenter to report to me on the state of the ship's boats."

Very slowly the opponents were coming together again, all probably realizing that it must now be a fight to the finish. There were puffs of wind and minutes between during which the sails flapped idly. It seemed to be a case of drifting into battle. Delancey paced the deck with mounting impatience and Northmore, deserting his post for a few minutes, came to join him.

"Shall we use the bow-chasers, sir?"

"No, I think a silent approach has a more menacing effect. Some would say, moreover, that it might slow us down. Or is that an old wives' tale?"

"I should have thought, sir, that the slowing down would be immaterial."

"Heaven knows. The men seem in good heart, don't they?"

"Your exhortations helped a lot, sir."

"The worst is still to come. It is bad luck the French having troops on board. They must be double our number even now., But they won't beat us, I think, in gunnery."

"We were lucky there, sir—in having the powder to spare for practice."

"Lucky? Ah, yes—most fortunate. We used about a year's allowance in ten days. Which reminds me—we may end this fight at close range. See that the forecastle guns have grapeshot handy—I'll give the same orders to the quarter-deck carronades."

Lewis ran up to the captain, panting.

"The carpenter reports, sir, that the launch is almost undamaged. There is one hole and his mate is now patching it with sheet lead."

"Thank you, Mr Lewis. What about the other boats?"

"The cutter's smashed, sir, beyond repair. The others are all right."

"Good. If we have a dead calm, Mr Northmore, as seems likely, we may need the boats to tow us out."

Seeing that the enemy was almost within range, Northmore went back to his post forward and Delancey trained his telescope on the *Clorinde*. Traces of visible damage were slight and the frigate was being handled confidently. He could see little of the

Fidèle but judged that she was further astern than was probably intended. He pointed this out to Cumner.

"I intend to engage the leading enemy ship from to windward but without shortening sail. I then mean to head for the gap between the two enemy frigates and will try to rake them both. They will bear up and we shall end with one on either beam, but not, I hope, within musket shot."

At long last the opponents closed, the two bowsprits level with each other, a cable's distance apart, and Delancey gave the order to open fire. The *Minerva* and *Clorinde* passed so slowly that the British seamen had fired three broadsides before they were ordered to cease fire. Then the helmsmen were given an order, the sail-trimmers sent to the ropes, and the *Minerva* altered course sharply to starboard, firing a broadside into the *Clorinde's* stern. It should have been possible, in theory, to fire simultaneously into the *Fidèle's* bows but the captain of that ship bore up too promptly, confronting the *Minerva* with his broadside. All hell broke loose again and now Delancey's men had the enemy on either side of them. Gunfire had become continuous, with mounting damage and loss on either side. There was a complex drill for fighting with both batteries, one which compelled men to dash backwards and forwards between the guns on either side. It was perfectly feasible until men were killed or wounded, but this created difficulties which could only be resolved, in the end, by deserting some guns and redistributing their crews. The noise was, of course, shattering and men would be exhausted the sooner.

There was now a dead calm (caused by the firing, as old seamen maintained) and smoke was accumulating between the opposing ships. Watching the smoke clouds which were tending to blind his gunners, Delancey heard an almighty crash behind him and saw that the *Minerva's* wheel had been shot away, both quartermasters killed and Cumner wounded, probably dying. There was a procedure for steering the ship after the wheel had gone but it was needless for the moment, in a dead calm. Two of the quarter-deck carronades went soon afterwards but there was no further damage and Delancey realized that the enemy gunners could no longer see their target. He promptly sent young Lewis to find the first lieutenant. "My compliments to Mr Northmore and ask him, from me, to take over gunnery control from the maintop. Inform Mr Topley and Mr Ledingham. Off with you—like lightning!"

When Northmore reached the maintop, with two attendant boys, he was almost above the smoke and could clearly make out the enemy topmasts. On either side of the platform there had been rigged up a sort of table on which had been painted a half-circle with its flat side outboard and marked out in degrees up to 180°. A peg was fixed at the half-circle's centre and to this was attached a moving arm, like the hand of a clock, with a peg attached to the free end. When the two pegs were lined up on a target, the bearing could be read off and passed down to the battery on that side. When first tried the device was made with the flat side inboard, which had seemed more logical, but time was then lost in working out the reciprocal and so it had been changed about. In half a minute Northmore read off a bearing for the *Clorinde's* main topmast, guessed a range of one cable, and sent a boy down to Topley with a written message. In another half-minute he took a bearing on the *Fidèle's* main topmast, guessed a range of a cable and a half, and sent the other boy down with a message for Mr Ledingham. Delancey heard all firing cease while the gun-crews trained their cannon on the given bearing and at the estimated range. Then came Topley's shout of

"Starboard battery—fire!" followed by Stock's shout from the lar-board battery.

Delancey noted with grim satisfaction that the enemy's shots were passing overhead or wide, their actual target clearly lost. Going down to the gun-deck, he decided to concentrate the fire a little. "Have your first three guns trained a little aft of the bear-ing you are given, your three after guns a little forward," he said to Topley and again to Ledingham. Then he went back to the quarter-deck, noting that the smoke cloud was as thick as ever. Some fifteen minutes later a boy came with a message from Northmore: "*Clorinde's* main topmast no longer visible, probably fallen I am taking bearings on foretopmast." Five minutes later followed another message "*Fidèle* target lost," and after that, "*Clorinde* target lost."

"Continue to fire on previous bearing" was Delancey's reply but he decided at the same time to shift his position. He was never one to waste powder and shot.

"Lower and man the launch!" was his next order, given to Forbes, another boatswain's mate, and the boat was soon in the water. "Take command, Mr Lewis," said Delancey, "and tow the frigate the way she is heading. When she has moved far enough we'll cast off the hawser at this end." The launch disappeared in the smoke, the hawser came taut, and Delancey was left to guess whether the ship was moving and to what distance. In the mean-while, he gave orders to cease fire and was gratified to note that the enemy continued. After ten minutes he had the hawser cast off and saw the launch return and be hoisted inboard. Report-ing back to his captain, young Lewis grinned delightedly:

"It would seem, sir, that the French frigates are firing at each other!"

"That is my hope, Mr Lewis, and I could only wish that their fire were more accurate. I suspect, however, that they are mostly firing into the ocean."

It was soon evident that one frigate, almost certainly the *Clorinde,* had ceased fire and that all the noise was being made by the other. At the same time a light wind sprang up and the smoke began to disperse. It gradually thinned and then, suddenly, it was gone. As when a theatre curtain was raised, the battlefield was suddenly visible.

On the *Minerva's* starboard quarter, under sail was the *Clorinde.* On the larboard quarter but half a mile distant was the *Fidèle,* with all her topmasts gone, a floating wreck with smoke still billowing from her last futile broadside. Blaming himself for his delay over this, Delancey bellowed the orders which would re-establish his control over the *Minerva's* helm. It would be hauled either way by men using tackles in the steerage and receiving their orders through a chain of intermediaries. The system was set up in about three minutes, beating the time of all previous rehearsals, but it involved a sad waste of manpower.

Meanwhile the *Clorinde* was moving into the attack. It seemed at first to Delancey that her captain was merely trying to close the range, but he presently realized that he was steering too close for that. The French plan was evidently to board, relying on their infantry to tip the scale in a hand-to-hand conflict. But if the *Clorinde* was under way, so was the *Minerva,* the distance between them altering little if at all. Delancey's first instinct was to meet the challenge by backing his topsails. If they cared to board they would soon wish they hadn't! But wiser thoughts prevailed. The longer the chase continued, the more distant the *Fidèle* would be when the fight took place. He decided, therefore, to hold his course and hoist topgallants as if in flight. The *Clorinde* made more sail in response and Delancey went round the gun-deck to explain what was happening.

"Listen, lads, the French are astern of us and will presently try to board. Our first move will be to load every gun with grapeshot. When we have cleared their decks, we shall board *them! So* be ready for the order "Boarders away!" and at that we'll board them in the smoke!" There were loud cheers at this speech, which was repeated at different places round the ship. Then Delancey returned to the quarter-deck where he had the marines drawn up as if to repel boarders. Only then, when the *Fidèle* was two miles away, did Delancey back topsails and allow the *Clorinde* to overtake him.

As the French ship came near, Delancey went through the motions of accepting a challenge to mortal and personal combat. Drawing his sword, he waved defiance and called for three cheers from his quarter-deck gunners, who waved cutlasses before returning to their carronades. As soon, however, as the *Clorinde*'s bowsprit approached the *Minerva*'s stern, he abruptly made sail again, altering course so as to frustrate any attempt at boarding. A minute later the *Minerva*'s guns fired almost together, sweeping the *Clorinde*'s decks with grapeshot. The French captain had foreseen this but his order for his men to lie down came just too late. His decks were covered by the wounded and dying and he lost all interest in the possibilities of hand-to-hand conflict. As if to taunt him, his opponent hove-to again, ready to meet his challenge. The French captain knew now what would happen if he renewed his attempt and rather doubted whether his men would respond again to any brave gesture. Uncertain what to do next, he passed the *Minerva* at fairly close range, firing and receiving a broadside and planning some further move the exact nature of which escaped him. Making sail again, Delancey steered for the French ship's beam and shouted "Boarders away !" As he dashed for the forecastle the *Minerva*'s bowsprit crashed into the *Clorinde* just abaft her forechains, bringing her foremast down with the impact. The two ships were hooked together by a tangled confusion of spars and ropes and the *Minerva*'s bowsprit provided the necessary bridge.

"Follow me!" Delancey shouted as he sprang forward. Mr Stock and the boarding parties were after him in an instant, a torrent of men armed with boarding pikes, axes, and cutlasses. From the quarter-deck the marines provided covering fire and men in the foretop threw grenades. There was pandemonium as the fight surged around the *Clorinde*'s forecastle, the clash of steel mingling with cheers and groans. Delancey was not actually the first man to reach the enemy deck—two or three seamen had passed him and one of them had already been killed—but he killed one opponent with his pistol and severely wounded another with his sword. A third man who attacked him with a cutlass was foiled by the speed with which Delancey threw a pistol in his face. David Stock, on Delancey's left, sent down a French petty officer with his cutlass. Tanner, at his captain's side, wielded a boarding pike with great effect and suddenly, it seemed, the French were gone from the forecastle but collected in strength on the quarter-deck. The secret, as Delancey knew, was to prevent them finding time to reorganize.

"Follow me!" he shouted again and his men surged aft with a mingled noise of cheering and blasphemy. For the only time in his career as a navy captain, Delancey was suddenly possessed by the devil. He ran at the enemy, screaming with fury "Kill the French bastards!" Raging on, he killed a private soldier but failed to extract his sword. Grabbing a fallen boarding pike, he stormed on, hurling it at another soldier and then grabbing the man's musket. He was now at the break of the quarter-deck, where he broke in a door with the butt and wounded a mess servant with the bayonet. For a few minutes he had literally gone berserk, creating a legend of ferocity his men were never to forget. Then he as quickly recovered his senses. He was in the main cabin of the French frigate, where the French captain was offering him his sword. Accepting it, he handed the weapon to Tanner and asked Northmore whether the French ensign had been lowered. This had apparently been done and the fight was over. "Drive the prisoners below decks," he said to Northmore, "and put sentries on each hatchway. You are in command of this frigate. It remains now to deal with the other one."

Back on board the *Minerva*, having left fifty sailors with Northmore, Delancey sent his other men back to their guns. Faithful as her name, the *Fidèle* had been loyally coming to the aid of her consort. She was now half a mile distant and could see the British ensign hoisted over the tricolour. Crippled as she was, escape for her was out of the question. But did her captain mean to make a fight of it? That query was soon answered. As soon as a gun was fired in her direction the *Fidèle's* colours were lowered. The battle was over and Delancey ordered his crew to man the launch. "Mr Topley," he said, "you are acting commander of the national frigate *Fidèle*. Take thirty men to board her and send her officers back to me. Mr Stock, you are acting first lieutenant of the *Minerva*. Mr Lewis, you are acting lieutenant in this frigate. Tell Forbes, someone, that he is acting boatswain . . ." He issued a stream of directions, attempting to produce order out of chaos.

That evening the three frigates were hove-to in close proximity while the final arrangements were made to proceed in company to the Cape. All French officers were brought on board the *Minerva,* most of the marines divided between the other ships. At Simonstown the bulk of the prisoners could be put ashore. In the meanwhile every precaution must be taken to prevent them rising against their captors; the first and obvious precaution being for the captured frigates to remain in company with the *Minerva.* On board the *Minerva* there would be no great problem over the French officers, who were likely to give their parole, but there was a nightmare shortage of navigators. With Stock, Ledingham, and Lewis, the *Minerva* had her theoretical quota but all had been midshipmen a few weeks or days ago. Ragley had died and there could be no proper replacement as master. Midshipmen he had none and the two prizes had just one officer apiece. The return passage was going to involve gross overwork for Delancey himself and an almost crushing responsibility for Northmore and Topley, who would scarcely be able to quit the deck until they reached Simonstown. Of all this Delancey was well aware but in the background to all his gloomier thoughts was his knowledge that he was on the way home. He would reach Portsmouth somehow and with two captured frigates in company. He would reach Guernsey and would be with his love once more. Would he ever go to sea again? He doubted it. For the first time in his life he felt that he had done enough.

Chapter Fourteen

HOME FROM THE SEA

My dearest Fiona—We sail for England in a few days' time and I have no certainty that this letter will arrive there before I do. Our passage cannot, however, be as fast as I could wish because the *Minerva* must sail in company with her two prizes, the *Clorinde* and *Fidèle*.

We fought an action off Madagascar in which these two frigates were finally made to haul down their colours. Northmore commands the one, Topley the other, and I am left with acting lieutenants (all recently midshipmen) to do duty in the *Minerva*. It was my hope that we might recruit some officers here at the Cape, if only invalids on their way home, but all I could find—and glad I was to offer him a berth—was a master's mate, Mr Rankin, who is now my acting master.

The voyage here following the action meant hard work for everyone, especially in refitting the almost dismasted *Fidèle*. Topley brought her in safely, nevertheless, and we have since rigged her (or at least jury-rigged her) in a fashion which should bring her safely to Portsmouth. With the help of the dockyard here, we now have the other two ships in fairly good order. I find myself in the position, in effect, of an Acting-Commodore commanding a frigate squadron. I should never have believed that there could be as much work to do! But we are all in good heart, having been feted as heroes at Capetown, and more indeed than we deserve.

If I have more praise now than I merit it may serve to console me for years of effort which brought me no credit. Admiral Pellew, for example, gave me the task of hunting down a single French privateer, the *Subtile*. You will remember her, I dare say, from my previous letters. It was a far more difficult operation than this recent action and involved heavier losses, at least through sickness, but I could finally claim that my orders had been carried out, that the *Subtile* had been burnt. Much good did it do me! Admiral Pellew had gone home before I was able to make my report. His successor had never heard of the *Subtile*. And what praise can anyone expect as a result of destroying a mere privateer? It means no more than squashing a cockroach with one's slipper! So if I should be praised overmuch now I can reflect that I did more on earlier occasions and had no praise at all.

I learn here at the Cape, and with great satisfaction, that Josias Rowley is to be made Baronet for the campaign in which he restored the situation after Pym's defeat at Grand Port. If ever a man deserves recognition it is he. His achievements were brilliant and should always be remembered. Unluckily for him, his battles were fought a long way from home, a success in the Indian Ocean having less appeal to the public than an action off, say, Cadiz. As against that, his victory immediately followed a defeat and was the more welcome, I should suppose, to the Admiralty.

I think I stand to gain a little from the same contrast,

my little victory doing yet more to wipe out the memory of that earlier setback. I am lucky in one other respect—even as compared with Rowley—for I shall have the chance to bring my prizes into Portsmouth, almost as if from a victory in the Channel. On this subject I must add—strictly between ourselves, please—that I shall cheat a little over the importance of the *Fidèle* (known to my seamen as the Fiddle).

According to my guest, Capitaine Peynier, recently of the *Clorinde,* she is a large corvette of 24 guns. In comparison with our ships, however, her dimensions are those of a small frigate. So I have taken the liberty of shifting four guns into her from the *Clorinde*—some of whose guns could have been and actually were destroyed in action—which allows me to describe her as a frigate, the *Fidèle* (28). This will do something to ensure the promotion of Topley; that of Northmore being, I take it, certain.

All my officers did extremely well, I may add, but I have since had to load heavy responsibilities on mere children. Alongside them, I feel as old as Methuselah. Young David Stock is now my first lieutenant, if you please, and it seems only the other day that he was a nondescript boy I picked up on the coast of Ireland when he was far too young to be a midshipman. He fought by my side, killing at least one Frenchman and disarming two others.

I should perhaps add at this point that I have acquired a scar on the left forearm. A French seaman aimed a cut at my head with a cutlass. I took the blow on my raised arm and Tanner ran the fellow through with a boarding pike, perhaps saving my life for the second time. Oddly enough, I felt nothing at the time and only discovered afterwards

that my sleeve was soaked in blood. I thought at first it
was the blood of my enemies but found, rather to my
annoyance, that it was my own.

Should this letter reach you before I do, you must understand that I am bound for Portsmouth. The *Minerva* will
be paid off there and I shall make my report to the Admiralty. Afterwards I shall return to Portsmouth and eventually
sail from Southampton for Guernsey. It would be wonder-
ful if you could meet me in London but I think we are
more likely to meet in Portsmouth—or Guernsey. At
Portsmouth I shall be staying, no doubt, at the George,
where the staff will be told to refer to me as Commodore.
I am, of course, nothing of the kind but merely a rather
senior captain. This fact makes me the more eager to quit
Portsmouth—I am just the sort of man who could be asked
to sit on a court martial or court of inquiry when all I want
is to be with you again at Anneville, at peace and at rest.

This service of mine in the East Indies has kept us apart
for longer than we expected, for longer than was fair. I
mean now to make up to you for all the time we have lost.
Much is made in the ballads and broadsheets about the
heroism of men in battle but all too little about what their
womenfolk have to endure.

I could wish that my services had gained me a large fortune but we have at least a small estate, a sufficient income
to keep a carriage, and some little repute. More than anything we have each other and I can give you my assurance
that I am little the worse for serving so long in the trop-
ics. My fear has been that I should reappear in Guernsey
without an arm, lacking a leg, blind in one eye, or the
worse for some more serious mutilation. There was still

greater danger, in fact, that I should die of malaria or hepatitis like so many other officers have done.

But I have been lucky and intend to run no further risks on the homeward voyage. Once I have dropped anchor at Anneville I shall not readily make sail again. Do please take great care of your dear self in the meanwhile. In years of separation I have never forgotten you for a minute. You have always been in my thoughts and now the moment is near when you will be in my arms.

Until then believe me always,

Your affectionate husband,
Richard Delancey

Delancey's homeward passage from the Cape was uneventful and he managed to keep his squadron together. On September 5th 1811, he sailed into Spithead and saluted the flag of the Commander-in-Chief. The day was fine and much of the Channel Fleet was there in magnificent array. The *Minerva* was followed by the *Clorinde* and *Fidèle* in strict formation, each captured ship flying the white ensign over the tricolour. The *Minerva* was cheered by all the other men-of-war as she came into the anchorage. When Delancey landed at the sally-port, on his way to call on the Port Admiral, he was cheered again by a crowd collected there. He had the unusual sensation of being the hero of the hour. That the hour would soon pass he knew, having no illusions about that, but it was a moment he would remember and a recognition which his men deserved. Nor was the Port Admiral other than friendly:

"Captain Delancey, I am honoured to welcome you home and am happy to assure you that your fame has gone before you. I have a signal from the Admiralty directing that you report at once to the Senior Naval Member of the Board, bringing with you Lieutenants Northmore and Topley. I now hand you an order to that effect, directing you to come ashore. Allowing you an hour or two in which to collect your gear, I have booked a post-chaise for you at midday and you will be at the Admiralty before their Lordships will all have left the office. I am honoured to be among the first to congratulate you but I know that I shall not be the last. Any officer who has captured an enemy ship of equal rate as the result of a single-ship duel has always been given some public recognition. To capture *two* enemy ships in such an action is an outstanding feat of arms, one for which I cannot recall an exact parallel. In a brilliant campaign, the details of which will be familiar to you, Captain Josias Rowley recaptured the *Afticaine,* retook the *Ceylon,* and received the surrender of the *Venus.* He was not, however, alone, and he did not meet all these opponents at the same time. My guess is that Lieutenant the Hon. Stephen Northmore will be given post rank and that Lieutenant Topley will be made Commander; promotions made out of compliment to you. His Royal Highness the Prince Regent is aware of your achievements, I should add, and has already expressed his approbation in what I understand to have been very generous terms."

Delancey knew better than to mention these possibilities to Northmore and Topley. He merely told them to wear their best uniforms and be ready to leave for London at noon. By the late afternoon their post-chaise rolled into the forecourt of the Admiralty building and Delancey hastened to present himself to the clerk on duty. In years past he could remember being told to wait on such an occasion, and had waited indeed for hours, but he now sensed a different atmosphere.

"Sir Richard will see you at once, sir," he was told. In a few minutes he stood in the presence of Admiral Sir Richard Bickerton, to whom he was presented by Mr John Wilson Croker, Secretary to the Board.

"Captain Delancey, Sir Richard," said Croker, "with two of his officers."

"Your servant, Sir Richard," said Delancey. "Allow me to present the Hon. Mr Stephen Northmore and Mr Topley."

"Glad to make your acquaintance, Captain Delancey, and glad to meet these other gentlemen. May I take the opportunity of conveying to you the approbation of the Board on the occasion of a notable feat of arms? The First Lord wishes to see you before he goes . . . Mr Croker, is the First Lord free?"

"Mr Barrow tells me, Sir Richard, that Sir Robert Barlow is with him at the moment but will be gone in a few minutes. Perhaps you will be good enough to follow me, gentlemen."

Delancey followed Mr Croker down a corridor and into an office adjoining that of the First Lord, the Rt. Hon. Charles Philip Yorke, son of a former Lord Chancellor. He there made the acquaintance of Mr Frederic Edgcumb, the First Lord's Private Secretary.

"The Commissioner of Portsmouth Dockyard is with the First Lord now but Mr Yorke will be free to see you very shortly."

Delancey responded with a bow and Edgcumb was promptly accosted by two other clerks who showed him a document and conferred with him on some obscure but urgent problem. Messengers came and went and there was a continued buzz of activity. Finally, an elderly gentleman emerged from the First Lord's office and Edgcumb showed him out with some little ceremony, saying finally "Good-bye, Sir Robert." A minute later he looked briefly into the inner room and, turning back, said: "Captain Delancey, the First Lord will see you and the other gentlemen now." And now Delancey was in the presence of Mr Yorke, a politician he knew only by name, a previous Home Secretary and one for whom his present office was actually to be his last. He was affable, bland, and careful to say no more than was fitting to the occasion.

"Captain Delancey, I am glad to see you and add my congratulations to all those you will already have received. I also have the honour of conveying to you the official approbation of the Board of Admiralty."

"Thank you, sir. Allow me to present the Hon. Mr Stephen Northmore and Mr Topley, both of His Majesty's frigate *Minerva*."

"Glad to make your acquaintance, gentlemen. I have to congratulate you on the success of your recent action, which was highly creditable to all who took part in it. In recognition of your gallantry on this occasion, the Board of Admiralty has decided to advance you, Mr Northmore, to post rank and you, Mr Topley, to the rank of master and commander. You both merit this promotion and I have no doubt at all will more than justify the good opinion of you which the Board is thus pleased to signify. Captain Northmore and Captain Topley, I will now ask you to retire while I have a further word with Captain Delancey."

Northmore and Topley murmured some words of thanks, bowed deeply, and withdrew.

"It is my privilege to inform you, Captain Delancey, that His Royal Highness the Prince Regent has instructed me to present you to him at tomorrow's levee—you and your two officers, on the occasion of their promotion. Be so good as to call here tomorrow at half-past nine. I shall then take you over to Carlton House. His Royal Highness leaves for Brighton in a few days' time—it is fortunate that you were able to reach London so soon, as you might otherwise have had to follow him there."

"I am indeed honoured, sir, by the Prince's kind notice of me and will wait on you tomorrow."

Delancey had never attended a levee and knew little or nothing about court etiquette. Many other officers would have seen a special significance in the First Lord's invitation but his chief concern was with the state of his uniform after years in the East. There was certainly no time to replace anything. If he was worried about his appearance, Northmore and Topley were more worried and probably with more reason. Northmore's sword was barely adequate and Topley's could only be described as shabby. They dispersed on leaving the Admiralty, each with some idea of borrowing from friends. Delancey, for his part, went to stay with old Colonel Barrington in St James's Square. Although almost bedridden, the Colonel was glad to see him and asked whether Fiona was also to be expected.

"Indeed I hope so," said Delancey, "but all depends upon whether and when she received my letter from the Cape."

"Ah, I have missed seeing her all these years. She is the sort of person one never forgets. And so you have returned in triumph at last? I read the gazette letters about your action. You have really excelled the hopes of all your friends. We shall yet see you commanding a fleet!"

"I don't think that probable, sir. I was not given post rank soon enough. But I've done sufficient to have gained some little reputation. I seek no more than a name for having done my best."

"Fiddlesticks, man! We all regard you as a hero and I shall be surprised if the Prince Regent fails to think as we do. In any case we shall dine here tomorrow and celebrate your return. And bring these two officers of yours! Where are they lodging? I must send a servant to find them." This was done and messages received that they would be happy to accept.

There was no sign of Fiona that night and Delancey told himself that he was unreasonable in thinking that she would go further than Portsmouth. She would know by now that he was in England or anyway she would know by tomorrow from the newspapers. On reaching Portsmouth she would learn that he had gone to London and would guess the rest. But she would, of course, be too tired after the voyage to go any further. He would find her at the George, no doubt of it; and indeed in Guernsey as likely as not. He had been guilty of the schoolboy error of thinking that facts known to oneself must be known to everyone else. He had no reason, after all, to assume that she even read the newspapers. As for his letter from the Cape, the ship to which it was entrusted could have been delayed. She would not have received it at all and it might not be delivered until some time next week. Poor Fiona had been compelled to learn patience over the years, almost like the wife of Ulysses, and it would be strange indeed if she showed impatience now instead of waiting sensibly at the one place where he was certain to present himself. He slept badly that night and woke several times to assure himself that Fiona was still in Guernsey and could not possibly be in London on the morrow.

Next day at the Admiralty the First Lord looked him over and all but deplored his shabby appearance. As for Northmore and Topley, he glanced at them and looked away again with an ill-suppressed shudder. He waved them all into his carriage, nevertheless, and they presently found themselves in a traffic jam. Pall Mall, St James's Street, and the Haymarket were all blocked with carriages and they did well to reach Carlton House in time. Delancey then found himself following Mr Yorke upstairs to the first floor room where the levee was to be held.

So far there had been an element of confusion but at this point equerries took over and began placing everybody in their proper place. The First Lord was now given due consideration as a Minister of the Crown. With Delancey and the other two officers he was placed at no great distance from the red carpet where the Prince was to stand. Military uniforms tended to predominate and the buzz of conversation was punctuated by the jingle of spurs and the clatter of swords. More junior officers looked awkward and nervous. More senior officers made it sufficiently clear that they had attended so many similar functions that the whole thing had become a bore. The First Lord fretted a little over the Regent's late arrival, hinting in effect that he had more important work to do. He presently fell into conversation with Lord Liverpool, the Secretary for War, who had with him a recently appointed Major-General and two Colonels, one of the Dragoon Guards and the other of the Royal Engineers. Delancey would have liked to tell Northmore who all the dignitaries were but he could himself recognize only two or three, Lord Moira being one of them and Lord Bathurst another. He knew that the Prime Minister, Mr Spencer Perceval, was supposed to be there but he failed to identify him. At long last a court official called out "His Royal Highness the Prince Regent," and the levee fairly began.

The Regent, whom Delancey now saw for the first time, was forty-eight but looked much older. He was grossly overweight although not quite as fat as he had been, and he had been crammed with difficulty into the elaborate uniform of a Field-Marshal. He was the more often so dressed in that the rank was one to which he had aspired in vain as long as his father ruled. Years of dissipation had left their mark on him but he was as charming as ever and as polite to everyone. With him was the Duke of Cumberland, of whom the Regent took little notice, and Lord Moira, with whom he was evidently on the best of terms.

There was much bowing and scraping and the Prince finally took up his expected position and the presentations began. When the First Lord of the Admiralty saw his opportunity, he led Delancey forward and said:

"I hope your Royal Highness will allow me the honour of presenting Captain Delancey, lately commanding the frigate *Minerva*."

"I had thought the Delanceys were all soldiers. Oliver Delancey is a General, surely, and William is doing great things in the Peninsula. Are you related to them, Captain Delancey?"

"We are cousins, your Royal Highness."

"And you, I gather, are rivalling your cousins in distinction. I heard with great pleasure of your successful action in the West Indies—"

A secretary whispered something in the Prince's ear. "I mean, in the East Indies. Your capture of a French frigate will long be remembered as a notable feat of arms and one very creditable to the Royal Navy."

The First Lord intervened at this point.

"Your Royal Highness should know that Captain Delancey fought *two* French frigates off Madagascar and captured them both; a most unusual achievement—one almost without example."

"Ah, to be sure. *Two* frigates! Most remarkable!" The secretary was whispering again in the Prince's ear.

"Yes, yes, of course," said the Regent. As if by magic a footstool was thrust into position and a sword placed in the Regent's hand.

"Kneel," was the First Lord's stage direction and Delancey knelt. The secretary whispered again, evidently to convey the first name correctly. The sword tapped Delancey's shoulder.

"Rise, Sir Richard Delancey!" said the Regent. Delancey rose, stepped back and bowed deeply. He then spoke his own piece.

"I thank your Royal Highness for the honour you have been pleased to bestow on me. I hope your Royal Highness will allow me the further honour of presenting Captain the Hon. Stephen Northmore and Captain Topley, both recently of the frigate *Minerva*."

The two officers bowed in turn and stepped back, the First Lord then motioning them aside as the next candidate for presentation—the Sheriff of York—came forward. So far as Delancey and his officers were concerned, the ceremony was over.

"Congratulations, Sir Richard," said the First Lord, leading the way to his carriage.

"By your leave, sir." said Delancey, "I am bound in the other direction, for St James's Square, only a short distance away, and I shall be there sooner on foot."

"Very true," said the First Lord, looking at the traffic. "I'll say farewell then. Perhaps these two officers will come with me to the Admiralty, however. We shall need to discuss their future employment."

Delancey parted from the others, walked into St James's Street, and was soon back at Colonel Barrington's house. He was shown up to the Colonel's bedroom and explained to his host that he had just received the honour of knighthood.

"What did I tell you, Delancey? The Regent thinks as highly of you as I do! I wish we could celebrate the occasion as we should once have done. I have to go easy these days, you know, and I dare say my physician does well to keep me on a tight rein. But it does me good to hear of merit being recognized, and especially the merit of a friend. I'll tell you what, though, I shall come down to dinner, if only to have the pleasure of drinking your health. Yes, we must dine together—perhaps for the last time—and I'll give orders to put the champagne on ice." The Colonel then pulled a cord by his bedside and there was a faint sound of a distant bell. The Colonel's valet appeared.

"Now, Dobson, you must know that Captain Delancey has just received the honour of knighthood. He is now Sir Richard Delancey. Please inform the other servants so as to ensure that they address him correctly."

After some further conversation and reiterated congratulations, Delancey took his leave—seeing that the old Colonel was tired—and went along to the drawing room, from which he could look down into the square. Would she arrive in the course of the day? He told himself that the idea was absurd. He would leave for Portsmouth in the morning and would find her at the George. What if they passed each other on the way, though? It seemed all too possible. He turned away from the window and picked up the newspaper which a footman had brought him. What was the news of the Peninsula? There was the sound of a carriage in the square but he had learnt to ignore that, for there were carriages passing all the time. He looked at his watch and was surprised to see that it was only the half-hour after noon. How would he spend the day? Restlessly, he went to the window again and at that moment a footman threw open the door and announced, with a certain emphasis:

"Lady Delancey!"

Fiona was in his arms, her tears wetting his cheeks, her voice a mere whisper.

"Fiona!"

"Richard!"

"You are much more beautiful than I had remembered . . ."

"You are no older than when you sailed for the East . . ."

"How long it has been!"

"Let's never be parted again!"

"Never again, Lady Delancey!"

"Does that mean—I thought perhaps the footman had made a mistake—are you really?"

"I was knighted this morning."

"And no one ever deserved it more. I've only just realized what you did in that action. All this hand-to-hand fighting should be left to more junior officers! And you were wounded, too! How proud I was to read the gazette letter but I shuddered to think of the needless risks you ran. Old Captain Savage told me what it means for one ship to fight two. He thinks you are the cleverest man alive and so you are! There are already ballads about you and the *Minerva* and I was shown a broadsheet in Portsmouth with a woodcut supposed to be of you but first intended, I expect, for Admiral Keppel. You are famous, darling, but you have done your share of the fighting and must stop now before you are more seriously hurt."

"Agreed, my love. And now to deal with our immediate plans: Colonel Barrington has asked us to dine with him and he is getting up for the occasion. He has also invited Northmore and Topley and maybe some ladies as well. We are to dine at two. Your maid will have unpacked for you by now and there will be plenty of time to dress for dinner."

"All the time in the world, my love."